For Love or Loyalty

Other Books by Jennifer Hudson Taylor

Highland Blessings
Highland Sanctuary

Path of Freedom (Quilts of Love series)

For Love or Loyalty

The MacGregor Legacy Series

Book 1

Jennifer Hudson Taylor

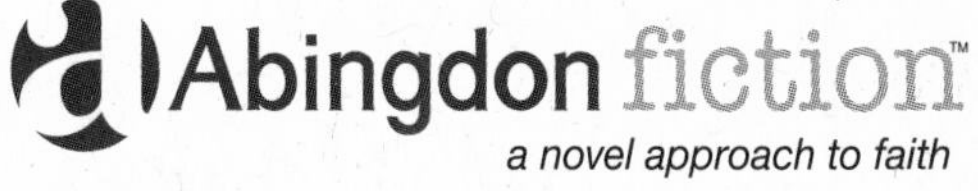

Nashville, Tennessee

For Love or Loyalty

ISBN-13: 978-1-4267-1469-6

Published by Abingdon Press, P.O. Box 801, Nashville, TN 37202
www.abingdonpress.com

Library of Congress Cataloging-in-Publication Data has been requested.

Printed in the United States of America

1 2 3 4 5 6 7 8 9 10 / 18 17 16 15 14 13

Dedication

To those whose lives may not have turned out as you planned due to either circumstances out of your control or poor choices, I pray that you can look back on your lives now or one day in the future and see God's sovereign hand of protection and guidance in your lives.

Acknowledgments

I would like to thank my husband, Dwayne, for being the first to read through this manuscript. I can always count on you for giving me the gift of truth. Thank you for sending me back to my computer to rewrite scenes that needed more work and for identifying those gaps that make the story flow better now.

To my daughter, Celina, thank you for your continuous understanding when I have to alter our routine to meet a deadline. It makes our quality time even more special.

To Abingdon's marketing team, thank you for the great new series title and the title of this new book. And I am thrilled with my cover! To my editor, Ramona Richards, thank you for caring about your authors and for your words of encouragement.

To my agent, Terry Burns, thank you for selling this series! Your prayers and support mean the world to me. I am so blessed to have a praying agent.

I know the thoughts that I think toward you, says the L*ORD*,
thoughts of peace and not of evil, to give you a future and a hope.
—Jeremiah 29:11

1

A feeling of foreboding crawled over Malcolm MacGregor like a colony of insects picking at his skin. He gripped the reins as he inhaled the crisp March air, but it burned his lungs with the residue of tainted fire. A cloud of dark smoke hovered over the wee village of Inverawe—home. Fear coiled inside Malcolm's gut as he urged his mount forward.

His brother kept pace beside him. At a score and four, Thomas was two years Malcolm's junior. He favored Malcolm with the same stubborn chin and broad shoulders from hard work.

Distant moors lined the overcast sky. Morning fog hovered over the glen, blending with heavy smoke. As they drew near, their eyes stung and the burned smell accosted them until they coughed. Keening scraped his ears like a tormented bagpipe.

They reached the stone huts, packed with dirt and topped by straw roofs. At least the village homes weren't on fire as he originally feared. Piles of furniture and personal items burned in front of each hut. Weeping echoed from every direction.

Malcolm's throat constricted. His chest tightened in a mixture of compassion and fear for his family. He maneuvered his horse between the huts, heading toward the center of the village, seeking the home where he had grown from a lad into a man. Engulfed in flames, it blazed to the sky.

"Mither an' Carleen . . ." The words fell from Malcolm's swollen tongue, stalling in the air as his thoughts shifted to their youngest brother, Graham. At only twenty, the lad would have done anything to protect the women in their absence.

"Malcolm, ye're back!" Heather strode toward him, her eyes red and swollen. Words stalled upon her tongue, increasing his anxiety as he waited for her to collect her emotions and continue.

"What happened?" Malcolm asked, pulling his horse to a stop and dismounting. It was an effort to keep his voice calm, but he tried for Heather's sake, though his insides quaked.

" 'Tis the worst." Heather succumbed to tears, shaking with grief.

"What is it, lass?" Malcolm shook her, hoping to force her out of her temporary stupor.

"Where's Mither an' Carleen?" Thomas strode toward them, his voice betraying his fears.

Heather sobbed, falling against Malcolm's chest. On instinct, his arms slipped around her. He looked up as the rest of the villagers approached with sorrowful expressions.

"The Campbells were here." Roy strode foward, his red eyes weary with similar grief—his right eye swollen and his lip cut. Even in his late fifties, Roy was healthy and robust. It would have taken several men to bring him low. "They took Iona an' Carleen."

"Took them?" Thomas gave the elder man a look of disbelief. "Where?"

"How long ago?" Malcolm pressed Heather into the arms of her mother, who came up behind her. He turned back to his horse and prepared to mount.

"Nay! There's too many o' them. Sixty or more." A strong hand grabbed his shoulder. "Listen to me, lad. Ye canna help yer mither an' sister if ye're dead."

"I've time to catch them if I leave now." Malcolm pulled away. More hands grabbed him. He didn't want to fight his own kinsmen, but they wouldn't deter him from his mission. He had to act now before it was too late.

"Let me go!" Thomas yelled, fighting a similar battle.

"I've got 'im, Da." Strong arms belted around Malcolm's neck and jerked him backward, cutting off his air. Malcolm coughed. He swung his elbow into Alan's ribs.

"Argh!" Alan relaxed his hold but didn't let go.

"Listen to reason, lad. The rest o' us are too auld an' wounded to be fightin' ye." A fist from another angle slammed into Malcolm's jaw. "But fight ye we will if it's the only way to save yer life." Roy's voice echoed over the multiple hands and arms keeping him down.

Never had the villagers fought him like this. More dread pooled in the pit of his stomach as he realized there had to be a reason for their adamancy. What had they not yet told him? They were right. How could he and Thomas expect to best sixty or more Campbell men? This feat would require his wits, and he wasn't thinking, only reacting.

"All right." He clenched his teeth, willing his body to relax against their resistance. "Tell me why I shan't go after them. It does not make sense to lose precious time."

Following Malcolm's example, Thomas also surrendered.

"Duncan Campbell came to collect the rents," Roy said. "But he arrived with an army of warriors. He did not come hither on business as he claims. His purpose was to cause trouble, an' he chose yer family to be the example."

"They were not supposed to come for another fortnight." Malcolm jerked away from Alan, who sported a bloody lip, already swelling, and a long sword gash upon his arm. Malcolm frowned. Only the Campbells would have been carrying broadswords. Blood soaked Alan's sleeve, probably more so from his skirmish with Malcolm. Guilt lacerated Malcolm's emotionally scarred heart.

How long must they go on living like peasant pawns for the Campbells' entertainment?

"They did all this over unpaid rents?" Malcolm lifted his hands in disbelief. "We took the cattle to market an' we now have the rent. 'Tis all for naught!" His voice cracked as he ran a hand through his hair. A deep ache twisted his gut.

"Listen to Da." Alan wiped the back of his hand across his lip. "We need a plan. The Campbells want us to come after them in a mad rage. They have the king's favor an' all the wealth they need. We canna fall into their trap again."

"We can gather more MacGregors an' break into Kilchurn Manor." Thomas walked over. The others stepped aside to let him through. "We'll get Mither an' Carleen out. We canna abandon them."

" 'Tisn't that simple. I wish it were." Roy rubbed a wrinkled hand over his weathered face with a broken sigh. "Even if we gather more MacGregors from other parts of Argyll, we may not be strong enough to break through Duncan Campbell's forces. He has too many allies. If we succeed an' bring them home, how will we stop the Campbells from coming again?"

Roy and Alan stood still, watching Malcolm and Thomas as though they would tackle them again if need be. More villagers crowded around. All of them looked like a sorry lot, the men having been beaten, the women wearing expressions of grief and sorrow. Soot layered their faces, arms, and clothing.

" 'Tis possible they have taken them to a debtors' prison," Mary MacGregor maneuvered around her husband and son, "since yer mither did not have the rent money."

"If that is the case," Malcolm said, "they will have to release Mither an' Carleen once I pay the rent."

"Duncan raised the rents again, plus he's charging interest," Mary said. "He took our furniture an' burned what he did not want." Tears filled her eyes. "William an' Graham are young an' foolish to try to fight them. They killed William this day. How many more do ye think we can stand to lose?"

"An' Graham?" Malcolm staggered at the news. He closed his eyes, rubbing his brows. William and Graham were inseparable. Had Graham suffered the same fate? Heather broke into more weeping, and Malcolm's chest tightened. The lass had been sweet on their youngest brother as soon as they could walk. Now he understood the extent of her grief. "Where is Graham? Did they take him too?" Malcolm clenched his fists at his sides, attempting to calm the rising tide of anxiety. "Is he alive?"

"Aye, but barely," Roy said. "I'm sorry, Malcolm. We tried to fight them, but there were too many . . ."

"Take us to 'im," Thomas said in a gruff voice, moving to stand beside Malcolm.

"Greg and Colin are tending to 'im. The Campbells beat him bad an' hung 'im on a tree." Roy's voice faltered. "To make an example out o' 'im."

"By the neck?" Malcolm followed Roy and Alan to their hut. Fear clawed at his heart and gripped his lungs, stealing the breath from him.

"Nay," Alan said. "With his arms spread out. We think both shoulders are dislocated."

They stopped before entering Roy's hut. "They left us only one bed so that is where we put 'im." Roy held up a palm and shook his head. "Prepare yerself, lads."

Malcolm bent through the threshold and blinked, allowing his eyes to adjust to the dim candlelight. Their small huts contained no windows for daylight to filter inside. He walked across the dirt floor to the tiny bed. Graham's long legs hung over the side. His height matched Malcolm's at six four. Among the three brothers, Thomas was the shortest, shy of them by a couple of inches.

Colin looked up from where he hunched over stitching a wound in the lad's side. Greg cleaned his bruised face from the other side. Neither of them spoke as they concentrated on their tasks.

Both Malcolm and Thomas dropped to their knees. Thomas groaned and gulped back a threatening cry. Malcolm searched for his voice, but it lodged in his throat as a sickening pain clutched his soul and wouldn't let go. They stayed that way for several moments, trying to make sense of it all.

Colin cleared his throat. "The lad fought bravely, like a Highland warrior if ever I saw one."

Graham disliked fighting. Unlike the rest of them, who thrived on the sword, Graham preferred his wits to outsmart the wretched Campbells. He held out in stubborn pride, believing forgiveness and reason would bridge the great divide between the Campbells and the MacGregors. Today, he discovered the truth, and his faith almost cost him his life.

"Is he . . ." Still unable to say it, Malcolm laid a hand on Graham's chest. A faint heartbeat pulsed beneath his palm. Malcolm closed his eyes in relief.

"He passed out from the pain when I reset his shoulders back into the sockets," Greg said. "As soon as Colin stitches his side, we'll bind his ribs."

"At least he's alive," Thomas said, shaking his head in disbelief. "I always teased him about being the bonny son. Now look at 'im. I fear he will never be the same again."

"Graham was never vain." Malcolm gripped Graham's limp hand. "I worry 'bout the lad's spirit an' his broken ideals. He will blame himself for not saving Mither an' Carleen. No doubt, he will feel naïve he ever thought reconciliation with the Campbells was possible."

"Aye, 'twill take him a while to recover," Thomas said with a sigh. "Did Mither an' Carleen see what happened to 'im?"

"Nay," Colin shook his head. "The Campbells split up. Scott Campbell took them away while his father stayed behind to cause more damage." Colin rubbed his eyebrows and sat back. "That one has the heart of the devil, he does."

"I shall get revenge for our family an' the whole MacGregor Clan. The Campbells have wronged us for two centuries. They have tried to wipe out the MacGregor Clan, an' here we survive against all odds." Malcolm raised a fist and growled. "This time, I care not what it takes." Malcolm turned to Roy. "We shall send a scout to Kilchurn Manor to see if Mither an' Carleen are being held there and also to the nearest debtors' prison. We will move our family to Glenstrae under the protection of the MacGregor Clan Chief." He shoved a hand on his hip and rubbed his eyebrows, fighting the onslaught of a headache and too much regret. "Should have done it a long time ago after Da died."

"Ye were but a wee lad." Roy shook his head. "Do not do this to yerself. 'Tisn't yer fault."

"Aye, I've tarried long enough. I almost lost my family because of it." Malcolm glanced down at Graham, fear spiking inside him. He hoped it wasn't too late.

"Where ye going?"

Lauren Campbell jumped with a start, throwing a hand over her hammering chest. She placed a finger across her lips to shush her sister of ten and two. A quick glance around the busy kitchen assured her no one paid them any attention. Cook put away uneaten food while the rest of the servants cleaned up where the Campbells had broken their morning fast.

"Do I have yer word to say naught?" Lauren peeked at her sister's wide brown eyes, curious as Blair twisted her lips into a mischievous grin.

"If ye take me with ye." Blair nodded, and her sandy brown hair slid over her face. She brushed the long strands out of her eyes with an impatient sigh.

"I canna." Lauren shook her head, biting her lower lip as she placed biscuits in a basket. " 'Tis dangerous where I'm going."

"Where?" Blair sidled up to the counter beside Lauren, excitement building in her tone.

"I'm going to the ancient castle of Kilchurn." Lauren's heart swelled as her sister's eyes widened in admiration.

"All alone? Ye know Da would not approve if he was home." Blair lowered her voice to a whisper. "He will be angry if ye do not take cousin Keith."

"Keith is studying to take orders next week and will give his first sermon," Lauren whispered, touching the tip of her sister's nose and grabbing a block of cheese. "I canna interfere with the Lord's work. Besides, Kilchurn Castle is part of our estate. 'Tisn't as if I'm leaving the grounds."

"But ye're leaving Kilchurn Manor," Blair said.

" 'Tis only a short ride." Lauren covered the basket with a cloth and tucked in the edges. She paused, considering her sister's hopeful expression.

"I want to go, please." Blair linked her fingers as if she was about to pray. She wore the Campbell plaid over a dark blue dress and frowned with a sulky pout as she crossed her thin arms. "Lauren?"

"Run along and get ready. Meet me at the stables," Lauren said. "I shall see that your horse is saddled and ready."

Blair disappeared. Her footsteps pattered down the hall. Lauren chuckled and shook her head, knowing the child ran in haste. She hoped Blair would not tumble into one of the servants. With her basket of goods in tow, Lauren let herself out the side door and made her way to the stables.

It was a crisp morning, bright with sunshine and promise. Lauren loved the ancient relic of Kilchurn Castle now crumbling on the far side of Loch Awe. The short journey would take them less than an hour on horseback. On the days she walked the grounds, Lauren loved imagining what it must have been like centuries ago when the castle passed from the MagGregors to the Campbells through marriage.

Lauren entered the shaded stables. "Aidan?" Lauren called to the stable lad. "Are ye there? Blair and I are going for a ride." No one answered. Strange. Lauren shrugged and stepped back, trampling on a pair of booted feet. A man's hand clamped over her mouth, shoving a piece of cloth inside to silence her scream. Another hand pulled her by the hair and jerked her back against his hard body. Her basket of goods flew over a nearby stall. The horse inside stomped and snorted.

"I took care o' the lad," said a gruff voice at her ear. "Just needed to get 'im out o' the way. 'Tis Duncan Campbell's daughter I want."

Lauren's heart pounded in her ears as she kicked behind her, but he slammed a fist against her temple. Pain sliced through her head. He wrapped an arm around her neck, cutting off her air, and dragged her into a dark corner.

"Lauren?" Blair called. Her footsteps came closer. "Are ye here?"

Closing her eyes, Lauren stopped struggling, praying God would spare her sister. The man breathed heavily at her ear, his grip intense. To Lauren's relief, he appeared to be alone, and he did not go after Blair.

"Aidan?" Her sister sighed with frustration. "Where did everyone go?" She stomped out of the stables and back toward the manor.

As soon as Blair disappeared, the man slipped a knife to Lauren's throat. "Go." The blade nicked her skin as he pushed her forward, leading her out of the stables on the other side. The gag tied in her mouth made her jaw ache and dried her tongue. He dragged her into the woods where a horse waited.

Lauren tripped over a fallen branch, but he caught her and shoved her against a tree. Her bruised hip stung as he pulled her arms behind her and bound her hands. The man slung her over his horse and mounted behind her. Between a dizzy spell and a wave of nausea, she caught a glimpse of his MacGregor plaid.

They rode toward Inverawe where Lauren often visited the poor and brought them food. Iona and Carleen MacGregor always welcomed her and shared their faith. Iona's sons were not quite as friendly, but Graham was open-minded and kind. Lauren supposed because he was the youngest he wasn't as set in his ways as the other two. He was closer to Lauren's age at twenty.

When they arrived at the village, Lauren wasn't prepared for the devastation she witnessed. Ashes simmered in gray piles. Grief-stricken faces glared at her with hatred. Several people spit at her, and one threw a rotten onion in her face. The putrid smell made her stomach roll.

They came to a pile of rubble that should have been Iona and Carleen's hut. Hot smoke still pumped from the smoldering remains. Lauren's chest tightened as tears sprang to her eyes. Her father and brother were supposed to arrive here and collect the rents. Surely, they were not responsible? Her heart ached, fearing it was the truth she wanted to deny.

Her abductor stopped at one of the huts where smoke pumped through the chimney. He grabbed Lauren by the arm and yanked her down. She stumbled to her feet, finding it hard to regain her balance. He pushed her toward the door as others surrounded them.

"Why did ye bring a Campbell 'ere?" a woman asked. "Do ye not think they have caused enough trouble?"

"Aye," a man said. "The whole lot o' them will come looking for 'er."

"Malcolm! Thomas!" Lauren's captor ignored them and banged on the worn wooden door. "Open up. I have Lauren Campbell."

The door swung open and Malcolm's tall form emerged. He crossed his arms with a menacing scowl. "Colin, ye were supposed to find my mither an' sister, not bring back a hostage."

"Iona an' Carleen were not at Kilchurn." Colin's words came out in a rush as he tightened his grip on her. "But she was."

"What are we supposed to do with her?" Malcolm pointed at Lauren, venom coating his tone. "This was not the plan."

"We have no plan since they were not at Kilchurn," Thomas said, coming to stand behind Malcolm. "Mayhap, she can be the plan. Who else is goin' to be as important to Duncan?"

"She canna stay here," another man said. "Her father will destroy the whole village lookin' for her."

"Aye, but she's here now," Mary MacGregor said. "The damage is done. Ye should make the best o' her situation. Could we exchange her for Iona or Carleen?"

Shock vibrated through Lauren. What had her father done? Although the MacGregors had never been cruel to her, most, except Iona and Carleen, were wary and reluctant to befriend her. Now that the villagers had good reason to be seething in anger and resentment, she had no idea how far they would go in using her. She wondered if anyone at home had discovered her disappearance.

"What if he comes back an' burns the rest o' our homes?" a woman asked.

"He owns all these huts. If he burns them all, he canna rent them out." Malcolm scratched his temple and glanced at Lauren. "Remove her gag. She may know something."

"How ye plan to get 'er to talk?" Colin asked, jerking at her bindings. The cloth fell from around her head, and Lauren spit out the other piece.

"Speak up, lass." Malcolm stepped toward her, his height more like a tower than a mere man. "Where did yer da take my mither an' sister? The sooner we find out, the sooner negotiations can begin an' ye can go home."

"All I know is that he intended to collect the rents and go to the harbor."

"The harbor?" Thomas joined his brother, his palm up against the side of his head, pondering the possibilities. "Why would he do that?"

"Only one explanation," an older man said, lifting a finger. All eyes turned to him. "To sell them. What else?"

The women gasped, some wept, while the men groaned and complained in outrage. Colin jerked Lauren by the arm and shoved her to the center. "We have one of their own!" She stumbled and fell to her knees. He pulled her hair. Fire burned her scalp. She prayed her neck wouldn't break from the pressure. Tears stung her eyes. *Lord, I thank You for sparing Blair.*

"What would Duncan do to save this bonny face?" An elderly woman bent to squeeze Lauren's cheeks. The others came at her all at once with raised hands. Lauren closed her eyes, expecting a beating.

"Stop!" Malcolm's firm voice sliced through the mob like a king. With the MacGregors scattered throughout Campbell lands that used to belong to the MacGregors, none of them had a clan chief. The exception was Glenstrae farther north in the heart of the Scottish Highlands. Yet no one laid a hand on her. They obeyed Malcolm out of respect.

"Let us think about our actions an' how the Campbells might retaliate." Malcolm lifted his hands and pointed in the direction of Kilchurn Manor. "As long as the lass lives an' remains unharmed, we have something to bargain. None o' us wanna worry 'bout being murdered in our beds at night or forced to flee to the hills again."

Eyes widened, mouths dropped open, and heads shook back and forth in slow motion. Some of the villagers' skin turned paler. They backed away from her.

"Duncan an' Scott Campbell have a good head start. At this point, we would be guessing which harbor they went to an' taking the lass at her word," Malcolm said.

"Taynuilt Harbor is the closest," Roy said. Lauren had heard one of the others call him by name. He was a middle-aged man who looked at her with so much malice her skin itched and burned. " 'Tis on Loch Etive an' leads out to sea."

"Aye." Malcolm nodded, rubbing the back of his neck. "First, I want to ensure Graham's safety 'til he heals, as well as the villagers'. I shall find her wretched father." His boiling gaze landed on Lauren, and their eyes met. If the good Lord hadn't been holding her together, she might have crumbled in fear, but Lauren not only found the courage she needed but also managed to lift her chin and keep her peace. Later in solitude she would bear her burdensome fear to the Lord.

"Let us bring her inside while we tend to Graham an' make our plans," Malcolm said, turning to the others.

Colin shoved her. Lauren stumbled into Malcolm. He reached out a steady hand and gripped her arm. She assumed the action was only out of instinct, not for her welfare.

"What happened to Graham?" The words tumbled through her lips. Of all the MacGregor men, he had always been kind to her.

Malcolm paused, his lips twisting in anger. "Yer da ordered him beaten. They tied him to a tree, pulled an' tortured him 'til his shoulders snapped out o' the sockets. They murdered his best friend, William."

Lauren cringed as her mouth drained dry and her stomach twirled. The temptation to deny his words frayed at the edge of her mind as she followed him inside.

Malcolm directed her over to a large figure lying motionless on a small bed. A candle burned on a makeshift table beside him. She took small steps, her heart pounding into her throat.

"Graham?" Lauren leaned over him, taking in the sight of his bruised and disfigured face. The memory of his handsome features was like a vision. Graham didn't respond. Deep sorrow filled her soul as she imagined what agony he must be enduring. "My . . . da . . . did this?"

"Aye," Malcolm's tone dripped with bitterness. "I was not here, but they tell me he tried to protect my mither an' sister—yer friends." He emphasized the last words as if she had betrayed them herself.

"They are my friends," she whispered, unable to wipe at her tears with her hands bound behind her. Bile rose to the back of Lauren's throat, threatening to overcome her. Graham's wounds would be branded in her brain forever. What would become of Iona and Carleen? She slid to her knees as grief wracked her body. Lauren had never been able to deny the emotional tug of compassion. While she wondered what was to become of her, Graham's grave condition weighed on her heart along with the spiritual state of the souls within her father and brother.

Lauren turned and tried to wipe her cheek on her shoulder. Malcolm strode toward her, his mouth set in a grim expression. She resisted the desire to cower and forced her muscles to remain still.

2

Malcolm paused in midstride, realizing what he was about to do. Lauren trembled and looked so pathetic weeping in the corner, but he refused to comfort her. He needed to keep his distance. The woman stirred too much confusion inside him. She leaned her head against the stone wall and closed her eyes as if shutting them out. When the villagers threatened to come against her, Lauren stood firm, unafraid to meet her fate, but at the sight of his battered brother, she wept as if he were her own kin. What kind of lass did such a thing?

Most likely, the tears were an act, a ploy to keep him from taking vengeance. Lauren Campbell knew the MacGregors took care of their own. The law was corrupt, siding with the Campbells at every turn. Ever since King James abolished the MacGregor name in 1603, the clan had to either renounce their name or suffer beatings, imprisonment, or worse, death. Many took other clan names. At times, his family used the surname Gregory. MacGregor lands were confiscated and handed over to the Campbells, but this problem with Duncan Campbell was personal. Malcolm would get his revenge.

"If ye do not need aught else, I shall go back to my own family to see what I can do to help," Colin said, looking from Malcolm to

Thomas. His nose and cheeks turned a shade darker, and he gulped with difficulty. "I'm sorry I did not find Iona or Carleen. I really thought they would be at Kilchurn."

"Ye did what ye could." Malcolm slapped him on the back as he walked him to the door. "I'm grateful ye went."

"Aye, an' for patching up Graham," Thomas said. "Now he will have a chance at living."

" 'Twasn't much, but ye're welcome." Colin opened the door and stepped outside.

Graham stirred. His mouth twisted in agony as he groaned. Malcolm's gut coiled as he and Thomas rushed to his side. Graham's eyelids fluttered, but he struggled to open them due to the swelling.

"M . . . Mith . . ." Graham's voice faded.

"Do not worry." Malcolm gripped his hand and bowed his head, hoping the Almighty would grant him the ability to keep the solemn promise he was about to make. "I shall get Mither back an' Carleen too. Ye have my word."

Malcolm tilted Graham's neck so he could sip a bit of whiskey. He hoped it was enough to dull the lad's pain. It dribbled down his chin. Thomas wiped his mouth with a rag. Graham didn't speak again as he dozed.

"Now that we have the lass, the Campbells will be back." Rising to his feet, Malcolm glanced over at Mary, Roy, and Thomas. He took three long strides to the table and kneaded the back of his neck. Malcolm rubbed his tired eyes. "Graham will live through this, but we have to get 'im safely out o' here."

"Where to?" Thomas lifted a dark eyebrow. "He canna travel. Not after what they did to 'im." Thomas leaned forward, resting his elbows on the table and linking his fingers. "We have no idea what injuries he has inside."

"He will be fine. I saw the determination in his eyes a moment ago," Malcolm said, refusing to believe otherwise.

"That was pain," Roy said.

Mary nodded in agreement where she sat at the wooden table on the other side of Thomas. "By the time Alan returns from the nearest debtors' prison, Graham may be doing better."

"We do not have that much time. The Campbells will soon know Lauren is gone an' they will come for her." Malcolm paced in thought. "Thomas, I want ye to take him to Mither's people. Uncle Athol Ferguson will take ye in after what they have done to Mither. Ye'll both be safe in Glenstrae under the protection of the chief."

"Roy, could I borrow yer wagon bed? " Thomas asked. "Or did the wretched Campbells burn it?"

"My cousin borrowed it," Roy said, nodding. "Otherwise, they would have taken it."

"Good. A flat bed for Graham to lie on will be the only way he can travel right now." Malcolm paused to rub his tense neck. "I do not want the two of ye here longer than necessary." Malcolm walked over and thumped the table with his fingers like a drum roll. "I am taking the lass with me to Taynuilt. I canna afford to let her out o' my sight. She is the only way I can be sure to get back at Duncan. He cares for naught else."

"Ye suppose the man has a heart." Thomas spoke in a gruff voice before looking down at the table and blinking.

"Everyone cares 'bout something or someone," Malcolm said. "We know he is greedy, but few have gotten to his family."

"No one has the courage to challenge 'im," Thomas said. "They say he was not good to his wife."

"Aye." Lauren's voice echoed across the room. "They say that and worse." She kept her eyes closed as she leaned against the wall. "I have heard all the rumors about my father. I do not remember much about their marriage, but I do know ye may not get the reaction ye hope. He hardly knows Blair and I exist. Ye should have taken Scott, his heir."

"Duncan is a prideful man an' ye belong to 'im." Malcolm straightened. "Believe me, taking ye matters."

"We shall see." Lauren shrugged, unconvinced.

Malcolm propped his fists on his hips and studied her. Was she attempting to make him think her father didn't care for her so he would let her go? Did she want sympathy, hoping he wouldn't hurt her? Lauren was a strange lass, to be sure.

"I have an idea." Malcolm snapped his fingers and whirled. The others stared at him with curious expressions. "When ye dig a grave for William, dig another one beside it. Put Graham's name on it. If the Campbells believe Graham is dead, there will be no reason to come finish the deed. Thomas an' Graham should leave tonight. Let them believe Thomas came with me to fetch Mither and Carleen. Mayhap, they will leave the villagers alone to focus on me."

"They will never leave us alone." Roy slammed a fist on the table.

"Ye're right 'bout that," Malcolm said, resuming his pacing. Being on the move helped him think. "As long as Duncan owns the lands, things will not change. The villagers need to leave." With a heavy heart, Malcolm turned to his brother. "Thomas, I shall find a way to write. I will slip yer letters inside the ones I send to our uncle."

"Aye." Thomas nodded as he stood. "To keep them from tracing me to Glenstrae. Good idea. I wish ye'd take Roy with ye," Thomas said. "Some of the other MacGregors too."

"Nay, no need to risk others." Malcolm glanced back at Lauren and winked. "Mayhap, people will think we are a couple."

"I doubt it," Lauren scoffed. "Not with my hands tied and a gag in my mouth."

"Looks like ye'll have yer hands full with the lass." Roy grinned. "Mary, give 'em a few extra plaids." He held out a hand, and Malcolm shook it. Unsure if he would ever see him again, Malcolm pulled Roy into a hug as emotion choked him. Ever since his father's death in the Jacobite rebellion in 1745, Roy had been like a father to him and his brothers. "Ye take care."

"I will," Malcolm said, nodding.

"Here ye go." Mary brought him a rolled bundle of plaids. "These will help ye stay warm an' give ye a change o' clothes." She reached up and wrapped her arms around his neck. Tears welled in her eyes. She brushed them away in haste.

Malcolm swallowed with difficulty and cleared his throat. He embraced Thomas. Malcolm leaned back and blinked several times. "I want ye to know, if I do not reach them afore they board the ship, I will not be coming back. I shall board the next ship to the colonies."

"I figured as much. Mither an' Carleen need ye." Thomas took a deep breath and slapped Malcolm's shoulder. "An' do not worry. I shall take good care o' Graham."

"I know ye will. Tell him bye for me when next he wakes." Malcolm took one longing glance at his brother lying on the small bed.

"Come on, Lauren. No need to gag ye now. No one 'round here would help ye escape." Without a word, she struggled to her feet with her hands still bound.

"They say the colonies are full of opportunities for men like us." Malcolm squeezed his brother's shoulder. "If it is as they say, I shall make a home over there an' I will send for ye both. Mark my words, brother." Malcolm gave Thomas one final grip before opening the wooden door. "This is not good-bye." He hauled Lauren out.

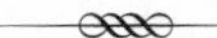

Lauren glanced down at her blue riding skirt, thankful she wore something warm and flexible. She had planned to enjoy a day of picnicking and exploring the ruins of Kilchurn Castle with her sister. Instead, she rode a brown mare, fenced in by Malcolm MacGregor's arms as he held the reins. As much as she hated to admit it, Lauren feared the gag and wondered when he would put it back on her. She loathed the idea of losing her freedom to speak.

"Even if we could not afford to pay our rents, the most yer father should have done was made us quit the premises. He had no right to sell Mither an' Carleen as if he owned them like slaves." Malcolm's bitter voice filled her ears. "They treated William an' Graham as if their lives meant naught."

Lauren didn't respond. She swallowed back the ache in her throat. Would they ride through the night? Would he stop and camp? Malcolm was one man she failed to understand. Even in the midst of so much chaos and tragedy, he kept his wits and temper. The feat earned her respect and was something she had never seen from her father and brother.

If he wanted to talk, mayhap she could learn more about the man himself. She would start by complimenting him. Didn't men like him need people to pump up their pride? "My da and brother would not have had such self-control under the same circumstances ye've endured," she said.

"I'd rather not talk about them," he snapped, his arms tensing around her. "Otherwise, I might be tempted to gag ye again."

Lauren clenched her teeth, chastising herself for antagonizing him. Of course, he didn't want to talk about the Campbells. He had been talking about his own family earlier. Why did she have to be so dim-witted? What made her think she could talk to Malcolm MacGregor? The man abducted her. He blamed her family and planned to use her as a pawn. It was as simple as that.

Her heart pounded with the steady steps of the horse. The late evening sun angled over the church steeple in the distance. They had almost arrived in Taynuilt. Fear pierced her heart and sent shivers through her body like tiny waves as she wondered about her destiny in this place.

Malcolm paused, shoved the gag in her mouth, and tied it behind her head. Dread pooled in the pit of her stomach. He unrolled one of the packs Mary had given him. "Put this on an' cover yer head and face with the hood. If ye try aught, I have a knife at yer back.

While I do not like the idea of hurting a woman, I refuse to die because of ye." He leaned around, making sure the results satisfied him before riding on.

Smoke from chimneys filled the air along with the aroma of mixed spices as they passed various cottages of all shapes and sizes. The sounds of a few rolling carts and carriages passed both directions. Most people had gone inside, but some lingered in the streets. It wasn't a large town, and before long the pleasant aromas and sights gave way to less pleasant odors and lurking shadows.

The stench of a livery stable caused Lauren to wrinkle her nose. The closer they drew to the docks, the more prominent the smell of whiskey, and the number of taverns increased. Some she assumed were brothel houses as loose women hung out the windows, calling to men on the streets. Masts on the taller ships reached above the lower rooftops.

At the end of the street, Malcolm rode toward a ship where a crowd had gathered around two men sitting at a rickety wooden table. One wrote down names on long parchment with ink and quill while the other spoke to individuals in a long line. Malcolm slowed and leaned forward, resting his blade against her side. Lauren wondered if he would really go through with hurting her. Was he as bad a man as he wanted her to think, or was this all bitter revenge?

"Pardon me, sir, but do ye know where this ship is headin'?" Malcolm called out to them.

"Pennsylvania. If ye plan to board, ye'd better get in back of the line." A middle-aged seaman shielded his eyes as he glanced up at them. "Looks like we will soon be full."

"I am lookin' for two women. Can ye check yer roster?" Malcolm asked.

"No time. I need to get to these people." He shook his head, his lips twisting in a frown as he gestured to those standing before him. The man looked as if he had not bathed in a while. Lauren was glad the hood hid her disgust.

"What are the names?" A man with a shadowed beard asked, waving a stack of parchment. His black hair hung in oily curls to his shoulders. Lauren imagined all these sailors must have come from pirate ships at one time. She glanced back at Malcolm, but he kept an expression of stone. If he was worried about Iona and Carleen being aboard this vessel with these type of men, he didn't show it.

"Iona an' Carleen MacGregor. They may have used the name Gregory," Malcolm's voice carried above the conversations around them as the water lapped against the docks.

The sailor scanned one parchment, then pulled out another. After he searched through three pages, he shook his dark head. "Sorry, but they are not on 'ere."

"Thank ye." Malcolm gave a small nod, but Lauren didn't miss his sigh of relief.

He rode down the row stopping at each docked ship and asked questions.

Dusk was now upon them, and soon no light would be left, save for the lanterns people carried and candles burning through the windows. A shadow came at them. An elderly man hobbled over. He wore spectacles perched on the edge of his bony nose. A bushy gray beard and mustache covered his mouth.

"Ye're lookin' for someone?" He coughed as if his words took the last of his breath. He bent over, bracing his hands on his knees and wheezed. "My son is cap'n of a ship bound for the Carolinas. I have a roster I will be submitting for Scotland's records. Most o' these ships do not go by the books, but my lad . . . he does." The man grinned with fatherly pride. "Too bad I am not well enough to go these days, for I dearly love adventure on the high seas."

"We are looking for Iona an' Carleen MacGregor," Malcolm said.

"*The Loyal Adventure* set sail this morn. In fact, she's headin' to Charles Towne, South Carolina, to be exact." He pointed a crooked finger at them. "But ye'll have to look at the roster yerselves. I canna read. Would ye be willin' to spare a coin to take a look?"

Malcolm reached in his plaid and tossed a coin to him. The man stumbled trying to catch it. He hobbled over to retrieve it from the dirt road. With slow effort, he made his way back and pulled a rolled parchment from his sleeve. "Here it is, just like I said." He handed it up to Malcolm, who grunted when his horse sidestepped as the man coughed and wheezed.

"To tell the truth, I canna read either." Malcolm unrolled the parchment. He held it up and squinted as if trying to make sense of it. Curious as to what happened to her friends, Lauren glanced at the slanted handwriting. She lifted her finger at the sight of the MacGregor name toward the bottom. A blot of ink made Iona's illegible, but Carleen's name was easy to read. She jabbed the paper to gain his attention. When he didn't respond, Lauren grabbed his hand, squeezed, and jabbed the paper where their names were.

"Lass, are ye sure?" Malcolm asked, the hope in his voice undeniable.

She squeezed him again. The warmth in his touch was like a lifeline, leaving her in complete dependence on him.

"What did ye say the name of this ship is?" Malcolm asked.

"*The Loyal Adventure*." The man scratched the side of his head. "Bound for Charles Towne."

"Thank ye, good sir." Malcolm tipped his hat and secured an arm around Lauren. "Do ye know of another ship heading there?'

"Aye." The man nodded with a yellow-toothed grin. "*The Sea Lady* sets sail just after sunrise in the morn."

"We will need to find an inn for the night," Malcolm lowered his voice near her ear. "But I warn ye, it shan't be the kind of place ye're used to, and I canna afford naught better. Ye need to be careful. The men there canna be trusted. If ye try to seek help, ye might end up in a situation worse than me."

Since Lauren couldn't respond, she listened, wondering if he wanted to intimidate her or if what he said was true. She would wait and see what she thought after they arrived.

Malcolm sat at a table with a mug of ale. He'd only taken a few sips. Now he waited for the liquid fire to dull the bitter taste and his senses along with it. The wee hours should have enticed his weary bones to sleep, but the blessed slumber once again evaded him. On the morrow he would leave bonny Scotland—possibly forever.

He could only afford one chamber at the inn, and in such a place of ill repute no one questioned his being with a woman. At least, the hood concealed her identity. Once she returned to her family, her reputation would still be intact.

In no way would he have harmed her with his knife, but it was necessary to threaten her. He needed to ensure her silence while he questioned the sailors. In spite of his behavior, she had helped him find his mother's and sister's names on the roster. He was grateful, but that didn't mean he could trust her. His mother and sister were indentured servants to the captain. In return, the captain would sell them in Carolina when they arrived.

Malcolm's heart was heavy with worry. He couldn't help wondering what kinds of hardships they were enduring. If only Duncan Campbell had been more patient. Resentment lodged in his chest, making it hard to breathe. He lifted his cup and took a long swallow. This time the liquid burned going down. He inhaled deeply and shook his head. Malcolm released the air in his lungs like a dragon blowing out fire.

After he drained his cup, Malcolm returned to their chamber. Lauren slumbered on the bed, lying on her stomach with her limbs spread out. She still wore her clothes. The warm fire he started in the hearth earlier would soon die. The tiny blue flames licked what was left of the smoldering logs. Cold air already sneaked into the room. Malcolm grabbed Lauren's red cloak discarded on a wooden chair in the corner. He spread it out over her before settling on his own makeshift pallet on the floor.

Lauren was a decent lass. What had motivated her to read the roster for him? Was she trying to win him over? The lass wasted her efforts. He would never trust a Campbell, not even one as bonny and as enticing as she.

He closed his eyes and allowed the drowsy effect of the whiskey to take over his mind. He wasn't a drinking man by habit, but tonight he needed something to ease his anxiety. One mug was enough to do the trick but not enough to put him in a stupor.

Sounds of people walking and talking in the hallway and laughter next door faded as waves tumbling to a sandy shore filled his mind. It didn't look like any beach he had ever seen in Scotland. The air was warm and the sky a brilliant blue. Lauren laughed as she rode by him on a brown mare. Her blonde curls bounced down her back as she leaned forward challenging him to a race. She glanced over her shoulder at him, her azure blue eyes mesmerizing and filled with . . . No, it was impossible.

Malcolm bolted up with a start, pulling himself from the dream. With his breathing erratic, he ran his fingers through his tousled hair. Lauren still slept. At least one of them had gotten some rest. He wondered about the time.

He strode over to the window and peeked through the drapes. Still dark outside. Dawn would arrive in an hour or two. It would give him enough time to find *The Sea Lady* and return with some food to break their fast.

Careful not to wake Lauren, Malcolm let himself out and used the key to click the lock in place. He didn't want Lauren escaping while he was gone.

Crisp air filled his lungs, and each time he breathed out, it looked like white smoke lingered from his mouth. The moon cast a silver glow that beamed off the surface of the ocean. A few ships had set sail, and others had docked since yesterday. Most were small vessels, but Malcolm noticed a larger ship toward the middle of the wharf. He hurried toward it.

A man with a steaming cup of coffee walked over the plank to the dock.

"Good sir, do ye know where I can find *The Sea Lady*?" Malcolm asked.

"Right 'ere." The man gestured behind him.

Malcolm grinned and thanked him. By the time, he arrived back at the inn, the smell of bacon and brewing coffee lingered in the air. His mouth watered and his stomach rumbled. A man sat at a table, ready to eat, while a serving wench adjusted her white cap and tied an apron around her bulging middle.

"Could I have two bowls of porridge and two cups of coffee?" Malcolm asked, sitting at the nearest table.

"Ye that hungry, are ye?" Her thick voice sounded low and husky, as if still trying to wake. Her lips lifted into a smile as she gave him a wink. "I would think a brawny mon such as yerself would need more'n a wee bit o' porridge."

" 'Tis why I have asked for two of each." He held up two fingers.

Malcolm braced his elbows on the table and linked his fingers as he waited. The server set his coffee down first. Malcolm gripped the warm mug in his cold hands and sipped the hot liquid. A moment later, steaming porridge arrived. While he ate, Malcolm pulled out a vial of valerian that Mary slipped inside the packed roll she gave him. He mixed some of it in the other bowl for Lauren.

"Pardon me, but could I have a wee bit o' whiskey?" Malcolm asked.

"Goodness, mon! 'Tis a bit early, is it not?" The woman turned a wide-eyed gaze at him.

"Aye." Malcolm nodded. " 'Tis why I only need a wee bit."

"All right." She shrugged and walked away. By the time she returned, he shoved in the final bite. She shook her head in disbelief as she set down the small cup of whiskey.

Malcolm waited until she left and poured more valerian in Lauren's coffee. With the coffee in one hand and the wooden bowl in the other, Malcolm set out for their chamber.

It took him a moment to maneuver the items in his hands while inserting the key and unlocking the door. He pushed it open to see Lauren at the washbasin cleaning her arms up to her elbows. She turned and glared at him. "Ye left me alone last night, and I wake up this morn all alone again."

"I thought ye might prefer it that way, wee privacy," Malcolm said. "Besides, I did not think ye wanted to spend time alone with yer abductor." He grinned and held out her food. "I brought something to break yer fast."

"I was not referring to spending time with ye, only that I did not want to be neglected." She grabbed a towel and dried her arms. "Ye covered me . . . with my cloak." Lauren pulled her shirt sleeves to her wrists and sat on the edge of the bed.

"Aye, I thought ye might be cold." He handed her the coffee and the porridge. "Eat all of it. I canna guarantee when we will eat again." He sat in the wooden chair across from her.

She sipped her coffee and grimaced, then took her first bite of porridge and frowned. "The food here tastes strange."

"Aye, mine was as well." He gestured to her food. "Eat. We do not have much time."

She must have been hungry. To his relief, she obeyed. After she finished the last bite, she blinked and swayed. She managed to lift her mug and sipped the rest of her coffee. "Are we leaving now?" Lauren blinked several times as if she couldn't focus. "Thank ye. I feel much better."

"Time to go." Malcolm stood and reached out to her. She tried to take his hand, but she stretched too far to the right. "This way."

Malcolm looped an arm behind her and under her knees, lifting her in his arms.

"What is wrong . . . with me?" Lauren mumbled. "I do not understand why I am so tired. Did ye poison me?" She touched the heel of her hand to her forehead, wrinkling her fair brow.

" 'Tisn't poison. Just something to help ye relax an' sleep a wee bit," he said. "How else could I get ye aboard *The Sea Lady* without resistance?"

"Ye brute!" Lauren tried to slap him, but her aim was off.

Malcolm chuckled and pulled her close. He had no doubt that by the time they reached the ship, she would be asleep and docile.

Malcolm carried Lauren's sleeping form down the boardwalk where a crowd had gathered in front of *The Sea Lady*. Two sailors were at a wooden table. A long line had formed in front of the first man, who was younger with no facial hair. He had a long parchment roll and wrote names down with other information. He pushed the quill across the page as fast as he could. The other man was a few years older with a brown mustache. He also had a parchment roll with quill and ink, but unlike his friend, he had a brown box with a lid.

"If ye can pay the fare for yer journey, I shall take yer coins right 'ere." The man with the mustache pointed at his box.

A well-dressed couple with two children stepped in front of Malcolm. He couldn't move as fast since he carried Lauren. His rolled pack looped over his shoulder, and his money pouch was fastened on his belt around his waist, holding his plaid in place. He strained to hear how much the fare would be. With the money he made from the cattle he and Thomas sold and from what he made selling his horse, he should have enough to buy both their tickets. As the people in front of him stepped away, Malcolm moved her over his shoulder like a baby to get to his money pouch. Lauren moaned. He winced and paused, waiting for her to settle. Malcolm hoped the rolled pack could serve as a cushion.

"How much for two?" Malcolm asked.

" 'Tis five pounds each for a total of ten pounds." The man grinned up at Malcolm with a lifted eyebrow as if he expected Malcolm to come up short. "O' course if ye do not have the total fare, ye can get in the other line and sign yerselves up for indenture."

"If I wanted to do that, do ye not think I would be in that line?" Malcolm inclined his head as he counted out the ten pounds and handed it over. "The names are Malcolm MacGregor and Lauren Campbell." He wanted to make sure that Duncan would be able to find a record of their travel. It was his first step in taking revenge.

"Ye're not wedded?" the man asked, frowning up at Malcolm and squinting at Lauren in suspicion. "What is wrong with her?"

"Naught to worry 'bout." Malcolm winked with a grin. "I gave her a wee bit o' medicine to help her with sailing. Had a few reservations, she did."

"Will ye need a cabin with other bachelors?"

"Aye." Malcolm nodded. "An' she will be fine with a few single lasses."

"Go aboard." The man waved him forward. "Find her a cabin, and she will be fine."

As Malcolm carried Lauren up the boarding plank to the main deck, the gray sky sparkled like a diamond in the east where the sun broke through the clouds. Shimmering light crystallized upon the surface of the sea as small waves rolled into the harbor like rivulets. A moment of fear seized him as he imagined being out in the middle of the ocean, surrounded by water. The idea of those small waves turning into large ones made his gut twist. He coughed to ease his tension. Lauren stirred.

She wasn't heavy, but after carrying her such a distance, his arms had grown weary and needed a break. Malcolm found a barrel and sat down for a moment. Lauren wiggled with a sigh but didn't wake. He pulled her close and stroked the back of her hair.

"Shush, 'tis all right," he coaxed her. He wasn't yet ready to deal with her wrath after she came to her senses.

"Do not leave me, Da." Her mumbled words pierced Malcolm's heart as Lauren snuggled closer and gripped his plaid. In her dreamy state, he saw a vulnerable side to Lauren that he hadn't allowed himself to consider. For the first time, he saw the woman beyond the Campbell name. He sensed she felt abandoned and unloved by her father. His mouth went dry at the realization she had told the truth. Lauren Campbell really believed her father wouldn't care enough to come for her. What if she was right? What would he do with her then?

Thoughts of his mother and sister languishing away in a field somewhere enduring hard labor stole his breath. Carleen was young and strong. She would survive until he found her. But his mother? She was getting old and frail. The years had been hard on her, raising four children as a peasant widow. After purchasing his and Lauren's passage, he doubted he had enough to purchase his mother's full indenture, certainly not both hers and Carleen's.

He looked down at Lauren and traced her golden hair along the smooth skin at her brow. Like his sister, Lauren was young. She could endure what his mother could not. If necessary, he would exchange her for his mother. It wasn't fair, but nor was it fair to sell his mother and sister into indenture. He loathed having to do this to Lauren, but what choice did he have? If anyone was to blame, it was her father. Fury rose inside him. If he ever got his hands on the man, Malcolm would make him pay for all the pain he'd caused the MacGregors.

Determined to ease his temper, Malcolm took a deep breath and let it out slow and easy. He surveyed all the busy activity around them. Crewmen whistled as they checked ropes and folded canvas sails, and others loaded barrels of food. Passengers were either saying good-bye to loved ones before boarding or giving instructions regarding their luggage. Babies wailed, children chatted in excitement, and people on the main deck waved to others waiting on shore.

Malcolm glanced at the stairs leading below deck. He needed to claim cabin space for them before all the good ones were full. He braced himself as he lifted Lauren. The narrow staircase proved to be his most difficult challenge. He had to turn sideways at an angle to miss scraping Lauren's head against the wall. By the time he reached the hallway below, he was quite out of breath and took a moment to recover. The quarters were tight, and people were crammed everywhere. It didn't appear as if there were enough beds for everyone. Malcolm grimaced at the thought of living like this for the next couple of months.

He came to a cabin and peeked in to see two women talking and sitting on two different beds. They didn't have five or six as some of the other cabins he passed. "Pardon me, but do ye have room for one more?" Malcolm glanced down at Lauren for emphasis. "She has no luggage an' the lass shan't take up too much space."

The two women looked at each other and nodded. "Of course." The redheaded lass stood and gestured to her bed. "Ye can lay her here for now. We only have two beds, but we shall figure somethin' out." She narrowed her gaze. "What is wrong with her?"

"I gave her something to make her sleep an' to ease her nerves." He carried Lauren over and bent to his knees so he could ease her onto the bed. "Her name is Lauren Campbell." Malcolm stood and gave them a brief bow. "I shall come back later to check on her, but right now I need to claim a cabin for myself."

"Aye." The woman nodded. "Ye can try my brother's cabin. Go down the hall and take a right. His name is Logan Grant. Tell 'im Deidra sent ye."

"I am much obliged." Malcolm gave her a quick bow before glancing one last time at Lauren. She looked so serene and peaceful, beautiful even. Warmth seeped through him at the realization, and he didn't want to leave her, but then he remembered how angry she would be when she woke. Aye, it was best to make his escape now.

3

Female voices on the other side of the room floated to Lauren's consciousness. She lifted her head with a groggy moan. Her eyelids were heavy as she forced them open.

"She is waking," a woman said.

Lauren blinked and tried to focus on the two fuzzy faces looming over her.

"Where am I?" Lauren pushed up on her elbows. Cheers escalated above, and she had the sensation that the floor moved beneath them.

"We are finally setting sail." Another woman clapped her hands. "I canna believe I am goin' to the Carolinas."

"Set . . . setting sail?" Lauren rubbed her eyes and sat up. She glanced around the room, but it was dark with little light and no windows. Two lanterns hung on the opposite walls, revealing only two narrow beds. Tears filled Lauren's eyes, but she blinked them back and swallowed, summoning her courage. "Where is Malcolm MacGregor?"

"Oh, ye mean the handsome brawn mon that brought ye hither?"

Now that Lauren's vision had cleared, a comely lass with brown hair bent toward her. "He said he would come back an' check on ye."

"How long ago was that?" Lauren stood and brushed her wayward hair out of her eyes. "Do either of ye know where he went?"

" 'Twas about twenty, maybe thirty minutes ago." Her second roommate stepped forward with wild curly hair falling past her shoulders in a sea of red. Green eyes sparkled as she smiled. "My name is Deidra Grant, an' I sent 'im to find my brother, Logan."

"Please do not think me rude for not introducing myself, but I am Kathleen Anderson." The other woman gave a brief curtsey.

"Look at yer formality," Deidra teased her friend.

"I am not supposed to be here." Panic rippled through Lauren's chest, gripping her with fear. "Please pardon me."

Lauren hurried from the cabin on trembling legs. Once she turned the corner, she leaned against the wall to catch her breath. What was she to do? She had no change of clothes, no money, and she was alone. A gentle reproach pressed inside her chest.

"Forgive me, Lord. I'm not alone. I have Ye," she whispered, closing her eyes. "Give me the strength to go to the captain. Please give me favor. Make them believe me."

"Are ye all right?" Deidra followed her into the hallway. Her long red hair showered her shoulders in tangled curls. She blinked in concern. Her compassionate expression was framed in pale skin layered with freckles.

"I need to find the captain. Where is he?" Lauren clenched her hands in front of her, determined to seek help. Her first instinct was to find Malcolm and rage at him, but she knew very well it would do no good. He was determined to make her pay for her father's sins. Arguing with Malcolm would only cause her to lose precious time. She needed to convince the captain to turn around before they got too far out to sea.

"The captain was up on deck at the wheel afore we set sail." Deidra pointed above. "He is probably still there."

"Thank ye." Lauren said, swallowing her fear. "I must go."

Lauren passed several more people who were trying to find their cabins with the intention of getting settled for the long journey. She reached the main deck and shielded her eyes from the bright sun as she searched for the captain. A middle-aged man with gray hair tied back in a ribbon wore a black hat and was dressed in a white shirt with a brown vest. Another man with long brown hair in his early thirties conversed with him. The elder man had a hand on the large wheel.

Taking a deep breath, Lauren strode toward them and climbed a set of steps leading to the quarterdeck. The younger man turned, lifted a brow, and walked to her.

"Please, sir, I need to speak to the captain. There has been a terrible mistake." Lauren scratched at her arm in nervous anticipation.

"The captain is busy. I am Hugh MacKinnon, his second in command. Ye may state your problem. I shall take care of it." His speech was more cultured than she expected, with a faint English accent.

"But the captain is right there." She glanced around his shoulder and pointed.

"Aye, but my job is to handle matters before they reach him." Mr. MacKinnon followed her gaze and twisted around. He nodded to the captain as the two men exchanged a glance. "So, what is this mistake you are worried about?" He grinned in the midst of his brown beard and mustache, revealing better-looking teeth than she would have anticipated for a sailor. His brown eyes assessed her attire, no doubt judging her character.

"I was stolen from my family and brought aboard against my will," Lauren said. "I am not supposed to be on this ship. Ye have to turn around and take me back before we go too far."

"I am afraid we are already too far for that." He laughed. "And where is this person who kidnapped you? How did you manage to escape?"

"He left me asleep in a cabin with two other women," she said.

"You do not look beaten or tortured." He assessed her and shook his head. "Did he not tie you up? Even your wrists look fine."

"He poisoned me so he had no need. Someone had to notice him carrying me aboard." Lauren stepped forward, ready to plead if she had to. "Please, ye have to believe me."

"My girl, if he was trying to hide you, then why put you in a cabin with others to come and go as you please?" He scratched his temple. "He did not try to hide you in a private cabin so he could have his way with you, nor did he sell you as an indenture. You could have easily been hidden in the hold with so many others." He shook his head in disbelief. "I am sorry, but your story sounds contrived."

Tears filled her eyes. Malcolm had known how they would react. The dirty scoundrel. "Please, believe me. I have no one else to turn to."

He narrowed his gaze and shifted his weight to one foot as he stroked his beard in thought. "Are you a stowaway then?" Mr. MacKinnon tilted his head. "The captain dislikes losing money. An' stowaways cost us."

"Nay, I'm not." Lauren fidgeted with the nail on her thumb. She needed to convince them of the truth. "I told ye, he gave me something. I was not awake when he brought me aboard."

"I suppose I could question the men who wrote the records." Mr. MacKinnon strode to the rail and leaned over. "Mr. Smith, fetch Mr. Todd Kerr at once." Folding his hands behind his back, Mr. MacKinnon walked back to Lauren. "And who brought you aboard?"

"Malcolm MacGregor." The words slid out in a rush.

"While we wait for the other men to arrive, tell me why this Mr. MacGregor would take such an aggressive action in kidnapping you." Mr. MacKinnon crossed his arms over his chest and waited, giving her a pointed look.

Lauren confessed the truth, the whole sordid detail of what her father did to the MacGregors, Malcolm's reaction, and her desire to go home. Mr. Kerr appeared standing at attention with his hands folded behind his back. A moment later, Malcolm arrived with his new roommate. His dark eyes met hers, and for an instant, she sensed his remorse. He averted his attention to Mr. MacKinnon as he approached.

"I understand you brought this young woman aboard. She says you stole her from her family. Is this true?" Mr. MacKinnon asked.

"Nay, I did not take her," Malcolm said, glaring at Lauren.

Heat rushed up Lauren's face, boiling her blood. An image of Colin MacGregor came to mind. Malcolm had not lied, but how dare he make her sound like a liar. "Ye poisoned me."

"True. I thought it would calm yer fears an' ease yer anxiety. I knew ye was not keen on sailing." Malcolm raised an eyebrow, twisting his lips into a patronizing grin.

"Aye." Mr. Kerr stepped forward. "The gel was asleep when he brought 'er aboard, but he did pay her fare. She is no stowaway."

"I knew someone saw us." Lauren lifted her chin. "Now, 'tis the matter of my abduction I want to set straight."

"What have I got to be ashamed of, Miss Campbell? I have paid for yer passage." Malcolm crossed his arms and emphasized her name. "I am not the one who sold yer family as indentured servants without their consent—like slaves at an auction."

"And neither did I!" She stepped forward on her tiptoes to meet him, but her head ached since she had to lean back so far to look into his eyes. "I am sorry for what happened to Iona and Carleen, but ye're a different matter—entirely."

"I only want the truth," Mr. MacKinnon said.

"I told ye the truth." Lauren appealed to Mr. MacKinnon. "Please . . . take me back. I am sure my father would make it worth yer time. He will pay ye well for yer trouble."

"Too late. We stand to lose more money than your father would pay to cover a hold of over a hundred or more souls." Mr. MacKinnon rubbed his jaw. "Things do not add up between the two stories, but it would take a simpleton to ignore the obvious history between you two."

"There is no history," Lauren said. "Please, ye have to believe me."

"All the signs point to a lovers' quarrel." Mr. MacKinnon raised a palm. "I do not care to know the details. We are not turning back." Mr. MacKinnon crooked a finger at Mr. Kerr. "Now if you will excuse me, I have a crew to manage."

Lauren glared at Malcolm. "I hope yer revenge against my father was worth selling yer soul for." She turned, unable to hide her contempt at how he had gotten his way. Tears blinded her vision as she stomped down the steps to the main deck.

Lauren's parting words still roared in Malcolm's brain like a prophecy of doom. Had he really sold his soul with his vengeful deed? The burning question was more than he could bear. No doubt, he would have to face the consequences of his actions at some point. At least he was able to save her from the misery of the hold. Relief filled him at the sobering thought of being responsible for her welfare while aboard. This way he could protect her from roving sailors and still exchange her for his mother when they arrived.

"I think I am gonna like ye." His new roommate grinned with a curious expression as he crossed his arms over his chest. Logan's blue eyes glimmered with a thirst for adventure. "Looks like ye'll be keepin' things lively 'round here. We shall need some of that while on this long journey at sea."

"Believe me, my life is full of unwanted controversy, but I am not sure I would call it an adventure." Malcolm scanned the main deck below, but saw no sign of Lauren. "Be careful befriending me. A black curse has been upon our family for generations now. Ye would not want to add to yer troubles, would ye?"

"I do not believe in that nonsense." Logan laughed. "Cheer up! Ye're about to enter a world full of promise an' a brand-new beginning. In the colonies men like us can make our own way rather than being born and stuck with whatever fate dealt us."

"Right now I need to find Lauren before she causes more trouble. She is quite angry, an' I am not sure what she might do." Malcolm followed the direction Lauren had taken.

"She will be fine." Logan followed.

"Aye, but this ship is full of questionable men." Malcolm shook his head. "She is young an' innocent."

"I see." Logan's voice took on a pensive tone. "I could check with my sister an' her roommate. Lauren might have went back to their cabin."

"Aye. Good idea." Malcolm looked over at his new redheaded friend. When they arrived at the cabin, Lauren wasn't there. Malcolm had to hold his patience while Logan introduced him to his sister, Deidra, and her cabinmate, Kathleen. Once he could break away, Malcolm checked the main deck. He went below and started on the opposite end from where his cabin was located. He walked the levels and talked a sailor into helping him search through the cargo in the hold and among the indentured servants. While he couldn't imagine her hiding in such a dark place with all the rats, he could see her making friends with those less fortunate.

He searched for an hour and began to wonder if she had found an ally and was hiding in someone's cabin. Malcolm rubbed his tired eyes, not liking the idea of having to knock on every cabin door. He could wait outside her cabin until she showed up. They were out in the middle of the sea. She couldn't very well leave the ship.

Hanging his head, Malcolm walked by the cockboat. A woman wept nearby. He paused, straining to determine the direction. It sounded like it was on the other side of the cockboat, but naught was there but a rail overlooking the wide-open sea. Fear coiled in the pit of his gut. If he startled her, she might lose her balance and fall.

Malcolm dropped on his hands and knees to crawl over to the bottom of the upside-down boat. He peeked over the edge, and Lauren sat on the side of the cockboat with her feet propped up against the rail. Her arms encircled her bent knees. She looked out over the blue sea as if seeking solace.

"Lauren?" Malcolm kept his voice steady and calm to keep from scaring her. "Please . . . come away from there. 'Tis dangerous."

She didn't respond, merely wiped her eyes and sniffled.

He took a deep breath and sighed. Guilt tightened around his heart like an iron fist. "I am sorry."

"Nay." She shook her head. "Ye would do it again if ye could." Her voice broke into a sob. "And . . . th-the worst part is, I canna blame ye. Iona is auld and special. If she were my mither, I would do aught to save her like ye."

"I . . ." His throat went hoarse. He expected anger. Why didn't she lash out at him with the bitterness and resentment he deserved? He wasn't prepared for her broken honesty, an admission to justify his own brutal actions. Was she playing a trick on him or trying to wear down his defenses? One thing was certain. She had always shown generosity to the villagers; she would not risk one innocent soul to save another as he was willing to do. Lauren would have found a more honorable way.

Lauren straightened and lifted her shoulders. "It is decided. The captain will not turn the ship around. There is naught more to say."

She crawled toward Malcolm. Her knee caught in the folds of her skirt, and she slipped. Lauren slid down the other side of the overturned cockboat. Malcolm feared she would fall through. He lunged for her, but her fingers were out of reach. With surprising agility, Lauren lifted her foot and slammed against the bottom of the rail, holding her body in place. She glanced up at Malcolm, her brow furrowed in worry. Biting her bottom lip, she considered her situation.

"Lauren, hold on," Malcolm said. "I am coming."

She didn't respond, merely stared at him. He crawled onto the smooth surface of the cockboat bottom and inched his way toward her. He braced his booted heel in a crevice and reached for her. Lauren placed her small hand in his. He gripped her tight, determined he wouldn't let her fall. Malcolm groaned as he lifted her toward him. When she was close enough, he wrapped his other arm around her and carried her as he slid on his bottom until his feet landed firmly on deck.

"Do not ever do that again," he growled through clenched teeth as images of what could have happened played across his mind.

"I am no fool!" Lauren jerked away. "I know I am being used. Otherwise, ye would be content to let me drown."

Her blue eyes blazed through red-rimmed lids. Malcolm's chest ached with fear he hadn't anticipated on her behalf. He blinked, giving his racing heart time to calm. He'd convinced her that he was a blackhearted MacGregor, and he might as well keep up the charade. The less emotion involved the better when he had to hand her over in exchange for his mother.

"Aye, my revenge against Duncan Campbell." Malcolm towered over her, settling his fists on his hips.

A sarcastic grin twisted her lips. "I am afraid ye've miscalculated on that score. My da will be angry ye took what was his, but I am not the revenge ye hope. He is not the doting father one might think."

"What do ye mean?" He leaned toward her, remembering what she mumbled in her sleep earlier. "Ye're spoiled, rich, and he gives ye everything ye've ever wanted." Malcolm narrowed his gaze, wondering what game she played. Her father gave her the life of a princess. Why would she have so little confidence in him?

"I appear to have it all, do I?" She shook her head with a scoff. "Deep down all a lass wants is her father's love. Malcolm MacGregor, why do ye not give it some thought as to who my father is, and then maybe ye'll come to realize what it might have been like to grow up in his household, without the love and protection of a mither. My biggest regret right now is leaving my wee sister behind. No one will be there to show her any kind of affection." Lauren poked him in the chest, her nail digging through his shirt. "The two of ye make perfect opponents. Ye're just as coldhearted as he is."

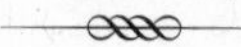

Lauren tried to calm her jittering stomach as she strode from Malcolm. She thought she would be safe from discovery, but the obstinate man found her in spite of her effort to remain hidden. She supposed her weeping gave her away. He could not have seen her.

When she nearly plunged into the sea, Lauren wasn't as afraid as she imagined most people would be. She felt confident of her life with Christ in the hereafter. For a moment, she was tempted to let go, but one look into the fearful eyes of a man she'd always known to be strong and powerful made her realize Malcolm didn't have that same assurance.

Mayhap he was her mission through this strange situation that led her aboard *The Sea Lady*. Her short time as an indentured servant was a small price to pay if she could win Malcolm MacGregor to Christ. Was she willing to let go of her own wants in order to make something good out of bad? She wouldn't win him over with preaching. It would take walking out her faith in all she said and did. Therein lay the *real* challenge. Malcolm had a way of vexing her like no other man she'd ever known—and her father and brother most definitely pressed her temper at times.

"I intend to survive what ye do to me no matter what it takes." She glared at Malcolm over her shoulder. "And Lord willing, I shan't allow bitterness to take root in me. 'Tis like poison."

"Yer tone does not sound like it." He grumbled behind her and said something else she didn't hear.

"What was that?" She whirled, causing him to nearly run over her, but she stood her ground and lifted her palms against him in protection. She glared at him. Lauren ignored his hard chest and hoped her elbows felt like spikes when he ran into them. Her toes would be sore for days after he trampled upon them.

"Och, lass! What did ye do that for?" Malcolm's eyes simmered like burning coal. "Are ye trying to get me flogged for running ye over an' causing bodily harm?" He pointed his thumb at his chest. "I am only trying to look out for yer welfare."

She lifted her eyebrows in acute shock. The man was daft. "Bringing me aboard as hostage is not looking after my welfare." She snapped her fingers as sarcasm dripped from her tongue. "I see. Ye have to make sure I am good and healthy to bring the best price in exchange for yer mither. Do not dare pretend 'tis naught other than personal gain. I am not that gullible."

"Lower yer voice, lass. Ye're starting to make a scene." Malcolm dropped the level of his tone and bent closer. His warm breath fanned her face. She closed her eyes and shook her head, concentrating on an appropriate response.

"I suppose it would make ye look like a thoughtless brute if everyone knew what ye've done." She twisted her lips. "Ye never struck me as the type to worry about what others think. I am surprised at ye." He rolled his eyes and looked out over the main deck below them, but his nonchalant attitude didn't fool her. She discovered two things about him. He loved his family and cared what others thought of him. Malcolm was a man of integrity, but if pushed to his limits, he would abandon the boundaries of his integrity—to get justice.

"Ye think ye're perfect, do ye not?" He scoffed, a taunting grin lifting his lips as he shoved his knuckles on his hip. "Well, I know how it is with people like ye, pretending to be merciful an' compassionate, but when it comes to giving up yer own comfort an' wealth, ye hold back, pitying the rest o' us."

"Nay, I am not perfect, but I know I am forgiven." Lauren swallowed, hoping his words weren't true, but how would she know unless she was tested? Could this situation be a test and not the mission of winning Malcolm to Christ as she thought? "I suppose my indenture will be a test of my true character. One thing is certain. I shall do my best to forgive ye."

"Do not be so quick to give what I have not asked for, lass." He stepped around Lauren and headed toward the cabins below. "Ye might change yer mind when all is said an' done."

She watched his broad back, hoping she could forgive him. Right now she had so much animosity built up toward him, it might take the whole voyage. At least she had God and the wisdom of the Scriptures she'd memorized. Malcolm walked alone. Compassion stirred her heart, threatening her defenses. Lauren clenched her teeth as caution rippled through her stomach. No matter the circumstance, she would have to be careful not to form an attachment to him. In spite of disliking him, he had a way about him that penetrated her heart.

He walked into his cabin while she lingered at the threshold. Logan sat on his bed sorting through a bag of clothes. He looked up and grinned at Malcolm. His gaze traveled to Lauren where she leaned against the door. "I see ye found 'er. He was quite worried 'bout ye."

Unsure what to say, Lauren didn't respond.

"Deidra is not too pleased with ye." Logan glanced at Malcolm as he strode to Lauren. "My sister considers herself a crusader for the poor an' defenseless." He chuckled. "I keep tellin' her we're the poor an' defenseless."

This news gave Lauren hope. Mayhap the arrangement with her new cabinmates would not be as unbearable as she feared. She smiled at Logan and joined him in walking down the hall. "It sounds as if yer sister and I will get along verra well."

"I am glad," Logan said. "She has been lonely since our mither died. Ye an' Kathleen will be good for her."

"I shall do my best to cheer her. I could use some friends as well." She pointed behind them. "Thanks to Malcolm, I have left everyone behind. I already miss my sister."

"Aye, sisters have a way of making things more bearable." Logan nodded in agreement. "Deidra an' I only have each other."

"Indeed, my only sister was stolen from us." Malcolm's bitter voice carried from behind. "I suppose it is a measure of justice that the Campbells experience the same."

Lauren closed her eyes on a sigh. This was going to be a long voyage—very long indeed.

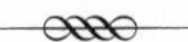

While unwanted guilt ate at Malcolm's soul like maggots, he was satisfied to see how well Deidra and Kathleen accepted Lauren. It amazed him how much Logan and Deidra favored each other. They shared the same red hair, green eyes, and a sea of freckles over pale skin.

"My brother told me 'bout yer unfortunate situation." Deidra's eyes turned to ice as she glared at Malcolm, a direct stare meant to reprimand him, no doubt.

Malcolm stood tall and met her gaze, refusing to back down. He'd let the lass pass judgment on him all she wanted. She knew naught of his family's plight, and her opinion mattered not. The only thing he desired of her was fair treatment toward Lauren.

"Do not be so hard on Malcolm. My da did him an injustice, and he is merely trying to right a wrong—even if he is going about it the wrong way," Lauren said, looking down at her feet.

"Why defend him? Did he not kidnap and drag ye aboard this ship?" Deidra glanced from Lauren to Malcolm. When neither responded, she turned to Logan. "Did ye tell me a falsehood?"

"Nay, I told ye what I knew, but I canna know all the details." Logan shot Malcolm a look of regret. "Forgive me, but I needed to tell her somethin'. She was demanding to know after Lauren left for the cap'n."

"Lauren, are ye on this ship against yer will?" Deidra asked, raising a red eyebrow.

Malcolm closed his eyes, knowing Lauren's answer. Once Lauren secured their sympathy and allegiance, she could solicit their help when they docked in Carolina.

"Aye," Lauren said, dropping her gaze in discomfort as her cheeks darkened. " 'Tis complicated. Malcolm's mither was wrongly sold by my father for a debt his family owed. She is a dear friend of mine, and I have known the MacGregors all my life. They are honorable people. I would do anything for her. She is auld and ailing. Even though I did not want to go to the colonies, now I am here, I would like to help Malcolm get his mither and sister back."

"Can ye trust 'im? He is out for revenge an' he will use ye," Deidra scoffed, glaring at Malcolm and pointing a finger at him. "There has to be a better way."

"Please . . ." Lauren covered Deidra's finger. "I would like for all of us to be friends. We have a long journey ahead, and we will need to depend on each other." Lauren turned full circle. "I was hoping to rest. Is there a place where I could lie down?"

"Aye." Kathleen stepped aside and pointed to the narrow bed where Lauren had awakened earlier. "Take mine for now. I shan't need it 'til tonight. I am too excited to sleep anytime soon."

"Thank ye." Lauren's shoulders slumped in relief as she walked toward it and sank on the thin mattress. "I am exhausted."

"Regardless of what ye think of me, thanks for welcoming Lauren," Malcolm said, determined not to allow them to deprive him of his manners. Tense silence filled the cabin as none of them responded. It was no more than he expected or deserved. He turned and strode out the door.

His feet carried him to the main deck where he sought the rail and looked out over the vast ocean. Peaceful swells carried them up and down as the bow plowed through the water and the sails caught the wind. Malcolm breathed the fresh salt air and tried to clear his mind and heart.

Why couldn't Lauren treat him with the disdain she owed him? He didn't want her forgiveness. If anything, he wanted her to punish him as he deserved.

4

Lauren slept most of the afternoon, dreaming of Blair at home. She woke feeling homesick and brushed her hair from her eyes. Someone had left a dim oil lamp burning on an iron hook extending from the wall. She sat up to gain her bearings. A small wooden table sat in a corner, bolted to the floor below the lantern. An empty narrow bed was against the wall on the other side with two bags below it. Lauren glanced under the bed where she sat and saw a worn satchel.

How long had she slept? The musty smell of the cabin made her long for fresh air. She donned her red cloak and left the security of the cabin. Lauren wondered how long she could wear her only set of clothes before everyone began to hate the smell of her. An ache welled inside, and she swallowed down the desire to let tears overcome her. Weeping would do no good, only make her more miserable.

A waft of salt sea air took her breath away as she stepped out on deck. The evening sun cast an orange glow in the sky. Passengers walked along the deck and leaned over the rails as if they couldn't believe their great fortune to be there. Under other circumstances, Lauren would have shared in their delight. Today, the vast sea trapped her. She feared God may not deliver her out of this mess, especially if He had a greater plan.

"There ye are." Deidra walked toward her with Kathleen by her side. "Do ye feel better?" She shoved her red locks over her thin shoulder.

"Aye." Lauren nodded, looking around for Malcolm. "I feel much better."

"I saved a biscuit for ye." Kathleen held it out.

"Thank ye." Lauren accepted the offer with a smile. "I am starving." Her mouth watered at the thought of biting into something edible. She had missed the noonday meal, and her stomach shrank like a dried prune. "I came up for a bit of fresh air."

Deidra and Kathleen followed her to the rail as she bit into the hard biscuit. The bread was difficult to chew, more so than she was used to, but she wouldn't complain. Her new friends were quiet as she ate in peace. She swallowed, wishing she had a cup of water.

When she rubbed the remaining crumbs from her hands, Deidra turned toward her. "Ye wept in yer sleep."

"What did I say?" Lauren tensed, wondering if she revealed something she wasn't ready to divulge.

"Ye cried out for Blair an' kept apologizing for leaving her behind." Deidra glanced at Kathleen. "Who is she?"

"Aye." Lauren stared out at sea, swallowing back the aching cry lodged in her throat. When enough time passed to recover her voice, she searched for the right words. "Blair is my wee sister. I am all she has in this world, and I pray our da and brother will not poison her with their lies and deceit. I fear they will strangle her faith from her." Lauren's voice broke as she closed her eyes, determined not to shed more tears.

"Did ye raise her, then?" Kathleen asked.

"Aye, and shielded her from our da's cruelty when I could. She does not remember Mither, so I shared my memories and taught her the faith Mither had taught me before she died giving birth to Blair."

"Such a heavy burden for one so young. Ye must have only been a wee lass yerself," Deidra said, leaning forward to peer at Lauren.

"I was eight, but Blair is now twelve." Lauren laid a hand over her chest. "I do not want her to think I abandoned her."

"How can she? Blair knows yer true character." Deidra patted her shoulder. "Ye have naught to worry about."

"I long for a bath and a warm fire to toast my toes." Lauren wrapped her arms around herself. "A change of clothes."

Kathleen laughed with sarcasm, scratching her temple. "I doubt we will see the likes of that until we dock in the Carolinas, but we might be able to find some clothes."

"Aye, at least we can come above deck an' breathe the fresh air an' see the sun," Deidra said. "The poor souls in the hold will only have rations of air, food, and water 'til landfall. Even then, they will stay aboard 'til sold at auction."

"Only if they live long enough to survive the journey." Kathleen twisted her lips in a frown. "To think I was almost one of them. I was a pence short for my passage, but someone paid it for me. Now I shall get a chance at my dream of being a schoolteacher in Carolina." She shrugged. "I never got to attend university, but the women I worked for taught me to read and do mathematics."

"I guess my situation could be worse." Conviction ripped through Lauren's heart. "I have always had more than enough. Mayhap, 'tis why Malcolm has always despised me so much, that and my Campbell name."

"I do not care if ye live like a princess," Deidra said. "Ye do not deserve this. He is a blackhearted scoundrel, he is."

"Nay," Lauren shook her head, surprised by the venom in her friend's voice. "Malcolm is forgiven by Christ, and we should forgive him as well."

"Ye're one o' them righteous women, are ye?" Deidra asked, narrowing her eyes in suspicion. "I say go ahead an' forgive him for his past wrongs, but do not let 'im keep hurtin' ye. Learn from livin', my mither always said."

"Malcolm has paid for my passage." She gave her new friends a sad smile. "I am afraid 'tis already too late. As far as he is concerned, he has bought me."

Malcolm found Hugh MacKinnon on the quarterdeck at the wheel. Approaching him from the side, Malcolm could only see his profile and beard. He hoped the man was in a good mood. Mr. MacKinnon turned and with a steady gaze watched Malcolm approach. Malcolm stood four inches above Mr. MacKinnon and hoped the man wouldn't be intimidated by his height. In his experience, many often were, and it had caused him trouble, especially with the less confident ones.

"What brings ye hither, Mr. MacGregor?" The first mate lifted a dark brow. "I would wager there is much more fun to be had below deck."

"We found a cabin for Miss Campbell, but she has no place to sleep," Malcolm said. "I was hoping ye might have a hammock I could install for her."

"I am sure we can find something." Mr. MacKinnon nodded in agreement. "Let me ask ye something . . . what exactly is yer relationship to the lass? Ye are not her brother or her husband?"

Malcolm tensed, wondering about the purpose of questioning. "Nay, I am neither, but as she said, we knew each other as children." Malcolm wanted to say that he looks out for her like a brother, but how could he claim it after what he'd done and planned to do when they reached Carolina? He had no rights regarding Lauren, but that didn't change the fact he wanted to try and protect her until he exchanged her for his mother. Sailors already watched her. Had Mr. MacKinnon taken a liking to her as well?

"So yer argument was not a lovers' quarrel?" Mr. MacKinnon's lips twitched in a devilish grin. "That pleases me."

"She is not like the others." Malcolm hastened to add, disliking the man's apparent interest. "She is verra religious an' comes from a well-bred, aristocratic family."

"How can ye defend them when she herself admitted how her family wronged ye?" Mr. MacKinnon asked, shaking his head with a chuckle. "If you worry about her innocence, you should not have let her come aboard without the protection of yer name, either as her brother or husband. Now she is fair game to any man who may want her, and sometimes a little convincing is all that is needed."

"Are ye sayin' ye've designs on the lass yerself or merely warnin' me of yer sailors?" Malcolm crossed his arms and stepped closer, meeting Mr. MacKinnon's dark eyes with a fierce glare of his own.

"Both." His twisted grin infuriated Malcolm, but he held his temper in check. Sailors like Mr. MacKinnon enjoyed throwing around their authority on the ships they sailed. Outnumbered and outranked, Malcolm would have to do his best to protect Lauren's innocence by his wits.

"Thanks for the warning." Malcolm gave the sailor a nod. "What about the hammock? Where can I find it?"

"Go toward the mizzenmast and follow the steps below. Take the hallway toward the back of the ship. The third door on the right will be a storage room with a crate of hammocks." Mr. MacKinnon cut a skeptical glance at him. "Should I send a sailor with you? I doubt you have the proper tools to mount it."

"Nay." Malcolm shook his head. The last thing he wanted was to encourage sailors to happen upon Lauren's cabin. He would make do on his own. "I am a peasant Scotsman an' used to making do."

"Suit yourself." Mr. MacKinnon shrugged, his dark hat angled to the side of his head. "I have work to do."

Malcolm followed the directions Mr. MacKinnon had given. The lower compartment on the backside of the ship smelled of molded wood and rotten food. He sniffed, wondering if he should be worrying about their meals. He lit a lantern hanging on a hook and grabbed it. Flour sacks lined the corner so at least their bread would be fresh. Other stocked barrels lined the hallway as he came to the third door. Though not locked, it groaned and took a bit of muscle with Malcolm shoving a shoulder against the heavy wood. It gave way, stirring up a cloud of dust and a musty stench. He wrinkled his nose in distaste.

A crate of coiled rope laid over another crate of hammocks hanging over the edges. Chests were stacked on one side with barrels on the other. Malcolm lifted the lid on one of the chests and found various tools inside. He sifted through them until he located something that would mount the hammock.

He removed the crate of ropes and sorted through the hammocks. He tossed a number to the side that had holes and needed repairs. After he'd gone through a handful, he discovered one that would hold Lauren's weight without putting her safety at risk. He righted the crates and put everything back.

Malcolm hurried through the dark hall and climbed the steps. He set the lantern back on the peg by the steps where he found it. If he wanted to hang the hammock before Lauren and the other lasses returned to their cabin, he'd better hurry.

Lauren stepped inside the cabin with her friends and paused. Hanging from the ceiling was a hammock. The thick, corded rope swayed with the movement of the ship. She exchanged glances with Deidra and Kathleen, wondering if she was to sleep in it. Tears stung her eyes. She blinked several times. Her throat muscles constricted in rebellion.

"The ship is out of beds an' I thought this would suffice." She didn't have to turn around to recognize Malcolm's deep, masculine voice.

Lauren closed her eyes, unable to meet his gaze just now. He already thought her a spoiled lass who had only known a good life of pampering. She would have to muster up enough strength to show that it didn't matter—that sleeping in a hammock like a sailor didn't bother her.

"Ye do not have to sleep in that thing," Deidra said. "We could share my bed."

"Nay, I do not want to be a burden." Lauren wished her tone sounded more confident.

"Ye're not a burden," Deidra said. " 'Tisn't proper for a genteel lady to sleep like that." She pointed to the swaying hammock.

"Lauren, may I speak with ye—alone?" Malcolm asked.

"Can it not wait until the morning?" Lauren turned and gave him a weary look. Anger coursed through her. It took all her strength to crush it. *I will not hate him.*

"Please, 'twill only take a few moments." His gaze tugged at the edge of her heart. How could he look like both a bewildered lad and a handsome rogue who wanted to devour her heart? There were moments when Malcolm MacGregor scared her with more than the brawny muscle and physical power he could wield. The emotional lure he had on her was more frightening, harkening an attraction she wanted to deny. *Lord, protect me.*

"Fine, but make it quick." She strode out of the cabin and waited in the hall with her arms crossed.

"Not here. Too many ears are around us." He grabbed her hand, led her down the hall, and up the stairs. The main deck was bare, with the exception of a few sailors. Most of the passengers had gone below for the evening.

Strong hands reached around her waist. Lauren gasped in surprise as Malcolm lifted her upon a barrel. His gaze met hers as a long silence passed between them. An uncomfortable warmth stirred in her chest, heating her neck and face.

While his holding her like this gave her a sense of security, it was false. Malcolm was anything but safe. Had he not already proved that? She laid her hands on his and pushed him away. He looked down and shifted his stance. He seemed reluctant to meet her gaze and cleared his throat.

"I know the hammock is not as nice as what ye're used to, but it was all I could do under the circumstances."

"Do not apologize. Ye plan to sell me as an indentured servant, or have ye forgotten? It would not do to become concerned about my comforts at this point, now would it?" Her voice took on a hard edge.

"I know I do not deserve yer trust," he said.

"Nay, ye do not." She glared at him, hoping he could sense all her rekindled anger.

"Still, I intend to look after ye while ye're in my care," he continued as if she hadn't interrupted him.

"Humph!" She shifted her fists to her hips and leaned forward. "Fine words from a liar. Ye need not act the gentleman now. By protecting me on this ship, ye're protecting yer interests. Ye want me fine and healthy when it comes time to exchange me for yer mither. I am not as gullible as ye think."

"Lauren, by purchasing yer passage on this ship, I saved ye from being thrown into the hold with all the other indentured servants who have sold themselves to pay for their passage to the colonies. I could have used the money to buy Carleen back and still exchange ye for Mither." He leaned toward her and lowered his voice to a dangerous pitch. Her heart thumped against her ribs. "That way I would get both of them back. I am not as bad as ye like to think."

"Is that supposed to comfort me?" She lifted an eyebrow, her tone sarcastic and biting. He wanted to confuse her, to melt her defenses against him, but she wouldn't allow it—she couldn't. Not if she wanted to keep her heart safe. The man had betrayed her and would do it again if he thought the means justified it. She needed to find a balance, to forgive him the way Christ wanted without risking her heart and giving him trust he did not deserve.

"It should. Half of them will not survive the journey." He gripped her shoulders and shook her. "Listen to me. They will be given rationed food of less quality than what we receive. They have no cabins or beds. Not even hammocks. They have a space no bigger than two by six feet to sleep on the floor with the rats. The only time they will be allowed to come up on deck is once a day for a short hour. Aye, yer paid passage should be a comfort to ye, even if it came about the way it did."

Lauren's head tingled as the blood drained from her face. "If what ye say is true, then 'tis no comfort to me at all." A shiver raced up her spine. "How can I enjoy the comfort of my situation when so many are suffering below—dying even?"

Malcolm sighed, stepping back and rubbing his face. "I did not tell ye this to make ye feel guilty, but to help ye understand that I did the best I could." He dropped his head and rubbed his neck. "In spite of what ye think of me."

"I will not say what I think of ye." She looked away, unable to meet his hazel eyes. How could the man who wanted to protect her from the vile conditions in the hold be the same as the man who wanted to sell her into indentured service? It didn't make sense. In contrast, why hadn't she even given the people in the hold more thought? When she first came aboard, there were many more people. It was as if half of them disappeared. "I should have wondered what happened to all the people I saw boarding." She shook her head, now disgusted with herself. "I was so caught up in what was happening to me that I did not pay attention . . . I did not think about it."

"I am afraid there is more." Malcolm ran a hand through his russet-colored hair. In the mixture of the light from the moon and the nearby lantern, it almost looked like the color of a pumpkin.

"I do not wish to hear more," she said.

"Well, ye must. It concerns ye." He took a deep breath. "Mr. MacKinnon said ye're at risk on board with no protection of a kinsman. Be careful around the sailors. I do not want ye goin' anywhere on this ship by yerself. Take one of yer friends with ye at all times."

"I see." She nodded, feeling a sudden discomfort. Lauren slid off the barrel, ready to go back to her cabin and rest. She wrung her hands at the distressing news.

"And, Lauren, be wary of Mr. MacKinnon himself. I dislike the way he was talking 'bout ye when he warned me."

"What do ye mean?" She paused, her heart pounding. Was she in trouble? Did he suspect her story to be false? She scratched the side of her neck, hating the nervous itch.

"He implied he might not be above indecent behavior with a bonny lass such as yerself. Just be careful." He held out his elbow. "I know I am not a proper gentleman, but I shall walk ye back to the cabin just the same."

Darkness claimed the cabin as Malcolm lay in his hammock swinging back and forth. The ship sailed over the swelling sea, and his thoughts kept returning to Lauren. Malcolm had always resented her visiting and bringing them food. He was too proud to admit they needed it. Instead of being thankful and gracious, he had kept to the fields or prowled the village to avoid her.

His mother and sister always looked forward to Lauren's visits. She told them news of the outside world, and his mother shared her wisdom and faith. The few times he managed to witness their discussions, Lauren sat on a wooden chair with her chin propped in her hand at the table like a doting child. Her cousin Keith always lounged in a corner or paced outside.

Malcolm wondered whether his mother survived the trip. She and Carleen would have been dumped in the hold and left to suffer like criminals caged in the dark. His heart ached at the thought. An image of Graham's battered face came to mind. He hoped Thomas would get him safely to Glenstrae and to their uncle before the Campbells returned.

Sleep evaded him, but he forced himself to relax as the hammock swayed. It was better than being tossed to and fro on a hard bed or dealing with bed bugs. Aye, a hammock would be better for Lauren whether or not she realized it. Her blue eyes taunted him like a burning torch in his soul. She confused, irritated, and gnawed at his insides with guilt until he wanted to protect her and amend his ways, but it was too late. The MacGregors had already stolen her and infuriated the Campbells. They would seek revenge, and he needed to save his mother and sister.

His cabinmates stirred. One of them lit a dim lantern. Other than Logan, Malcolm met Archibald Clark and Patrick Stewart when he returned to his cabin after dealing with Lauren. Archie swung in the hammock beside him, scratching his red head. The lad was young at ten and eight, but he had lots of energy.

"Good mornin', lads." Patrick's wispy voice floated across the room, still filled with sleep. He rubbed his eyes and blinked.

"Lads? I am five years yer senior," Malcolm said. "And who lit that lantern so early?"

"Aye." Logan groaned. "If I do not have to be up to plow a field afore dawn, I might as well sleep in a wee bit."

"I set it on dim. Stop yer complainin'. Ye sound like a bunch o' lasses, ye do." Archie leapt out of his hammock and stood, stretching his arms. "I am starvin'. Ye had better get up if ye wanna break yer fast."

"I like yer spunk, my friend," Patrick said, yawning. "I think I shall grab a bite to eat and write my journal for yesterday. I plan to keep an account of the trip and sell my articles to the newspapers when I arrive in the colonies."

"Just as long as it does not contain any of our personal lives." Malcolm lifted a finger, pointing in his direction. The last thing he needed was the Campbells reading about them. He had no doubt that Duncan would find him, but he wanted the man to work at it as he wondered about Lauren's fate.

"I will not use names if that bothers ye." Patrick sighed, running his fingers through his blond locks. "Malcolm MacGregor, ye can be a testy one, I see."

"Aye." Malcolm stretched his cramped legs and arms. "An' do not be forgettin' it either."

"Go on with the lot o' ye. I am tryin' to get some sleep." Logan threw his plaid over his head.

"I shall break my fast as well. No tellin' what kind of mischief Miss Lauren Campbell has waiting for me today." Malcolm grinned as he swung his legs over the hammock. His bare feet hit the cold wooden floor. He winced in distaste.

"Ye had better make yerself more presentable than ye are right now." Patrick chuckled. "In fact, I am looking forward to meeting the lass. Yer sister, too, Logan."

"Argh!" came the response from the beneath the plaid.

"Never mind him." Malcolm stood and raised his arms above his head. His joints popped, loosening his muscles. Now he felt better. "I shall introduce ye to them. Just mind yer manners."

Up on deck a few people leaned over the rails. Sailors were busy with various tasks, but they didn't miss whistling as Lauren and her cabinmates appeared. Malcolm's stomach tightened in knots as he remembered Mr. MacKinnon's warning. Lauren's golden hair coiled and lifted in the wind, striking a bright contrast to her red cloak. Her high cheekbones and pearl white skin gave her a regal beauty he should have seen before. At least her blue eyes looked well rested as she scanned the deck. He wondered if she looked for him or if she surveyed her surroundings out of general curiosity.

Her gaze landed on him. She paused. He took a deep breath, wishing things could have been different between them. Their births into opposing clans had always separated them. Her wealth and his poverty created an even deeper divide. Before, only circumstances were against them, but now, he made it personal. Lauren Campbell had every reason to hate him, and the knowledge didn't sit well with him.

"Come, lads, I shall make the introductions." Malcolm strode toward the women. Deidra twisted her lips into a sour expression but forced a smile when acknowledging his cabinmates. Kathleen's greeting turned out to be more welcoming.

Once the introductions were over, Archie drew Lauren into conversation with his animated chatter. Patrick and Kathleen seemed to find common ground regarding their studies. As an aspiring writer, he approved her goal to be a teacher.

"Where is my brother?" Deidra asked, stepping in line beside Malcolm where they waited for a cup of black coffee and a biscuit.

"If he does not have to get up to plow a field afore sunrise, he would just as soon sleep," Malcolm said.

"Sounds like him." Deidra grinned. "I shall save half my biscuit for 'im."

"Ye do not like me, do ye?" Malcolm asked, determined to air their grievances. He preferred to know his enemies, not guess at them.

"On the contrary, I am sure I would like ye fine if I had met ye under better circumstances." Deidra turned a green-eyed gaze at him. "I dislike what ye're doing to Lauren."

"I am not happy 'bout it either, but I shall do what I must to save my mither an' sister. At least her family can afford to buy her back. My family does not have that luxury."

When her cabinmates went below, Lauren stayed on deck where she could enjoy the fresh sea air and the bright sunshine. She missed her long walks around the estate of Kilchurn Manor as well as the long talks with Blair. The breeze lifting off the ocean's surface gave her chills, but it was just what she needed after spending the night in a stuffy cabin.

Lauren wrapped her arms around herself as she thought of the hammock Malcolm had hung for her. The swaying motion had rocked her to sleep. Unlike her cabinmates, she never feared being tossed onto the floor as the ship sailed over the great swells. Kathleen complained of itching when she woke this morning.

"Paid passengers, please return to your cabins for the next hour." Mr. MacKinnon made the announcement on the quarterdeck steps. "The indentured servants will be up from the hold. They are dirty and carry illnesses you should not be exposed to."

"I am commissioned as a minister in the Carolinas." A man stepped out from the crowd as others lined up to return to the cabins below. "I should like to attend to the spiritual needs of the poor." He wore a black tricorn hat and round spectacles. A hint of gray layered his brown hair at the temples. His dark coat contained brass buttons, and the length reached his knees. Tan breeches complemented a brown waistcoat topped with a white cravat.

"You may wait on the quarterdeck with the captain while the sailers inspect those who are well enough to come up for food and fresh air." Mr. MacKinnon pointed up the steps behind him.

"May I wait as well?" Lauren stepped beside the pastor. "At home I often brought food and medicine to the poor. Mayhap, I could be of assistance."

Mr. MacKinnon hesitated, looking up at the captain standing behind the wheel. The gray-headed man nodded. His hard expression never wavered.

"Pastor, you shall be responsible for Miss Campbell," said Mr. MacKinnon.

"Indeed." The pastor held out his elbow with a wide grin. "God's favor is upon me this day to put me beside such a bonny lass."

"Thank ye." Lauren placed her hand on his arm and allowed him to lead her up the steps.

"Ye remind me of my daughter, Megan. She is about yer age. I daresay, over the course of the next year, I shall miss my bonny wife and all five of my children."

"I am sorry. I also left family behind," Lauren said.

They turned around at the rail, overlooking the main deck. Lauren removed her hand from the pastor's arm and gripped the rail as the last of the paid passengers disappeared.

"My name is Pastor Braddoch Patterson of Argyll." He bowed, tipping his hat. "I give ye leave to call me Pastor Brad as most of my former congregation did. The idea of Pastor Patterson does not sit well with me." He waved a hand in the air. "Never has."

"I am Lauren Campbell of Kilchurn Manor of Argyll." She dipped into a curtsey while holding one hand on to the rail.

"Ah, I know the place well. I believe I visted the parish a couple of times when ye was a wee lass. Would yer father happen to be Duncan Campbell?" He raised a dark brow.

Lauren bit her bottom lip, unsure if she wanted to admit to the connection. While she loved her father, he had made few friends among the clergy. In fact, he infuriated many of them. Since he held the king's favor, few could complain without making an enemy of her father and incur his wrath.

"Aye, he is my da." She watched his reaction, wondering if it would change his behavior toward her.

"Oh, the others are coming out on deck now." Pastor Brad turned his attention toward the poor souls below them. It was an effective way to change the subject and one she welcomed.

"What happens to those who are too weak to come up on deck?" she asked, watching as two sailors inspected each person before allowing him or her to get in the food line.

"A sailor will throw some bread down the hold, and each person will be allowed to refill their flasks before going back down." The pastor grew silent as he watched.

Lauren's heart constricted at the sight of some with bare feet, the filth and grime on their faces, hands, and clothing. Most were thin with protruding bones. Many blinked at the bright light. Red-rimmed eyes looked around as they squinted in the sunlight. Some of the children cried while others exclaimed in excitement. A few coughed and wheezed.

"Pastor, now you may go down and minister to the ones who have been inspected." The captain waved to them. "And keep the gel with you."

On deck Lauren could see their misery up close. A woman grabbed her arm. "Please, do not let 'em send us back down. The air is awful an' makin' my children sick." She clutched her baby to her chest.

"I'm sorry." Lauren shook her head. "I have no authority here." She looked to Pastor Brad for help, but several people had surrounded him with cries of pain, outrage, and despair. They ministered to those who would listen with encouraging words and prayers. By the time it was over, Lauren was exhausted.

"Ye did verra well, child. I am grateful for yer help." Pastor Brad looked down at her. New lines now strained his face that weren't there before. He patted her arm. "Go rest. 'Twill do ye some good."

Lauren's feet weighed her down like anchors as she made her way to the next level below. Malcolm stood outside her door with his arms crossed. When he saw her, he stood to his full height and towered over her.

"Where have ye been?" Anger laced his tone. "I was worried when they would not allow me on deck to look for ye. One of the sailors finally told me ye were with a pastor. What were ye thinking, Lauren?"

"Not now, Malcolm." She shook her head and tried to squeeze past. "Please."

"Answer me! Did naught I said last night mean anything?" He shook her shoulders. Her headache intensified. Images of suffering faces tormented her mind until she burst into tears.

"Lauren, I am sorry." Malcolm's strong arms crushed her against his chest.

5

The next morning, Malcolm waited in line with his cabinmates. His stomach rumbled with hunger. The rations on this ship were not equal to the amount of food they managed to produce at home, in spite of being peasants. He worried Lauren's health would soon suffer since she was used to even better.

The way she wept for the indentured servants below depleted his heart of the numbness he attempted to build against her. How could a woman with so much passion for the well-being of others be anything like her father? It wasn't possible. By all accounts, he had wrongly misjudged her.

Deidra and Kathleen appeared without Lauren. His chest tightened in fear. Could she have gotten ill from the peasants? Malcolm had never lacked patience until now. He stood in line beside Logan. Deidra saw her brother. A smile lit her face, and she hurried over with Kathleen.

"I am glad to see ye've come to yer senses and got up in time to receive all yer daily rations." She squeezed his arm.

"Aye, these blokes would not let me sleep." He gestured to Malcolm, Archie, and Patrick.

"And I say well done, blokes." She giggled as Archie and Logan chuckled.

Malcolm managed a weak smile while glancing at the stairs, hoping to see Lauren appear. Pastor Brad stepped up on deck with another gentleman, who looked to be a few years his senior. With a sigh of disappointment, Malcolm turned away, determined to broach the subject with Deidra or Kathleen.

Deidra stared at him, as if trying to understand his character. He didn't need her approval. He only wished to know what she knew of Lauren. Deidra stepped toward him, and for once, there was no disdain in her green eyes.

"Lauren wept most of the night. The condition of the indentured servants below has convinced her that yer mither never made it." Deidra dropped her gaze. " 'Tis as if she is grieving for her."

"She is verra fond of my mither." He nodded, hating the sharp pang shooting through his chest.

"More'n that, Lauren said that yer mither was like her own." Deidra gripped his arm with more strength than he would have imagined. "Now I understand why she is not fighting harder against yer plan to replace yer mither."

If her words had been a dagger, the blade would have sliced through his heart and twisted as it sank deep. The sounds of the lapping water against the ship and the buzz of conversations around them faded as his thoughts took over. The line moved forward, but Malcolm didn't budge. Logan nudged him. His feet stepped into motion like a wheel rolling on momentum. Malcolm accepted the bowl of porridge and refilled his flask.

"I am taking this to Lauren. She should not go without." He spoke to Logan, but he knew that Deidra also heard him by how her expression turned into a smile of approval.

A dim light glowed under the door to Lauren's cabin. It was ajar. If she had fallen asleep, he didn't want to wake her. Placing his ear to the open crack, he listened. Someone whispered.

Who was she talking to? Unable to help himself, Malcolm maneuvered his head so he could see better through the opening.

Lauren must have been on the other side. All he could see was her empty hammock.

More whispering continued. Mr. MacKinnon's words haunted his mind like poison. Lauren wasn't the type to allow a man to touch her, but that didn't mean one of the sailors wouldn't try to force himself on her. Yet there wasn't a struggle on the other side of the door. What if she had been gagged or, worse, knocked unconscious?

His heart pounded in fear for her. If someone tried to take advantage of her, he would have a better chance at surprising him. No need to knock on the door and give him time to come up with a plan.

Malcolm took a deep breath and slammed the door against the wall. His labored breathing was the only sound save for Lauren's gasp. She whirled from where she had been kneeling by a narrow bed against the wall, her hands clasped in a peak.

He groaned, realizing he interrupted her private prayer. Torn between relief and a strange sense of embarrassment, he turned and, without a word, walked out to get the porridge and water he'd set in the hallway.

"Malcolm, wait!"

Taking a deep breath to calm himself, he returned to see her sitting on the bed where she prayed. With clasped hands in her lap, silent tears crawled down her cheeks. If she looked at him with those sad blue eyes, he might come unhinged. Thankfully, she kept her gaze cast at the floor.

Malcolm sat beside her. The bed sank under his weight, and the straw mattress crunched like the sound of walking through fall leaves. He placed the bowl of porridge in her hands. "Eat. 'Twill make ye feel better."

"Nay, I canna." She shook her head. "It belongs to ye."

He placed his hands on both sides of her face and turned her toward him, tracing the pad of his thumbs along the path of her tears. "We shall share. Ye eat a bite, then I will. 'Twould be a shame to let it waste."

"Not fair." Tears welled up in her eyes again. "Everyone on board should get the same amount of food."

"I agree, but starving yerself will not put one extra morsel into their bellies." He dipped the spoon into the thick porridge and held it to her lips. "Now eat."

She opened her mouth to say something, and Malcolm shoved the spoon inside. Her words died in her throat as she ate. Malcolm then ate a bite, hoping to keep encouraging her.

She swallowed. "What I was going to say is, what if Iona and Carleen were treated like that?"

"Shush." He touched a finger to her lips. "Each ship is different. They could have been on a better ship." He dug the spoon in for another bite. "Deidra told me ye think my mither did not make it. Let us not dwell on it and instead concentrate on the possibility she did."

"Carleen was strong enough to survive." Before she could close her mouth, Malcolm shoved in another bite.

"Lauren," Deidra said from the doorway. Kathleen stood behind her, wearing a concerned expression. "Mr. MacKinnon is requesting yer presence up on the quarterdeck."

Lauren made her way to the quarterdeck with Malcolm close on her heels. Pastor Brad awaited her with the captain and Mr. MacKinnon. The pastor offered her an encouraging smile that managed to calm her rapidly beating heart.

The captain stood before them with his hands linked behind his back. His tricorn hat shaded his dark eyes. As a middle-aged man, he wore a full beard and mustache, but it covered only a portion of the pockmarks digging in the right side of his face. Lauren had never before been close enough to see them. A small gray patch in his brown beard drew her attention.

"I am Captain Edward Shaw, and I have summoned ye both here for a dire situation. Several of the peasants in the hold are ill. I fear the majority will not survive the journey." He paused, looked down at his feet, and paced back and forth in front of them. "Let me be frank. If they die, I cannot sell them, and I lose money."

Lauren gasped. His gaze shifted to hers. He chuckled, looking down at her as if she were an obscure animal. "This is a business, Miss Campbell. I do not have time to be sentimental. I must be practical. I will not be able to pay my sailors their wages and buy more food and stock for the next journey. And if my ship needs repairs, I cannot pay a shipbuilder to make them."

He held up three fingers. "This is my third trip carrying indentured servants to the colonies, and I learn something from each trip. This time I hired a physician."

"Ye want me to pray for the dying?" Pastor Brad asked, confusion layering his expression.

"Aye, and minister to their families. I shall need ye to perform a seaside ceremony for the dead. I can do that myself, but I prefer a man of God to do it."

The captain crooked his finger, and a man with a wiry frame strode forward from the shadows. He wasn't much taller than Lauren.

"This is Dr. James Taylor." The doctor bowed and tipped his hat. He had thin brown hair combed to the side over a balding head. The captain gestured to Lauren. "Miss Campbell and Pastor Brad."

"I am not completely heartless, Miss Campbell." Captain Shaw turned to her. "The other day I saw ye caring for them. I believe ye will make a helpful assistant to these men. Can ye read and write?"

She nodded.

"Good. I have plenty of parchment paper and ink. If any of the dying want to write letters to their kin, if I am able, I shall see that they are mailed." He motioned to someone behind her, and a moment later, a young sailor brought her a quill, a bottle of ink, and a stack of parchment paper. "These items are yours to do with as needed." He looked at the physician. "Dr. Taylor, tell them the rest."

"I have quarantined eight souls in a storage room in the back of the ship. 'Tis directly below the poop deck and above the tiller. The location is not the best and quite noisy, but well away from others to keep the disease from spreading."

"What is . . . the disease?" Lauren asked.

"Some stomach illness causing vomiting, fever, chills, and dysentery. I expect that some will die." Dr. Taylor leaned forward, met Pastor Brad's gaze, and then settled on Lauren. "They are contagious, and both of you would be putting yourselves at risk. Of course, I shall teach you to limit that risk as best as I can, but there are no guarantees. No one would blame you if you chose not to do this."

Lauren clasped her hands and walked over to the rail to stare out at the wide blue ocean. If something happened to her, she couldn't help Malcolm recover his mother. Yet there was always the possibility Iona hadn't made it. Once they made landfall, another family would purchase her services and essentially own her for the next seven years. At least this way, she could ensure her last free will would be in service to the Lord, an act of faith that God would be with her through everything.

"I will do it." Lauren whirled and met their expectant and curious gazes. "I am ready to learn all that ye wish to teach me."

"Are you sure?" Dr. Taylor lifted an eyebrow above his spectacles. "The risk is quite high, and there is the concern of forming an attachment to some, especially the children."

"Children are sick?" she asked, unable to hide her surprise.

"Aye, few below the age of eight survive a journey across the ocean," Dr. Taylor said.

"Indeed, 'tis the very reason I left my own family behind," Pastor Brad said. "My youngest is seven. We decided it would be best to wait until she is a bit older."

"I see." Lauren thought back to the other day when Pastor Brad said he would miss his family. By making this decision to serve the Lord in Carolina, he made a great sacrifice. She could do no less, not if she wanted to truly love the Lord and His people. A biblical proverb came to mind: *He that giveth unto the poor shall not lack, but he that hideth his eyes shall have many a curse.*

She needed no curses upon her head. Her situation already appeared very grave. She would do naught to incur the Lord's wrath. Her decision was made.

Malcolm sat on deck enjoying the fresh air and open sea as he and his cabinmates played a game of whist. To their annoyance, the breeze kept flipping the cards, and they finally gave up.

"I shall take a stroll in that direction. Ye never know, I might run into her on an errand for supplies." Malcolm turned and strode away.

Malcolm stepped below deck. He moved with caution on the narrow steps to keep from losing his balance. A dim lantern hung on a wall peg, lighting up the hallway enough to see the barrels along the wall. He came to a door with muttered voices behind it. Malcolm lifted his hand to knock. The door swung open, and his knuckles tapped thin air. Dr. Taylor paused, his eyes wide behind wire spectacles. He blinked as if trying to focus. Fatigue showed in his hunched shoulders, and the lines in his face made him look older.

"I came to see if Miss Campbell is well," Malcolm said. "She has been putting in some long hours."

"Aye, considering the circumstances, she is doing well." Dr. Taylor glanced over his shoulder and rubbed the back of his neck. "Would you do a favor for me?"

"Of course." Malcolm straightened. " 'Twould be an honor to help if I could."

"We have lost two souls within the hour. Please tell the captain the sad news." Dr. Taylor pressed his eyebrows. "We have four more patients who were brought in this morning. We will need to prepare for a burial at sea. One was a child."

"I shall do it at once." Malcolm nodded, ignoring the sorrow rising in him for people he didn't even know. "Sir, may I ask, are we facing an epidemic?"

"I am afraid so. For now it only seems to be plaguing the indentured servants in the hold. Their conditions are filthy and their rations so little. I feel that cleanliness will help keep bacteria from spreading. It may be the biggest difference between them and those in the cabins."

"Is Lauren in danger?" Malcolm asked, holding his breath as he waited for the answer.

"She is at risk, but I do not believe the disease can spread through the air. As long as she limits her physical contact with the patients and washes when she leaves, I believe she will be fine. In fact, I am sending her up for a bit of rest within the hour."

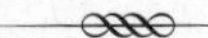

Exhaustion consumed Lauren as the overcast sky brought a gray hue over an already depressing day. Lauren stood beside Malcolm and Deidra listening to Pastor Brad speak Scriptures over the deceased lying on the deck. She stared at the small lad as tears obscured his image.

On the other side, his mother wept into her husband's shoulder, while older siblings grieved beside them. At the foot stood a middle-aged woman weeping for the loss of her husband lying beside the lad. The rest of the passengers and crew crowded around the deck with their heads bowed.

Pastor Brad prayed for their souls and asked God to ease grieving hearts, heal the sick, and preserve the health of the rest of the crew and passengers. After prayer, two sailors pushed the bodies into the sea. The mother and wife screamed in protest and ran to the rail. The husband grabbed his wife and wrapped his arms around her. Their other five children circled them, comforting each other.

The wife continued clinging to the rail until her legs failed her, and she slipped to her knees. Lauren looked around, but no one else moved to comfort her. People had tears in their eyes, but they seemed rooted in indecision, unsure whether or not to intrude. Lauren couldn't take it. She stepped around Malcolm and walked toward her. Lauren sat beside her and laid a hand on her shoulder. "Ye're not alone."

The woman nodded her brown head and broke into wailing sobs as her shoulders shook. After awhile she shifted to lying on the deck, making soft groans as she wept. Lauren stayed with her, keeping a hand on her back. The indentured servants were sent to the hold while the rest of the passengers scattered to their cabins. The crew went back to work at their stations.

Malcolm stayed on the main deck with his cabinmates, Deidra, and Kathleen. They stood talking with Pastor Brad while Lauren bowed her head and prayed for comfort and strength for this woman whose name she didn't even know. Having them nearby and hearing their voices gave Lauren courage. She hoped the grieving widow felt the same. More time passed as the sun faded in and out of the clouds.

"Thank ye." A hoarse whisper carried in the breeze. Lauren's hopes lifted. "Ye've been a comfort. I have been lying here thinkin' how I would like to help the sick if I can be of use." She sat up and wiped her red eyes.

"I shall ask the doctor. What is yer name? If he agrees, I will have them fetch ye from the hold."

"Amy Murray." She moved to stand, and Lauren assisted her.

A sailor escorted Amy back to the hold.

"Do not go back to the quarantine room. Ye need rest." Malcolm appeared at Lauren's side.

"Dr. Taylor released me for the night. To be honest, I am bone weary." Lauren brushed a lock of golden strands from her forehead. "I fear more may die. We have more people arriving at the sickroom each day."

"Which is why I wish ye would stop risking yer life like this," Malcolm said. "I do not intend to leave ye out here in the middle of the ocean." His last words ended on a whisper as he looked over the rail where the bodies had been tossed.

"Nay, ye plan to leave me in the middle of a field working a plantation." Her words came out bitter. His discomfort was evident as his eyes faltered, unable to meet her gaze. "In my case, I do not have much to lose, now do I?"

"Lauren, I have been thinking 'bout that." He sighed, rubbing his stubbled jaw. "I give ye my word, I shall do my best to find work an' save enough to buy the rest of yer indenture."

"Indeed, after I have already worked half of it off?" She raised an eyebrow and suppressed a yawn with a hand over her mouth. "Do not make unrealistic promises ye canna keep. I am tired, Malcolm, and I would like to retire for the night."

Distant thunder rolled in the sky. They both turned to the east, glimpsing a quick flash of lightning.

"Looks like we are in for a long night," Malcolm said. "Ye should go to yer cabin an' rest. 'Twill take a wee bit o' time afore the storm arrives. Be sure to warn the others below."

More flashes lit the sky. If they had been on solid ground, she would have thought the silvery clouds beautiful, but out here in the middle of the sea, fear twisted her heart. As much as she needed it, how could she sleep now knowing a storm lurked upon their sails?

The ship dipped to one side and bobbed for several seconds. Malcolm, Logan, and several sailors slid toward the opposite rail. It seemed as if all gravity had disappeared at the mercy of the sea. One of the sailors hit his head while trying to lower the sail on the foremast. The gusting wind whipped the heavy rope against him. He lost his balance and fell. It took both Logan and Malcolm to finish the task while other sailors dealt with securing sails and cargo and calming passengers.

A wave crashed over the deck and flipped the ship on the left side. The force caused Malcolm to lose his grip. He catapulted in the opposite direction and slammed into the base of the mainmast. Wrapping his arms around the wooden structure, Malcolm hung on as he tried to catch his breath. He shook the wet hair from his eyes and blinked the sting of salt water away. The ship righted itself again, but he knew it wouldn't be for long. The storm was far from over.

His bruised ribs ached from the impact. He couldn't afford to concentrate on the pain. Malcolm closed his eyes and focused on an image of Lauren, but that only heightened his fear for how she fared below. He hoped she had taken refuge in her hammock so she wouldn't be thrown about the cabin.

The rain continued to soak them, pounding their bodies like bullets. Thunder cracked above them, and lightning slashed through the sky looking for a victim to strike.

A lad around the age of eight ran onto the deck. Tears streamed down his cheeks as he looked around, blinking from the splashing waves and pouring rain.

"Laddie, come back! 'Tis not safe up here." Lauren appeared, gripping her long skirt as she chased after him. A gust of wind blew her back. Lauren faltered, taking two steps backward. "Yer da will be fine."

Fear swelled in Malcolm. The ship leaned right, causing them to lose their balance. The lad fell and slid down the incline. Lauren tripped over her skirt when she reached for him. Malcolm let go of the post he had been clinging to and lunged for her.

"The child! Save him!" Lauren yelled over the noise of the crashing waves rising over the deck.

Malcolm swerved and fought the wind to rescue the lad. The ship shifted to the other side as a wave washed over the deck and took a man into the sea. Lightning struck and the foremast split. The rolled-up sail limped to the side as a rope slipped from its knot and swung around, slashing a sailor across the back like a whip. Thunder cracked above them, drowning out voices. Malcolm refused to give up. He crawled on his hands and knees until he reached the child. The salt spray upon his lips tasted bitter as he swung an arm around the lad's middle and pulled him close.

The child's frail body shivered in the cold rain, and Malcolm wondered if he was already mad with fever. Something caused him to run out on deck in a fright. Was his mother hurt below?

The boards beneath his palms creaked. An eerie feeling swirled in his gut. He peeked over his shoulder. A wave the size of a mountain peak curled toward them, roaring like a lion. If this one didn't flip the entire ship over, he couldn't imagine what would. Malcolm glanced over at Lauren. She lay against the wall near the steps leading below. There was nothing secure enough for her to grasp.

Malcolm rolled to his back, lifting the child across his chest and holding him tightly in one arm. He lifted his legs and allowed the gravity of the ship to tilt him in Lauren's direction. This way he could slide toward her faster than he could run to her.

He slammed into the wall as pain shot through his back and whole body. Now only a few feet from Lauren, Malcolm braced his body against the wall and crawled toward her. He grabbed her with his other arm and purposed in his heart that he wouldn't let go.

"Lauren, pray!" If God would hear anyone's prayers, it would be hers. He had no right to expect anything from the Almighty. He kissed the top of Lauren's wet head. "I am sorry, Lauren. Please forgive me."

He would never know if she heard his whispered plea. The tidal wave crashed the ship, rolling it over. They tumbled. Seawater engulfed them, but Malcolm hung on to Lauren and the lad. Wedged between the quarterdeck railing and a couple of secured barrels, they gasped for air. When the ship bobbed back up again, screams came from every direction. Malcolm dragged in a ragged breath, desperate for air. The child in his arms whimpered, flooding Malcolm with relief. He set the lad at the rail.

"Hold on with both hands an' do not let go no matter what," Malcolm said. "I need to help Miss Campbell."

Gulping with fear, he lifted her limp body and adjusted her on his lap. He tilted her chin toward him, but she didn't awaken. A bloody gash slashed across her scalp at the hairline. Tears blinded his eyes as he crushed her against him.

"It should have been me an' not ye." He groaned against her ear, allowing the raw pain to etch deep into his soul. When had he come to care so much? The answer was simple. When he had seen her give so much of herself to everyone else with no expectations in return—even from him. It was her caring heart that had made her visit Inverawe and his family. And how had he repaid her? By betraying her kindness and using her as revenge.

Malcolm tightened his arms around her. She sputtered and coughed. Relief filled him as he bent her over his arm and pounded her back. She choked and coughed up more water.

"Thank ye." Her words were a hoarse whisper but a blessed sound to his overjoyed heart.

The ship tilted again. Taken off guard, Malcolm had no time to brace himself or grab anything to hold onto. Instead, he used his body to shield and hold onto her as the raging storm thrashed them about the deck. Blows slashed against his back, legs, and arms. Searing pain sliced through his head. His vision went black, and the last thing he heard was Lauren's voice.

"Malcolm?"

6

Lauren woke partially sheltered under Malcolm's body. She glanced over his arm to see morning had come. They survived the stormy night. Lingering clouds cast a bleak fog around them. Water splashed up over her fingers as the ship swayed back and forth, now floating in the calm sea. It was cold with a bittersweet smell like seaweed. Water sloshed across the wooden deck.

A few sailors stirred. Some tended to the wounded while others inspected the damage. Lauren shoved Malcolm's arm off her shoulders, but it only flopped to the side like dead weight. Fear pierced her heart.

"Malcolm?" No answer. She crawled up on her knees and shook him. No response. "Malcolm? Speak to me."

Lauren rolled him over and gasped at the bloody wound above his left temple. She pulled his jacket open and bent to listen to his chest. A faint heartbeat pressed against his ribs. Breathing a sigh of relief, Lauren tapped his cheek. "Malcolm, ye're scaring me. Wake up." Nothing. She shook his shoulders to no avail.

She sat back on her heels, unsure what to do. Lauren glanced up at one of the sailors hammering the foremast where it split. Two other sailors retied a sail in place. Another poured excess water over the side.

Malcolm was too heavy for her to lift, and she didn't want him to fall facedown in the remaining water on deck. She moved behind him, gripped under the arms, and hauled him toward the wall, inch by inch. Her skirt caught under her foot. She tugged it free and kept going. "I knew ye to be a big mon, Malcolm MacGregor, but not so heavy," she said against his ear, hoping he would wake. His chin continued to rest against his chest. "Mayhap, a better insult will wake ye up then?"

By the time she set him against the wall, she breathed heavily and took a short break. Lauren wiped her brow and swallowed, realizing how parched her throat had become. Her own needs would have to wait. Right now she had to clean Malcolm's wounds and assess the damage.

She hurried below deck to where the doctor kept his supplies. The sight that awaited her was a mess. Glass bottles were shattered. Liquid contents and powdered substances poured out and leaked from the top shelves to the bottom. Narrow beds had shifted, and patients were tending to each other.

"Has anyone seen the doctor?" Lauren asked.

"Nay." One gaunt man shook his brown head, dark circles haunting his eyes. "We were told he was wounded in the leg and could not walk down the steps."

"From what I have seen, the rest of the ship looks as bad as it does down here." Lauren grabbed a bar of soap and stitching supplies from a drawer still intact. "There are plenty of wounded everywhere. Can ye manage down here?"

"Aye." He nodded. "I suppose we will have to. Do not forget about us at mealtime."

"Let us hope that we still have a cook and that the food was not destroyed," Lauren said. "I shall do what I can. I promise."

"I see that gash on yer head." The man pointed at her. "It needs tendin'."

Lauren touched her forehead, suddenly aware of the tight feeling. Dried blood caked her hair. Other than a slight headache and extreme fatigue, she felt fine. Too many were in far worse shape, like Malcolm. An image of his unconscious face came to mind, and her heart beat with concern. "Thank ye, but I shall be fine." She turned and strode out and made her way down the dark hall. *Lord, please let Malcolm wake up. And give us all courage to survive this.*

Lauren arrived on deck to see Logan bent over Malcolm, smacking his jaw. Deidra stood behind him, wringing her hands in distress.

"Logan, nay! He has suffered trauma to his head." Lauren rushed toward them.

"Yer alive an' well." Deidra whirled, relief flooding her face. "Ye had us worried, ye did!"

"I am sorry. Malcolm took care of me." Lauren bent to his side and cleaned his head wound. "At least he is not awake to feel the pain."

"Too bad he neglected to take as good care o' himself," Logan said, rubbing his forehead. "I would wager he was worried 'bout ye."

"Aye." Lauren nodded. "He probably got this nasty cut and bruise because of me. He shielded me and would not leave my side. Saved a wee lad's life as well." Lauren glanced around her. "I wonder what happened to the poor lad? He got scared when his da hit his head and ran up here for help, right into the brewing storm."

"He may have went lookin' for his da. Sounds like yer Malcolm MacGregor is a hero," Deidra said, grinning. "Ye should be proud."

"He is not my Malcolm. 'Tis enough if he wakes and lives. I will not be thinking on more than that."

"Ye there!" Mr. MacKinnon pointed at Logan. "We need all the help we can get to repair the ship, restore order, and tend to the wounded. My men took a beating in last night's storm, and two were permanently lost." He pointed to one of his sailors climbing a mast. "You can help repair the sails."

"What do ye mean . . . lost?" Deidra asked.

"Washed out to sea. There was no way to save them." He motioned to Lauren. "If you will help Miss Campbell tend to the wounded, I would be much obliged. Miss Campbell will show you what to do."

"Mr. MacKinnon!" Captain Shaw waved a compass in the air from the quarterdeck. "We need to discuss our whereabouts."

"Pardon me." Mr. MacKinnon dipped his head and turned to follow his captain's bidding. His clothes were just as wet, dirty, and rumpled as the rest of them. Mr. MacKinnon's brown hair was usually swept in a ribbon at the back of his nape, but now his dampened locks had curled askew all over his head and down to his shoulders. Even the captain wasn't wearing his usual wig and proper attire.

"Our whereabouts?" Deidra exclaimed once he was out of hearing. "Does he mean to say we are lost at sea?" She clutched her stomach as fear etched across her face.

"In a storm like the one last night, 'tis possible we have blown off course. We could be anywhere," Logan said.

Pain burned Malcolm's head. He tried to escape it, but the fierce sting followed him to where there was no escape. He reached up to push it away.

"He is waking up. Help me hold him down."

Lauren's voice. Where was she? He tried to open his eyes, but his lids were too heavy.

"L . . . Lauren?" His voice croaked. What was wrong with him? "Lauren?"

"I am here, Malcolm." Her voice came near. He reached for her, eager to touch her. Lauren's hand found his, and he gripped her tightly. He couldn't explain why, but her touch and her voice calmed him.

Something twisted and burned the top side of his head. He reached up as he blinked. A string? What were they doing to him?

"Nay!" Lauren grabbed his other hand. "Malcolm, I need to stitch yer wound. 'Twould have been better if ye had stayed unconscious a wee bit longer, but I canna tell ye how relieved I am to see ye awake."

"The storm . . ." Images pressed his mind of the ship rolling, thunder, lightning, and monstrous waves. "Did we make it, then?"

"Aye." Lauren squeezed his hand. "Now listen, I'm stitching yer head, but ye must be still. Promise me, Malcolm."

"Look into my eyes. I need to see ye, Lauren." She leaned forward. Her worried blue eyes peered at him from a ring of purple circles. He swallowed, but his throat felt swollen and dry. Taking a deep breath to summon his strength, Malcolm reached up and cupped her cheek. "Ye look tired, lass. Is there no one else who could tend to me?"

"I am here," Deidra said, her lips twisted into a mischievous grin he didn't trust. "I could take over yer stitches."

"Nay, there are so many others that need attention." Lauren shook her head, her damp golden hair hung over her shoulders. "I shall finish what I started with Malcolm."

"But who will hold 'im down for ye?" Deidra asked. "Ye will need my 'elp."

"I have been stitched afore," Malcolm said, closing his eyes and resting his head against the wall. "I daresay, Lauren will manage, an' I shall do my best to stay still."

As the rest of him awakened, Malcolm grew more aware of the aching bruises and soreness throughout his body. Was there no spot on his person that hadn't suffered a beating? He wouldn't complain. He had no idea what Lauren might have endured while he was lying unconscious.

"Are ye sure?" Deidra sounded hesitant.

"Aye, Malcolm and I have weathered many unpleasant situations in the past." Lauren tightened her grip upon him for emphasis. The action alerted him to the task at hand and helped him stop concentrating on the throbbing aches. He opened his eyes to see her gazing at him, her expression one of concern and uncertainty. She smiled, lighting his heart with a hope he had been afraid to allow before the storm. "We shall be fine."

Lauren pulled the needle through his skin. The sting of every prick and the thread sliding through his skin felt like a razor blade slicing him. He clenched his teeth, determined to keep his word about not flinching. Malcolm longed to be invincible in Lauren's eyes while he struggled to mask his pain. How else could he prove that he was worth more than the Campbell Clan deemed him?

He had always believed people of wealth couldn't be true Christians. They had everything and no opportunity to test their faith time after time like the poor. Lauren had come along and shattered that idea. In watching her these last few weeks, he knew he had witnessed true faith. She had lived a life of comfort, and he had despised her for it.

"Ye're doing well for someone who has been given no laudanum or whiskey for the pain." Lauren tied off the thread into a knot as Malcolm gritted his teeth. If she didn't soon finish with her task, he might slip back into unconsciousness. If only he had remained in such a condition, then none of this manly prowess would be necessary.

When Lauren finished, Malcolm leaned his head against the wall and closed his eyes. "Ye did not have to do this. Deidra was right. She could have tended to me."

"I am not good at letting others finish what I started." Lauren touched his wound, now so sore it was numb. "I wanted to take care of ye. 'Twas the least I could do after all my family did."

"Forget that, Lauren. I know what yer da is guilty of, an' I know his sins are not yers to bear." Malcolm blinked and waited for her to deny it. When she didn't, he continued, "Yet that is what I have tried to do to ye."

"Shush! Ye need yer rest now." She brushed a lock of hair off his forehead.

The tender gesture sank a hole in his chest, and the back of his throat throbbed as much as his wound. He didn't want her to leave him, not yet, and he couldn't find his voice to speak. Malcolm grabbed her wrist. His thumb circled her soft skin, while he blinked away emotion and gulped to find his voice.

"What is it?" She leaned over, her damp hair tumbling past her shoulder. The scent of the fresh sea carried with her. At home, she had always smelled of heather and pine. It was how he had known when she had paid his mother and sister a visit in his absence.

"Why did ye visit us so many years? Was it merely charitable work, or was there something more?" He covered her hand with his. "Please, lass, I need to know."

"At first, it was charity." A faraway look came into her eyes. "But then I came to know yer mither and sister, especially yer mither. She was different than any woman I knew. I had lost my own mither and craved a mither's love."

She paused, leaving him on edge. He wanted her to continue but forced himself to be patient.

"The other women who came to visit Kilchurn Manor were beautiful, clothed in colors and fabrics of wealth, but their conversations and personalities lacked substance. I came to realize it was yer mither's faith that drew me. She talked about God and the Bible the way my mither did before she died. My mither had planted the seeds of the gospel in me, but God brought yer mither into my life to water those seeds and teach me."

Unshed tears filled her eyes as she swallowed and met his gaze. "Malcolm, ye've always thought I came out of pity for yer family, but it was the opposite. I was the one living in poverty."

"How is that?" Malcolm eyed her with a familiar criticism that always threatened him whenever he compared their lives. "Ye had everything!"

"Nay, I did not." She shook her head. "There was no love in our home. I needed love, and yer mither knew how to love me."

Over the next few days, Lauren helped stitch and bind the wounded while those in the worst shape finally succumbed to their illnesses and mortal wounds. They held a massive ceremony for as many as thirty souls. Several supplies were ruined, but they still had enough to carry them through the rest of the journey.

Malcolm was on the mend and joined Logan in the effort of replacing some of the lost and wounded sailors. Ever since their discussion, he treated her differently. He watched her more and inquired about her health and comfort.

"He is in love with ye." Deidra sidled up to the rail beside her. "A person would have to be daft or blind not to see it."

"What? Who?" Lauren turned to her friend, gripping the rail until her knuckles turned white.

"Malcolm MacGregor." Deidra lifted a red eyebrow. "Do ye really need to ask?"

"Then I must be daft and blind." Lauren burst into laughter. "Ye're mistaken. Believe me, Malcolm is only feeling a wee bit of guilt for what he intends to do to me once we land in Carolina."

"Nay, I think 'tis more 'n that." Deidra shook her head. Long red curls flew in the breeze. "At times, the way he looks at ye reminds me how my da used to look at my mither." Sadness crept into her tone. "Makes me miss them, it does."

"I am sorry. I know ye must miss them a great deal." Lauren wrapped a plaid shawl around her. A husband who lost his wife gave it to her after the storm. "I barely remember what my mither looked like. My da is not one for showing emotion. I doubt she felt loved by him."

"We did not have much growin' up, but love was something we had plenty of," Deidra said. "An' that ye canna buy."

"Aye." Lauren shivered as she turned to look out over the ocean. How could it be so calm and blue one minute and a raging life taker the next? The sea was as fickle as a man's love. She had to tiptoe around her father's moods, pleasing him as best as she could. Only then could she ever earn his approval. Love wasn't part of the deal. She was his daughter, a piece of property he hoped to use in negotiating a marriage that would best benefit his goals.

"Believe me, I shall be shocked if Malcolm does not change his mind afore we make landfall." Deidra gripped her arm. "Have faith. Ye've so much for everyone else. Why not save some for yerself once in a while?"

"If he does, 'twill be out of guilt and naught else," Lauren said. "I refuse to believe it could be from anything more." They stood in silence as Lauren wondered about the colonies, things she had heard, and the way indentured servants were treated. "What do ye suppose it is like in Carolina?"

"When our cousins could not afford rent, they sold themselves as indentured servants to Carolina. Once they work off their indenture, they will receive fifty acres of their own land an' tools. That would never 'appen in Scotland—least not for a peasant."

"But how are they treated? And what kind of work do they do?" Lauren knew she shouldn't fear the unknown, but being at the mercy of someone else for her livelihood filled her with trepidation. If Malcolm succeeded in exchanging her for his mother, would her master be kind or harsh?

For we walk by faith, not by sight.

The verse rose from memory, encouraging her to let go of her fear and trust the Lord. She could do this—go to Carolina and take Iona's place. Still, her insides quaked at the thought.

"One of the sailors grew up in the colonies," Deidra said. "I would be willing to bet he has some interestin' tales. He told my brother 'bout it during one of their card games."

"Who is he?" Lauren asked, scanning the deck for a sign of which sailor it might be.

"Mr. Todd Kerr." Deidra pointed toward the watchtower at the mainmast where a man looked through a long telescope. "Quite handsome with the sailor's look about 'im. Sun-browned skin, blond hair, and bright blue eyes."

"Och! I doubt he will want to have much to do with me." Lauren frowned, remembering her first day on board when Mr. MacKinnon questioned him about seeing Malcolm bring her aboard.

"Why not ask 'im what ye wanna know?" Deidra grabbed her arm. "Life is full of uncertainties. Ye must grasp the moment. For all we know, a band of pirates could come upon us next."

An image of a ship firing guns upon them in the midst of the high seas made her breath hitch in her throat. Lauren touched her hand to her chest. "That is not a verra comforting thought. Are ye trying to give me nightmares?"

Music floated through the hallways luring passengers to the main deck. Although she was extremely weary from hours in the infirmary, the sound of lively music drew Lauren like a caged animal full of curiosity.

"Come on. It has begun!" Kathleen scrambled from her bed to the door, motioning for them to follow.

"What?" Lauren asked, swinging her feet over the side of her hammock.

Deidra and Kathleen exchanged a secret glance, both grinning with excitement as their eyes glowed. "I suppose she has not heard since she spends so much time in the sickroom," Kathleen said.

"Heard what?" Lauren slipped from the hammock and stood with her hands on her hips.

"The cap'n has given 'is permission to celebrate tonight." Deidra walked to Lauren and took her hands in a firm grip. "Those with instruments may play them while the rest o' us dance."

"But why?" Lauren scratched her temple, wondering what could have brought this about.

"Somethin' about reaching Carolina within a fortnight." Deidra tilted her head. "Honestly, Lauren, must there be a reason? Ye've worked so hard. Ye deserve a night o' fun."

"The indentured servants will not be allowed up from the hold, will they?" Lauren couldn't mask her feelings at the unjust way they were treated. Her words and tone reflected her disappointment.

"Nay, but that does not mean ye shan't take advantage of yer good fortune," Deidra said.

"Aye," Kathleen nodded, leaning around Deidra. "Ye would not stop eating just because others are starving. 'Twouldn't fill their bellies any more than ye denying yerself a wee bit of fun would get them out of the hold tonight."

Lauren sighed in frustration and crossed her arms. Kathleen was right. With her being a teacher, she had a way of stating facts that always made one think.

"Come on, Lauren." Deidra tugged on her arm. "We will not allow ye to waste the night. Ye're comin' with us."

Kathleen grabbed her other arm, and the two of them led her out of the dark cabin and up the steps to the main deck. A couple of fiddlers were already playing with a woman hitting notes on her tin whistle. One man pounded a stack of metal spoons in rhythm, while another beat the bottom of a barrel like a drum. Couples were already swinging around and dancing to the lively tune of "Speed the Plow, Mrs. MacLeod."

Even the sailors had taken a break to celebrate. The captain smiled as he walked around, watching the dancing. He nodded to the beat of the music with a cup in his hand. Lauren assumed it was whiskey since the smell drifted in the salty air.

Lit lanterns hung in each corner, and a bright moon gave them plenty of light as the reflection on the water bounced to cast more beams. Malcolm stood talking to Logan and his other cabinmates. They seemed to be relaxed and enjoying the evening.

Logan was the first to spot them. He said something to Malcolm, who turned and met Lauren's gaze. Of all the balls she had attended and the gowns her father had ordered for her, this was the first time she wanted to look her best—and she looked her worst.

She longed for a bath and clean clothes and wished her hair was washed and combed. To her utter amazement she wanted to impress no one save Malcolm MacGregor—the very one who was responsible for stranding her here. She blinked, allowing the realization to take root. If she had been drinking, she could at least blame her wayward feelings on that, but she had naught to blame except her own madness.

If he could have his way, Malcolm would no doubt dispose of all the Campbells, including her. He held a deep grudge against her father, and she would do well to remember it. She couldn't risk giving her heart to him regardless of how tempting. He risked his life to save her in the storm but in doing so ensured a replacement for his mother.

The men approached, grins broadening their faces. Malcolm had his sights upon her. Lauren's stomach twisted at the thought of having to reject him if he asked her to dance. She had already worked through all the reasons why she should avoid him and save her heart in the process. Stepping back, Lauren wrapped her arms around herself in consolation. She should have listened to her instincts and not come.

A hand reached out and grabbed her. Deidra sensed her retreat and looked at her brother. "Logan, it took some convincing, but we managed to drag Lauren up here to enjoy herself."

"Did ye now?" His blue eyes peered at her in curiosity. "Mayhap ye will like my bagpipe." He pointed to a set of pipes lying on a nearby barrel.

"I did not know ye played the pipes," Lauren said, her interest piqued. "I always enjoyed hearing them at home. 'Tis one of the things I have worried I might miss in the colonies."

"Never. We have many cousins already settled in Carolina, an' they assure us in their letters that they still play the Highland pipes. We are a people who carry our traditions with us."

"Afore ye start in on yer pipes, why not dance a wee bit yerself?" Deidra asked. "Even if she will not admit it, Lauren is well deserving of it after all the hours she has put into the sickroom."

A gleam lit Logan's eyes, but he hesitated with a glance over at Malcolm. Quick anger burned through Lauren. Neither of them needed Malcolm's permission. The man didn't own her—at least not yet. He could produce no papers on her.

Malcolm didn't respond right away, and it gave Lauren the chance she needed to take matters into her own hands. Deidra lifted Lauren's hand toward Logan. Lauren smiled up at him. "I promised yer sister I would do my best to enjoy myself tonight."

"In that case," Logan gripped her hand, "the others will have to wait their turn. If Malcolm's expression sours any more, we may be inclined to think the mon's in pain an' will not be able to take his turn with ye." Logan winked at her and turned to Malcolm with a friendly pat on the shoulder. "Patience, my friend."

Malcolm grinned, his gaze landing upon Lauren's with a promising glint and a brief nod in her direction. "Indeed, I have more than enough to last me 'til later."

7

As promised, Malcolm waited patiently while Lauren and Logan danced. After the second song, Logan grabbed his bagpipes and joined the others in a lively tune. Lauren stood on the side, tapping her toes to the beat and clapping. It was refreshing to see her smiling and enjoying herself.

Archie swung by with a young lass on his arm. The two laughed as their feet pounded the wooden deck in unison. As people ambled onto the main deck, more couples joined in the dancing.

Lauren made her way to the water barrel and waited her turn to dip the ladle. Malcolm approached her, but before he could reach her, Lauren glanced up with a welcoming smile.

"Mr. Kerr, so good to see ye. How are ye enjoying the celebration?" she asked.

"Well enough. Each time we make it this far, the cap'n throws a party. It started out with only the crew, but last time he let the passengers take part." Mr. Kerr paused beside her.

Malcolm stepped aside and watched. He didn't deserve to dance with her. Deep down he had known it, but the ambience of the ship and the distance from their homeland made anything seem possible. At home, Lauren would be forbidden—forever out of his reach. The colonies were different, or so he heard. As a free man, he could make of himself whatever he chose. The ban on the MacGregor name would no longer matter, so why should all the reasons that would have kept them separated in Scotland apply here?

The answer seared his heart as if someone opened his skin and branded him with a hot iron like a slave. At home, all the things that separated them were due to rules of society and the animosity between their clans. When he made the conscious decision to hold her captive on this ship and exchange her for his mother, it became personal. He didn't succeed in taking revenge against her father or striking against the Campbell Clan. All he'd done was betray Lauren. He wronged her and in doing so cut off any opportunity to win her heart. How could he have known he would be severing his own heart?

Malcolm slipped into the shadows, bracing his back against the wall. All of a sudden he didn't feel like dancing. The music now sounded as if someone kept scratching at his ears. The smell of whiskey made his stomach churn. His heart beat fast as Lauren nodded and placed her hand on Mr. Kerr's arm. They joined the line of dancers.

There were plenty of bonny lasses, but none captured his heart the way Lauren did. He had no desire to ask any of the others. Malcolm folded his arms and crossed his ankles.

"Ye're a well-fitted mon. Ye ought to join in the fray." Pastor Brad stood beside him tapping his toes. "If my wife were here, we would be enjoying the night on the sea."

"Aye, few things compare to the beauty of the sea." Malcolm turned to revel in the bright reflection of the moon against the water's surface. It looked like shiny white diamonds in the midst of a black curtain.

"Many lasses are glowing with merriment tonight." Pastor Brad waved a hand, gesturing to all the dancers.

"Ah, but the verra one I would have will not have me." Malcolm lifted a finger, trying to match the pastor's good mood with a grin. "An' therein lies the problem."

"That is not a problem unless ye let it be, laddie." The pastor gripped his shoulder much like a father doling out advice to his son. "When I first met Mrs. Patterson, she would have nary a thing to do with me." He chuckled at the memory. "Almost made me mad, it did."

"This is different." Malcolm shook his head. "We have a lifetime of disagreements, and my latest sins against her are full of bitter betrayal."

"Lad, I know. 'Tis no secret how ye an' Lauren Campbell came to be on this ship. Besides, she needed someone to confide in." He scratched his graying temple. "Mind ye, someone who would not mislead her or judge ye, someone who could help her see things from a godly perspective."

"Aye. Her faith is verra important to her." Lauren swung by on Mr. Kerr's arm. Jealousy twisted his gut. "Even if she finds the strength to forgive me, I canna expect her to trust me."

"That comes with time, I assure ye." Pastor Brad rubbed his brown mustache. "One of the reasons people run from God is because they do not trust Him to do what the gospel says. They spend too much time lookin' for God to prove Himself—to earn their trust. They forget that it should be the other way 'round."

Pastor Brad's words penetrated Malcolm's heart like an arrow hitting its target. Malcolm had no idea what to do with the pastor's imparted wisdom. In many ways, he was guilty of doing exactly what Pastor Brad said, expecting God to give him a reason to trust Him. Where was his own attempt to give something back? Aye, he worked hard to provide for their family but not for the Lord. He always expected to receive, never to give.

Could it be his family wasn't cursed, after all? What blessings had they received that he could be thankful for? None came to mind. All he could think of was the painful loss of his father from the Jacobite war, the shameful poverty, the hunger, the taunts, and the betrayals of the Campbell Clan, the wrongful beating Graham took, and the unfair treatment of his mother and sister being sold as indentured servants against their will. Nay, he couldn't think of one blessing for which to be thankful. How could he trust a God who had turned His back on his family so many times? Malcolm hardened his heart, determined not to hope in something that would only hurt worse if he was once again disappointed.

"If ye do not heed any other advice, heed this. Lauren is not like any other lass. She is trying her best to forgive ye without any bitterness between ye. Take advantage of her goodness. 'Tis rare in a world full of sin." Pastor Brad sipped from his cup. "We do not have the strength to forgive and love as we ought, but through Christ, we can do all things. Ye can undo the damage ye've done by doing right by her now."

"If only it was that easy," Malcolm said with sarcasm.

"What was yer quest when ye boarded this ship?" Pastor Brad asked.

"To free my mither and sister no matter the cost and get revenge against Duncan Campbell."

"Ah, a noble cause in the eyes of most men. A cause filled with rage, pain, and revenge—all the forbidden fruits leading nowhere but further pain." Pastor Brad lifted his palm as if to stop an advance. "Has your quest changed now that ye've come to know Lauren better?"

"The quest in freeing my mither an' sister has not changed and will not." Malcolm crossed his arms, his chest tightening in concern at where this conversation was headed. "But I will admit I now have reservations of using Lauren as I had originally planned."

"Good." Pastor Brad nodded in approval. "That is because yer cause is a noble one, but the execution is flawed. The desire to get back at Duncan Campbell is not as strong as it once was, is it?" He raised an eyebrow.

"Nay, not if it has to be at Lauren's expense." Malcolm looked down at his feet, hating the shame that rolled through him.

"Then change yer course now before ye've more regrets. Mark my words, ye'll not only give her freedom back but begin to rebuild her trust again."

The dance ended, and Lauren settled her hand on Mr. Kerr's arm. They took a stroll toward the quarterdeck. Mr. MacKinnon had been leaning against the mizzenmast and turned to follow them. "Pastor Brad, thank ye for the advice. I think I shall go see what Lauren is up to."

Malcolm maneuvered around the dancers with a nod toward Logan, who played the bagpipes with excellent skill. He stepped around someone hanging another lantern. An older sailor manned the wheel and tipped his hat to Malcolm. "I may be too auld for a wee bit o' dancin', but I can still handle the wheel."

"Aye, that ye can." Malcolm grinned.

"Mr. Kerr, leave us a moment. I have a matter I would like to discuss with Miss Campbell."

Malcolm raced toward the poop deck.

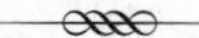

Lauren gripped Mr. Kerr's arm as they stared at Mr. MacKinnon. "Whatever ye wish to say can be said in front of Mr. Kerr."

Malcolm's warning echoed in her mind. She looked around the dark shadows on the poop deck, wishing he were here. What if Mr. Kerr had led her up here on purpose at Mr. MacKinnon's demand? Mr. Kerr was under his authority. Did he not have to obey his superior?

"Todd, you know very well that on this ship either I or the captain give the orders." He motioned toward the steps. "Now do as I said and move along."

"Why must he go?" Lauren kept a firm grip on Mr. Kerr. "If I do not mind him hearing what ye have to say, then ye should not."

"Go . . . now!" Mr. MacKinnon raised his voice but not loud enough for anyone to hear over the music and dancing.

"Nay!" Lauren panicked as Mr. Kerr tried to wrench her fingers from around his arm. "Ye canna leave me here alone with him."

"I am sorry, Miss Campbell, but he is right. I must follow orders." Mr. Kerr stepped away from her. "You have naught to fear, Miss."

She stared at him, but he refused to meet her gaze. "I see. Ye led me back here, pretending we were on an innocent stroll, and all the while this was planned." She jabbed a thumb toward Mr. MacKinnon.

"Naw, that ain't the way it happened." Mr. Kerr shook his head as he moved to stand beside his boss. "All I planned to do was talk like we did before." His thin frame shook as he looked from Lauren to Mr. MacKinnon.

"Get on with yourself, lad." Mr. MacKinnon shoved him toward the steps. Before he disappeared in the shadows, he took a lingering glance at Lauren. Guilt etched into the strained lines of his young face.

"I shall scream," Lauren said, backing away until her back hit the rail and she had nowhere else to go.

"They cannot hear you over the music," Mr. MacKinnon said as he lunged forward, an arrogant grin widening his face. He looked as if he was about to open a new package.

"Help!" Lauren brought her knee up into his groin as someone grabbed him by the neck.

"Ye're wrong." Malcolm bellowed in fury as his breath gushed. "I heard her." Malcolm gripped Mr. MacKinnon's collar and jerked him away from Lauren. The man stumbled back and spiked his elbow in Malcolm's ribs. A deep grunt escaped his throat, but Malcolm gritted his teeth in determination and used the momentum of his body to ram Mr. MacKinnon against the rail.

Malcolm reared back and planted his fist against the sailor's jaw. Mr. MacKinnon's head snapped back, knocking him off balance. With his back against the rail, Mr. MacKinnon lifted his foot to kick Malcolm, but he sidestepped and Mr. MacKinnon's foot landed in Malcolm's thigh. The brute force shoved Malcolm backward, his boot heels scraping against the wooden deck.

Lauren rushed to aid him, but Malcolm motioned for her to stay safe in the corner. He took a deep breath, keeping his opponent in sight and assessing the man's next move. The music on the main deck switched to a new tune as Malcolm stalked toward Mr. MacKinnon, who wore an arrogant grin.

Mr. MacKinnon's mustache twitched as he lunged for his boot to grab something. Suspecting it to be a weapon, Lauren screamed, "Malcolm, watch out!"

Malcolm paused to glance at her. It was just enough time for Mr. MacKinnon to slip out his knife from his boot. They circled each other like prowling tigers. Mr. MacKinnon charged him. Malcolm braced himself and grabbed his wrist, squeezing. The man swung his other fist at Malcolm's face, but Malcolm ducked, pulling the man's wrist and twisting his arm. Mr. MacKinnon groaned at the pain.

Lifting his knee at Malcolm, Mr. MacKinnon prepared to kick him again, but Malcolm slammed his left fist into the man's knee. The blow made him cringe and loosen his grip on the blade.

"I should have known ye would not fight fair." Malcolm took advantage of Mr. MacKinnon's agony and shoved him back against the rail where he beat his hand against the iron bar until he relinquished the blade. Malcolm kicked it toward Lauren, who picked up the knife and threw it overboard. He slammed his fist into Mr. MacKinnon's nose. Bone cracked and blood gushed. "Now 'tis a fair fight."

Malcolm stepped back, waiting to see if Mr. MacKinnon would rush at him again. Instead, he dropped his head back on his shoulders and looked up toward the starlit sky to slow the bleeding. He brought his good hand up to cover his nose and winced in pain.

" 'Tis only part of what I shall do if ye try to touch Miss Campbell again." Malcolm placed his hand on Lauren's back, guiding her toward the steps. "We shall go see the cap'n an' explain why one o' his sailors has a broken hand and nose. To make sure he is told the right version of the story."

Malcolm gripped her hand and led her down the steps from the poop deck. They passed by the old man at the wheel on the quarterdeck. The sound of the music grew louder as they drew closer.

"Are ye all right, lass?" Malcolm asked.

"Aye. Ye came at the right time." She squeezed his hand to let him know her gratefulness. "Thank ye."

"There is the captain." Malcolm pointed across the dancers to where the captain stood by the water barrel, talking to Pastor Brad and Dr. Taylor. He pulled her along, hurrying toward the captain.

Lauren struggled to keep up, taking two steps to each one of his. She was out of breath by the time they arrived at the captain's side. Malcolm relayed the details of the incident. Pastor Brad expressed his concern for her, and she assured him she was fine.

"I am sorry for the discourtesy of my first mate and relieved to know your honor was not compromised." Captain Edwards gave her a brief bow. "While I cannot do without the skills of my first mate, he shall be properly reprimanded, I assure you."

"He should be locked up," Malcolm said, his tone fierce as he rubbed the back of his neck and paced. "He canna be trusted."

"I have been trusting him for nigh on three years now. A beautiful woman caught his attention, and he had a weak moment. I refuse to destroy a man's position for one mistake."

" 'Twould be a dishonorable mistake." Malcolm turned and met the captain's gaze. "His behavior is no better than a lewd pirate, and if ye allow 'im to behave like that, ye're no different."

"I told you he will be punished. Now if you will excuse me, I shall see the deed is done." Captain Edwards walked away.

"Strange, how everyone is dancing and merry as if naught has happened." She took a deep breath to calm her nerves. Laughter and music filled her ears, but her heart wasn't so merry.

"Lauren, ye need time to recover. Stay with me a wee bit afore ye retire for the night. I want to make sure ye're well."

"I shall be fine. What amazes me is how I never thought I could be so grateful to ye, but tonight, I have never been more relieved to hear yer voice." Lauren reached up to cup his cheek and searched his hazel eyes in the lantern light. "Thank ye."

Malcolm couldn't sleep. He slipped out of the hammock and crept across the room to grab his boots. The boards creaked beneath his feet, but his cabinmates continued to snore as usual.

Outside in the hallway, he pressed one foot inside his boot and then the other. After lacing them, he slid along the wall until his toes hit the bottom step. He climbed up to the main deck.

Fresh air filled his lungs, tinged with the salty sea. White stars filled the black sky with a bright moon shining down upon them. The wee morning hours beckoned Malcolm through the fog hovering over the water's surface.

He shivered in the cool air, wishing he had thought to bring his plaid. Malcolm rubbed his hands and blew on them. The aroma of brewing coffee teased his nose. What he would give for a warm cup of coffee. He followed his senses as his mouth watered.

Voices brought him up short as he blinked to make out the figures in the fog. Pastor Brad sat on a barrel with an open book on his lap, reading in a monotone voice. People sat on the deck floor with various expressions, but no one could doubt how intensely they listened.

Malcolm took slow, steady steps toward them, careful not to disturb anyone. Curiosity drew him like a moth to lantern light. He assumed Pastor Brad read from the Bible, but what had these people so mesmerized?

He wasn't such a heathen that he'd never attended church. On many Sundays, he had taken his mother, but the boring sermons caused his mind to wander to different places. There was only so much talk he could tolerate on judgment and eternal damnation. His list of sins was quite long. What to do about it eluded him. It seemed God expected him to be a perfect and loyal subject. It was impossible when the Campbells were forever provoking the MacGregors to hunger and poverty.

"Coffee?" The cook pointed to a steaming pot. He held up a wooden cup. Malcolm had never seen the ship's cook, but the man wore an apron around his bulging middle so Malcolm assumed he was the cook. At Malcolm's nod, he poured the dark brew. "We only serve it black." The cook whispered as he held it out.

Malcolm wrapped his fingers around the warm cup, thankful for the warmth. He sipped the coffee, reveling as the hot liquid heated his insides and pooled in his empty stomach. For a man as large as he, it must have looked comical to see him shivering like a wee child.

"Malcolm." Someone whispered his name. He turned to scan the people sitting on the floor. One pulled a plaid from her head, and he recognized familiar blonde locks. Lauren motioned for him to sit by her. Her bright blue eyes sparkled, and she awarded him with a brilliant smile, the kind he'd hoped to see when she looked at him.

He walked toward her, but it was as if his feet floated. All night he had worried about her after Mr. MacKinnon's near attack. Had she cried herself to sleep? Would she be afraid for her safety during the rest of the journey? As he lowered himself beside her, he sensed no reservation or fear in her.

She turned her attention back to Pastor Brad, a look of awe and adoration upon her face. She closed her eyes and swayed at the words as if they were music to her ears. Her hands clasped in front of her, and the angelic, peaceful expression on her face caused a longing in Malcolm he had never felt before.

Malcolm shook his head to clear it, but the cloud over his mind lingered. He took a deep swallow of coffee, allowing the liquid to burn down his throat. It gave him the jolt he needed. The foggy haze over his mind faded, and he blinked, glancing over at Lauren's profile again. Her expression had not changed, but her eyes were now open.

Lauren stared up at the orange glow now budding in the skyline where it met the ocean in the east. She sighed in contentment and grabbed his hand. "God's glory is about to rise," she whispered. "Did ye know His mercies are new each morn?"

He shook his head. The coffee helped, but it wasn't able to shake off this strange effect Lauren had on him. Pastor Brad's voice penetrated his mind as he sat beside Lauren and watched the sunrise.

"For God hath not given us the spirit of fear, but of power, and of love, and of a sound mind," Pastor Brad said.

Malcolm contemplated the verse. Could that be why Lauren wasn't frightened after last night's incident? Malcolm didn't have the same security as she. What if he wasn't around the next time Hugh MacKinnon wanted to take advantage of her? Men like that didn't give up so easily. They took what they wanted while others beneath their authority looked away and pretended they didn't know in order to save their livelihood.

The pastor bowed in prayer, and the rest of them did the same, including Malcolm. He closed his eyes out of respect. When it was over, Lauren touched his arm.

"Ye surprised me in coming to our morning devotions," she said.

"I could not sleep." He motioned around them. "Ye do this every morning?"

"Aye." She nodded. "Except the morning after the storm. It helps to remind us of God's love and His promises when things seem so bleak. It gives me hope when I am tempted to give up."

"To give up yer faith?" Malcolm asked. It never occurred to him that she felt that way.

"Nay, not in my faith or in God, but in people." She smiled. "God always works through people."

Several days turned into a few weeks, and with the illnesses that the indentured servants came down with, Mr. MacKinnon's untoward behavior faded to more urgent matters—death and disease. If the captain ever punished Mr. MacKinnon, none of them knew it.

Lauren brushed her hair from her face as she made her way from the sickroom to her cabin. It was late, and once again, she had missed dinner. A painful headache pressed against her temples, and her shoulder muscles had tightened into knots.

During the past two weeks, Lauren spent more time working in the infirmary. An illness spread among the passengers in the hold, and several lost their lives. Tonight, it was Amy Murray's turn to care for the ill while Lauren and Dr. Taylor caught up on their rest.

It was rare to see Malcolm. If she made it back to her cabin, she fell asleep in her hammock before her cabinmates returned.

Lauren's stomach rumbled as she pushed open her cabin door. A lit lantern hung in the corner, casting shadows on the dark walls. Voices came to an abrupt stop as several pairs of eyes looked up at her.

"Each of us saved a portion of our dinner for ye." Deidra carried a wrapped package to her.

"Aye, ye're working too hard," Kathleen said, her eyes filled with concern.

They sat on the floor with Logan, Malcolm, and Archie. A stack of cards had fallen over between them. Malcolm held out a wooden cup of water. "Here, ye'll need this to wash it down."

Lauren dropped beside him with a grateful sigh. "Thank ye. I am starving, and I have a headache that feels like an ax in my skull."

"If ye do not rest more, ye could end up as sick as the rest o' them." Malcolm lifted an eyebrow. "Then who will care for them?"

"If we had more volunteers, those of us helping would not have to work so hard or long." Lauren bit into the beef jerky. The salty meat tasted better than she remembered. She must be hungrier than she thought. Beef jerky had never been her favorite. In fact, she had forced herself to get used to it the first couple of weeks on the ship. An endless supply of it seemed to be their main course.

"Well, then, I suppose the rest of ye can pitch in on my behalf or in my memory." Lauren touched the side of her head, hoping the pounding would soon fade with a bit of food.

"Ye're not already sick, are ye?" Malcolm leaned forward with a frown. He pressed the back of his knuckles against her forehead.

"Nay, merely tired and hungry." Lauren took another bite. "With a satisfied belly and some decent sleep, I should be back to myself in the morn."

"Lauren, I do not think ye should go back on the morrow. Yer body is fighting exhaustion. I read about it in one of my health books while teaching." Kathleen touched her hand and looked into Lauren's eyes. "When ye wear yerself down like that, 'tis easier to get sick. Ye've got to take care if ye want to keep serving people."

"I want ye to rest for the next two days." Malcolm crossed his arms and set his chin at a stubborn angle she had come to recognize.

"Well, ye do not own me." Lauren's ire rose. She clenched her jaw. "I will not allow it. Those people deserve to be cared for as if they matter. Everyone else on this ship is too afraid to go around them lest they become sick themselves. I have naught to lose. I know where I am going when I pass. I will stay with them until they breathe their last, and no one will stop me, not even ye, Malcolm MacGregor."

He stared at her with an unchanging expression. Tense silence spread among them, but Lauren refused to budge. The others stared back and forth between them.

"Um, I think the lass knows her own mind, Malcolm." Archie gave a nervous chuckle.

"I do not care. I canna risk it." Malcolm's unwavering tone pierced Lauren like a sword. "Ye shall rest the next two days an' we will see how ye feel afterward. I dislike this headache ye have. Ye never complain."

"Ye canna fool me, Malcolm. Ye're a good mon, but I know the real reason ye want naught to happen to me." Lauren swallowed, blinking back hot tears stinging her eyes. "Ye're afraid ye will not be able to exchange me for yer mither if I am not healthy or do not make it."

"Lauren, 'tis more 'n that an' ye know it, lass." Malcolm's gruff voice lowered as he glared at her. "If only that is all it was, I might have gotten more sleep in the last fortnight."

"Guilt," Lauren snapped. "Take heart. It only affects those of us who have a conscience."

"Think of me what ye will. I took the liberty of speaking with Dr. Taylor earlier today an' he is not expectin' ye tomorrow." Malcolm shifted his large legs, crossing them at the ankles.

Lauren stared at him in disbelief. Anger flared through her, pumping the blood in her veins until her hot cheeks no doubt flamed her skin. "How dare ye, Malcolm! Ye had no right." She lifted her chin in defiance. "I will not leave my patients at the mercy of no one, an' the doctor has his hands full."

"Lauren, calm down." Kathleen touched her arm. "Malcolm has more to tell ye."

"Aye." Malcolm nodded. "I knew ye would say that, and 'tis why I shall be taking yer place tomorrow." He rose to his feet. Logan and

Archie followed. "I will be goin' now so I can get my rest. I have an early start in the morn."

"Night." Logan said with a brief nod.

" 'Til the morrow." Archie grinned.

As soon as the men left, Deidra turned to Lauren. "A man who is only interested in sellin' ye off would not be riskin' his own health an' life to cover for ye in the sickroom. I think we might have misjudged 'im."

8

Glad to be free of the stench of sickness, Malcolm scrubbed his hands, arms, and face clean. He climbed to the main deck and blinked as the waning sun cast angled rays in his eyes. His boots clicked against the wooden floor as he nodded to other passengers and breathed fresh sea air.

Lauren stood looking out over the ocean, her elbows resting on the rail and her fingers linked. She had pinned her hair upon the crown of her head. Her profile left a striking portrait revealing a slender neck with creamy skin that begged for gentle kisses. Malcolm shook his head and rubbed his tired eyes, wondering what sparked such a thought.

He strode forward, joining her at the rail. Neither of them spoke. She spared him a momentary glance that assured him she had finally gotten enough rest. The red circles around her eyes were gone. She carried better posture in her shoulders and back rather than the weary dragging she had shown last night.

"Thank ye for making me rest today. I needed it more than I realized." She sounded sincere, and the knowledge pumped him full of satisfaction that he had finally done something right by her.

"Ye're welcome." He leaned toward her with a grin. "If I might say so, ye look all the better for it."

"Is that so?" She teased, arching a golden eyebrow. Her pink lips curled, and his heart overflowed with warmth. "Are ye saying I looked all that bad before?"

Malcolm studied her face and longed to touch her skin—to tell her how he really felt, but he dared not since he didn't deserve her. Instead, he settled for truthful flattery to appease her and disguise his deeper feelings.

"Lass, ye could be covered in mud from head to toe, an' I would still believe ye beautiful." She flushed crimson. "But as an elder brother, I have come to recognize the signs of a lass needing rest." He touched the tip of her nose as he would a child. "An' ye most definitely needed a break."

"Goodness, Malcolm, what a fine da ye'll make one day. Please keep in mind that I am not a wee child." She turned away and sobered her voice. "Tell me, how did things go today? Did we lose anyone else?"

"Nay, we were fortunate in that, at least. Dr. Taylor seems to think the worst is over."

"Good." She laid her hand across her neck and breathed a sigh of relief. "I have seen enough death to last me all the days of my life. I never knew how hard the voyage would be on those in the hold." She bit her bottom lip as she paused. "I daresay, many of them would have lived if they were not locked up in those dark and cramped quarters like wild animals."

"Indeed," he said, lapsing into silence. She was right, but encouraging her to talk and think about it would only compound the guilt she felt at being in a better situation. If he could have changed their plight, he would have done so, including that of the MacGregors. One thing he could do was rectify what he had done to Lauren.

"I negotiated an agreement with the captain to work in place of a wounded sailor. In exchange, I shall receive a small sum once we arrive in Carolina." Malcolm took her hand in his. To his relief, she didn't resist. "I promise, when I earn my wages, I shall spend them buying my mither's release or at least shorten her indenture."

"That is verra noble of ye." Lauren gave him a skeptical look. "What about yer sister? Will ye not need to free her as well?"

Every nerve in his body tensed at the reminder. An image came to mind of Carleen's sandy brown hair and innocent hazel eyes. His chest ached, and he hated the frustration of his limitations. He could only work with what he had, which wasn't much. Malcolm needed a miracle, and so far, God had done little to help his family in their plight.

"I will figure out something," Malcolm said, the burden upon his heart deepening. He hoped he would be able to keep his word. After all, he had no idea what to expect once he arrived. Regardless, he wanted Lauren to know his true intentions.

"Please forgive me for trying to use ye to get revenge against yer da." The words tumbled off his tongue, releasing him from the guilt that had plagued him throughout the voyage. "Once I raise the money to buy my mither's an' sister's indenture, I shall do what I can to help ye get home. If ye write Duncan, he may arrange for yer passage home afore then."

"It could take ye years to raise that kind of money from mere wages." She curled her fingers around his, and her azure blue eyes searched his face. "Malcolm, do not make promises ye canna keep. I know why ye did what ye did, and I hold my da entirely responsible."

"I do not deserve yer forgiveness, lass." An uncomfortable lump formed in the back of his throat. Lauren was beautiful inside and out. He wished . . . no it was better not to let his mind go there.

Lauren stood on her tiptoes and cupped a gentle hand on his roughened jaw. She met his gaze. He couldn't look away if he'd wanted to, but he treasured this moment, knowing he might spend the rest of his life cherishing it—cherishing her—a woman far above his station.

"Malcolm MacGregor, this world has undervalued ye far too long, but let me assure ye that Christ values ye more than anything money can buy. And through His eyes, I see a mon of honor with a kind and decent heart. Ye need not take revenge against my da. Ye've already won. Ye're the better mon."

Her thumb caressed his cheek as she blinked back unshed tears. Without another word, her breath caught, and Lauren turned, leaving him to contemplate her words. He ignored those who might have witnessed their tender moment. None of them could have imagined what she said or how deep it quaked his heart and soul.

Lauren stood on the bow of the ship with her hand cupped over her eyes. A sailor had spotted land from the lookout tower more than an hour ago. A mixture of fear and excitement raced through her.

They sailed between two islands and into the harbor. As they approached a piece of peninsula land, Lauren marveled at the various two-story homes along the water's edge bordered by a gray stone wall. The captain steered the ship to the right into the mouth of a river. She counted at least eight wharfs, with vessels already anchored at a few. Two were merchant ships with cargo goods unloaded.

The Sea Lady headed straight for the empty wharf in front of a wooden two-story building with a balcony on the second level. It stood on a man-made sea wall shaped in a semicircle. She scanned the rows of rooftops that seemed to go on for miles. A few church steeples peeked above the rest of the buildings.

Lauren gaped in awe. Charles Towne didn't look like the primitive town she had imagined, surrounded by a forest with wooden homes no larger than small cottages. Their buildings and homes were colorful, many of brick and stone. Even a stone cathedral stood in the midst of the city like a proud monument. The city was larger than Taynuilt in Scotland.

"Welcome to Charles Town, Miss Campbell," Mr. Kerr said. She turned to see him approaching with his hands gestured wide to include the bustling city. Malcolm followed, his gaze meeting hers over Mr. Kerr's head where he towered above him by at least four inches. Still reeling from Mr. Kerr's betrayal the other night with Mr. MacKinnon, Lauren braced herself, knowing she needed whatever information he was willing to provide about Charles Towne.

"That is the Court of Guard." Mr. Kerr pointed at the wooden building with the balcony. "Stay away from the lower floor. They keep prisoners in there. The upper level is a public meeting place. Charles Towne is a beautiful city but has a dark side as well."

"Mr. Kerr!" Captain Shaw called. "We need your assistance to set up the tables for the auction while MacKinnon an' the others manage the sails."

"Aye, Cap'n!" Mr Kerr motioned to him with a brief nod.

"The auction will take place on the ship?" Lauren glanced at the busy docks where so much room would afford the indentured servants space to stretch their legs and take the fresh air. "Would it not be better someplace else? On the docks, for instance?"

"Nay, Lauren, half of them would run away," Malcolm said. "Canna say as I blame them. Many signed their indenture out of desperation not knowing what would be expected o' them."

"Do not forget, Mr. MacGregor, ask for directions to the courthouse. That is where they shall have the records for the auctions of your mama an' sister." Mr. Kerr walked away.

Malcolm leaned toward Lauren's ear. "Gather yer things an' wait here for me. I shall go ask for my wages after I gather my things." He squeezed her hand. "I realize ye'll be free to go as soon as we're anchored. While I would not blame ye, I hope ye'll wait for me to return as I intend to see ye well settled for the night. No tellin' what dangers might await an innocent lass unfamiliar with Charles Towne."

"Indeed, I understand." Lauren's clipped tone was harsher than she intended. It boiled her temper to realize he was right. She knew naught about the people here other than what she heard by hearsay, and she had no idea if such reports were accurate. Judging by what Mr. Kerr said, she would be safer with Malcolm. She still didn't know if she could trust him in spite of everything.

"Do not look so frightened." Malcolm laid a comforting hand on her arm. "I shall return shortly," he said.

The ship's hull bounced against the wharf, and one of the sailors threw the anchor overboard. They finally came to a stop. The auction tables were now in place with two chairs at each. Lauren watched in fascination as they lowered a walking board to the dock. Sailors tied ropes to the dock. Men lined up waiting to board, eager to peruse the selection of indentured servants and cast their bids.

The hold opened, and several servants lined up in rows to be inspected like pieces of horseflesh for auction. Buyers judged their hair, teeth, skin, and posture. It was the most humiliating thing she had ever witnessed. Her heart sank at the thought of what Carleen and Iona must have endured.

While Lauren watched people leave the ship as buyers purchased them, she couldn't help wondering what kept Malcolm. Someone grabbed her shoulder from behind. Lauren gasped in fright.

"Shush, 'tis only us." Deidra's whispered words floated to her burning ears. Deidra and Logan stood behind her. "We only wanted to say good-bye afore we leave." She reached out and drew Lauren into a tight hug. "I shall miss ye. I hope we will see each other again."

"Me too." Lauren returned her hug. "Malcolm said he would try to raise the funds to buy back his mither and sister, but I am afraid he will become discouraged and change his mind."

"Never ye mind that." She took Lauren's hands in her own. "He loves ye, even if he does not yet know it. Ye're a woman of faith, if I ever knew one. Do not lose faith now."

"My sister is a bit of a romantic." Logan elbowed Deidra in the side and stepped forward when she moved. "I was hoping to tell Malcolm good-bye. Will ye let him know we were lookin' for 'im? If ye stay in Charles Towne, I am sure we will be seeing each other again."

"Aye, I shall tell him. He will be pleased to know it. I had hoped he would have already returned. I suppose the captain has a lot to deal with at the moment. Malcolm went to collect his wages before we disembark."

With a final wave good-bye, Deidra and Logan gathered their belongings and left. Once again, Lauren stood alone, wringing her hands, wondering how much longer Malcolm would be.

The indentured servants in the best shape went first. Amy was gone before Lauren could tell her good-bye. They brought up more indentured servants from the hold. The second group was not as healthy as the first. One buyer's eyes kept falling on Lauren after he viewed the selection of what was left. Most of the free passengers were already gone, and Lauren lingered where Malcolm left her.

The man eyeing her went to Mr. MacKinnon. He lowered his voice where she couldn't hear and pointed at her. Lauren tensed. *Lord, please let Malcolm return in time.* She whispered the brief prayer as Mr. MacKinnon and the man walked toward her. Lauren glanced in the direction where Malcolm had disappeared, but there was no sign of him.

"This one is special and slightly resistant. She was not a peasant but is well educated. Her family has come upon hard times." Mr. MacKinnon motioned to Lauren. The man's brown gaze lit up in eager delight.

She lifted her chin and squared her shoulders. "I am not for sale, Mr. MacKinnon, as ye verra well know. Malcolm MacGregor paid for my passage."

"I beg to differ," Mr. MacKinnon said. "He owes me quite a bit after our last encounter." The buyer feasted his eyes on her. "Name your price and be generous. I will not allow this one to go for just anything."

"I am not for sale!" Lauren turned to run, hoping to reach the captain or Malcolm for help.

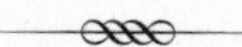

Malcolm left the captain's office pleased with the few coins he now had in his possession. The captain had tried to pay him less than they agreed upon, but Malcolm refused to give up and argued his case. The man finally gave in, no doubt just to be rid of him.

Malcolm searched the main deck for Lauren, but she was nowhere to be found. His gut clenched as he gritted his teeth. He should have known he couldn't trust her. Disappointment crushed his spirit as he whirled in a circle.

"Lauren? Where are ye, lass?" Malcolm strode across the deck and went below to her cabin. It was empty. Fear coiled in his stomach as he stood in place and contemplated the situation. As much as Lauren wanted to be free of him, something wasn't right.

He charged from her cabin back up to the main deck. The last of the indentured servants were purchased and final contracts written. He walked over to the table where Mr. Kerr wrote out the contracts and leaned his palms on the table.

"Where is Lauren? I canna find her." Malcolm tried to keep his voice calm, but blood pumped through his veins faster than a raging river. Mr. Kerr cleared his throat and glanced in Mr. MacKinnon's direction, who stood talking to a buyer with his back to them.

"Tell me now." Malcolm clenched his teeth in a rumbling growl.

"I . . . I . . . wrote a contract for a Mr. Lee Davidson." Mr. Kerr's gaze slid over to Mr. MacKinnon, still occupied in conversation. "She tried to fight it, but they would not listen an' MacKinnon was determined."

"Why did ye not fight for her?" Malcolm swallowed the rest of what he wanted to say. He needed Kerr's cooperation to find out where they had taken Lauren, and insulting him might not be the best way. "Give me the contract." Malcolm held out his hand.

"I canna do that," he whispered. "MacKinnon will have my head."

"If ye do not give it to me, that will be the least of yer concerns." Malcolm's hands curled into fists. He had to keep those papers from being filed in the courthouse. If there were no official record, the man wouldn't be able to hold Lauren. "There is naught to stop me from huntin' down the Kerr family to see they enjoy the same fate."

"Ye would not!" He started to rise from his chair, but Malcolm leaned closer, and he lowered himself. "I suppose I could let the wind carry it overboard. As long as he sees the paper tumble like a leaf, he will never know the difference."

" 'Tis the least ye could do. Her passage was paid. What MacKinnon did was wrong," Malcolm said.

Kerr flipped through the sheets with dried ink and pulled one out. With smooth swiftness, he folded it in half and then again and twice more until it was small enough to hold in one's hand. He looked around him, ensuring no one watched them and slipped it in his shirt sleeve. He held out his hand. "A pleasure getting to know you, MacGregor."

Malcolm shook his hand as Mr. Kerr twisted his wrist and flicked the folded paper into Malcolm's palm. He grasped it tightly into his fist and folded his arms over his chest, slipping it into the folded pocket of his plaid.

"Kerr, what is taking so long?" Mr. MacKinnon demanded. "We have a buyer eager to go." He narrowed his eyes at Malcolm.

"MacGregor, why are you still on board? I would have thought you would be long gone by now. Are you wanting to join our crew on a permanent basis?"

"I would not give ye the satisfaction." Malcolm backed away from the table with a brief nod at Kerr. "Just sayin' farewell to a good friend is all." Malcolm shrugged, ready to unleash the anger stirring inside. "Not that ye would know what a friend is."

Malcolm left the ship, thankful to be back on solid ground. The muscles in his legs felt strange as he walked. Hired carriages waited on the docks to carry new passengers wherever they wanted to go. Malcolm didn't dare waste his money and ignored the drivers who called out to him. A merchant woman in a corner booth held up a red cloak in admiration. It looked very similar to Lauren's. Malcolm pushed his wobbly legs in determination as he strode toward her.

She looked up with a broad grin, revealing yellow teeth. Wrinkles lined her eyes, giving away her advanced years. "An elegant cloak for the missus?"

"Please, where did ye get it?" Malcolm slowed to a halt in front of her table.

"That is not important, lad. Look at this fine detail. A nice lining to boot." She opened the cloak to show the inside.

Malcolm touched the sleeve and fingered a dark brown stain near the wrist.

" 'Tis only a small stain an' I am sure 'twill wash out."

" 'Tis coffee. I remember the morn Lauren spilled it on herself." He crushed the garment in his fist and tried to ignore the aching hole in his chest as he peered into the woman's eyes. "Please, tell me where he took her. I intend to get her back."

"Oh, I see." She pointed up the street. "I bet you are after the pretty one with the blonde hair an' striking blue eyes. He had about ten o' them chained on a wagon, but she is the only one who stood out from the rest."

"What did the man look like?" Malcolm wiped his face and took a deep breath.

"He is middle-aged with brownish-gray hair to his shoulders." She motioned to one of her own thick shoulders. "He has got a mustache an' beard. You better hurry if you wanna catch 'im."

"Thank ye." Malcolm stepped back. "An' do not worry. I will catch 'im, an' when I do, he shall be sorry."

Lauren tugged on her bound hands, but the rope was so tight it rubbed her skin raw. She and nine other indentured servants from *The Sea Lady* sat on a bed of straw as a horse pulled the wagon through the busy streets of Charles Towne, alternating between dirt roads and those laid in brick and stone. The horse clip-clopped along, his shoes pressing against the hard stones.

The man who purchased them sat up front, guiding the wagon through the busy traffic. Mr. MacKinnon had called him Mr. Davidson. He wasn't a well-versed gentleman, but one with bad manners and an ill temper. When Lauren tried to explain that she wasn't for sale and that they were making a mistake, he shoved her toward the other indentured servants and ordered all of them bound. Her protests and struggles against them were in vain.

She glanced behind them, seeking a sign of Malcolm. Surely, he would come after her, wouldn't he? Even if he did, how would he catch them without a horse? Doubt pressed her like a heavy burden, throwing her mind into survival mode. She would have to depend on her own faculties and pray for God's wisdom and favor to guide her.

Lauren glanced at the dirty and thin faces around her, wearing pale expressions of no hope. How many of them were here against their will? Of those who had chosen this path, were they already sorry?

The wagon rolled along, wobbling from side to side between uneven stones. Conversations buzzed in all directions from the town's citizens. The smell of liquor drifted from taverns, mingling with the stench of horse droppings still in the street. The sun warmed the day and brightened the world, making her wish she could use her hands to shield her eyes. Instead, she closed them. They burned as she allowed herself to be still and rest while she could.

It was no use to make plans at this point. Lauren had no idea where they were going and what would happen. The ten of them might be going to different places, or all of them could land at the same location. Their destination might be around the corner or take days.

One thing was certain. She needed to eat and rest to maintain her strength so she could make her escape at the first opportunity. They turned off the cobbled street and onto a smooth dirt road. The wagon wobbled less, allowing Lauren to relax more. The background noises faded. Lauren imagined herself at home in bonny Scotland, riding in her father's wagon to market as a child.

The sound of a lone rider approached from behind. Horse hooves pounded the compact dirt road and grew louder. People around her shifted to stare. Someone's foot touched hers.

"Halt that wagon!" a man called. He sounded like Malcolm.

Lauren's eyes flew open. Her heart pounded with hope. Where would he have gotten a horse? He had planned to save what money he had earned on *The Sea Lady* to purchase his mother. Her heart thumped against her ribs as hope rose in her chest.

"I said halt that wagon. Now!" Malcolm passed them in a blur as Lauren scrambled to her knees and tried to peer over the side.

Lauren had never been so glad to see Malcolm MacGregor. In the last six weeks, her feelings for him had changed more than she ever thought possible. She was determined to forgive him, but more than that, she had come to depend on him and trust in his judgment.

"Who in the blazes are ye?" Mr. Davidson yelled over the rattling wheels and the heavy breathing of the horse. "If a thief, ye should try a rich man."

"Pull over!" Malcolm raised his voice and pointed to the side.

"Nay." Mr. Davidson shook his head.

Malcolm manuvered his horse closer, pulled his left foot out of the stirrup, and swung his leg over. He lunged from his horse and jumped onto the wagon seat. Before Mr. Davidson had a chance to react, Malcolm steadied himself and swung a fist into his jaw. The man slumped over to the side while Malcolm grabbed the reins and pulled them back. The horse slowed as he steered the wagon to the side.

People paused in their yards and on the front steps of buildings to watch. A woman beside Lauren gasped. "Is the mon crazy?"

The wagon slowed to a stop. Malcolm jumped down and strode to the back. Lauren hobbled on her knees, but her long skirts kept getting in her way and others blocked her path. He unlatched the back and pulled the gate down.

"Lauren? Where are ye, lass?" Malcolm asked, ignoring the questions and pleas from the other servants.

"Right here." She had fallen in her struggle and lay on her side.

"Move aside." The others scrambled back. Malcolm leaned in and lifted her into his arms, pulling her close.

"She is mine!" Mr. Davidson said. "I just bought 'er."

"Mr. MacKinnon cheated ye. She is not an indentured servant. Her passage was paid. I paid it myself." Malcolm carried her to his horse where he untied her.

"I paid good money for 'er, I did," said Mr. Davidson. "I signed a contract an' all. I can prove it once filed in the court records."

Malcolm kept a reassuring hand upon her arm as he pulled out a piece of paper with his other hand. "Ye mean this?"

Mr. Davidson reached for it, but Malcolm jerked it away. "Not so fast," Malcolm said, shaking his head. "I canna trust ye, and I am not about to let this document get into the wrong hands. So place them behind yer head." Mr. Davidson stared at him in confused defiance. "Now!"

The man jumped and threw his hands behind his head. Malcolm stepped forward and held up the paper for him to see. "Does this look familiar?"

"Aye, 'tis the agreement I signed when I bought 'er." Mr. Davidson glanced over at Lauren. "That is why ye do not have the right to take 'er."

Malcolm ripped up the agreement into tiny pieces. "Since it will never be recorded in the courthouse, ye would have a hard time proving it."

"How did ye get it?" Mr. Davidson demanded.

"It matters not," Malcolm said. "Go on about yer business. Now that I have Lauren back, I shall go about mine."

Malcolm mounted up behind Lauren. His arms wrapped around her to take the reins. She had never felt so safe and secure. Leaning back against his muscular chest, Lauren closed her eyes. "Lord, thank Ye for answering my prayers," she whispered, content to go wherever Malcolm took her.

Malcolm savored the feel of Lauren in his arms as he carried her back toward an inn with a tavern he had seen earlier. This one didn't reek as much as the others near the docks. It appeared to be kept in better condition, and the people were less offensive.

"Where did ye get the horse?" Lauren asked.

"I ran into Logan and Deidra after I met the woman who purchased yer red cloak. He had already bought a horse and was more than willing to let me borrow it when they learned what happened to ye."

"They are such loyal friends. Will they be staying where we are going?" Lauren asked over her shoulder.

"Aye, ye shall be sharing a chamber with Deidra this night. Logan and I will find a comfortable spot under the stars."

"Why can ye not stay in a room as well?" Concern laced her voice. "The two of ye can share it and the expense."

"We are already doing that with yer chamber, lass." He squeezed her in a tight hug. "Do not worry. I am told the April weather is rather mild 'round here."

"So it is." Lauren covered his hand with hers. He closed his eyes feeling blessed to be the object of her favor, even if only for the moment. "Thank ye for coming after me."

"He did not hurt ye, did he?" Malcolm asked.

"Nay, but I did not want to go with him. I belong here, wherever ye are," she said.

"Do ye mean that, lass?" He leaned close to her ear. The scent of the sea mixed with straw drifted to his nose. She fascinated him, and he loved everything about her. He would have done much more to get her back. Was she right? Did she really belong here with him? Or would she be better off at home in Kilchurn Manor where she had every luxury and comfort—food in abundance, beautiful gowns, servants who catered to her. What could he offer her? Very little.

When he dreamed of Lauren Campbell at his side, he dreamed of the impossible. She deserved better, and he wouldn't be that selfish—he couldn't—not if he truly loved her. To his dismay, he did love her. He knew it now, as sure as he knew that dusk would soon come and the moon would shine with the stars.

"Aye, I mean it, Malcolm. I have never felt more safe than when ye're by my side." Lauren's tone grew pensive as she dropped her head and looked down. "Not even my own da ever made me feel so secure. He protected me, but he did it in a way to make me feel like property—a possession to claim and keep. Ye take pains to make sure I am comfortable and oft ask me what I prefer as if I matter."

"I care, lass. Make no mistake 'bout that." Malcolm wrapped his arms tightly around her. He dropped his chin upon the soft strands of her hair, wishing he could run his fingers through it. A deep ache rooted in his chest. In her mind, the recent comforts she had given up were temporary. Soon she would write her father, and Malcolm would have to let her go.

They came upon a two-story building with faint candlelight in the windows. Malcolm pulled the horse to a stop and tied him to a nearby post. The sun now lowered below the trees, and dusk had finally come upon them. He intended to see Lauren settled before tending to the horse.

Lauren yawned as she leaned down and laid her hands upon his shoulders for balance. Malcolm lifted her and settled Lauren on her feet. She wavered as if gaining her boundaries and then smiled with satisfaction. "I am still getting used to my legs on solid ground."

"Me too." He took her arm and led her toward the door. "Are ye hungry, lass?"

"Aye." She nodded, rubbing at her wrists. "And verra thirsty. The water on the ship had become stale."

After almost losing her, he loathed the idea of letting her out of his sight. At least she and Deidra would be safe for the night, and tomorrow he would inquire about renting a more permanent room.

Malcolm swung the right side of the double doors open. Conversation and laughter erupted. The smell of liquor and baking bread drifted toward them. They stood in a small foyer with a brass candle chandelier hanging above them. An archway to the left led into the dining area. A wood counter faced the archway, beside a set of stairs along the corridor wall. His stomach rumbled as he led her toward the dining hall.

Dim lanterns hung on each side of the wall, casting the room in moving shadows. It had twelve tables of varying sizes occupied by patrons—mostly men enjoying a hearty meal and a few mugs of whiskey. He tightened his grip on Lauren's elbow, determined to protect her if need be. A bonny lass as beautiful as Lauren could prove too much of a temptation for a man deep in his cups.

Rather than be irritated by his possessive manner, Lauren drew close as if sensing the danger. She scanned the room, her expression drawing into a disappointed frown. "There is not an empty table to be found."

"Malcolm!" Logan's voice boomed behind them.

He whirled to see Logan and Deidra waving at them from a corner table.

"Thank God ye found her, Malcolm." Deidra bounced from her chair and hurried to them, holding out her hands to Lauren. She released Malcolm's arm to greet her friend. Deidra turned Lauren's hands over and gasped. "What did they do to yer wrists?"

"He bound me with a rope. Malcolm found me just in time." Lauren sat beside her. "No telling where I might have ended up."

"What will ye do now, Malcolm? How will ye get yer mither an' sister back?" Logan asked, tipping his mug and taking a long swallow.

"I do not know, but I shan't be askin' Lauren to pay the way by replacing my mither or Carleen." He covered her hand with his and offered an encouraging smile. "But first, I will have to find them. On the morrow, I plan to visit the courthouse to ask about indentured servants auctioned in the past couple of months."

"Seems like a good plan." Logan nodded, pushing his empty mug aside. "A wee bit ago, a mon told me 'bout a nearby mill lookin' for loggers an' saw cutters. When I go see them for a job, ye want me to ask if they have an open position for ye as well?"

"Aye," Malcolm said. "The sooner I have a steady income, I shall be able to purchase proper boarding rooms for Lauren and me. Eventually, I hope to rent a house large enough for all of us after I find Mither an' Carleen."

"Och, mon!" Logan leaned forward. "I know ye wanna do right by Lauren an' all but think on the cost of two rooms. Ye'll never be able to save up enough to buy both indentures for yer mither an' sister." He lowered his voice. "Ye could share a room if ye wed 'er."

Malcolm blinked and stared at his friend as if he had lost his mind. If truth be told, he rather liked the idea, but he didn't deserve her nor would she have him. She gasped, and judging by the shocked expression on her face, he had his proof.

"Do not look at me like that. Anyone can see plain as day ye're taken with 'er." Logan gestured to Lauren. "An' the way she looks at ye is just as tellin'."

"Logan, stop it," Deidra said. "Ye're embarrassing them." Deidra slapped at her brother's arm, but the grin on her face and the rosy blush to her cheeks showed she shared his opinion. Malcolm wondered if they had even discussed the matter among themselves.

"That will not be necessary." Lauren's firm voice carried above the conversations around them as well as the clinks of forks against plates and spoons upon soup bowls. "I intend to find a suitable job and will support myself. Malcolm is not responsible for me." She shook her head, her face darkening in color as she pressed her palms flat against the wooden table. "Besides, I would never dream of trapping Malcolm or myself in a marriage of convenience. We are in the colonies now, where I am told things are quite different."

9

Lauren woke at dawn. Deidra washed in the basin and donned her day clothes. A small candle burned on the dresser, affording a bit of light. Deidra stood before the looking glass in the corner by the fireplace, twisting her body to the side. She wore a simple emerald green gown she had been saving for such an occasion.

"Ye look lovely," Lauren said, her voice cracking with sleep. She rubbed her eyes and brushed her wayward hair from her face.

"I am sorry. I did not mean to wake ye." Deidra whirled. "How do ye feel?"

"Much better. Thank ye for letting me stay here." She glanced between their two narrow beds and noticed that Deidra had already made hers.

" 'Tis naught." She waved a hand in the air and placed a white cap upon her head, adjusting it over the bun in which she had swept her red hair. "Besides, Malcolm paid Logan for yer share and 'tis as much yers as mine." She sighed, patting her head. "This will have to do. I hope I look presentable enough to secure a position."

"No doubt about it." Lauren flipped the covers to the side and swung her legs over the edge until her bare feet hit the cool wooden floor. "I, on the other hand, am another matter. I have no references nor have I ever been in the employ of another." Lauren stood and glanced at her discarded gown draped over a chair. "Not to mention I own one gown in dire need of a washing. Oh, what I would give for a few things from my wardrobe at home."

"Ye plan to write yer father today?" Deidra raised an eyebrow as she walked to the door.

"Mayhap later." She shrugged. "Right now, I intend to help Malcolm find his mither and sister. Even if I mail a letter today, 'twill take several weeks for him to receive it, and several more to act on my behalf. In the meantime, I must find myself a job so I do not become a further burden to Malcolm." Lauren didn't share her worries over what her father might do to Malcolm. He would consider Malcolm's actions a grave insult and would never admit his own behavior had led Malcolm to react the way he had.

She had no idea how extensive her father's connections were. Could he know people as far away as here in the colonies? If so, Malcolm could still be in danger. She longed to protect him and delay her correspondence, but she couldn't delay long. She needed to let her father know how she fared, if only for Blair's sake.

"I shall see ye this evening." Deidra closed the door behind her, and Lauren launched into action. She wanted to be ready when Malcolm arrived.

An hour later, Malcolm escorted Lauren down Meeting Street where a two-story building stood on the corner. A balcony overlooked three archways at the entrance. The lobby echoed every footstep, voice, and clink of a cane. An elegant staircase led to the balcony on the next level. Lauren stared in amazement. People back home would not believe how robust Charles Towne proved to be.

"All parties attending the court case of the Willie Blade trial, come this way to room C8." A man waved people toward him. He wore a dark blue vest over a white shirt with gray trousers and hose. His white wig was neat and fashionable with a ribbon tied at his neck.

"May I help you?" Lauren and Malcolm turned to see another man with a white wig peering at them over a pair of spectacles. He sat at a large wooden desk with a quill in hand. A thick book lay open where he wrote.

"I want to know where I can find a list of auction records." Malcolm strode toward him, tugging Lauren along. " 'Twould be for indentured servants who arrived a few weeks ago."

"Do you know the name of the ship?" The man rubbed his shaved chin between his thumb and forefinger.

"Aye, *The Loyal Adventure*." Hope lingered in Malcolm's tone. Lauren glanced up at his profile and marveled at the strong contours of his face. No one else would know his eager hope unless they had the pleasure of knowing him as well as she did. He loved his family, and it showed. She admired him for it.

"Knowing the name of the ship is helpful. Give me a moment to see what I can find." The man stood and disappeared behind a closed door.

Malcolm took a deep breath, pressed his fingers over his eyebrows, and pinched the bridge of his nose. He shifted his stance in worried agitation.

Lauren's heart filled with compassion as she laid a hand on his arm. She reached up and cupped his cheek. "We will find them." The words sounded more certain than she felt, but it was what he needed—encouragement.

"Aye, we will, lass." His haunted eyes met hers. The dark skin around his eyes showed his lack of sleep. "I will not rest 'til we do." He turned and kissed her palm. His lips were warm and tender. Lauren's hand tingled all the way up her arm, paralyzing her like a captured scene on a painting.

"Here you go." The man returned carrying another book similar to the one he had been writing in earlier. He flipped past the middle and shoved it toward Malcolm, turning the volume around so they could see it. "These are the entries for *The Loyal Adventure*."

Malcolm stared at the page and squinted. She leaned up on her tiptoes and read the names over his arm. After she read the list and saw no entry for MacGregor, she waited for Malcolm to turn the page. He didn't move.

"May we read this on the bench over there?" Lauren asked, pointing to a wooden bench by the far wall.

"Aye, 'twill be fine." The gentleman nodded.

Malcolm marked his place and carried the volume across the lobby. He sat with a heavy sigh. "Thank ye for helping me avoid further embarrassment that I canna read." He lowered his voice as he leaned toward her ear.

"Ye're welcome." Malcolm was a proud man, and he wouldn't appreciate any pity. She looked down at the book.

He turned the page and gave her time to read more names. When Lauren didn't see them, she shook her head and Malcolm moved on. By the time they reached the seventh page, Lauren found them. Iona MacGregor sold to the overseer of Mallard Plantation north of Charles Towne, while a man by the name of Benjamin Shore purchased Carleen.

"What is it?" Malcolm asked, gripping her wrist. "Tell me. All of it."

" 'Tisn't much to tell. They have been separated, but at least now we know where they were taken."

It took a couple of hours to reach Mallard Plantation by horseback. While Logan worked on his new job, he let Malcolm borrow his horse for the afternoon. Lauren rode behind him with her arms wrapped around his waist.

He had no idea what kind of condition he would find his mother, but at least he now knew that both she and Carleen had survived the voyage. That alone gave him hope she might prove to be healthy and well.

The horse clip-clopped along the dirt road between two plowed fields. Birds chirped and flapped above them. The sun shone bright, and Malcolm wished he had a decent hat to shield his face and eyes.

They came to a brick archway and a white sign with Mallard Plantation written across it. Malcolm rode down a dirt road that circled in front of a porch with white pillars to a three-story brick house. A carriage house was on the left, and a stable stood behind it.

"I hope they will talk to me," Malcolm said, breaking the solemn silence around them.

"They will. Just appeal yer case to the butler, and let him determine how best to proceed." Lauren lifted her head from his back where she had been resting against him. "Ye've naught to lose and everything to gain."

Her words were encouraging. He was glad he brought her along. Lauren had a way of making him feel as if he could accomplish anything. With her around, everything seemed better. He hated to think about how lonely and lost he would feel once she returned home to her father.

Planters sowed crops into the earth in a distant field. Malcolm wondered if his mother was one of the hardworking souls. More than anything, he wanted to free her from such backbreaking labor, but he would have to keep his temper in check and negotiate as if he had something to bargain with beyond a few coins he had managed to save.

They rode to a stop. Malcolm dismounted and reached up to assist Lauren. She leaned down, trusting him with her care. He swung Lauren to her feet. To his increasing dismay, she felt natural in his arms—as if she belonged there. With reluctance, Malcolm let her go and held out his arm. She accepted his escort with a willing smile she wouldn't have offered six weeks ago.

He followed Lauren up the steps past the four giant pillars. Reaching around Lauren, Malcolm pulled the pine leaf knocker that vibrated throughout the house. They waited. A few moments later, a well-dressed Negro opened the heavy door. He bent his gray head in a bow. "May I help you?"

Malcolm stared. Since arriving in Charles Towne, he had seen persons of such color, but this was the first opportunity to speak to one. He blinked and opened his mouth to answer, but no words came forth.

"We have come to inquire about a particular indentured servant who may have been sold to this plantation by mistake." Lauren spoke up in Malcolm's obvious silence. "Who should we speak with?"

"Why, that would be our overseer, Mr. Stanley Fairbanks. Wait here while I fetch him."

He started to close the door, but Malcolm slipped his booted foot in the way. "Are we not welcome inside?"

"No, I do not allow any strangers inside the big house without permission from a member of the family or Mr. Fairbanks." He met Malcolm's gaze, an expression of pleading in his eyes. "Please, sir, I am only doing what I have been told. I do not dare make the master or Mr. Fairbanks mad at me."

The plea stirred Malcolm's compassion. He stepped back, a piercing discomfort centered in his gut. There could be only one reason this man feared his master's ire. Abuse—physical or mental torture. Once again fear for his mother coiled in his stomach and traveled to his throat, almost choking him. The butler closed the door and disappeared, leaving them standing on the front porch.

Malcolm's gaze slid to Lauren's. Her azure blue eyes looked haunted with the same fear paralyzing his own thoughts. She swallowed and patted his arm.

"Do not worry, Malcolm. I have seen my father deal with such men as Mr. Fairbanks. He will come out of curiosity and the possibility he might be passing up on a good deal that would please the master of the house. If he can strike a bargain with ye to make him look good, he will do it."

"Aye, that is the trouble, lass. I have naught else to offer 'im." Disappointment reverberated through Malcolm like an avalanche.

"Ye have more than ye realize," Lauren said. "I know the MacGregors, and the whole lot of ye can survive anything. Even when the king did away with yer name in 1603 and tried to abolish the clan, his efforts were in vain and did not succeed. Ye're dealing with much less here in the colonies. We shall find a way to free yer mither. Have faith. God has not forsaken us."

The butler reopened the door. "This way, please." He led them through a dim foyer and down a hallway with even less light. They passed a staircase along the wall and continued walking on the pine floor until they paused by a closed door. The butler knocked twice, paused, and then twice. Malcolm lifted an eyebrow. Why would a secret coded knock be necessary?

"Come in," a male voice called from the other side.

The butler turned the knob and pushed the door open. "Mr. Fairbanks is waiting," he said, motioning them inside.

Dark panels covered each wall, but two windows on the other side of a large carved pine desk angled the morning light, brightening half the room. Thick burgundy drapes pulled back by a cord hung to the floor where no speck of dust could be traced. An unlit fireplace encased on the left wall had a white marble mantel. A small oval clock stood in the middle, ticking away, while matching vases of dark blue flowers aired the room. Malcolm had no idea what kind of flowers, but it spoke volumes to a woman's touch. No man would worry with flowers in his study.

"Welcome to Mallard Plantation. I am Mr. Fairbanks, the overseer." A middle-aged man stood up from the chair behind the desk and motioned to two chairs in front. His gray hair was pulled back at the nape by a string. His clothes were simple but tidy in a white shirt with ruffled sleeves and a gray vest. He wore black breeches, and he had a tight smile upon his unshaven face. His expression befit one who wasn't pleased with being disturbed but who was determined to make the most of it. "I hear one of our indentures was not meant to be hired. What an unfortunate incident."

"True, sir." Malcolm said, meeting the man's piercing gray eyes. "My name is Malcolm MacGregor, and records at the Charles Towne Courthouse say that my mither, Iona MacGregor, was sold into indentured servitude for three hundred pounds to Mallard Plantation."

"We have so many slaves and indentured servants here that I canna possibly remember them all." Mr. Fairbanks shrugged and tilted his head. "We do keep our contracts under lock and key."

"I was hoping to see her. She is an elderly woman about sixty-two, gray hair," Malcolm said.

"You describe about ten percent of our servants. Do you plan to buy back her indenture? As you know, we have money invested in her. 'Twill need to be recouped, plus a small profit, or the master of the house will not be satisfied." He lowered his voice in a firm tone. " 'Tis my upmost concern to keep him very happy."

"How much of a profit?" Malcolm crossed his arms and planted his feet in a warrior-like stance. His heart beat heavily against his ribs, knowing he could hardly raise the original fee. Anything more would be impossible.

"Her commitment is for seven years. I would say a ten percent profit for each year would be good enough to persuade me to let her go early."

"What if we replace her with a younger, more able person?" Lauren asked, stepping around Malcolm. Mr. Fairbanks glanced down at her, unable to hide his surprise. "That would be more than ten percent profit each year. Ye would be getting at least thirty percent more work. In fact, 'twould be more than fair to cut the length of the term."

Mr. Fairbanks threw his head back and roared in laughter. "I did not realize you had brought a little lady to do your bargaining for you." He dropped his hands on his hips. "And who do you have in mind to take her place?"

Malcolm grabbed Lauren's arm in protest, but she jerked away from him with her blue eyes flashing. "Before I tell ye, just answer me one thing. Would we have a deal? Would ye let Iona MacGregor go free this day and shorten the term?"

"Go free?" He nodded. "Yes, if the girl is young and able. Your mither may go free today, but I want to know about her skills and what she has to offer before I agree to a shorter term. Now who is she? I would have to meet her, and if I approve, the exchange could take place today."

"Mr. Fairbanks, allow me a moment to discuss this sudden arrangement with Miss Campbell." Malcolm grabbed her arm and tried to lead her away, but she pulled free and dug in her heels.

" 'Tis me," she said. "But ye have to cut the term from seven to four years since I can produce double the amount of work as someone her age."

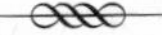

Mr. Fairbanks gave Lauren a mischievous smile. Her heart vibrated in her ears as she waited, hoping she wouldn't regret her decision. Malcolm's earlier plan was the only thing that would work. To her relief, he couldn't go through with it. She had underestimated him. He was a better man than she had given him credit.

"Lauren, this is not necessary," Malcolm growled through clenched teeth and grabbed her arm. "Now that I know the terms, I will figure out some other way."

"Do not worry, Malcolm." She patted the top of his hand on her arm. "I know what I am doing."

"Well, is this not sweet?" Mr. Fairbanks folded his arms and scratched his chin in obvious amusement. "I must admit, this new turn of events has taken me by complete surprise."

"Believe me, sir, I am not doing this for yer entertainment." Lauren lifted her chin as she mustered enough courage to do what she had to do. She couldn't back out now, even though the thought was more than tempting. Lauren imagined Iona's face and prayed in her heart that God would be with her and bless her decision. This was only temporary. God would provide Malcolm the means to buy her indenture, or her father would come for her. Unlike Iona, she had other options, and her youth would see her through, in addition to her faith.

"You must love this young fool a lot." Mr. Fairbanks nodded toward Malcolm. "I only hope you do not come to regret this foolish mistake. Servitude on a plantation is not easy, and many do not survive the time to reach their freedom."

"All the more reason for me to take Iona's place." Lauren struggled to keep her voice steady. " 'Tis my Christian duty."

"Call it what you like, but I see the way you look at him." Mr. Fairbanks laughed. "You are besotted, and perhaps you prefer he not know the real reason you do this."

"I love Iona like a mither," Lauren said. "Now please, have Iona brought here. I will not sign a contract until we see her."

"Very well." Mr. Fairbanks went to the door, swung it open, and called, "George! Come here."

A moment later, the butler returned. "Yes, sir?" He bowed his head in submission.

"Have one of the field hands fetch Iona MacGregor and tell them to be quick about it." He scratched the side of his head as he stepped around the large desk and sat down. He pulled out a long piece of parchment paper, quill, and ink. "In the meantime, I shall begin writing the contract agreement."

While he scratched his quill across the paper, Malcolm shook his head and stepped forward, leaning his palms on his desk. "Nay, ye canna do this. Lauren Campbell is the daughter of a wealthy overlord in Argyll, Scotland. She left without his permission, and he could already be on his way to the colonies to collect her as we speak."

"Good." Mr. Fairbanks didn't bother looking up as he continued writing. "Then her indenture will be short-lived, and the master of the house will be sure to make a profit if her father is as wealthy as you claim."

"Ye do not understand," Malcolm said. "He is a man of great importance with friends and allies in many places, especially the Duke of Argyll, who has the favor of the king. I realize this is a colony, but it is still governed by the king of England, is it not?"

"Indeed, Mr. MacGregor, but you fail to understand that things run a little different here in the colonies." His firm voice grew louder with marked impatience. "The colonies exist for the sole purpose of trade and commerce—all to fatten the king's coffers. The girl has chosen to put herself under indenture of her own free will as stated in this document. How she came to be here is of no concern of ours. If you brought her here against her will, then you shall be the one to answer for it, not me or the master of the house." He waved the paper to dry the ink. "If her father wants her back, he will have to pay the price. I shall have a signed legal document, which will hold up in any English court here in the colonies or the mother country."

"Malcolm, he is right," Lauren said, trying not to let her nerves get the best of her. "Besides, ye'll have yer mither back. That is the most important thing."

Malcolm whirled. Anguish lingered in his eyes as he blinked and slowly walked toward her. "I once thought it was, but not anymore." His voice was low. "Do not do this, Lauren. Please . . . I have a bad feeling. I could not bear it if something were to happen to ye."

"Then set yer conscience free, for I do this of my own free will." She cupped her hand on his cheek and smiled up at him. Her heart skipped a beat as it grew heavy with the knowledge of how much she had come to care for him in spite of everything. "My time will not be long. My da will come for me. Have faith."

Someone knocked on the door.

"Come in," Mr. Fairbanks called.

The door opened and in walked the butler, leading a limping figure into the room. Her hair was a matted gray that looked as though it had not been washed in months. She wore a dirty and torn gray skirt not fit to be a rag, much less someone's clothing. Her oversized and rumpled blouse wasn't much better.

Lauren's stomach plummeted. This couldn't be Iona.

"M . . . Mither?" Malcolm's haggard voice broke the silence. "What have they done to ye?" Malcolm rushed to her side and bent to examine her.

"I remember her now," Mr. Fairbanks said. "This is how she arrived. I took pity on her. There is no telling what might have happened to her if I had not bought her."

Lauren gulped as Iona's faraway gaze strayed to Malcolm and recognition dawned. The wrinkles on her forehead and her weary brown eyes and thin lips had deepened and multiplied. Her hollow cheeks and bones were evidence of how little she had eaten since they had last seen her. In that moment, Lauren's doubts disappeared. Iona wouldn't survive another month if Lauren didn't take her place in the fields.

Aching remorse shuddered through Malcolm as he stared at his mother's frail and weak body. His heart lurched when her gaze landed on him, but she didn't seem to recognize him. Had they stolen her mind as well?

"Mither?" He cupped her cheek and willed her to see him. "I came to take ye from this awful place."

He knew the moment she recognized him. Relief poured through Malcolm. She ran her gnarled fingers over his face as a slow smile lit her weather-worn features. "Malcolm, my lad, 'tis ye. I was afraid to let myself believe it."

"Well, believe it. I'm right here in the flesh." Malcolm wrapped his arms around her shoulders and tried not to wince at her sharp bones. "We shall fatten ye up an' have ye back to yerself in no time at all."

She shook her gray head, now layered with strands of white hair that hadn't been there before she had left Scotland. "Nay, son, I will not ever be the same again. Ye must not get yer hopes up." She looked around the room. "I see ye brought Lauren, but where are yer brothers?" Alarm widened her brown eyes.

"They are back in Scotland. Thomas is taking good care of Graham. I sent them to yer brother, Athol. They will find protection from the Campbells among the Fergusons in Perthshire under the MacGregor Clan Chief."

"Well done, lad." She gave him an approving pat on the cheek.

"Do ye not want to gather yer belongings afore we go?" Malcolm asked. "The sooner we get ye away from this place, the better."

"I came with naught but the clothes on my back." Her gaze flicked from Lauren to Mr. Fairbanks. "However did ye manage to convince them to let me go?" Suspicion laced her voice as she raised a thin eyebrow.

"Do not worry, Iona." Lauren stepped forward and took his mother's hands in her own. Unshed tears brimmed her eyes, and her nose turned pink as she tried to hide her emotion. "I came to undo what my wretched father has done. Ye go on with Malcolm now, while I stay behind to finish the details." Lauren kissed Iona's cheek and gave her over to Malcolm.

He led his mother to the door, but he felt like he was leaving part of himself behind. Agony shot through him at the thought of abandoning Lauren to a similar fate of what his mother had endured. Once they reached the hallway, he turned to his mother. "Wait here, I need to tell Lauren something."

"I think not." Mr. Fairbanks blocked the threshold.

"Please . . . just let me say good-bye." Malcolm pressed forward, but Mr. Fairbanks pushed an arm against him.

"No, I will not allow it," Mr. Fairbanks said.

Malcolm struggled against him, careful not to use the bulk of his strength lest he make things worse for Lauren. Taller than Mr. Fairbanks, he glanced over at Lauren and saw the silent tears crawling down her face. "Lauren, I shall come back to visit an' check on ye."

"No, it is not permitted," Mr. Fairbanks said. "Here at Mallard Plantation, indentured servants are not allowed visitors from the opposite sex. It cuts down on unnecessary problems."

Panic rose inside Malcolm. What if he couldn't raise the funds to buy her indenture? It could be years before he got another chance to tell her how he felt about her. He mouthed the words, *I love you.*

Lauren tilted her head as if uncertain. She closed her eyes and turned her back on him in a gut-wrenching sob. Mr. Fairbanks shoved him out the door.

"You have your mother. Now go take care of her," Mr. Fairbanks said. "I daresay, she could use a bit of attention."

At the reminder of his mother, Malcolm stopped struggling and accepted Lauren's fate—for now. He vowed he would get her out of here—somehow. Malcolm offered his arm to his mother. "Let us go, Mither."

"What about Lauren?" she asked.

"Do not worry. Everything is fine." His mother took his arm and leaned upon him. He patted her hand. "All will be well. I promise."

But would it? The nagging thought kept digging at his mind, like termites on a piece of wood. He rubbed the back of his neck as he guided her through the hall and out the front door. She hobbled down the steps with a limp.

"Mither, what happened to yer leg?" Malcolm asked.

"I fell," she said. "An' do not try to distract me. I may be feeble in body, but not in mind an' spirit. Somethin' does not feel right about leavin' Lauren here." She lifted a skeptical gaze, pinning him with one of those stares that had always managed to wrestle confessions from him. "She is not just stayin' behind to handle the details, is she?"

"In a manner of speaking, aye, she is." He dropped his gaze, unable to meet his mother's eyes. It was encouraging to hear some of the fight back in her voice. No doubt, her grit and determination helped her survive the horrible ordeal of these past few months. Still, he dared not tarry. He needed to find them a decent, affordable place to stay before the evening. Once he had his mother settled, he would try and figure out what to do about Lauren.

"Lad, I can smell when something 'tisn't right." She crossed her thin arms and set her stubborn chin at an angle. He had seen this reaction many times throughout his childhood, but the weary wrinkles and circles under her eyes tugged at his heart.

Without a word, Malcolm swept her up and set her upon Logan's horse. She gasped in shocked surprise. Back in Scotland, Malcolm never would have considered such an action. His mother had always been strong and independent. She would have boxed his ears for not waiting for permission, but things had changed. She was too weak to mount up on her own and possibly still too stubborn to admit it.

"Mither, I will tell ye everything by an' by." Malcolm mounted the horse behind her. "But not 'til we leave this place."

Dazed, Lauren stood staring at the door where Malcolm had disappeared with his mother. She couldn't be sure, but she thought he mouthed the words, *I love you*. Placing her palm to her aching forehead, Lauren wondered if her hurting heart could be playing jokes on her vivid imagination.

"So you are mine to do with as I please." Mr. Fairbanks stood in front of her, blocking her view of the empty door. She couldn't keep staring at it as if Malcolm would walk through it again. Sighing, Lauren lifted her gaze to the man who now controlled her life.

"Actually, my indenture belongs to Mr. Robert Mallard, at least that was the name on the contract." Lauren met his gaze with a challenge in spite of her watery eyes. She cleared her throat, straightened her posture, and lifted her chin. "I am ready to hear my list of duties."

His face turned a shade of red as a vein pulsed in his right temple and looked about to pop. He strode toward her, his breath coming out in quick puffs. Raising his hand back, Mr. Fairbanks struck her across the face. The slap reverberated through the room as Lauren's head snapped back. Her skin stung while her mind reeled in shock.

"Get one thing straight, girl. I do not take any sass. Mr. Mallard may be the master and owner, but he has given me full power to oversee his property and to make sure his servants and slaves stay in line." His voice rose and strained with his angry temper, shaking his body with each fierce word. "All you got to do is give me no lip, and do what I tell you to do. Is that clear?" The words rang through her ear where he hovered over her.

Lauren nodded.

"What was that?" He lifted a hand to cup his ear and turned his head at an angle, while keeping an eye on her.

Lauren cleared her throat, trying not to wince. She willed her body to remain still and strong in front of him. "Aye, that is clear."

"Good. Glad we have an understanding. I do flog indentured servants for rebellion and insolence. Do not be thinking that you are any different from the slaves here just because you shall be getting your freedom back at the end of four years. Compared to that other woman, I came out with the upper hand. I shall get more work out of you in four years than I could have dreamed from her in seven years. She would not have lasted anyway, but you will."

He took a calming breath and rubbed his chin as he walked behind the desk and sat down. "This study also belongs to Mr.

Mallard, but he gives me use of it from time to time. He prefers for me to do all my record keeping right here," he tapped the top of the cluttered desk with the tip of his finger, "so he can see and approve all that I do. Do not be thinking you can go running to him for help if you get in trouble with me. It shall only earn you a flogging."

Lauren's mind raced as he talked. She had seen cruel men like him before, but she had never been under the ruling thumb of one of them until now. It would take her time to observe him and figure out how to placate him and avoid being beaten. Fear coiled through her, wrapping around her heart like an iron fist. *Lord, what have I done by putting myself here in this man's hands? Please be with me. And above all, give me wisdom.* She prayed the silent prayer as he continued to talk.

"I shall put you in the fields for now. We need as much help as possible planting the tobacco, but once that is done, you might serve here in the main house. 'Tis obvious you read and write by the way you read your contract and signed your name. How did you come by your education?"

"My da had us educated by a governess." Lauren clamped her teeth to keep her expression from showing her thoughts. She didn't want him knowing how much she hoped to move from the fields to the main house where her labor would be easier. She suspected few educated servants came to them. Perhaps it could be her saving grace from the backbreaking labor that would steal her youth.

"Can you do sums as well?" He lifted an eyebrow.

"Aye, and I am fluent in French and Gaelic," she said.

"We have no need for other languages. Everyone who comes had better learn English and quickly, or they will earn the whip. Some of the field servants do not count as well as I need. I may have you help with the harvest count."

Lauren's stomach sank. That wouldn't be until fall. First, she would have to make it through the whole summer laboring under the sun in extreme heat. Her shoulders drooped in disappointment.

"In the meantime, you shall do whatever else I need." He set her contract on the side of the desk and strode to the door. "I shall take you to the field where you will begin. The sooner we get you trained, the better."

"What about my room?" Lauren asked, following him out the door and down the hallway to the back of the house. They passed a black slave woman who carried a basket of clothes and kept her head down.

Mr. Fairbanks burst into laughter. His shoulders rocked in mirth as he turned the corner and led her through a spinning room where two other servants were at the wheels. They kept their attention on their tasks, and no one looked up to greet them or smile in acknowledgment. He didn't bother to introduce her to them. She wondered if the servants were even allowed to talk to each other.

They came to a side door. Mr. Fairbanks set his hand on the knob and glanced down at Lauren. His mirth faded as his expression turned sour. "You still do not get it, do you? Girl, you are a field servant. You do not get a room. Only house slaves and servants get rooms, and they share. The field servants and slaves sleep in huts near the fields. I may later use your reading and writing, but you're going to pay your dues in the field first. 'Tis the fastest way to break you in. Gets you used to hard work and humility."

Lauren followed him out of doors. The bright sun hurt her eyes as she tried to adjust. She blinked back tears, unwilling to cry in front of Mr. Fairbanks, but she longed to weep. Even if Malcolm raised enough funds to buy her indenture, would he not first be obligated to buy his sister? Her only hope lay in getting word to her father. Why didn't she take the time to write him before she sold herself to these cruel people? Now how would she get paper and ink? Money for postage? She had to find a way. The thought of spending the next four years in this place made bile rise in the back of her throat, and she feared she would be sick.

10

Malcolm sighed as he guided his mother to the bed in her new boardinghouse room. On the way he confessed everything. She wasn't pleased to learn of his initial plans for using Lauren to get his revenge but understood the remorse he now felt.

"Mither, I am sorry I canna afford more than a simple room, but after a few days' wages, I shall try to find us a house to rent." Malcolm sank on the straw mattress beside her and draped an arm over her frail shoulders.

"Believe me, lad, this is much better than what I have been used to." Iona leaned over and kissed his cheek. "I am grateful ye came for me but sorry Lauren took my place."

"Aye, I must find a way to help her." He slammed a curled fist into the palm of his other hand.

"Let us get some sleep. Tomorrow we can think with clearer heads." His mother yawned and covered her mouth as she closed her eyes. "The Lord will not forsake her anymore than He did me."

Guilt slashed through him. He had no right to unburden his worries upon her. She had been through more than he could imagine. It was his responsibility to see she got all the rest she needed and time to replenish her strength and health. Malcolm leaned over and kissed the top of her wrinkled forehead. "First, ye must bathe.

I ordered a bath, an' the woman of the house has offered to give ye one of her auld nightgowns."

"Praise be to God!" Tears sprang to her eyes. "Do ye know how long 'tis been since I had a nice, warm bath?" She glanced down at the smudged dirt on her aging hands and arms and lifted the coarse linen fabric of her soiled gray gown. "To feel somethin' besides this against my skin would be a blessin', indeed."

"Aye, tomorrow when I come home from work, I shall bring ye a new set of clothes," Malcolm said, glad to at least provide her that.

"What a blessed mither I am!" Suddenly revived with new energy, she threw her arms around him, Malcolm smiled as he embraced her. She no longer smelled of the rose water scent as she always had in the past, but he hoped her faith combined with Lauren's would be rewarded and his mother would soon be back to herself again.

A knock sounded at the door. Malcolm pulled away to answer it. Two men carried in a tub as Malcolm stepped out of their way. A woman followed with a set of towels and a white nightgown. She looked from Malcolm to his mother sitting on the side of the bed and strode to her, bending to her knees.

"My mother asked me to bring you this." She set the folded towels on the bed and held the gown up for inspection. "She said you could have it."

"I could not accept it, but that is verra thoughtful of her." His mother fingered the sleeve with a thoughtful expression. "Please tell her I am grateful."

"I will, but she insists that you keep this." The young girl laid it upon his mother's lap with a gentle smile. "There is a bar of soap between the towels. Now be sure to let us know if you need aught else."

As she left, four other men came in carrying steaming buckets of hot water. They took turns pouring the contents into the tub. A haze of steam hovered in the air and spread around the room like a mysterious mist.

"It should cool off in a few minutes—enough for her to get in." The elderly man said, wiping his brow. By the look of the younger men, Malcolm assumed they were most likely his sons.

"Thank ye," Malcolm said. The men filed out. Malcolm turned to his mother. "I have a few things I need to go over with Logan. I shall be back in a couple of hours. Then I will make a pallet on the floor." He closed the door behind him. His mother sighed with contentment on the other side. He smiled, knowing she needed some time alone. Regardless of what the Campbells had done against his family, he would never forget the compassion and generous sacrifice Lauren made this day. He vowed to help her.

Malcolm headed to Logan's room and knocked on the door. To his relief, his friend answered rather than his sister. "I need to talk to ye." He glanced over Logan's shoulder but didn't see Deidra. "Alone." He lowered his voice. Right now, he didn't have the energy to deal with the anger he knew Deidra would have once she discovered that Lauren had stayed behind in his mother's place.

"All right. Let me tell Deidra." He stepped away for a moment. Lowered voices murmured inside the room, and then he came back and closed the door behind him. "I could use a drink at the tavern. Today was a long day. I shall probably reek of pine for weeks."

"Is it that bad?" Malcolm asked as they walked down the hall.

"I am sure I will get used to it in a few days." Logan grinned as they stepped into a tavern and settled at an empty table. "The work is hard, but it will make a man strong."

"Did ye tell them about me?" Malcolm asked.

"Aye." He nodded. "Ye can start in the morn. Be there by six. Yer wages will be the same as mine, two shillings a day. We have Sundays off." Logan waved a servant over to take their order.

"I appreciate everything," Malcolm said, rubbing his hands over his face as he mentally added up how long he would have to work before he could earn enough to buy back Lauren's indenture. It would be a decent living to provide for himself and his mother, but it didn't leave much else left over for savings. His gut clenched at the thought of not seeing Lauren. Were they treating her well? Was she miserable? Did she hate him?

"What would you two be wantin'?" a woman asked in a squeaky voice. She leaned over the table and gave Logan a taunting grin. Ample cleavage showed from her low-cut gown.

"I shall have a mug of ale, and bring one for my friend as well," Logan said.

"I want naught." Malcolm shook his head and rubbed the back of his aching neck. "I need to keep my wits. I have a lot o' thinkin' to do."

"Nonsense, mon." Logan waved the servant away. "Whatever it is, ye canna let it get ye down. We can put our heads together an' come up with somethin'. Now confess, my friend, what is it?"

Malcolm told Logan everything, how Lauren willingly sacrificed herself for his mother. Once he had seen her poor condition, he couldn't bear the thought of leaving her there one more night.

"At this rate, Lauren will work off her indenture faster than I could pay it." Malcolm pinched his eyebrows.

"I have an idea how ye could make some quick cash, but ye might not like it," Logan said.

"What is it?" As Malcolm straightened and faced his friend, hope rose in him for the first time since leaving Lauren behind. He gave Logan a skeptical look. "Is it legal?"

"I do not know all the laws here." Logan laughed. "Although I suspect some would disapprove, including that sweet mither of yers." He shrugged. "Ye'll just have to decide if Lauren Campbell is worth it."

The sun was much hotter than Lauren imagined. She feared her skin was blistered the way it burned and pulled tight across her face. Her back ached from bending over and digging small holes in the plowed rows where they planted the tobacco. No wonder so many poor women who worked out in the fields with their farming husbands developed a round posture in their backs.

Lauren glanced up and wiped her brow. The rows seemed to go on forever. They were only halfway through this one. She couldn't tell how many hours it had been since Mr. Fairbanks left her, but the sun began to set in the west, dropping inch by inch. A bell rang in the distance, and the women around her sighed. They gathered their tools and walked toward the wagons at the end of the rows. Lauren followed their example.

As soon as she stood, her back cracked. She lifted her arms and tried to stretch her muscles, then rolled her aching neck from one shoulder to the other.

"You will need to make a straw hat like mine to give your face and neck some shade." A girl stepped beside Lauren as they filed out of the row and followed the others to the north side of the fields. She had blonde hair and blue eyes. Slight freckles dotted her nose. "My name is Alice Burton. I came last spring an' had to learn things the hard way. After one whipping, I decided to do whatever it takes to get to the end of my indenture. Anyway, the hat will help you keep from getting these." She pointed to her freckles, which gave her more of an endearing look than anything revolting.

"I am Lauren Campbell, and I do not know how to make a hat like yers." Lauren wondered what the poor lass had done to deserve a beating. She looked around for a sign of Mr. Fairbanks. No one had talked much all day, and she couldn't help wondering if it was all right to talk now. A few were engaged in whispered conversations.

"I shall show you tonight. Where will you be bunking?"

Lauren gave her a blank stare.

"What hut did they give you?"

"I have no idea." Lauren lifted her shoulders. "No one has told me much of anything. All I know is I took Iona MacGregor's place."

"Oh, no." Alice's eyes widened as she reached out and touched Lauren's arm. "Did somethin' 'appen to her? I wondered about her when they called her out of the fields an' she did not return."

"Nay. Her son came for her." Lauren shielded her eyes as a man on a horse rode toward them.

"All the way from Scotland?" Alice tilted her head with a sharp expression. "Are you sure?" She lowered her voice and leaned closer. "These people cannot be trusted. They are cruel to those beneath their station."

"I know because I was there. Her son could not afford to buy her indenture. Malcolm was afraid Iona would not survive the harsh conditions here, but I am younger and I can."

"How noble . . ." Alice turned to stare at her feet as they walked along. "My family would have done the same thing for me had they all not already been auctioned off themselves."

The indentured servants parted to make room for the man on the horse who rode between the two adjacent tobacco fields. Much younger than Mr. Fairbanks, he had brown hair pulled behind his neck under a tricorn hat. He wore a dark green jacket made of fine material and tan riding breeches that disappeared into tall black leather boots.

"Who is that?" Lauren asked, nudging her friend.

"Rob Mallard, the young heir." Alice smiled and lowered her voice. "Rumor has it from the slaves at the main house he is quite a ladies' man. He is sort of handsome. Do you not think?"

The word *handsome* brought Malcolm MacGregor to mind and a familiar ache at being separated from him. "Nay, I am afraid only one mon will ever be handsome to me, and since I am to be separated from him for an indefinite time, I do not wish to think on him."

The man on the horse drew closer. More servants parted for him. Lauren and Alice moved to the right as he passed. A satchel strapped to the side of his saddle came undone. His horse bounced with each step until a small book fell onto the ground. Afraid it would be ruined, Lauren rushed to pick it up.

"Sir! Ye dropped yer book." Lauren called after him. She glanced down to see that it was Shakespeare's *Hamlet*. Rob Mallard paused and gave her a quizzical glance, his lips twisted in distaste. Other servants around her gasped in shocked concern. Lauren realized their concern was for her. Had she done something wrong? Her insides began to quake. Perhaps she wasn't allowed to speak to the Mallards unless first spoken to.

"My what?" Rob demanded. His tone wasn't one of anger, but more like someone who was impatient and ready to move on. "Who spoke?"

Fear paralyzed her, but she couldn't afford to invoke his wrath or let anyone else take the blame for her folly. Lauren stepped forward, lifting her chin. "I did. My name is Lauren Campbell." She held out the book as she approached him with hesitation. "I am sorry to bother ye, sir, but I thought ye would want to know yer book fell. 'Tis such a lovely copy of Shakespeare's *Hamlet* and 'twould be a shame for it to be ruined."

Surprise lit his brown eyes as he took more time to study her face. He reached out to accept the book and tilted his head. "How did you know it was *Hamlet*?" He raised a speculative eyebrow.

"It says so on the binding." Lauren pointed to the book and gulped.

"Open it and read from any page." Rob handed it back to her.

Lauren took the book and flipped to the opening scene. "Who's there?" She read the first line from the character Bernardo.

"Nay, answer me. Stand, and unfold yourself," Rob said, reciting the character Francisco's part of the play. He watched her closely.

Lauren looked back at the page and cleared her throat. "Long live the king!" She read Bernardo's next line, hoping that was what she was supposed to do.

"That is enough." Rob held out his hand for the book. "Indeed, you can read. Why, then, are you out here in the fields?" He gestured around them.

"This is where Mr. Fairbanks put me." Lauren backed away, dropping her gaze.

"I can tell from your accent that you are Scottish. Did your indenture buy your passage to America like the others? When did you arrive?"

"I came earlier today. No, my passage was purchased on *The Sea Lady*. I volunteered to take the place of a frail elderly woman who needed to be with her family."

"You volunteered?" His skeptical look worried Lauren. She bit her bottom lip. *Lord, please do not let them beat me*. "Why on earth would someone do that? Especially someone with your education. It does not make sense." Rob turned his impatient horse around to face her.

"My family had wronged her family back in Scotland. 'Twas my Christian duty to right the wrong against her," Lauren said, hoping she didn't sound like she wanted special treatment or boasted of her faith.

He leaned forward. "And was your Christian duty worth it? Several years of hard labor, an ocean between you and your homeland, no chance of marrying and starting a family of your own while you are young and in your prime. People always talk about Christian duty, yet they behave with animal-like qualities." He grinned at the confused expression on her face. "Perhaps I have been reading too much *Hamlet*. I am starting to sound like him." He held up the book. "Thank you." Turning his horse, he spurred the animal to a gallop.

It wasn't often Rob went out to the fields. He disliked the harsh reminder of how his family earned their wealth. This evening he offered another excuse to avoid dinner with his parents and decided to sneak out of the house. He headed in the opposite direction of his usual haunts, opting instead for a ride south. He planned a relaxing read by a small fire at the bubbling spring.

He hadn't counted on meeting Lauren Campbell with her intriguing blue eyes and expression that dug deep at a man's soul. While he sensed fear in her, there were also quiet strength and boldness he didn't often see. The fact she could read only added to her mystery, one he intended to discover. What was she doing here? His father assured him they only had arrangements with indentured servants who were poor and had no other means to better themselves. Here, they spent time in the fields and were taught trades that would enable them to support themselves when the indenture was over.

Rob reached the end of the field and paused. He hadn't seen Mr. Fairbanks on his way out here, but then again he had avoided being seen. Soon he would lose what was left of daylight.

To his knowledge, Mr. Fairbanks wasn't invited to dinner at the main house. That meant he would be leaving the fields and heading to his own humble house for a warm, cooked meal with his family.

With a quick flick of the reins, Rob urged his mount northwest. He found Mr. Fairbanks outside washing up by the well. He dipped his cupped hands into the bucket and splashed water over his face and the top of his shaggy hair. Beads of water dripped from him as the crickets hummed in the background.

He looked up at the sound of Rob's horse clicking his hooves against the hard ground. Mr. Fairbanks ran his long fingers through his gray hair, which looked black when wet. He shook off the dripping water and rubbed his eyes, trying to focus on Rob.

"Good evening, Rob." Mr. Fairbanks kept a light tone, though his expression was one of perplexity. "Allow me to invite you in to visit with the wife and children and take supper with us."

"I appreciate it, but I shan't be staying long." Rob forced a grin and leaned over the pommel. "I came to ask about an indentured servant I met. I believe she said her name is Lauren Campbell. Do you know anything about her?"

"She arrived this morning. I am breaking her in so she will become familiar with how things are around here." Mr. Fairbanks's expression tensed, and Rob didn't care for the glint that now burned in his eyes. "Whatever she has done, I assure you, I shall take care of it."

"The girl has done naught, so she should not be punished." Rob was more than familiar with how Mr. Fairbanks dealt with the slaves and servants under his authority. He despised the abusive tactics their overseer used, but his father claimed it was part of business and chose to allow Fairbanks to do as he pleased. It caused many heated debates between them, so he chose to stay out of the family business, at least until he inherited it and could run things the way he wanted.

"I see." Mr. Fairbanks lowered his voice and walked around the well, folding his arms. "Have you taken an interest in the girl? Should I bring her to the main house?" A grin sliced the older man's face and made Rob's gut clench.

"I dropped my book and she recognized the title." Rob decided to ignore the man's suggestive remark. He already had enough issues with his parents growing weary of his dandy ways with the ladies. The last thing he wanted was to cause trouble for this girl. "I asked her to read a page to test her skills, and it turns out that she is well read."

"Yes, she said she was educated by a governess in Scotland," Mr. Fairbanks said with a nod of acknowledgment. "I planned to keep her in the fields during planting season, just enough time to lose a bit of her high-handed pride."

"She did not strike me as being very prideful. I dislike wasting a servant's skills in the field. She is not used to the work, and judging by her white skin, the sun will fry her if not already." Rob lowered his tone to a warning. "You know I am different from my father. I believe a wounded servant in pain is of little use and causes lost revenue."

"Where should I put her?" Mr. Fairbanks asked. "An educated servant like her has few labor skills. I doubt she can even cook."

" 'Tis your responsibility to find out." Rob shook his head as if displeased. "I'm surprised you neglected to find out all you could when she arrived."

"She says she speaks French." Mr. Fairbanks stepped forward, his tone more of a plea now.

"Does she speak it fluently?" Rob asked.

"I have no way of knowing since I do not know the language." Mr. Fairbanks lowered his head.

"Never mind." Rob sighed. "Bring her to the library after we break our fast, day after tomorrow. "I shall speak to the girl myself."

"But your mother will have to approve any of the women servants brought into the house," Mr. Fairbanks said. "Since your father is leaving on business in the morning, he will not be here to reason with her. How will you get her to approve of the girl? She dismissed the last one I sent to the main house and sent her back into the fields."

"Leave my mother to me." Rob turned his horse, nudged his flanks, and rode away.

The crowd roared as individual men rallied for one boxer over the other. Malcolm kept his feet planted and tried to ignore everyone around him to concentrate on his opponent. With both hands balled into a fist, he jabbed his left at the man's face. His head snapped back.

Both of them bounced around in a circle as a cut above the man's eye poured blood and sweat into his vision. A couple of inches shorter than Malcolm, he didn't have the same stamina to keep up. Malcolm didn't want to hurt him and wished he would go ahead and give up the fight.

He swung a right at Malcolm. Leaning to the side, Malcolm avoided the hit and swung his right fist in an upper cut, landing in the man's ribs. Hoping to end the round, Malcolm thrust his left fist into the side of his head and landed a hard right into his nose, shattering the bone.

His opponent staggered back with a dazed look. Malcolm knew that feeling well, having been in a number of fights in his youth. An image of his brother, battered and bruised, came to mind, and Malcolm lowered his hands. He didn't want to fight anymore. Logan promised he would earn fifty pounds if he won, but now the fight didn't seem worth it.

Someone threw in a white towel on behalf of the other man. Men who bet on Malcolm cheered while others grumbled. Money exchanged hands as someone lifted Malcolm's arm in victory. He didn't feel victorious. His opponent might be suffering from broken ribs and definitely had a broken nose. No doubt, he would be sore for a fortnight.

"Ye did it, Malcolm!" Logan broke through the crowd. "A few more nights like these, and ye'll have the money ye need to buy Lauren's indenture."

A bitter taste filled Malcolm's tongue. He was about to tell Logan there would be no more nights like this, but the reminder of Lauren's plight slammed into his gut. Was there no better solution than this? His swollen lip felt tight against his teeth. The bruise on the side of his jaw would be hard to hide from his mother. Winning had come with its own set of problems.

Malcolm shook hands with the loser and endured several pats on the back and shoulder as people congratulated him. Logan stayed nearby as Malcolm pushed through the crowd in the street. He wanted his pay.

A man dressed in black approached Malcolm with a grin. He tipped his tricorn hat and pulled out several notes as he counted them. "Here is your cut. Your friend Logan was telling the truth. He said you would win this in a few short rounds." He held out the money. "I am glad I invested in the right man. Listen, if you get a hankering for more, we have these fights every Friday."

"Thank ye." Malcolm took the notes with a nod, careful not to make any promise.

"We will be back," Logan said with a grinning nod and a quick slap to Malcolm's back.

"I have not made a decision about future fights." Malcolm gave his friend an irritated glare but turned to grin at the man who had given him his pay. His split lip stung. "But I never rule out a profitable prospect." Malcolm held up the notes before slipping them inside his jacket pocket.

"That sounds like a good philosophy." They shook hands and parted on amiable terms.

Logan followed Malcolm out of the side alley. "That would have taken ye months to earn. I told ye it would be worth it."

"Logan, I am tired, sore, and ill. Now is not the time to try an' convince me to do this again." Malcolm turned a corner, feeling light-headed. "I need some water. "

"Aye, let us go to the tavern." Logan weaved in and out of people moving about the street. Some stared at his swollen lip and bruised cheek. Malcolm wondered if he looked as bad as he felt. What would Lauren think? Would it matter that he did this for her?

By the time they reached the tavern, Malcolm's limbs felt like heavy boulders. Logan found an empty booth, and they both slid onto benches facing each other. Malcolm sighed, grateful to rest. He had no idea how he would be able to function at work tomorrow. He had worked his new logging job for three days now, but tomorrow might prove to be his most difficult after tonight's fight.

"There has to be a better way," Malcolm said, glaring at his friend. "This is pure torture, an' I am not sure I can endure it week after week."

"I do not know of aught else that will bring ye as much money so quickly," Logan said. "Ye held up well. A strapping Scot is bound to win over a puny Brit any day."

"He was not puny, and he has a solid arm on 'im." Malcolm rubbed his jaw. "I would not feel so tired if I had not worked all day afore the fight."

"Ye could try gambling." Logan shrugged and tilted his head.

"Nay," Malcolm sliced his hand through the air. "I am not 'bout to lose what I just earned."

"Ye could try investing it." Logan leaned forward and folded his hands on the table. " 'Twouldn't be as risky as gambling."

"Let us concentrate on adding to the sum I have, not losing it." Malcolm plopped his elbows on the table and watched the waitress sauntering toward them. He could hardly swallow—his throat was so dry.

"I shall take a mug of ale," Logan said.

"I want a glass of water. I am too parched for aught else," Malcolm said.

The woman nodded and disappeared.

"I thought I would go by Mallard Plantation and see how Lauren is getting along." Malcolm folded his hands.

"Did ye not say that the overseer would not allow ye to see her? Ye wanna get her in trouble?" Logan shook his head in disbelief. "Besides, ye might want to wait 'til ye look more like yerself."

"True." Malcolm sat back with a sigh of discontent. Being around Lauren every day for several weeks and now being apart made him realize how much more he had grown to care for her. He missed her spiritual inspiration when he felt defeated. Memories clung to him, their conversations kept playing through his mind, and whenever he needed to make a decision, he longed to confide in her. Worst of all, her lovely image compared to no other, the way she looked up at him and felt in his arms the night he held her through the storm.

"Malcolm?" Logan peered at him and waved a hand in front of his face. "Did ye hear me?"

"What?"

"If ye're willing to fight the Norwegian, ye'll get triple the price if ye win," Logan said.

"Why?" Malcolm watched Logan's expression with suspicion. "There has to be a reason I get more for fightin' him."

"From what I have heard, he has not lost a fight in over a year, and he is huge."

"Are ye tryin' to get me killed?" Malcolm slammed a fist on the table, drawing attention from nearby patrons.

"Just listen." Logan lifted both palms. "Everyone has a weakness. All ye've got to do is watch 'im in a few fights an' figure out what it is."

"Ye make it sound so simple, but for what I have done to Lauren, I suppose I deserve the punishment."

The sun burst through the haze of the morning clouds at dawn two days later. Lauren breathed a sigh of momentary contentment. If it was already so hot this early, then the afternoon would be stifling. Her new hat would be a blessing.

Lauren's nose and cheeks pulled tight, and her skin felt hot. If she had a looking glass, she knew she would see a burned face. It would be easier to endure if she had gotten a decent night's sleep. Instead, she spent the night tossing on a straw mattress thin enough to fall through, or so she feared.

She yawned, covering her mouth as she walked in line with the other servants up the aisle between the fields. A man she had never seen before strode from the opposite direction. When he reached

Lauren and the other servants, he stopped and crossed his arms. "I am looking for Lauren Campbell." His voice boomed over them.

Everyone paused, and Lauren cringed as the other servants turned to look at her. They didn't need to say anything as their expressions gave her away. Taking a deep breath for courage, she stepped forward.

"I am Lauren Campbell."

Without an explanation, he crooked his thick finger and turned to walk away. Not knowing what else to do, Lauren followed him. He looked to be in his forties. His shoulders were wide, but his height wasn't quite as tall as Malcolm.

Her thoughts stalled. Since when had she started comparing every man she met to Malcolm MacGregor? She shook her head, but the action didn't clear her mind of his image. Malcolm was always there, pressing on her memories, until she longed to see him again—to be in his protective presence. She never thought it could be possible, but she missed him.

They left the fields and headed toward the main house. Lauren tensed. She hadn't been here long enough to cause any trouble. What could she have done to be called to the main house? They climbed the hill and passed the barn and stables.

He took her through a side door leading into a hallway. It was dark, but not scary, only intimidating as she realized how many decisions made in this house concerned so many lives. In the next few minutes, her fate would be revealed.

Lauren assumed that she would go to the same study where she had met Mr. Fairbanks. Instead, the man led her to a room across from the study. The door was ajar and creaked as he opened it.

"Mr. Mallard, I brought 'er just like ye asked," he said.

Lauren stepped into a library filled with shelves of books from floor to ceiling on each side except for the fireplace and two long windows. Although it was smaller than the library at home in

Kilchurn Manor, she would venture to guess they had squeezed more books in here.

"Thanks." Lauren whirled to see the young man she met on the horse. "You may go." He waved away the man who brought her.

"Welcome, Miss Campbell." He gestured to the chair across from him. "Please, have a seat."

Lauren walked to the chair and sank onto the cushion as bid. If her weary bones could respond, they would be sighing in contentment right now. Determined not to get too comfortable, Lauren kept a straight spine and waited, hoping her behavior was appropriate.

"We are moving you to the main house." Rob sat adjacent to her and crossed his ankle over his knee. He wore the same black boots as before. Relaxing his back against his chair, he studied her. "Does that suit you?"

"Indeed, it does," she said. "As ye can tell, I do not do well in the sun." She pointed to her red face.

"I am sorry for that." He grimaced in genuine concern. "I hope 'tisn't too painful?"

"I shall manage." Lauren glanced down at the floor as sudden embarrassment heated her face. She wondered if her burns were worse than she originally thought.

"I told my mother about your education and convinced her you belong here in the main house." He shook his head in disbelief. "She is not completely convinced, so she may come by later and test you."

"What sort of test?" Alarm passed through Lauren. What if she couldn't remember a few facts from her previous studies? What would happen if she failed?

"She plans to converse with you in French." He grinned, his brown eyes glinting. "To assure herself that you know enough proper French to help me with my speech, reading, and writing in the language."

"Am I to be your governess?" Lauren couldn't hide her surprise and confusion.

"Not exactly." He chuckled. "Someone I can practice and converse with. I have also arranged for you to help in the kitchen. You may be required for other duties as needed, such as assisting Mr. Fairbanks keep the books."

"I see." Lauren looked down at her lap. God had answered her prayers. He had delivered her from the fields. She wanted to sing His praises but forced herself to sit still.

"I am sorry that I could not get a better chamber for you, but my mother agreed to let you have the attic chamber. It can be very hot in the summer but is the warmest room in the house during winter."

"I am verra grateful," Lauren said, trying not to fidget. "Will I need a uniform like the others?"

"Yes, although you would not be required to wear a uniform when we are practicing French. In fact, I might feel better if you were not in uniform during those days." He scratched his shaved chin in thought.

"I have naught else, sir." Lauren shrugged. "I am sorry."

"Nonsense." He waved her concern away. "I shall take care of everything. Just leave it to me." He stood. "I will have one of the maids show you to your chamber."

A few days later, Malcolm managed to rent a proper house for his mother and bought a horse for travel. The swelling in his lip wasn't quite as severe, but a slight scab remained. The bruise on his cheek was still prominent, but there was little he could do about it. Today, his mother wanted to go to church, and he intended to escort her. Since he had no carriage or wagon, they would walk the short distance. If there was a chance to see Lauren again, it would be at church.

He waited on the front porch while his mother stepped out of the small one-story house. A number of larger homes with varied colors, including brick, surrounded it. Perhaps God had broken the curse that he often worried plagued their family. He made a decent salary, more than what he could ever hope to attain in Scotland. His rent was much less and in a convenient location within walking distance to church and the market. Best of all, he was now reunited with his mother. For the first time in a long time, he looked forward to worshiping in church.

"I am sorry I have not been able to purchase us a proper carriage yet," Malcolm said once she reached his side.

"Nonsense, lad. Ye've done well in the short time we have been here." She waved his concern away and awarded him with a doting smile. "Yer da would have been verra proud."

"I am unsure 'bout that." Malcolm held out his elbow and offered his arm. Since he didn't have a sidesaddle, he knew better than to push the idea of her riding astride on the Sabbath. "Especially after what happened to ye an' Graham. As soon as I can, I hope to find a trustworthy person to write a letter for me to post to Thomas."

"Aye, an' we need to send out inquiries for Carleen as well. I long for my family to be reunited." His mother looked away as he guided her west down Society Street. "I hope her situation is much better than mine has been."

"Do not worry, Mither." Malcolm tried to ignore the pinch in his heart and sighed. Independent Church was only a half mile from their house, but he wanted to arrive early enough to find a decent seat and to determine how he might approach Lauren if she was there without getting her in trouble with the Mallard family or Mr. Fairbanks.

When they reached the street corner, Malcolm turned left onto Meeting Street and marveled at the sight of all the carriages, wagons, and individuals heading in the same direction. Horses clopped along the pebbled road at a slow pace. Families varied in station, wealth, and sizes. It never occurred to him that a church might be overcrowded, but today he could imagine it. Even if Lauren was here among all these people, how would he find her?

They stepped under the branches of a tree with Spanish moss hanging over the road. The shade gave him a better view of the church without the need to squint from the bright sun. It was a circular church made of dark red brick. The arched windows indicated various levels, and the front entrance was through an archway. The thick wooden door was painted a maroon color, and the hinges looked to be of black iron. No steeple or church bells were evident.

A brown carriage rolled by with three wagons following close behind. Several other prominent citizens had already passed in expensive carriages, some with inscriptions, but most were without.

"Malcolm, there is the Mallard family." His mother pointed at the brown carriage now pulling to a stop on the side of the road ahead of them. "The wagons are carrying their servants."

"Which one would have Lauren?" he asked, keeping his eyes trained on the last wagon from which people were now climbing out.

"The one right behind the carriage would be the house servants. The rest are full of the field servants."

"What about the slaves?" Malcolm glanced down at her, so thankful color had begun to return to her cheeks. "Are they not allowed to worship God?"

"Aye, but they have their own minister on the plantation, and they meet in the barn on Sunday mornings." She squeezed his arm. "Mr. Fairbanks stays behind to ensure they behave an' none o' them run off."

"I see." Malcolm turned his attention back to the wagons. At least, he wouldn't have to deal with the watchful eye of Mr. Fairbanks. It increased his chances of speaking to Lauren.

He scanned the servants as they walked toward the building. Granted, their backs were facing him, but he would recognize

Lauren's gait. For hours, he had observed her on *The Sea Lady*, her posture, profile, and expressions. He felt quite confident that he could pick her out of a crowd. Yet he saw no sign of her. Disappointment plummeted in his chest.

They filed behind others as they drew closer. Some individuals were in groups conversing around the churchyard. A lass stepped out of line and leaned against the brick wall as she bent to adjust her shoe. Malcolm recognized the blonde pieces of hair that framed her oval face beneath her hat.

" 'Tis her, Mither." Malcolm patted her arm. "She appears well."

"Go to her, lad." His mother nudged him forward. "Ye only have a few minutes afore she goes inside with the others."

Unable to miss this opportunity, Malcolm rushed to her side. It was all he could do not to take her in his arms and thank the Lord for this moment. Instead, he leaned down. "Lauren, 'tis me, Malcolm."

"Malcolm?" Blessed excitement laced her voice as she glanced up at him. A bright smile lit her face, but he disliked the dark circles under her eyes. The skin on her nose was peeling from what appeared to be a sunburn. Concern flared in his gut. He had known working out in the fields would be too much for a gentle lass like Lauren. "I thought a pebble might be in my shoe."

"Do ye need help?" he asked, wishing for an excuse to touch her, to stay with her.

"Nay." She shook her head and straightened. "I have already taken care of it."

"I thought ye might be in the last wagon with the field servants, but I did not see ye earlier."

"They moved me to the main house." She lowered her voice. "The son of the house discovered my education, and now I assist him with his French and helping out in the kitchen as I learn new tasks."

"Lauren!" A lass called from around the corner.

"That is Alice. I had better go."

She started to walk away, but Malcolm grabbed her hand. "Please, meet me by the well after church. I shall stay hidden until then."

"All right." She nodded. "I want to know about yer mither." Her intense blue eyes met his. "And I am verra glad to see ye, Malcolm."

In an instant, she was gone, but Malcolm had her promise.

11

After church, Lauren helped prepare the midday meal, and afterward the cook gave her free time. She took a bucket to the well, hoping Malcolm would be there to greet her. She stood still and listened. The leaves in the trees swayed in the air as birds chirped and fluttered from branch to branch. The afternoon crickets sang, but no other sounds indicated Malcolm's presence.

What if he had fallen asleep waiting for her? She searched for a plausible excuse about why he might not have waited. She who risked a flogging, not he.

A shadow in the trees caught her attention, and hope soared in her chest. Was it a squirrel, or could it be Malcolm? Glancing around to ensure her privacy, Lauren approached the woods on the other side of the well. A hand reached out and pulled her into the shadows.

The sudden, unexpected motion frightened her into releasing a cry when a pair of lips crushed her into silence. The masculine scent of leather and pine invaded her senses. Lauren's resistance fled as she relaxed in Malcolm's arms and crept her hands around his neck. His lips were gentle but firm as he explored her mouth. Heat ignited between them, sparking a pleasant rush to the head that made her giddy. This moment of passion shattered the tiny walls in her heart that had been holding back tender feelings for him. They burst forth in a tidal wave she could no longer deny. She loved Malcolm MacGregor. Any uncertainty fled.

Malcolm pulled back, and they both gasped for air. He pressed his forehead against hers and cupped her cheeks in his palms. "Lauren," he whispered, "I know that I should apologize for taking advantage of yer frightened state, but please do not make me, lass." His thumb trailed a light circle on her cheekbone. "The truth is, I have wanted to kiss ye for a long time now."

Lauren gripped his shirt in her hands and pulled him closer as she stood on her tiptoes and met his lips again. This time she smiled as they parted. "If ye do apologize," she whispered, "I shall have to think of something dreadful to get back at ye."

He sighed in relief and wrapped his heavy arms around her, squeezing her tightly until she thought he might cut off her air. "I have been so worried about ye. Tell me ye're all right an' they are treating ye well. I could not bear it if they were not." His whispered voice came out in a rush at her ear. Tingles rippled down her neck from the warmth of his breath until she shivered.

"I am fine. How is Iona?"

"She is recovering an' getting better each day." He settled his chin upon her head. "I have a logging job now. I will get ye out o' here. I promise."

Lauren leaned back and traced the tip of her finger along his bruised cheekbone. "So what happened? Did ye get into a fight with a logger?" She pressed her cheek against his chest.

"Not exactly," he said. "Do not worry 'bout me." He stroked the back of her neck where her hair was pinned up. "I'm sorry it is taking me so long to raise the money."

"Ye have a job now." Lauren closed her eyes and reveled in the woodsy scent of him. "At one time I would have questioned yer motive but not anymore. I know ye'll do what ye can. I trust ye, Malcolm."

"Lauren, I'm not like the Campbells. I have no property, no money, and naught to recommend me. I do have my honor, an' thanks to ye, a growing faith in the Lord again. 'Tis my fault ye're here in this mess."

"Nay." She shook her head. "I chose to take Iona's place."

"But ye did not choose to board *The Sea Lady* an' cross the Atlantic." He bent and kissed the tip of her nose.

"True, but now I am glad I did." Lauren smiled up at him, her heart filled with light and peace. "Now promise me, ye will not do any more knuckle fighting."

"I canna." Malcolm shook his head, his lips thinning into a stubborn line as his hazel eyes hardened with resolve. "I will do anything to get ye out o' here an' back into my arms again."

The sound of a cantering horse broke their conversation before she could respond. Lauren peered over Malcolm's arm and around the tree where he leaned his back out of view. At least the woods hid them.

Rob Mallard rode toward the main house. He slowed his horse and dismounted, taking the reins and walking toward the well. He lowered the bucket and pulled up water. Cupping his hands, he dipped them into the water and drank.

"That was a good ride. Very invigorating, my boy." He rubbed the horse's neck and patted him. "Now we shall clean up and invite Miss Campbell for an afternoon of tea and French lessons." Rob led the animal away.

"Who is that?" Malcolm demanded once he was gone. An angry scowl now appeared on his face. "Are ye teachin' that young fop French lessons?"

"He is the only heir to the estate, and the one who demanded I be removed from the fields. Rob already knows French, but I am the only one around with whom he may practice with the exception of his mother."

"I can imagine why he demanded to have ye removed from the fields." Sarcasm dripped from Malcolm's tone. He crossed his arms. " 'Tis Rob, is it?"

"Only because his father goes by Robert. They needed some way to keep junior from being confused with senior." Lauren rubbed his arm, hoping to ease him back into good temper. "Do I detect a wee bit of jealousy? My heart is in danger of no one else. Not when ye've already stolen it, Malcolm MacGregor."

"Truly, lass?" He brushed his roughened knuckles across her cheek. "Ye might change yer mind once ye're free again, an' I have naught to offer but a poor life of poverty."

"I care naught for any of that. In fact, I do not miss my auld life at Kilchurn Manor. The whole time I have been here serving others, 'tis ye I have missed."

Malcolm crushed her to him, folding her in his warm embrace. "I love ye, Lauren."

"And I love ye, Malcolm." She reached her arms around his neck as he enveloped her and lowered his head to give her one more parting kiss. "I must go," she whispered, pulling back. At first, he wouldn't let go, but then with an agonizing sigh, Malcolm released her.

Malcolm returned to find his mother pacing on the front porch. He made a mental note to make a wooden rocker for her. First, he needed to finish carving out the kitchen table he had started making a couple of days ago.

"How is the lass?" She paused to lean over the white rail as he climbed the four steps to the landing. "I have been worrying about 'er somethin' fierce. I know how hard the fields can be for a lass who has never known hard labor."

"She is fine." Malcolm smiled, curling his fingers around the pole on the rail. "Much better than ye. It seems Mr. Rob Mallard discovered her education an' had her moved to the main house."

"Praise be the Lord!" She clapped her hands in glee. "I knew my prayers would be answered. She has been a faithful servant, an' God looks after 'is own."

Even though Malcolm hoped God would lift the curse from his family, he still had so many questions. "An' ye've always been a faithful servant, Mither. Where was God when Duncan Campbell sold ye into bondage against yer will? At yer age, ye could have died on that voyage 'ere."

"Och! Lad, that was not the Lord's doin'." She stood on her tiptoes and laid a wrinkled hand on his jaw. Her brown eyes held so much tenderness and love, it made him wallow in guilt. "That was the devil, it was. Workin' through the heart of an evil man. The Lord took care o' me. He brought ye an' Lauren to deliver me." She gave his cheek a gentle pat. "Ye've no need to fight, Malcolm. 'Tis dangerous an' I wish ye would stop."

Malcolm wanted to believe like his mother. "I know ye're disappointed, but I have no other way to get the money I need to free Lauren."

"If ye're willin' to abandon yer lust for revenge against her father, then I am sure the Lord will give ye all the desires of yer heart, Malcolm. But ye've got to forgive an' let go of the hate. Otherwise, I do not know that a relationship will work between ye and the lass. He is still her father, and she loves him."

Malcolm walked around her and leaned his elbows over the rail beside her. "I meant God could deliver Lauren from her indenture as He has done for ye. Aye, I love the lass, so much so this forced separation hurts worse than a physical pain." He shook his head and rubbed his eyebrows. "I do not think I can let Duncan Campbell off so easy. Lauren will not be my revenge. The lass knows what her father did. She told me so."

" 'Tis God's place to take revenge, Malcolm." He chose to ignore the warning in her tone. It was quite similar when he was a child.

"God can have His revenge, but I am getting mine as well." Malcolm straightened and stepped back from the rail.

"After church, Logan an' Deidra came by to invite us to dinner. Do ye know if either of them can read or write?" She turned and opened the door to the house. Malcolm followed her inside and paused at the smell of fresh flowers and steeping tea. All the windows were open to let in the breeze and sunlight. She kept the hardwood floors swept clean.

"Nay, but we met a friend who hopes to be a teacher. I am sure she can be trusted with our letters 'til Lauren returns to us." His booted heels clicked across the floor. He sat in a wooden chair by the window and left the couch for his mother. The house came with a few furnishings, most plain and well used.

"I started writing a letter to Mr. Benjamin Shore, the man who purchased Carleen, but I am afraid my writing is not good enough just yet." She sighed in frustration as she went to a scarred corner table and lifted a piece of paper for him to see. "Lauren started teaching me an' Carleen, but we did not get much practice afore everything happened."

Guilt slammed into Malcolm like an iron cannon ball. He had spent so much time concentrating on freeing his mother and Lauren that he had done naught about his sister. What kind of hardship could Carleen be enduring? The worry must have been evident on his face, for his mother dropped her letter on the table and hurried toward him.

"I have been praying for Carleen. If she was not all right, I believe I would feel it in my soul." She laid a hand on his arm and gave him an encouraging smile. "We shall find her. I know we will."

"Mither, when we go to dinner at the Grants tonight, I shall ask if they know where Kathleen Anderson is. And I promise, if they do not know, I will check all the local schools. We shall get a letter to Mr. Benjamin Shore. I will not rest 'til we do."

The dark housekeeper came into the kitchen. The middle-aged woman shifted her gaze from Lauren to the cook. "Could ya spare Miz Campbell for a while? I was informed our supper guests will be stayin' da night an' we need to prepare chambers for 'em. In da meantime, we have several baskets dat need to be hung out on da line."

"Aye." The cook nodded. "She already chopped da carrots an' taters." She turned to Lauren. "Be gone with ye, gel." She waved Lauren away.

Moments later, Lauren stood in the bright sunshine with a basket of washed bed linens. She threw a white sheet over the line and spread it out, setting pins in place to hold it in the breeze. Voices carried from the main house where the windows were open.

"My boy, you are the heir of this estate. I will not entertain the idea of you going into the clergy. I forbid it." Mr. Mallard's voice rose.

"Father, just listen," Rob said. "I will not be inheriting the estate for many years. Can I not do as I please until then?"

"Absolutely not," the elder responded. "You need to learn all there is to know in managing this great estate. 'Tis an honor, my boy, and you act like it is a burden."

"I would not be so unwilling if you would only be open-minded to my ideas."

Lauren bent to grab another sheet. She shook it out, now distracted by the voices. She swallowed and prepared to hear the rest. They spoke loud enough for all the house servants to hear.

"Out of the question. We cannot have paid field workers. We would go broke in less than a year."

"If we must continue to prosper on the backs of slaves, then ensure they are better treated. Mr. Fairbanks is wearing them out in their prime. They will last longer and produce more if they are not whipped, beaten, and half-starved to death. You do not even treat your horse half as bad. How can you do this to God's people?"

"Tell him, Rob," Lauren whispered to herself. She wanted to clap for him but dared not. Instead, she bowed her head and whispered a prayer for God to help Rob in his battle. "Lord, soften Mr. Mallard's heart. Help him to see the value of what Rob is saying. Please help these slaves out of bondage as You did the Israelites in Egypt." She concentrated on keeping her voice low.

"Rob, I shall make a compromise if you agree to meet me halfway." A pause of silence followed. Lauren found herself straining to hear Rob's response. She lifted a pillowcase and pinned it to the line.

"Do you mean it, Father?"

"I do."

"Then what do you propose?" Rob asked.

"I will tell Mr. Fairbanks there will be no more whippings or severe beatings of the slaves or the indentured servants with the exception of runaways."

Lauren bent to retrieve another sheet. She hoped Rob would agree. Gaining some ground was better than nothing at all. As she threw the sheet over the line, Lauren closed her eyes, willing the Lord to give Rob wisdom in this situation.

"And what do you wish of me if I agree to these new terms?" Rob asked. "There must be something you want of me."

"Of course, I want you to take a more active role in running this estate. You need to learn the books Mr. Fairbanks is keeping. I want you to ride out to the fields and take over the inspections each week."

"Fair enough. I accept," Rob said. "But if I catch Mr. Fairbanks whipping or beating any slaves or servants who have not attempted to run away, he himself will suffer the same punishment he is attempting to impose upon them."

"You really dislike him that much?" Mr. Mallard asked, his tone one of bewilderment.

"Give me leave to dismiss him . . . immediately."

"I realize you are young and the responsibility of running this estate seems daunting, but the profits would be more endearing if you had a wife, someone you wanted to keep comfortable and happy. I know it seems unfair for us to push you into marriage at the tender age of twenty, but I am not getting any younger. With four daughters older than you, I am much older than you realize."

"Father, you are as robust as I am. I daresay, you might outlive me. We have come to an agreement, so let it rest."

"There is one little matter I would like to discuss." A woman's voice interrupted, surprising Lauren. "About Miss Campbell."

Lauren froze as she bent over her basket to retrieve another pillowcase. What could she have against me? Lauren wondered.

"What about her?" Rob asked.

"I realize she is well educated, but she is still an indentured servant," his mother said. "I think you have been spending way too much time alone with her."

Rob chuckled. "Mother, we have only had tea a few times and discussed the weather and a few religious topics in French. 'Tis good practice for me. You agreed to this arrangement."

"True, but it seems as if you concentrate on her all the time. At church this morning you were more occupied with where she might have gone than taking your seat with your family as is appropriate."

"I only noticed that she was missing and wondered what might have happened. You act as if I chose to sit with her over the family."

"I should hope not!" Her voice rose to a new level. "I believe you are infatuated with her. I want you to limit the amount of time she spends in your company."

"Well, you have both succeeded in interrupting our tea this afternoon," Rob said, irritation lacing his tone. "Whether or not she spends time in my company, Lauren does not belong in the fields. She is too well educated and unused to hard labor."

"See? That is exactly what I mean." His mother sighed. "Since when are we concerned with the comforts of our slaves and servants? And now you are on a first-name basis?"

"Do not become so distraught, my dear," Mr. Mallard said. "The boy has always had a soft heart. He disliked the mistreatment of others long before this girl came along. I am sure naught will come of it. For now, let us assume the best of him."

"He was not talking about going into the clergy until she started influencing him. And he did admit to discussing religion with her."

"That is not true," Rob said. "I have mentioned the clergy several times before."

"Not that I recall." His father's firm tone silenced them both. No one spoke for a few moments. "I think I am ready for an afternoon nap."

Their discussion faded into silence. Lauren continued hanging the bed linens, reeling from the shock of being part of their discussion. She couldn't believe Mrs. Mallard would think there could be anything more to her and Rob's relationship than amiable friendship. To make matters worse, she was certain the rest of the household staff had heard the discussion.

It didn't matter. Lauren picked up the empty basket and lifted her chin. She would hold her head up, especially since she had nothing to hide and did nothing wrong.

To Malcolm's relief, Deidra had kept in touch with Kathleen Anderson. She took a position as a teacher at a nearby grade school. Deidra met with her and arranged for Malcolm and his mother to visit her on a Wednesday evening. After a long day of cutting down trees, Malcolm returned home to a warm bath waiting for him. His mother's excitement was a deep concern. She had such high expectations of locating Carleen with the prospect of contacting Mr. Shore.

Malcolm wanted to enjoy the warmth of the water upon his sore muscles, but he needed to hurry and dress so they could make it on time to Kathleen's home. All week his thoughts kept returning to Lauren. He chastised himself for allowing her to take his mother's place, but each time he looked at his mother and witnessed her increasing health, gratitude swelled in him. It made him love Lauren even more.

He had asked his logging buddies about Rob Mallard. Many had heard of him, but few had met him in person. None of them kept the same circle of friends. The one thing he was able to learn is that the young man had an excellent reputation among the servants of the house. In fact, it was rumored that many of them preferred the son over the father.

The other thing he learned was that Mr. Fairbanks had earned the reputation of being a tyrant. Knowing that Lauren was under his authority made him cringe. Knowing she had transferred to the main house helped him cope, although now he worried Rob Mallard might make inappropriate advances toward Lauren. How could any man resist her innocent charm and genuine warmth?

They arrived ten minutes before seven. Deidra and Logan were already there. Kathleen rented a small suite that was part of the west side of a large house. It was cozy, warm, and inviting. Now that she was no longer on *The Sea Lady*, her skin bloomed with health. No doubt, a better diet helped as well.

"Mrs. MacGregor, I am so delighted to finally meet ye." Kathleen sat beside her on the couch. "Malcolm was so worried about ye. I can only imagine his relief to learn ye arrived safe an' sound."

"Indeed." His mother nodded. "Which only brings me to the purpose of our visit. 'Tis been so hard to set my mind at ease after I was separated from my daughter, Carleen."

"Of course. I am honored to help ye write a letter to Mr. Benjamin Shore." She reached for his mother's hand. "And please know, I shall be happy to help ye write any letters ye need in the future."

Malcolm gave Deidra and Logan the news of his visit with Lauren while his mother worked on the letter with Kathleen.

"Pardon me, Malcolm, but it sounds as if ye're besotted with the lass." Logan reached over and chucked him with a playful fist on the shoulder. "Do I detect somethin' more than a mere friendship?"

"Logan!" Deidra slapped his arm with a laugh. "Ye're incorrigible, but I must admit I am eager to know the same thing." Deidra glanced over at Malcolm. "Lauren always did have a fondness for ye. If I said aught 'bout ye, she would defend ye no matter what."

"And pray tell, what complaints did ye have against me?" Malcolm grinned, knowing well what her grievances were. "Whatever they were, I agree."

Malcolm awarded her with a grin, hoping to set them at ease. "In truth, I am grateful Lauren has ye as a loyal friend."

"I knew it! Ye're in love with her." She covered her open mouth with her hand and shoved her brother with the other. "See? I told ye."

"Aye, I was quite aware of his attachment, my wee sister. A man would not go through a knuckle-buster fight in an alley for naught."

"Speaking of which, I know I said I was not interested in another fight, but after seeing Lauren on Sunday and knowing the risk she took in meeting me, I am most eager to raise the remaining funds to buy her indenture. The longer we are kept apart, the worse the torture."

"Oh, how romantic." Deidra lifted her shoulders in a dramatic sigh.

"Even though ye're on bad terms with Lauren's father, have ye considered contacting him? He certainly has the means to purchase her indenture."

Malcolm gulped. She was right, but the thought of appealing to her father after all he had done was unbearable, especially when Lauren seemed to be in decent health and doing well under the Mallards' care.

"If I thought Lauren was in dire circumstances, I would write to him straightaway. At the moment, Lauren is in no immediate danger."

"Ye can raise the funds yerself an' make a fine impression on Lauren. 'Twould certainly prove ye can take care o' her no matter what." Logan scratched his temple in thought.

"Aye." Malcolm nodded, sitting back in his chair. "I agree. I shall try to manage Lauren's release without the help of Duncan Campbell." Malcolm stroked his chin in thought. "Although we would appreciate help in writing my uncle an' brothers."

Rob ordered the maid to bring him and Lauren tea at the afternoon table. They sat outside in the shade under the full branches of a circle of oak trees. Birds chirped all around as the sun shone bright and the heat of the summer day grew to a stifling degree. He was pleased to see Lauren wearing the new gown he had ordered for her. The purple floral print suited her.

"*Salut*, Rob! *Comment allez-vous aujourd'hui?*" Lauren asked him how he was doing.

He grinned and settled back in his chair.

"*Je suis bien.*" Rob answered that he was good and then went on to ask her in French if she wanted tea.

"*Oui.*" She nodded. Rob reached over and poured her a cup. It felt strange to serve her rather than the other way around.

She pulled out a sealed letter and handed it to him. It was addressed to Mr. Duncan Campbell in Argyll, Scotland.

"*Merci, pour le papier et encre.*" She thanked him for the paper and ink he provided a few days ago and explained that she wanted him to mail the letter to her father.

Rob nodded in agreement, slipping it in the pocket of his brown vest. He would do as she asked but not right away. Such a letter would bring her wealthy father here to demand her release back to Scotland where Rob would never again get to see her. While he didn't like her being an indentured servant, he wasn't ready to let her go. He enjoyed her company. She was the only one who understood him and didn't judge him for wanting to abandon his father's estate and join the clergy.

Perhaps his parents were right. He had become too besotted with Lauren. If so, he wasn't sure how to break the spell she had cast over him. Everything about her was so pure and innocent. It was refreshing to have a candid conversation with a woman who wasn't pining for his inheritance but who believed in him as a person. Lauren had a way of making him feel like a man, but not just any man—a man who had the ability to honor God. Yet here he planned to hold her letter longer than he should. How was that honorable? Guilt coiled in his gut and settled on his stomach like a lead ball.

As they finished their first cup of tea, his parents appeared. Rob greeted them both in English for his father's benefit.

"We have some news." His mother announced, glancing over at Lauren and curling her mouth in distaste. "We have decided to take a brief holiday and visit your sister in New York. We just received the invitation this afternoon."

"What about all the work that needs to be done here on the plantation?" Rob asked. "Should I stay behind to see that things are handled properly?" He lifted an eyebrow at his father. The interest of the family plantation always came first, and he had no desire to go on holiday with them. It would only serve as a means to wear down his defenses in giving them their way, which meant living his life to please them, not himself.

"Mr. Fairbanks has everything under control. 'Tis why we hired him." His father waved his concern away with an agitated expression.

Rob didn't trust Mr. Fairbanks, but they already knew that. Repeating the same conversation over wouldn't do any good. He shook his head. "I think it is a great idea for the two of you." He pointed to himself. "As for me, I shall stay here and finish what I started. I have been going out to view the fields each day as you wanted. I have started reviewing the books with Fairbanks."

"I am pleased to hear it, but there are some new developments that we think you ought to know." His Father glanced at Lauren and inclined his head. "Miss Campbell, will you please excuse us? We have some family matters to discuss."

"Of course." Lauren nodded and started to stand, but Rob leaned forward and covered her hand with his.

"*Non, restes.*" He shook his head at her and then turned back to his father. "Can we not have this discussion later?"

Lauren looked down at his hand still covering hers but remained silent. Her discomfort was visible in her expression, and it angered Rob even more. He disliked the way they treated her, especially since he much preferred her company to theirs. It wasn't fair to drag her into their family battles, but he refused to allow his father to dismiss her as if she didn't matter. He looked forward to spending time with her, and they wouldn't get away with ruining his afternoon again. All week he and Lauren had endured one interruption after another. They would do anything to keep him away from her.

"Can this not wait until later?" He looked up at his father, keeping his tone calm.

"Rob, how could you?" His mother exclaimed, tears filling her eyes. Rob frowned, not understanding her strange behavior.

"No, it cannot wait!" His father growled through clenched teeth. Anger shaded his face in a darker hue as the muscles in his neck and forehead strained. "We must leave immediately. If you must know in front of this girl, your sister is in poor health and has been confined to her bed for two months. We may lose both her and our grandchild."

His mother burst into tears and hurried inside the house. It was rare for her to cry. He knew she had been waiting for a letter from his sister, and it wasn't like her not to write. Fear twisted inside his chest like a funnel. What if they weren't using this ploy to manipulate him? What if his sister truly was in danger with her first child?

"Why did you not tell me? You made it sound like a little holiday for fun and relaxation." The words tumbled from him. "I wondered why she neglected responding to my last letter." Rob pressed the heel of his hand to his forehead as sudden pain shot through his temples.

"We only received the news a few moments ago. Her husband sent word." His father pointed at Lauren. "But you have been so enamored with this chit that you cannot be concerned with naught else."

"That is unfair." Rob stood and pressed his knuckles on the table as he stared at his father. "She has done naught to deserve your contempt."

"Her presence here is tearing this family apart. You have no interest in the family business because you spend all your time with her." He pointed again at Lauren, who now looked frightened. His father tilted his head and regarded Rob with a different expression, linking his hands and pressing two steepled fingers against his lips. "You know, I am beginning to think your mother is right. You are so infatuated with this girl you have lost all ability to be sensible."

"Lauren makes me sensible. She has an understanding of the Bible I have never received in church. She has a way of making me think deeper. What is wrong with that?"

"What nonsense!" His father slashed his hand in the air. "You can follow the Lord without making it your profession. Do not start with me about the clergy. I do not want to hear it." He pointed at Lauren. "And if she keeps filling your head with religion, she must go."

"Are you listening to yourself? I wanted to go into the clergy long before Lauren came here. Blaming her will not change things. And she is not tearing this family apart. The damage was already done long before she arrived." Rob sat down and took a deep breath. "If I go to New York with you, 'twill not be because you demand it, but because I care about my sister, and I want to be there in her time of need."

"I suggest you get packed. We will be leaving before the end of the day." His father turned and stomped away.

Rob poured himself another cup of tea and took a long swallow. "I am sorry you had to hear that. I daresay, even if you had left, you would have still heard our heated discussion, as the rest of the servants no doubt did." He set his cup down and, as he looked into her eyes, regret lingered in them. "None of this is your fault. My father and I have been at odds since I was twelve when I witnessed my first slave whipping. Something inside me snapped, and I have not been the same since. I lost a great deal of respect for my father that day."

"I am sorry about your sister. I shall pray for her and the babe while you are gone." Lauren stared at the table, either unwilling or unable to meet his gaze.

"Thank you. I would be most appreciative." He touched her arm. "And, Lauren, do not worry about them sending you away and selling your indenture. You belong here until you are free again."

12

Lauren dipped the thick cloth into the soapy bucket and scrubbed the brick floor in the kitchen. Her bruised knees ached from the hard floor, and her shoulder and neck muscles burned. Ever since the Mallard family departed three days ago, her tasks had become harder. She wouldn't complain since she was too thankful to be out of the fields.

As she shoved the cloth across the floor, it made a swishing sound that soothed her. A cooking fire danced in the large fireplace where black iron pots hung over the flames. A slave cut vegetables while another cut pork. Before coming here, Lauren knew very little about cooking since servants had always prepared their meals at Kilchurn Manor. All she had to do was plan the meals and turn them over to the cook.

Booted footsteps walked across the floor and stopped in front of her. Lauren paused as she gazed up the black breeches to the unbuttoned vest over a dirty, rumpled white shirt. Mr. Fairbanks scowled at her with narrowed dark eyes and an evil grin that made her shiver.

"Stand up." He crossed his arms as he waited for Lauren to crawl to her feet. "You are leaving."

"Leaving? To where?" Lauren tried not to panic as an unnatural fear tempted her. She glanced over at the two slaves she had been working with, but they looked just as surprised and confused as she.

"My boss, the senior Robert Mallard, ordered me to wait three days after they left to ensure his son would not change his mind and try to come back. My job is to get rid of you. He did not say how, but I know exactly what to do."

" 'Tis all a big mistake," Lauren said. "I do not have that much influence over Rob."

"No matter. You have to go . . . now." He grabbed her by the arm and dragged her out. Lauren tried to scramble to her feet and keep up. Outside, he had a horse waiting. He slammed her over the saddle, knocking the breath out of her. She tried to regain her wits, while Fairbanks mounted behind her. He spurred the horse into a gallop as the animal bounced into her ribs, making her nausea worse.

Fairbanks kept a firm hand on her back while he guided the reins with the other. Lauren coughed as the horse kicked up dust and sand in her face. Grit flew into her eyes, stinging and blurring her vision. She wept and blinked until her eyes were free of the offending dirt. It didn't stop her from breathing in the dust. She sputtered as her lungs squeezed and contracted.

They left the secluded roads of the country and arrived in Charles Towne. Lauren struggled to stay conscious as the blood pooled in her head from being upside down so long. She hoped someone would stop Fairbanks and question why he swept a woman upon his horse in such a manner, but people only laughed and pointed. Lauren had seen other men hauling women over their shoulders, but she had assumed they were women of ill repute. Could they be assuming the same about her?

"Lord, please help me." The whispered prayer came out in a rush of air.

They turned a corner and left the dirt road for a cobbled street. Some walked, while others rode wagons or carriages and hired coaches.

"Help me!" Lauren tried to scream, but no one heard her over the scattered conversations, the clip-clopping of horses, and the rolling wheels of carts and carriages. As they grew closer to the sea, Lauren could smell the heat mixed with the sea air and fish, sweating body odor, and tainted whiskey. She gagged.

Women with low-cut dresses, lots of perfume, and powdered faces walked the sidewalks and called to men as they passed. Lauren struggled, not caring if she fell in the path of trampling horses.

"Sit still or it will not go well for you." Fairbanks popped her in the back of her head.

"Help me!" No one heard her over the laughter at a nearby house. Fairbanks slammed a fist into her back, crushing the breath from her.

"I told you to shut up." He leaned forward.

He pulled behind a house into an alley. The horse came to a stop. Fairbanks dismounted, grabbed the back of her dress, and jerked her down. Lauren fell to the ground, coughing to catch her breath. Her legs trembled, and she couldn't stand. Tears stung her eyes as she tried to make sense of what was happening.

A woman came out the back door of what looked like a pink building. Two large men with muscled arms followed her and stood on each side. They crossed their arms and stared. Their eyes were focused and intent, assessing her. Each one possessed a square jaw with tight lips. Their height varied by a couple of inches. She wondered if they were brothers.

"Is that her?" the woman asked, pointing at Lauren. She wore an expensive gown in a dark pink color that looked to be made of satin and lace. White powder covered her face and neck down to her exposed cleavage. A white powdered wig crowned her head, and red rouge covered her cheeks.

"Aye, this is her. The girl's looks are lacking, but I daresay, she shall clean up well. I promise." Fairbanks stepped over Lauren. "She is a little resistant."

"She had better clean up well. This is an investment for me, naught else." The woman gestured to both men with her thumbs. "My men will take care of any resistance. We have not had a girl come through yet that we could not tame."

"Where is my money?" Fairbanks held out his hand. "I believe we had a deal."

"Indeed." The woman snapped her fingers, and one of the men tossed a small bag of coins at him. Fairbanks caught it with a grin. "I appreciate it. Nice doing business with you."

Fairbanks stepped around Lauren as she struggled to her bruised knees. Once Fairbanks disappeared on his horse, Lauren stood to her feet and met the woman's gaze. "My name is Lauren Campbell."

"Not anymore." The woman pressed her hands on her hips and gave her a mischievous smile as she sniffed. "What were you? A kitchen maid? Smells like . . . cinnamon. From now on that is what we shall call you. Refer to me as Adelle."

Malcolm arrived home from work to see a carriage parked in front of his house. Fearing something had happened to his mother, he hurried up the front steps and across the porch. Malcolm threw open the door.

"Mither! What is wrong?" He stopped short at the sight of Deidra and Kathleen sitting in their small parlor. Kathleen broke the seal and unfolded a letter.

"Malcolm, I am so glad ye're home, lad." His mother smiled from the chair where she perched on the edge. "Mr. Benjamin Shore has already responded. Is that not delightful?"

"Indeed. An' what does the good gentleman say?" Malcolm looked from his mother to the other two women.

"We do not know yet," Deidra said. "We only sat down to read it. Will ye not join us, Malcolm?"

"Aye, but I shall stand since I am still dirty from work." He held out a hand indicating that they should proceed. "Please, continue. Mither an' I are most anxious to learn the news of what happened to Carleen."

Kathleen held up the letter and cleared her throat. "Dear Mrs. MacGregor. I did indeed purchase the indenture of a young lady by the name of Carleen MacGregor from *The Loyal Adventure* as soon as it arrived. I made the purchase along with eight other individuals and delivered them into North Carolina to various families. I sold Miss MacGregor's indenture to a Mr. Oliver Bates in Wilmington. I am sorry I do not have more information as to your daughter's health and well-being, but I can assure you that she was in decent health when I last saw her."

Silence filled the room when she finished reading. Malcolm stroked his chin in thought. Carleen was hundreds of miles away from them. He would have to prevail upon Kathleen in writing a letter to Mr. Oliver Bates.

One decision he had made since arriving in the colonies: he intended to learn how to read and write as soon as he could find the time and opportunity. He wondered how long it would take before he received a letter from Uncle Ferguson or Thomas. Malcolm hoped Graham was healing and still safe from the Campbells.

"Although I am pleased to know she is well, I had hoped to see Carleen soon." His mother broke the silence. The sadness in her tone was unmistakable—at least to him. "I hope she is among kind-hearted people an' they treat her well."

"What will ye do now?" Deidra asked, looking at Malcolm.

"I suppose we shall try and track down Mr. Oliver Bates." Malcolm took a deep breath. "We need more information. How large is Wilmington an' where is it? My logger friends assure me although North an' South Carolina are twice the size of Scotland, most of the area is a vast wilderness."

After taking tea, Kathleen and Deidra departed. Malcolm went to clean up from all the wood dust on him. That night he didn't get much sleep as he continued to think about Carleen and Lauren. He couldn't wait until next Sunday so he could see her again.

Out of desperation, Malcolm took on another knuckle-buster fight on Friday night. Once again, the event turned out to be quite profitable. Saturday he spent the day logging and nursed his wounds that evening, most of which were minor. He had a bruised jaw and a black left eye. His mother was most displeased.

On Sunday, they arrived at church. The Mallard family was not present, but their servants arrived as usual with the exception of Lauren. Unease entered his soul. Malcolm hated the unrest inside him. He needed to know something. Why wasn't she with them?

He approached one of the servants after church in the churchyard. "Excuse me," he said to a young lass, "do ye know when the Mallards might return?"

"No, sir." She shook her head as she glanced up at him. "All we know is that they have gone away to New York."

"What about their servant, Lauren Campbell? Do ye know if she went with them?" Malcolm held his breath, hoping for some news.

"I do not know. She was removed from the fields an' stationed at the main house."

"I see." Malcolm nodded in disappointment. "Thank ye."

He took his mother home, but he wasn't good company as he brooded in restless thoughts. Malcolm couldn't rest until he knew what happened to Lauren. While his mother cooked, he departed for the country to Mallard Plantation. It would do no good to barge in and demand to speak with Lauren. Mr. Fairbanks would never allow it.

He hid in the woods by the well, hoping Lauren would appear. She didn't. Instead, a slave came for a bucket of water, but Malcolm was hesitant to approach her. He needed to be careful not to cause anyone to be reprimanded or get caught himself.

The heat soon had him sweating and swatting at flies. He kept a constant lookout for snakes and mopped his brow several times. Frustration added to his agony as one hour turned into two, then three. By late afternoon, Malcolm was convinced Lauren had either been assigned to another task besides the kitchen or something else had happened.

Malcolm left and stopped by Logan and Deidra's house before going home. He shared his concern since they attended First Presbyterian Church down the street from Independent. They wouldn't have known that Lauren had gone missing.

"Deidra, I was hoping ye could visit some of the vendors tomorrow and find out if any of them will be making any deliveries this week to the Mallard Plantation and offer my services to make the delivery for free for them. That way I can sneak past Mr. Fairbanks since he knows who I am. 'Twill afford me the opportunity to question the kitchen staff without seeming out of place."

"Forgive me, my friend, but that black eye will be sure to give ye away," Logan said. "I shall go in yer place. That way ye will not have to risk Mr. Fairbanks recognizing ye or wait 'til that eye of yers heals."

"Are ye sure, Logan?" Hope leaped in Malcolm's chest. He leaned forward.

"Aye," Logan nodded, "if ye trust me."

"I do, indeed." Malcolm held out his hand, and they shook in agreement.

"And I shall be more than delighted to inquire 'bout delivery services. We are verra concerned as to what happened to her as well. Ye can count on us, Malcolm."

"We shall find Lauren, and no matter what has happened, we will bring her home where she belongs," he said, determined to make his words true.

Against her will, Lauren was hauled into the Pink House, past the rowdy tavern to the second floor, where a dozen half-dressed women lounged, most with lovers. It was a large single room with no doors or privacy. Her heart beat into her throat and stomach as they climbed to the third floor to her new prison. It was another large room, much like a finished attic with a single bed and nothing else.

"You are not the first to arrive against your will. I, myself, was once in your shoes, but once the damage had been done against me, I learned to play the game, and so, here I am." Adelle held out her hands. "Your old life as it once existed is no more."

Lauren gulped. Tears streamed down her face. How was she to prevent them from taking her virginity against her will? *Lord, please save me from this.* The whispered prayer stung as silence followed. Hadn't she been faithful? What had she done to deserve this?

"I can imagine all the thoughts running through your pretty head," Adelle said, smiling wide, as if she had just won a round of poker. "You will no doubt lose any religion you once had. God does not frequent a bordello. I gave up on that a long time ago, and in time, so will you."

Fear coiled inside Lauren. God may not dwell in this place, but He most certainly dwelled inside her. She refused to believe their lies. Was the devil himself now tempting her?

Her voice failed her. All she had were her thoughts. She stood still, determined not to provoke them or cause herself an unnecessary beating. The men standing behind Adelle looked like bodyguards who could do more damage than she could imagine.

"Due to the special education Mr. Fairbanks assures us you have, I have determined your virginity will be saved for the highest bidder at auction. Some of the gentlemen only prefer women like you and me. They are the wealthy ones who pay the best. If one of them takes a liking to you, he may set you up as his mistress, if you are lucky. In the meantime, 'tis my job to ensure you are quite prepared."

Adelle turned to her men. "You have my permission to do whatever you need to acquire her cooperation. All I ask is that you do not injure her face or any part of her body that will show to the public."

Both men bowed in understanding without saying a word. Fear swirled inside Lauren. She trembled and struggled to continue standing. She feared her legs would fail her.

"Men, you know the routine. The first thing she must learn is humbleness. Strip Cinnamon of her garments."

"Nay!" Lauren screamed, but it did no good. The men stripped her garments as she fought them. One slammed a fist into her ribs. Lauren fell to her knees, hoping that her ribs were not shattered. When she clung to her chemise, the other one slammed his fist into the back of her head. Dazed, and barely hanging on to consciousness, Lauren tried to stand, but a fist slammed into her back as the last of her garments stripped from her.

She slid to the floor in a puddle of tears. Adelle had made a fire in the large hearth. "I realize it is not cold out, but a fire seems to be a small comfort to the girls during their humiliation lesson."

Adelle snapped her fingers and pointed at the door. The men stepped outside. "Cinnamon, I want you to be aware that this process can be as smooth or as difficult as you choose. The bottom line is this, I will have my way."

"I shall never agree to this." Lauren managed to say through her tears. "Ye can kill me if ye like. I do not care."

Adelle walked toward her and kicked her in the side. "Do you not understand, you stubborn wench? I know all the possible tortures necessary to get you to do my will. I have plenty of patience, but eventually, I will win. I always do."

"Not this time." Lauren managed to whisper. The pain in her chest and back was so severe, she could hardly breathe.

Adelle laughed. "That is what they all say." She bent to Lauren's ear. "Over the next three days you shall receive no water or food. The door is locked. By the time I return, you shall be so weak, you will beg me for food. Your convictions will be a distant memory. After a bit of nourishment, you shall remember your convictions, but more starvation will bring you back to an amiable state of mind. I am an expert at this. Do not think you can outwit or outlast me."

"Go ahead and think what ye will," Lauren said. "But God shall deliver me, or I will die in the effort. My soul belongs to the Lord, and that ye canna take even if ye do away with me."

Lauren's words earned her another kick in the ribs. She groaned, but her spirit wasn't yet broken. She prayed God would give her the ability to endure what she needed or bring her deliverance soon. She had never been tested like this before, and in truth, she had no idea how strong her earthly body could stand against such torture.

Adelle walked out, closing the door behind her.

Alone, Lauren crawled to the bed. Her body was in such pain that it took her several minutes before she could manage to climb onto the mattress. She curled in the center like a wounded kitten and cried out to God until she was out of breath and energy. "Lord, please lead Malcolm to me."

Slumber finally overcame her. Only in her dreams did she find the peace she sought.

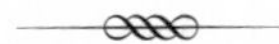

"Timber!" Malcolm called with his hands cupping his mouth as the large tree tottered and hesitated. He pressed his palms against it, braced his feet, and pushed. The tree tumbled over. Large branches snapped in two as the trunk smashed to the ground. Some of the heavier limbs took down several other nearby tree limbs with it.

"Malcolm, I have never known a man who could put down as many trees as you in such a short period of time," his boss called from nearby, his tone quite pleased.

"He is only showing off!" one man said. "MacGregor is determined to prove the brawn of a Scotsman."

"No true Scotsman has to prove a thing." Logan spoke up, joining Malcolm's side as he shoved on a pair of thick gloves. "I got the crosscut saw. Ye ready to cut off these extra limbs?"

"Aye." Malcolm nodded, wiping his brow with his sleeve. "Have ye any news 'bout Lauren?"

"I do, but I needed ye to slow down on plowing through the trees long enough to hear it." Logan shook his head as he picked up one end of the saw and pointed to the handle at the other end. "Ye wanna help me?"

"Ye had better keep up. I got a lot of frustration to work off," Malcolm warned, picking up his end of the saw. They placed the saw across one of the larger limbs at the bend next to the trunk. "Ready?"

"Aye." Logan nodded. The two of them pulled the saw back and forth until the blade sliced through the wood at an even pace. "I made the delivery yesterday."

"I thought ye were goin' today?" Malcolm lifted a brow, a scowl twisting his lips into a frown. "Are ye holdin' back on me?"

"Nay." Logan met his gaze as they sawed back and forth. "I planned to tell ye first thing this morn, but ye've been going at it with a vengeance."

"Just tell me what I wanna know," Malcolm said, unable to hide his irritation. "Did ye see her?"

"She is not there. One of the kitchen slaves told me Fairbanks took her away last week. He waited 'til the Mallard family went up north. Rumor has it, the master's son developed an attachment and his parents disapproved."

"Where did he take her?" Malcolm gripped the saw tighter until his palms ached. He clenched his teeth.

"None o' them know, but they suspect she was sold to some other family." Logan paused. "We could check the courthouse records an' see if there was a recent sale."

"True. Sounds like the next step." Malcolm blinked, wishing he had more information. "I canna give up."

"Of course not. Ye're not alone in this, Malcolm. 'Tisn't right." Logan kept time with Malcolm's rhythm in sawing the wood. "We will find her. Deidra is beside herself with worry."

Lord, please let her be safe. The silent prayer burst from Malcolm's heart. Once the words were part of his thoughts, he realized he meant them. As much as Lauren believed in God, if anyone could help her, it would be the Lord. She had served Him faithfully. If God ever had a reason to save a lass, Lauren would be it. Malcolm had never known anyone who had so much faith or who sacrificed herself to serve others as she did. Hope sprung up inside, giving him an inner strength he lacked a moment earlier. Was this what it was like to have faith?

He took a deep breath, and his chest felt a bit lighter. Malcolm glanced up at the blue sky with dotted white clouds. For the first time in his life, he didn't feel cursed but blessed. He was in love with a beautiful woman, he had a new start here in the colonies, and he had learned that both his mother and his sister were alive. Soon he would find Lauren and Carleen, and they would all be together. How had he lived all these years with so little hope? And how could everything change with one single prayer?

It was as Lauren had told him. Belief. Without belief, what did one have but despondency? He didn't want to live that way. This world was too complicated not to have a Creator who understood more than all the people in it.

The limb broke off the tree trunk. He and Logan worked on another branch. They brought down several more trees before an afternoon thunderstorm rolled in. Their boss let them go early since the rain made things hazardous.

Malcolm took advantage of the extra time to stop by the courthouse. Water dripped from him as he stepped inside with others who were trying to avoid the rain. All the benches were full as they waited out the bad weather. Malcolm walked over to the man behind the counter.

"Excuse me, but I would like to know if a lass, uh, young girl, was sold from Mallard Plantation within the last two weeks. Her name is Lauren Campbell." Malcolm scratched his temple.

The clerk shook his head. "That is easy. I do not have to look. No plantation auctions have taken place in that time. All we have had are auctions from the ships docking at port."

"What about the ships leaving Charles Towne?" Malcolm asked.

"Only exports of dry goods and things." The man shook his head.

"An indentured servant was taken from Mallard Plantation an' sold to someone. How would I find out if they neglected to register it?" Malcolm rubbed his chin, perplexed by what to do next.

"There is always that possibility, or they took her out of the area and sold her someplace else. We simply do not have the people to track 'em down like that."

"Would ye mind lookin' in the book? In case somethin' was logged in while ye stepped out for a short break?"

"All right." He flipped through the large book on the counter and pressed his finger on a page, turning it so Malcolm could see. "Here are the logs starting April first. We have no sales like you are looking for through late May." He flipped more pages.

"Thank ye." Malcolm sighed with disappointment.

"You might try visiting some of the taverns and asking 'round. 'Tis one way to hear useful gossip that might lead to a hot trail. I have heard some of the local investigators talking about it."

"Good idea." Malcolm turned and left the courthouse, not caring about the rain. Water poured on his head, matting his hair to his scalp. He needed to find Logan. They would start making the rounds at the taverns tonight.

After three days of no food or water, the door opened. Lauren scrambled to her knees in the center of the bed. The pain in her ribs was acute, but she had no idea what to expect.

A young girl walked in carrying a tray of fresh brewed coffee, toast, a slab of bacon, and scrambled eggs. Lauren's mouth watered, and her stomach tightened in response. Weakness claimed her body to the point of a severe headache. Tremors quaked through her.

The girl sat on the bed and placed the tray upon her lap. "I have brought you somethin' to eat." Her childlike voice reverberated through the large chamber.

"Do ye think I might be allowed some clothes?" Lauren asked.

"If ye behave." She nodded her dark head, her violet eyes wide with concern. "Are you cold?" She glanced toward the hearth. "I could build a warm fire."

"At first I tried to keep it going, but then I decided it was not worth the effort. 'Twould be better to die than endure the sinful life they want to force on me."

"I do not know much about all that. All I know is 'tis less painful if you do what they want." She shoved the tray toward Lauren. "Now eat. Three days is a long time to go without anything. I know . . . because they once put me through it."

"But ye canna be more than fourteen." Lauren's stomach churned at the thought of what must have happened to her.

"To be exact, I am thirteen. I will not be fourteen for five more months." She picked up a piece of bacon and held it out to Lauren. "What is your name?"

"Lauren Campbell, but Adelle said I shall be called Cinnamon." She accepted the bacon and bit into the crisp meat. Lauren closed her eyes, savoring the taste. For now she would replenish her body and worry about their intentions later.

"My name is now Violet. What it was before no longer matters. I have tried to forget my former life, so I can better survive."

"What has happened to ye is not right, nor what is now happening to me." Lauren grabbed the fork and speared the eggs. "What about the clothes. Please? May I have some?"

"I shall see what I can do." The girl bowed her head and stood to her feet. She reminded Lauren of Blair. A pang of longing pierced her heart.

Once the girl left the room, Lauren came to her senses and rushed to the door. She peered outside and recognized one of her brutal tormentors from the other day. He turned to stare at her, an evil grin upon his thin lips. Lauren slammed the door closed. There was no way past him, especially unclothed.

Lauren shuffled back to the bed and downed the glass of water Violet brought. She wiped her mouth with the back of her hand. Picking up a piece of toast, she took a bite and closed her eyes. Never before had food tasted so good.

Lord, I canna believe it is Yer will for them to make a sinning prostitute of me. What would Ye have me do? Please, if I must die, let it be swift. I pray I am not tortured or starved to death.

Tears spilled onto her cheeks. Over the last three days she had cried often and prayed until her voice failed her from dehydration. Scriptures came to mind that she had forgotten. She hoped it meant God's word was buried so deep inside her it had become part of her. Wouldn't that be the only way for her not to give in to their demands, even at her weakest moment? She feared she wouldn't be strong enough.

"God, give me strength," she whispered into the empty room. "And wisdom."

Lauren couldn't finish all the food on her plate, but she ate what she could. It seemed as if her stomach had shrunk. Even though she drank all the water, her throat still felt dry.

The door opened again. Violet returned carrying a beautiful satin gown of blue with lace trimming. "Madame said she noticed the blue in your eyes and thought this gown might do well for you until we can have you fitted for new garments of your own."

She laid the dress out on the bed as well as the accompanying undergarments. "I hope it fits. Madame has an eye for detail so I am certain it will."

Eager to cover herself, Lauren moved to her feet with renewed energy after eating. "Please, help me."

The gown was cut much lower than Lauren would have preferred, but after three days of nothing, she could hardly complain. No doubt that was their intention. Once the new gown covered her, Lauren felt so much better. Their tactics were inhumane. Lauren turned to face Violet and sat on the bed. "Now what?"

"I am not sure." She shrugged. "All I know is that like you, I am to be auctioned as a virgin to one of the highest bidders."

"How long have ye been here?" Lauren asked, shocked by the child's candid attitude toward everything.

"Almost a year. Madame Adelle likes to make sure us younger women have started our monthly courses and have been trained and prepared for what is to come."

"Does that mean I have a year?" Hope soared inside Lauren but deflated as Violet shook her head.

"I do not think so. I heard Madame tell one of the bodyguards in the hallway that she wants you ready within the month."

Lauren cringed. That didn't give her much time to plan her escape. She would have to pretend to go along with their scam, to make them loosen her privileges. Once she earned their trust, she would make her move.

"Why did Adelle allow ye to bring food and a gown?" Lauren asked as Violet buttoned her up in the back.

"Sometimes the other girls can get jealous of each other and fight over the men who come here. I suppose she thought I would be less of a threat than the others." She patted Lauren's shoulder and stepped around to face her. Only a couple of inches shorter than Lauren, Violet was a beautiful girl but still so much a child. Lauren's throat constricted. How could she leave Violet here when she made her escape? Although she didn't realize it, Violet needed to be rescued as well.

"When will I be allowed out of this chamber?" Lauren asked.

"Madame Adelle will come in after I leave, and she shall begin your training. If she suspects any resistance in you, your confinement will last longer." Violet grabbed Lauren's hands. "Please . . . do not do anything to make them hurt you. I hope she will let you out. I like you and know we can be great friends. You are not like the others."

Lauren gave her a reassuring smile and squeezed her hands in return. "Do not worry. I shall do my best."

Lord, help me get through this without dishonoring You.

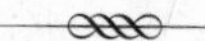

Each night Malcolm and Logan visited a new tavern and made inquiries about Lauren. Their efforts were in vain, and Malcolm had no more knowledge of where she had disappeared than the day he started looking. Desperation made him turn to prayer. He needed hope. Often, he remembered something Lauren had said or a scripture that gave him encouragement.

"Tomorrow we will start at the taverns on Chalmers Street," Logan said as they walked down Meeting Street. "From what I understand many are beneath the bordellos located on the upper floors above them. 'Tis definitely not a part of town I would take my sister."

The moon provided enough silvery light to walk by while sparkling stars scattered across the dark heavens. Fewer people were out this late at night. Those who did venture out were men who frequented the taverns.

Malcolm massaged the back of his aching neck. "I did not want to have to consider it, but it looks more like we shall have to check the less reputable places around Charles Towne. She could not have vanished like this without a trace."

"Aye." Logan shook his head and clucked his tongue. "There is somethin' underhanded with the whole thing. The Mallard family must be involved somehow."

"Ye think they could have sent her to a convent?" Malcolm asked.

"My friend, ye canna afford to be in denial any longer." Logan touched his arm. "Why would they do that? They could not make any money off her, and the convent would expose them since she would have been dumped there against her will." He shook his head. "Nay, I think a bordello is more likely. That way they could get payment for her, an' no one would talk. They all have somethin' to hide."

"Ye're right." Malcolm fisted his hands at his sides. "I canna imagine Lauren in a place like that. She is a godly woman and does not belong there."

"I doubt she had much of a choice." Logan's tone turned to one of disgust. He cleared his throat. "Will it change the way ye think 'bout 'er?"

"Of course not!" Malcolm snapped in irritation. His stomach churned, and he had to swallow several times to keep from casting up his counts.

"All right." Logan raised up his palms and stepped over, allowing a wider gap between them. "I just wanted to ask because ye need to know where ye stand if we find her in such a place."

Malcolm's eyes burned and his ears rang. He could feel a headache coming upon him. "I will not abandon her, ever." The conviction in his words helped strengthen his resolve. "Do ye have any other suggestions?"

"Nay, not unless they took her away from Charles Towne, but we canna begin to consider that if we have not checked every place here in town."

"True." Malcolm wrapped his arms around his unsettled stomach. "I never thought losing her would feel like this. I mean . . . I knew she might go back home to her father, but this . . . "

Tears stung his eyes. He blinked, trying not to let his mind imagine what might be happening to her right now. His throat constricted, and the pain inside him stung and clawed at his insides. He had to keep it together. Could a bullet through his stomach feel any worse?

"I need to find Pastor Brad. Do ye know where he might have gone?" Malcolm asked. "To talk to him. He was so close to Lauren."

"He is a pastor at a Presbyterian church north of Charles Towne. 'Tis too far to walk. Ye'll need a horse." Logan stopped walking. "Here is where I need to turn. Promise me ye will not do anything stupid."

"It depends on what ye think is stupid." Malcolm shrugged. "I will not be at work tomorrow. I canna sleep tonight. I have got to find her. I will not rest 'til I do."

"Are ye going to Pastor Brad's tonight?" Logan asked.

"I think I need a voice of reason right now. I am not thinking too clear, and I do not feel well. I want to break somethin'." He slammed a fist into his palm.

"I have seen ye fight." Logan stepped back. "The last thing ye need is to end up in jail. Ye will not be able to look for Lauren if that happens." He sighed. "Mayhap Pastor Brad can help ye. I wish I knew what to say." He lifted his empty hands. "I am sorry, my friend."

"I appreciate all yer help," Malcolm said.

"I canna afford to give up my job, but I will be happy to help ye again tomorrow night."

"That sounds reasonable. I will be startin' the search again in the morn. I canna wait 'til the evening. I hope ye understand."

"I do." Logan gulped and rubbed the back of his head. "If 'twas Deidra, I do not know what I would do."

"Just be glad it is not. I feel like I am about to lose my mind." Malcolm reached over and patted his friend's shoulder. "See ye tomorrow."

"Wait, I have one more thing to tell ye." Logan gave him directions to Pastor Brad's church. A few weeks ago, he had taken Kathleen and Deidra for a visit.

Malcolm couldn't go home and face his mother in his brooding mood. She had been crying for the past three days, feeling guilty over Lauren's disappearance. In her mind, none of this would have happened if Lauren hadn't taken her place at Mallard Plantation. He walked to the livery and saddled his horse and set out north.

He traveled for half an hour before the image of a steeple matching Logan's description came into view in the moonlight. He dismounted and banged on the door.

No one came. Malcolm would not give up. He continued knocking. "Pastor Brad! Please, answer the door. 'Tis Malcolm MacGregor!"

Feet shuffled on the other side. Finally, the door swung open to reveal Pastor Brad in a white nightgown and cap. "Malcolm? Come in an' tell me what is eatin' at ye."

"Lauren has been kidnapped an' I need ye to give me a good reason not to do what I am tempted to do."

13

Lauren received permission to mingle with the other girls, but none of the visiting men were allowed to touch her. All they could do was admire her across the room and enjoy her piano playing. This arrangement suited Lauren quite well as she pretended to go along, learned their schedules and habits, and tried to figure out a way to escape.

Madame Adelle had her fitted for a couple of new gowns, specifically for the event where she would be auctioned. Lauren spent most of her time in training on how to please various men, to recognize mood swings and personality types and to divert anger in an attempt to prevent a beating.

To Lauren's increasing despair, the opportunity to escape never presented itself. None of them had single rooms, and she was never alone. The second floor was one huge room where they all slept and did things that Lauren wished she had never witnessed. Why hadn't God answered her prayers? Had He forgotten her? She feared her virginity would be forcibly taken before God delivered her to safety. If so, what would that mean for the rest of her life? To Malcolm?

Violet was forbidden to men as much as she. The one thing that unsettled Lauren was the fact the young lass had started flirting with young men, mimicking the actions of the older prostitutes around her. Lauren prayed for her and was mocked by the others for praying, but she didn't care.

God was her only voice of reason in a place mad with the love for sin. She longed to be free but feared she could be tainted, never able to fully return to the life she once knew.

"Cinnamon!" a woman called across the tavern. "Play us a happy ditty."

Lauren glanced at the only door of escape. One of the bodyguards stood nearby, with his legs spread and his arms crossed over his chest. She had already experienced the brunt of his fists in her stomach and sides enough to last her a lifetime. Her ribs weren't healed, but it helped that Adelle now allowed her ribs to be bound tightly so she could at least walk and sit, providing she moved slowly.

Lauren turned and placed her hands on the keys as she tried to remember a familiar tune lively enough to please them. An arm draped across her shoulders, startling her. A man in his midtwenties leaned in her face. His breath smelled of strong whiskey. She turned away so he wouldn't see her disgust.

"Ye are new, are ye not? What is yer name, gel?" With slurred words, he leaned too far to the right and swayed back.

"Lauren Campbell."

"I thought they just called you Cinnamon?" He coughed and leaned closer.

" 'Tis my new nickname." Lauren hoped the explanation would satisfy her captors enough to prevent another beating.

"She is off limits." The bodyguard slung the man's arm away from her with so much force that he staggered into a nearby table. "Anyone interested in Cinnamon will need to be at the auction in a couple of weeks. Madame Adelle will post the details."

Mumbled conversations followed as all eyes turned upon Lauren, ruining her hope of not being noticed. With burning cheeks, Lauren turned back to the piano and did her best to ignore the discussions about her.

Tuning out everyone else, Lauren pretended to be at home in Scotland and let her fingers fly across the keys. A new tune bellowed in the air, and soon, other things distracted them. It was how she preferred it. Otherwise, how was she to make her escape while in the midst of their attention?

The tavern was on the first floor as one large room with long trestle tables where patrons ate and drank well into the night. A few couples retired to the second level where she loathed to go. She wondered where she would find a place to sleep tonight. Most of them slept during the day, which proved to be the only time she could find a few hours of solace after surviving the late night parties.

Lauren glanced up at the ceiling as she played the piano. Mayhap God couldn't hear her prayers in a place so full of sin. She once feared laboring in the fields under the sun, but this was much worse.

At first, she hoped Malcolm would find and rescue her. Now she felt too ashamed to be discovered here. If she couldn't make her escape before the auction, she hoped her loved ones would forget about finding her and remember her as she was. Lauren didn't want to become one of the dead in spirit, but if she lost her hope and faith, she would be nothing.

After a while, her sore ribs throbbed even more. She needed to move to another position. Ending her final song, Lauren stood and strode to Madame Adelle and bent herself to a humbling position. "Madame, my ribs hurt. May I go rest on the third floor?"

"I would have thought you spent enough time alone in that chamber." She raised an eyebrow in suspicion.

"Indeed, which is why I asked to be let out. I enjoy being around people and playing the piano, but my ribs are paining me. I hope to rest them to be in my best shape before the auction."

"I see." She touched Lauren's cheek. "Very well, you may retire for the evening." She glanced up and snapped her fingers at the bodyguard to follow Lauren.

Stepping inside the chamber and shutting the door, Lauren breathed a sigh of relief and closed her eyes as she leaned against the door. Once her ribs healed, she could wait until early morning when they were all asleep and try to climb out the window using the bed sheets. She hoped they would be long enough from the upper floors. What other option did she have with a bodyguard stationed outside her door?

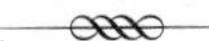

After his sister's miscarriage, Rob convinced his father to allow him to return home alone. His mother refused to leave, and his father felt he belonged at their side. To help his cause, his father didn't want the plantation to be without direction for too long.

Once he was certain that his sister would recover, Rob purchased a horse and departed. Riding horseback helped him make better time. He stayed at various inns along the way. When he finally arrived home, Rob was exhausted, hungry, and thirsty. He dismounted as the stable lad came to meet him.

"I am sorry, Mastah. I did not know yous be returnin' today." Henry hurried to take the reins.

"No one knew." Rob gripped his thin shoulder. "Take care of my weary horse. He deserves some extra oats for the length of road he carried me."

"Yes, sir." Henry nodded and led Rob's horse away.

Rob strode across the yard as he glanced up at the overcast sky. It was early afternoon, but he had missed the midday meal. Birds chirped nearby as he crossed the threshold at the side door. His heels made a steady rhythm against the wood floor with each stride.

"Mastah Rob, is it you?" George, the butler, walked down the hall.

"Indeed, just returned and starving. Would you have the cook bring a meal to the dining room?" He stretched his arms and yawned.

"I shall tell her right away," George said. "Glad to have you back home, sir."

Rob gave him a brief nod as he continued to the dining room. It was quiet, barren, and dark. Very little light passed through the two long windows. Rob lit a couple of candles, which made the room better but still barren. With the exception of servants walking across the floor in other parts of the house, it was too quiet. A grandfather clock ticked in the foyer. Rob disliked being alone. Where was Lauren? He always enjoyed her company and conversation, and his disapproving parents weren't here to interrupt them.

George returned. "Mastah, a warm meal will be served directly."

"Thank you, George. Would you ask Lauren to attend me?"

Silence greeted him. George stared at the floor and coughed in obvious discomfort. "I am sorry, Mastah, but she is gone."

"Gone?" Rob tensed. "What do you mean?"

"After you all left, Mr. Fairbanks took her away an' none o' us seen her since."

"How long ago was this?" Rob demanded, standing to his feet. The chair scraped back against the floor.

" 'Tis been a couple o' weeks now." George linked his hands in front of him but stood in place.

"Where is Fairbanks? In the house or out in the fields?"

"He is out, but I do not know at which field."

"Have Henry saddle a fresh horse for me. My meal will have to wait."

"I shall tell the cook after I speak to Henry." George turned and disappeared into the hall.

Anger burst inside Rob as he tried to make sense of what he just learned. He always knew that Stanley Fairbanks took advantage of his position, but this went beyond the boundaries. Since when did he have a right to remove people from the estate? It was grounds for dismissal, and if Stan didn't have a reasonable excuse, he would see to firing the man. Unlike his father, Rob had always thought the estate would benefit from a better overseer.

He rubbed his temples, mentally preparing himself for the upcoming confrontation. Rob took a deep breath and stomped from the dining room. He stormed down the hall and out the side door toward the stables. Henry met him with a fresh horse.

Without a word, Rob mounted and took off toward the small house where the Fairbanks family lived. Slaves and field servants stopped to greet him as he rode past. He nodded in acknowledgment but didn't slow his pace.

Stan sat on the front porch, rocking in a wooden rocker. The sliding motion beat a smooth rhythm against the wood floor. A jug of whiskey sat at his feet. He smiled. "You back already? Are your parents back as well?"

Rob didn't respond as he dismounted. The cocky grin on Stan's unshaven jaw and the mischievous glint in his eyes infuriated Rob. How dare he act as if all was well? He secured his horse to a nearby tree, strode up the porch steps, reared back, and slammed his fist in Stan's nose. His head snapped back against the rocker, and blood spattered down to his chin and dripped, soiling his white shirt. "That is for having the nerve to dismiss someone from this estate without permission. You had better tell me where you took Lauren or you will not like the consequences."

"I do not have to tell you a thing." Stan held his head back as he tried to stop the bleeding with his hand. "I was told to do it."

"By whom?" Rob leaned forward, bracing his hand on the rocker's arm. " 'Tis in your best interest to tell me everything." Rob lowered his tone as he glared at the man who had enjoyed carrying out so many beatings of others.

"Ask your father!" Stan pointed in the direction of the main house.

"He is not here. Right now I am in charge." A cold sweat broke out on Rob's back. He gulped at the betrayal. Pain pushed deep into his soul. Even though he had never agreed with the way his father ran the plantation, Rob himself had never known his cruelty. "Are you saying he is aware of what you did?"

"Of course. I do not take orders from anyone else." Stan leaned to the side away from Rob. "I will not tell you where she is. I cannot risk your father's ire."

"He is not here, and you cannot afford to risk mine." Rob grabbed his shirt and hauled Stan out of the rocker. "Now tell me where she is, or you can leave the plantation right now. Think about it. Do you want to be responsible for your family's homelessness?"

"I only did what your father told me to do. He said to wait three days and get rid of her." Stan stumbled back against the porch post. "He will not like what you are doing to us."

"Tell me where she is, and you can keep your job." Rob clenched his fists at his sides. Rage surged through him in waves. He took several steadying breaths. "What will it be?"

"If I do what your father wanted, then I have a chance at being rehired when he comes back." He shook his head while holding his bloody nose. "You have been wanting to get rid of me."

Rob shoved his fist into Stan's stomach. Air gushed from him as he hunched over. "You have one hour to get out of here. Ten of my best field hands will escort you off the estate. After the way they have suffered under your cruelty, I am certain they will enjoy the privilege." Rob shoved him toward the house. "Get packing. I shall find Lauren without your help." Rob bounced down the steps and mounted his horse and rode away.

He selected ten men as promised, gave them instructions, and rode into Charles Towne. Rob pulled in front of the courthouse. Inside, he strode to the counter and cleared his throat. The clerk looked up from his recordings, pausing with a quill in his hand.

"I am looking for a woman by the name of Lauren Campbell. She might have been sold from Mallard Plantation at a recent auction," Rob said.

The clerk tilted his head with a perplexed expression. "A man was in here asking about the same woman not too long ago. I'm sorry to say that no transaction has taken place with that name."

"Who was asking about her?" Rob leaned closer, hoping for a lead to track her down.

"His name is MacGregor." He lifted a finger. "He is a large Scotsman with a noticeable accent. Rust-colored hair, at least it looked to be when wet. 'Twas raining that day. Said something about getting the rest of the day off from logging due to the rain."

"So he must be a logger. Thanks." Rob tipped his hat and left.

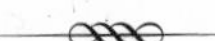

Pastor Brad managed to convince Malcolm not to hire vagabonds to raid the bordellos along the docks and on Chalmers Street. Most of them were protected by burly men who were well paid, loyal, and ready to defend their domains. It could cause a scandal and make things worse for Lauren if word spread before they discovered her. Malcolm couldn't imagine making things worse, but he didn't want to be the cause of further embarrassment to her.

Once Malcolm calmed enough to listen to reason, Pastor Brad prayed with him. Malcolm discovered that releasing his frustration through prayer was more effective than pounding someone. It left him with a feeling of hope compared to his old habits that only sufficed to give him temporary satisfaction with no hope.

Malcolm woke with clarity and a renewed resolve. He listed all the known bordellos on Chalmers Street and his mother wrote down each name. As they finished, a knock sounded at the front door.

"I will get it." His mother stepped from the parlor into the small foyer. The lock clicked and the door squeaked open. "May I help ye?"

"Please pardon my unannounced visit, but my name is Rob Mallard. I came to inquire about Miss Lauren Campbell." A man's voice floated into the hall. "She has gone missing from our plantation."

His mother's fingers flew over her mouth. In a speechless state, she turned to gaze at Malcolm, seeking guidance concerning the gentleman at the door. Malcolm strode to his mother's side.

"We were told that Lauren was forcibly removed from Mallard Plantation. She has disappeared without a trace." Desperation dripped in his tone, but Malcolm didn't care. He would do anything to find her. The aching pain in his heart burdened him, soaking up his strength and maddening his mind. He couldn't concentrate on anything else, not even the search for his sister.

"After questioning some of my field hands, I may have discovered a clue, but I need your help." Rob glanced from Malcolm to his mother as silence lengthened between them. "May I come in?"

"Indeed." Malcolm stepped back, widening the entrance.

Rob removed his hat when he stepped inside. They led him into the parlor where he sat in a chair by the window. Malcolm and his mother took a seat on the couch.

"My father believes that I am infatuated with Lauren and told our overseer to get rid of her once the family left to visit my sister in New York. I returned home before the others and discovered the deed."

"Why did ye not question Mr. Fairbanks and the people who work for ye? Someone there knows somethin'." Malcolm clenched his jaw, determined he wouldn't yet accuse him of negligence, at least not until he heard everything.

"I did. Fairbanks would not tell me where he took her, but he admitted to getting rid of her for my father. I fired him. I went to the courthouse for records of an auction sale. The clerk told me about you. I started asking around about a Scottish logger by the name of MacGregor. You have quite a reputation at being in knuckle-buster fights and visiting all the bordellos seeking a lost lady love. You were not hard to find."

"Is this what people are sayin'?" Malcolm shifted in discomfort. Lauren was his lost lady love, and it tore him apart.

"Indeed." Rob nodded. "I questioned several of my field hands. It seems that Stan got drunk and was bragging about taking Lauren to the Pink House. I confess, I am not familiar with the place. I thought I would see if you had made any progress. If we join forces, we shall have a better chance of finding her."

"How do I know I can trust ye?" Malcolm gripped his knees, tensing.

"Malcolm, he is offerin' his help. Do not be so stubborn to know when the Lord is blessin' ye." His mother's scolding tone filled the room.

"How do I know he will not take her back to the plantation after we find her?" Malcolm pointed at Rob and stood to his feet. He paced around the small room, rubbing his throbbing temples. "I will not let her go back. She does not belong there. She never did."

"I agree," Rob said. "Lauren is too well educated. She was born and raised to be a lady. As much as I would like to bring her back, she would still be in danger of my father's heartless schemes." He met Malcolm's gaze. "The other reason I wanted to find you is to make sure she would be safe."

"Aye, she would," his mother said, linking her hands in her lap. "I am not her mither, but as a God-fearing woman who is a mither, I know what the lass needs to heal. God willing, I can help her if ye bring her to me."

"That brings me more relief than you know, Mrs. MacGregor." Rob breathed a sigh.

"Ye are infatuated with her." Tense jealousy seized Malcolm. Did Lauren feel the same way about him? Betrayal struck his heart at the thought.

"True, but only because she helped me find my faith again. I had become bitter and cynical in battling my father's evil ways and almost gave up. Lauren gave me renewed inspiration and helped me see things differently." Rob's gaze slid to the wall. "She has a way of awakening the soul. 'Tis a gift she has. Now I am determined to step into my role as my father's heir. I intend to change the way our plantation runs. The beatings and the floggings will stop."

"Was Lauren beaten?" Malcolm's head snapped up, his tone sharp.

"Not while I was at home," Rob said, shaking his head.

Eager to find her, Malcolm pulled out the list of bordellos. "I believe the Pink House is on this list. 'Tis on Chalmers Street. Logan and I plan to go there tonight. You are welcome to come along. We may need yer help."

The stench of stale whiskey and gaudy perfume made Lauren's stomach lurch as she gripped the stair rail and descended the steps. If she moved too fast, her aching ribs protested against their binding. She had tried to escape too soon out the kitchen door the night before. One of the girls caught her. The blows she suffered to her already wounded ribs cracked them again. They resorted to punching her jaw and the side of her head to keep from giving her black eyes or busting her nose before their precious auction.

Adelle waited at the bottom of the stairs. She wore a burgundy gown with a matching ribbon necklace from which hung a silver heart trinket. Sparkling diamonds in silver drops dangled from her ears. Her lips shone ruby red, and her cheeks glowed. It was her piercing dark eyes that brought Lauren's knees to a fearful tremble.

Disgusted with her own weakness, Lauren glanced ahead at the busy tavern. Men were already on both sides of the trench tables. Some feasted on mutton and whiskey while others dallied with the wenches eager to take them into their beds for the night and lose whatever coins they earned. Two men arm wrestled upon the wagers of the men standing over their shoulders.

"I hope you intend to behave yourself tonight." Adelle reached out and touched the bruised knot on the right side of her chin. Lauren winced and closed her eyes. " 'Twould be a shame to ruin the rest of your face. And do not worry. If you are not ready for this auction, I shall save you for the next, even if I have to lock you up until that time."

Lauren did not respond. Her jaw hurt too much. Why didn't the Lord go ahead and end her misery? Why did she keep surviving these beatings? Would it not be best to die and go home to heaven than to allow her body to be used and raped in a life of sin and prostitution?

"I have no strength to cause ye any trouble tonight." Lauren hated it, but it was true. If she were to escape tonight, it would be by a miracle from God, not her own stubborn will. Still, she hoped God would reward her efforts.

"I admire your spirit, but be warned, I will break it if need be," Adelle said, lowering her voice as Lauren passed.

"Ye'll have to if ye expect me to stay." Lauren mouthed the words under her breath, thankful Adelle hadn't heard them. Tonight she would have to survive. The fight for her freedom would have to wait for another day.

"All you have to do is play some lively melodies and keep our customers happy." Adelle's taunting voice floated behind her. Lauren gritted her teeth at the pain in her midsection and made it to the wall. She paused to lean against it.

"She has a strong will," said a man. "I do not know that we can break it with our usual methods." Lauren glanced over her shoulder to see one of Adelle's bodyguards now standing by her side.

"I never intended for my life to turn out this way," Adelle said. "I was the strongest person I have ever known. If I could be broken, anyone can—even Cinnamon."

The bitterness in Adelle's tone spoke volumes as a new realization crawled up Lauren's spine. She was more than a girl Adelle could make money on. Lauren had become a personal challenge. If Adelle couldn't break her, then Adelle's justification for the path her life had taken would cease to exist. Her belief that no one could be strong enough to endure this torture would shatter. She was forced to admit her own weakness and failure.

A month ago, Lauren would have pitied her, even prayed for her. Instead, she shut the knowledge out of her heart and resolved to concentrate on her purpose—to survive. Adelle didn't deserve her compassion, not while she remained a formidable opponent with absolute power over her.

God had chosen to abandon her. She didn't know why, but the reality of her situation pained her deeper than any heartache or betrayal she could ever imagine from a person. If she couldn't depend on God, who could she depend on? Was there any point in this horrible existence she had now? She could see why Adelle succumbed. Lauren had no right to judge her, but she did despise her. She hated Adelle for what she had done to her and what she intended to do.

Lauren inched along the dark paneled wall for support. With the pianoforte in sight, she swallowed and pushed herself toward it. Someone slapped her on the rump. Lauren jerked as something stabbed her in the side. She cried out, tears stinging her eyes.

"Been wonderin' what happened to our music queen." A deep voice boomed beside her. Hearty laughter followed, but Lauren couldn't bring herself to respond. It took all her energy to keep going. How she would get through this night was beyond her. Mayhap she wouldn't have to worry about it if she managed to pass out. *Lord, if You haven't forsaken me and You won't free me from this place, be merciful and let me lose consciousness so I can at least escape the pain.*

She slid onto the pianoforte bench and placed her fingers on the cold keys. Lauren closed her eyes and let her mind drift into a Scottish hymnal that rested in her memory. It was lively enough to please them, but unknown to the average soul stuck in a bordello. Lauren smiled as she glanced up at the dark wall. At least, she could get away with this one small gift.

After Lauren played several more songs, she took a break to massage her stiff neck. She turned and heard a familiar male voice speaking in a Scottish accent. Prickles rose on her skin, up and down her arms. She sat still, afraid to hope, worried what he might think of her in a place like this. How could she look Malcolm MacGregor in the eyes after she had lectured him about her faith? Would he think her a hypocrite?

She scanned the faces of those busy in conversation and laughter. A myriad of sailors, labor men, and pirates filled the tavern. Many were deep in their cups and choosing their mates for the night. Lauren's heart ached to erase the last few weeks and pretend none of it had ever happened. Even if Malcolm no longer thought her worthy of him, Lauren longed to be free of this place. She took a deep breath, willing him to look up and find her.

Her gaze fell on swords and pistols hanging on the hips of men who were more than capable of murder. Fear gripped her insides and coiled in a tight ball, almost cutting off her air. Mayhap, it would be best if Malcolm didn't see her. She didn't want anything to happen to him.

Hazel eyes met Lauren's. Recognition lit Malcolm's face as he twisted his lips in angry disgust and strode toward her. Lauren's heart lifted in a mixture of hope and anxiety. She didn't see a weapon on Malcolm, but she knew he was too cunning to come here unprepared. He lifted a finger to his lips, indicating for her to keep quiet and not give him away.

Rob and Logan came in, separating around the room. More men came in whom Lauren had not seen in the last few weeks. She noticed them exchanging glances with Malcolm, Rob, and Logan.

"Cinnamon, play some more." A man with a thick brown beard thumped the table in a rhythm she didn't recognize.

Lauren turned and placed her fingers on the keys, releasing a light-hearted melody. A commotion took place behind her, but she kept playing, knowing that fights were quite common at the Pink House. Chairs scraped against the floor, voices grew louder, and punches hitting flesh caused a flood of emotion to swirl through her already tight nerves. Lauren fumbled the keys. Anxiety crawled from her hands, up her arms, and around her throat, gripping her in a mind-numbing state.

"Lauren, let us go." Malcolm's blessed voice appeared at her ear. Relief rushed through her, and she abandoned the pianoforte.

"Leave her alone!" Adelle yelled across the room. Logan held a pistol at her head as Rob fought one of the bodyguards. Some of the servants from Mallard Plantation were fighting others in the room. Girls screamed, crawled under tables, and cowered in the corner. A mug went flying over Lauren's head and smashed against the wall, landing on the pianoforte. Its contents dripped from the wall to the floor.

One of the guards finished a fight and stomped toward them.

"Malcolm!" She pointed behind him.

He swung in time, grabbed a sword from a fallen man, and slashed the bodyguard in the arm. Blood soaked his sleeve, but he didn't stop. The bodyguard swung his good arm in an arch. Malcolm lunged to the side, missing the blow.

Lauren stood and pressed her back against the wall. Several of Adelle's bodyguards had fallen. Two appeared dead. Logan tied Adelle to a chair as he shouted and pointed a finger in her face. One of Rob's servants lay lifeless as the rest continued to battle pirates and raucous sailors. Some whom she had never met fought alongside Malcolm and Logan. How had Malcolm convinced these men to risk their lives to rescue her? Another servant from Mallard Plantation fell. Pain sliced through Lauren's chest and side. Her breath came in short gasps, swelling against her broken ribs. Her vision faltered, and she blinked to stay conscious.

Malcolm slammed his fist into the guard's face and kicked him away. The guard staggered, tripping over a fallen bench and striking his head on the table, knocking him out. Malcolm turned back to Lauren and grabbed her arm to lead her out, but a man stepped back and bumped into her.

"Ohhh!" Pain ripped through her, and she slid to her knees, gasping for breath. She wrapped her free arm around herself. Tears pooled in her eyes as she blinked, staring at the dirty floor.

"Lauren, come on." Malcolm tried to help her rise.

"My ribs are broken." She struggled to her feet, wincing. Each breath was too painful to endure. "I canna ride."

"Pastor Brad is outside with a wagon. We came prepared with loggers an' some of my fighting friends. Pastor Brad figures if ye're here against yer will, there may be others, an' he wants to free them."

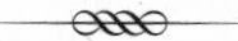

When they reached the front door, Lauren faltered. Malcolm swept her in his arms. She shut her eyes and went limp. He suspected she lost consciousness. Fear spiked in his gut as he rushed to the door, eager to assess her injuries. Malcolm carried her to the waiting wagon, where Pastor Brad paced. He unhooked his hands from behind his back and rushed to Malcolm.

"Ye found her." Pastor Brad paused in midstride. Malcolm laid Lauren on a bed of straw in the wagon. "What is wrong with her?

"I do not know." Malcolm shook his head, ignoring the increasing pressure rising inside him. "I believe she is suffering from a beating. She said her ribs are broken." Malcolm touched her chin, trailing a finger along her face. "Her jaw is swollen an' bruised. They tried to cover it with powder, but 'tis coming through."

"Poor lass." Pastor Brad clicked his tongue and shook his head. "I canna think of anyone who deserves better than Lauren Campbell. Do not worry, lad. She has a strong faith an' the Lord is with her. He led ye to her, did He not?"

"Aye." Malcolm nodded. "We need to get her home an' send someone for a doctor."

Logan and Rob returned with two women. One looked to be Lauren's age, while the other couldn't be more than ten and four. Malcolm's stomach tightened, almost making him ill. He swallowed the bile in the back of his throat and forced his mind on the task at hand.

"These two were forced to be here like Lauren. Given the opportunity, they wanted out." Logan assisted them into the back of the wagon as if they were both princesses. "We ought to burn that place down." His tone held the same bitterness that Malcolm felt.

"We shall fight them through the church," Pastor Brad said. "There are more people who are against these bordellos than for them. For now, let us get these lasses out of here to safety."

"Agreed." Malcolm strode to the front of the wagon and climbed up to take the reins. He waited for Logan and Rob to settle in the wagon bed beside the women. Pastor Brad and Malcolm's logging and fighter friends loaded in another wagon. They watched for signs of followers from the Pink House, but none came.

Malcolm flicked the reins, and the horses launched forward. He urged them to keep a brisk pace as he led them down Chalmers Street. He couldn't get away from this place fast enough. They passed other bordellos where prostitutes called out to men on the street. The smell of whiskey overcame the fresh scent of the nearby sea. It was shameful how rotten some people could make a place with such potential. At least, the rest of Charles Towne wasn't like this.

Soon they rolled down Meeting Street, and the change in scenery allowed Malcolm to breathe a sigh of relief. Now that he had Lauren, he would never let her out of his sight again. He could only imagine what she had endured and seen in that place. Now wasn't the time to think on it. Right now, he needed to stay focused on her recovery.

The sound of the rolling wagons must have alerted his mother to their return. She stepped out onto the porch and hurried down the steps to greet them.

"Where is Lauren? Did ye find her?" She leaned over the side as they rolled to a stop. "Oh my, what is wrong with the lass?"

"They beat her because she tried to escape." The younger girl said, glancing down at Lauren and touching her arm in concern. "But I have never seen her pass out before. You think she will be all right?"

"We hope so," Pastor Brad said. "Rob, would ye fetch the doctor?"

"Of course." Rob nodded, swinging his legs over the side and landing on his feet. "I shall get my horse. He should be well rested by now."

Malcolm set the brake and jumped down. He strode to the back and unlatched the gate. "Mither, before she fainted, Lauren told me her ribs are broken. Ready my bed so I can take her in directly. She can have my chamber."

"Aye, she will need a soft bed to rest an' recover." She rushed into the house while the other two girls scooted to the edge.

"Is there aught we can do?" the younger one asked. "I am Violet."

"Hold the front door open for me," Malcolm said. He glanced at the other girl. "If ye do not mind, make some tea for us."

They both nodded and left to take care of their tasks. He turned and met Pastor Brad's gaze. With a brief nod, both men maneuvered Lauren to the edge where Malcolm lifted her into his arms.

She groaned, and her eyes fluttered. "Malcolm." He coveted the way she whispered his name. If she intended to say anything else, it died upon her lips with another wince. Her face contorted in pain, and Malcolm's gut twisted in reaction.

Lauren had lost too much weight. He swallowed the rising emotion as he cradled her thin body against him. Did they starve her as well? Swift anger engulfed him. She moaned as he placed her on the bed.

Her eyes opened, registering on him. A slight smile lifted the corner of her pale lips. "Thank ye."

"I declare, lass, we shall have to fatten ye up, we will." His mother spread a quilt over her and patted the top of her hand.

"Iona." Lauren's eyes filled with tears. "I am so glad ye look well." She swallowed as a deep breath gushed out. Her shoulders shook. " 'Twas awful. I thought the Lord had forsaken me." Lauren sobbed, clutching at her side. A wrenching cry filled the chamber.

His mother leaned over to hug her as if she were her own daughter. "There, there, lass. Tell me all 'bout it." She motioned for everyone to leave.

Malcolm turned and strode from the room, shutting the door behind them. Lauren deserved this moment of privacy, and he wasn't sure he could handle hearing the intimate details—not yet, at least. He wouldn't be able to keep from retaliating against the hateful woman running the bordello. If he ended up in jail, how could he protect and care for Lauren? How would the townspeople react toward her once they heard of her disgrace? Would Lauren blame him for not rescuing her sooner? Malcolm closed his eyes and swallowed a new rising fear. Would she want to go home to her father in Scotland? Would he lose her?

14

Grateful to be alone with Iona, Lauren sobbed until she was so stuffy she couldn't breathe. Lauren confessed all that Adelle had done to her and intended to do if Malcolm hadn't rescued her. Iona sat on the edge of the bed and listened in silence. To Lauren's relief, her expression wasn't condemning but consoling. Her soft brown eyes filled with compassion and wisdom as she refrained from speaking, no doubt waiting for the right moment.

A knock sounded at the door, and Violet walked in with a tray of steaming hot tea.

"Violet, what are ye doing here?" Lauren asked.

"Your friends asked if anyone else wanted to come along." She shrugged. "I figured it might be my only chance to escape. Madame Adelle could not do aught with a gun pointed at her head."

"My son didn't have a gun, did he?" Iona laid a hand across her chest and turned a shade darker. Her wide eyes blinked in disapproval.

"I believe his name is Rob." Violet poured tea in both cups. "Sugar?" She lifted an eyebrow.

"Two lumps." Iona nodded, her shoulders releasing tension.

"The same," Lauren said.

"Pastor Brad was upset when I told him I am ten and four. He said he is going to help me find my parents." She handed Iona her tea and held out Lauren's. "Do you think he can really help me?" A wide smile brightened her face, and she straightened with a slight bounce. " 'Tis been almost a year since I was taken. Almost too good to believe."

"Well, believe it." Iona patted her arm in encouragement. " 'Tis a shame what those people are doing to young lasses."

"I shall be getting back to the kitchen. I do not want to leave Rose alone for too long." Violet headed for the door.

"Rose came too?" Lauren asked. "Who else?"

"Just us three. I think the others were too afraid." Violet swung the door open and gasped. A man with a black bag stood with a raised fist as if he was about to knock on the door.

"I am sorry." He grinned. "I am Dr. Drake."

"I was just leaving." Violet sneaked around him and ducked out of the chamber.

He walked in and set his bag on the side of the bed. "Looks like someone tried to break your jaw." He reached under Lauren's chin and nudged her head to the side so he could get a better look. "At least they did not succeed. You have a solid bone. Any trouble moving it when talking or chewing?"

" 'Tis tender and sore," Lauren said. "My ribs hurt more. I can hardly breathe. Feels like someone is piercing me with a broadsword."

"I am sorry, but I will need to take a look." Dr. Drake glanced at Iona. "Will you be able to assist me?"

"Aye." She nodded. "Tell me what to do."

The next few minutes proved to be torture as he moved Lauren around to examine her from front to back. He asked her a series of questions. Dr. Drake unbound her ribs and reset her with something sturdier.

He questioned her about personal details and the possibility of rape. Lauren could relieve his concerns on that score. She didn't share all the despicable things she witnessed, only what she thought might relate to her health. How could she explain the horrible nightmares and that she feared the marriage bed?

Much of the damage lingered in her mental state, taunting and torturing her as if she had been part of the acts. She felt dirty and ruined for having witnessed them and for being in the Pink House. Her bruises would eventually disappear, but her tarnished memories would remain. How could Malcolm want a woman like her? How would he feel when people talked about her? And she had no doubt that gossipers would talk.

"You have broken ribs on both sides," Dr. Drake said, leaning over her. "Breathing will be uncomfortable for a while. I recommend staying in bed with as little movement as possible for three weeks." He held up a finger and lowered his voice in severity. "Even if you begin to feel better, do not get up and start moving around. That is when the healing is critical. It may be better but not complete."

"I shall be tendin' to her an' I assure ye, she will be as still as a root." Iona walked to the foot of the bed and inclined her head at the doctor. "What about the pain?"

Dr. Drake pulled out a brown bottle from his bag and handed it to Iona. "I only want her taking this when the pain is unbearable during the day. Just a spoonful at night for the first three nights. 'Twill help her sleep, but I do not want her to become dependent on it.

" 'Tis a mixture of several things from my herbal garden. The starvation she has endured caused her to lose weight, and she is dehydrated. Start out giving her chicken broth and gradually increase her portions with vegetables, then breads and meats."

He placed his black hat on his head, picked up his bag, and walked to the door. Glancing over his shoulder, he said, "Send for me if you need me."

"We will." Iona pulled the covers up to Lauren's chin. "Lauren, I know ye need yer rest, but Rob asked if he could come in to see ye afore he leaves."

"I am feeling much better now that Dr. Drake is not moving me about." The pillows behind her helped prop her up so she could breathe better.

"Good, I shall get 'im." She walked across the hardwood floor. Lauren closed her eyes and listened to Iona's steps and the click of the doorknob with the creak of the hinges as it opened. Male voices rumbled from the hallway. Dr. Drake spoke with Rob and Malcolm about her condition.

Footsteps came closer. "Lauren, I am sorry for what my father had Fairbanks do while we were away." Remorse filled Rob's voice. She blinked and tried to focus on his face. His skin heated with shame. She reached out her hand. He dropped to his knees, gripping it. "I am so sorry." The whispered plea came out in a tremor.

" 'Tis not yer fault." She swallowed with difficulty. "What about my indenture?"

"I brought the original contract with me." Rob wiped his eyes and produced a rolled parchment. He pulled the string tying it together and opened it. Without a word, he ripped it in two. "I am taking this to the courthouse and officially releasing you. As far as the Mallard family is concerned, you are a free woman. The Pink House never exchanged written records with Fairbanks. 'Tis the risk Adelle took in being in the kind of business she is in." Rob turned to his new friend.

"Malcolm, you are my witness to tearing up this contract."

"Indeed, I am." Malcolm slapped Rob on the back in a friendly pat. "I am much obliged." The two men shook hands.

Rob turned back to Lauren and kissed the top of her hand. "I appreciate your forgiveness. I plan to return home and do as you suggested: take over the plantation, and run things better than my father did."

Lauren smiled. "Does that mean no more floggings?"

"None. They are now forbidden." He sliced his hand through the air. "I plan to hire someone to replace Stan Fairbanks before my father returns. Otherwise, he might try to rehire the man."

"Logan Grant might be a good overseer," Malcolm suggested.

"Actually, I was thinking you might." Rob raised a brow at Malcolm.

"Thank ye, but as soon is Lauren is well, I plan to resume the search for my sister. I may not be staying in the area."

Fear pierced Lauren's heart, and she couldn't suppress a gasp. It hadn't occurred to her that Malcolm and Iona might leave Charles Towne. What would she do?

"What is wrong?" Malcolm leaned toward her, touching his knuckles to her forehead.

"Where might ye be going?" she asked, hating how her voice now sounded like a croaking frog.

"Wilmington, North Carolina."

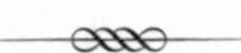

After everyone left and while Lauren slept, Malcolm and his mother settled in the parlor. She sat in her wooden chair and picked up her sewing kit. Too much silence grated on Malcolm's nerves and left him to imagine the worst. He turned to his mother. "What did Lauren tell ye, 'bout the Pink House? What did they do to her?"

"I am surprised at ye, Malcolm." She frowned, looking up at him from her sewing. Lines formed around her mouth as she gave him a hard stare. Malcolm shifted in his seat across from her, feeling like a lad once again. Her stern tone sounded as if it belonged to a robust woman half her age. "Ye know I will not betray Lauren's trust, no matter that ye're my son. I will tell ye this. She has been through quite an ordeal. Ye'll have to be patient with 'er. 'Twill take time for her to heal, both physically an' emotionally."

He stood and paced in front of the dark fireplace, rubbing the back of his neck. "One minute I want to know the details, an' the next I would rather not know a thing." He leaned an elbow on the wooden mantel next to a vase of wildflowers his mother had picked. "A fickle mind has never been part of my character."

"Do not be so hard on yerself, lad. 'Tis a difficult situation, to be sure." She poked her needle through the fabric. "Ye'll hear naught from me."

"I shall try to get another job over the next few weeks while Lauren heals."

"Mayhap the loggers will take ye back." Her hopeful tone tugged at his heart. At least the fighting money he had earned would last them for a while.

"Lauren seemed a wee bit distant toward me earlier today," Malcolm said, worried she had changed her mind about him. He shrugged. "I am not sure what to expect."

"Give her time." His mother looped her needle and thread, pulling until it stopped. "She may never be herself again."

"I understand, but somethin' is not right." Malcolm shook his head, unconvinced. "She will not look me in the eye. She has naught to be ashamed of."

"She will come 'round. Ye will see."

Over the next three days, Lauren slept a great deal and talked very little. Malcolm watched her at times, taking turns with his mother. He bought her a new Bible, thinking she might enjoy reading it while she healed, but it still lay on the table by her bed in the same position. If he hadn't known her before her experience at the Pink House, he wouldn't have guessed her to be a faith-filled woman. The knowledge seared him through to the heart, especially since she was the one who inspired his returning faith.

His mother took Lauren a plate to break her fast. Malcolm followed a few moments later with a fresh cup of coffee. Lauren sat up, wincing at the effort as his mother propped pillows behind her. Then she placed the tray on Lauren's lap.

Malcolm handed the steaming cup to her. Their gazes met as she accepted the mug. His warm fingers touched hers, sending a tingle through his hand and up his arm. Her pleasant expression shifted to instant dislike, and she jerked away.

Her reaction stung. He swallowed his disappointment and tried to hide his embarrassment by pretending nothing had happened. "Did ye sleep well?"

"Aye, and yer mither spoils me with her great cooking." Lauren bit into a warm biscuit.

" 'Tis enough ye like it." His mother strode toward the door. "I have a few things to do in the kitchen. Malcolm will keep ye company for now."

Malcolm stood in awkward silence while she chewed. Even if she wanted him to leave, this time he would not. He had been too accommodating in the last few weeks. He ached to be near her, to help her overcome the bad memories. If only she would allow him to love her beyond the hidden chambers of her heart, he would show her how much he cared for her.

"I am glad to see ye eating more. Ye've lost so much weight." Malcolm sat in a chair and scooted it closer to the bed. "Kathleen will be coming over today with Deidra and Logan after work."

"What about ye?" she asked, fingering the patterned quilt his mother just finished making last week. "I thought ye planned to go back to work?"

"Why do ye want me gone?" Malcolm leaned his elbows on his knees. As he studied her, he willed Lauren to look at him. "Lauren, do I make ye uncomfortable, lass? It seems as if ye're avoiding me."

"Nay, not ye, Malcolm." She picked up a slice of ham and paused. " 'Tis me. I am the one who has changed."

She bit into the meat and chewed, keeping her gaze averted. Frustration welled inside Malcolm, but he forced himself to remain still. He didn't know what to say, but he refused to give up.

"Lauren, I do not know what ye're thinking, but I want ye to know that my feelings toward ye have not changed." She gulped. Anxiety increased his pulse. "Do ye not believe me?" When she didn't answer, Malcolm reached for her hand. "Lauren?"

"I believe," she snatched her hand away, "that ye want things to continue as before." She shook her head and tears filled her eyes. "But they canna."

"Why?" He gripped his knees to keep from grabbing her. "I do not understand. Even if they took yer innocence, 'tis ye I care 'bout. I am sorry they hurt ye, but I do not want them to win. Ye canna let them steal our happiness, Lauren."

"They may not have stolen the innocence of my body, but they took it in every other way." Tears filled her eyes. "Everything I believed has been shattered. I had so much faith." A bitter laugh erupted from her, scorching him inside. "I actually thought that God would protect me—that He would keep me from harm. I prayed and prayed." A sob broke from her. "Why would He let them do those things to me if He loves me?" Her voice broke into a fading whisper.

An ache in the back of Malcolm's throat stalled his voice. He blinked back tears of his own. Her pain ran so deep, he could feel it, and it made sense he would. They both had the same Holy Spirit residing in them. He realized that now.

He lunged out of his chair and braced himself on his knees beside her. Malcolm gripped her face in his hands and forced her to look at him. "I do not have all the answers, nor do I know all that happened to ye or what ye witnessed. It does not matter." He wiped her tears with his thumb. "What does matter is, I shall be right here as ye heal. I will not let ye go through this alone."

"Malcolm, I do not doubt yer love. I know that ye would have saved me sooner if ye could."

"Then why doubt God's love?"

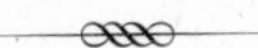

Malcolm's simple question made Lauren sound illogical. How could he be so different? It was only a few months ago he thought the Lord had placed the MacGregors under a curse. He of all people should understand her feelings—at least her anger.

"I question God's love over yers because unlike ye, He has the ability to protect me from all harm and evil. He can do what ye canna." Now that the words were spoken aloud, it felt as if her heart cracked open and bled out all her emotions at once. She shoved her tray aside, blinking to keep the threatening tears away. "Please, I am tired. I want to rest now."

She lay back and closed her eyes, listening for the sound of his departure. Instead, he sighed, and the chair creaked with his shifting weight. Would she have to ask him to leave?

She waited. Silence followed. The stubborn man! He knew she wanted to be alone. Could he not give her privacy to cry alone?

"Malcolm, would ye call yer mither? I need assistance with the chamber pot." That would guarantee his removal. To her satisfaction, footsteps walked to the door, and the lock clicked as he turned the knob and swung it open. "Lauren, do not be like me. Blaming God will not change what happened. Bitterness only makes ye feel worse—rotten."

His parting words brought tears to her eyes. She sniffed and wiped her face. To keep from hurting her ribs, she let her breath out slow and easy. Months ago, she would have been thrilled to hear Malcolm say that. Confusion swirled inside her.

After Iona helped her, Lauren dozed into a fitful sleep. She dreamed she and Malcolm were back on *The Sea Lady*, and this time her family and all of Malcolm's were aboard. She stood beside Malcolm at the rail, facing both their families. Frowns marred their expressions, and they spewed accusations. Malcolm glanced down at her with a mischievous grin, not caring about their displeasure. He grabbed her hand, and the two of them jumped into the sea.

Lauren screamed, certain they would drown so far out in the deep. She woke thrashing. Gentle hands grabbed her arms. "Shush! Lass, it was just a dream. 'Tis all." Iona sat on the bed and embraced her like a daughter. She stroked Lauren's long hair. "That is better."

"I am sorry," Lauren said. "I wish I was not so much trouble."

"Not at all." Iona patted her arm before standing. She strode to the dresser and grabbed Lauren's brush. "Let me brush yer hair an' make ye presentable to yer visitors when they arrive."

Having Iona tend to her in such a loving manner made her long for a place in the MacGregor family. Her thoughts shifted to her own family. She wondered if her father had gotten her letter by now. Was he heartbroken because he missed her and worried for her welfare? Or was he merely angry at having lost a possession and being bested by a MacGregor? Lauren wasn't even sure if he would come for her. Most likely, he would be too busy with other matters and would send a few men to bring her back. When they arrived, would she return with them?

By the time her friends arrived, Lauren felt better. Kathleen and Deidra were in lively spirits, and their good moods brightened Lauren's. Logan kept Malcolm occupied, while she and Iona were able to enjoy the women's company.

"How do ye like yer new teaching position?" Lauren asked Kathleen, pleased to see her in a new floral print dress, trimmed in lace around the wrists and across the neckline. She now wore the proper corsets to bring the skirt out around her hips and to accentuate her waist. "Ye look lovely."

"Thank ye." She glanced down at her clothing before sitting in a chair that Malcolm had placed by the bed. Wearing a simple brown dress and matching bonnet, Deidra sat in another chair beside her.

"Being a schoolteacher is all that I hoped it would be. 'Tis solid, respectable work an' I can afford to live alone 'til I marry."

"Logan says I do not need a job now that he is a logger." Deidra crossed her arms with a frown. She cast her blue eyes toward the door where Logan and Malcolm talked in the parlor. "I would like to do somethin' besides keep house an' cook."

"Be thankful ye have each other." Kathleen leaned toward her. "I miss my family terribly. It is hard once they are gone. The sea took my father, and my mother died of consumption. As an only child, I would love to have an older brother who could care for me."

Lauren thought about her brother, Scott. Would he bother to care for her if he were here? At home he rarely noticed her. He spent most of his time trying to please their father and impressing his friends, especially the lasses. A dull ache pressed her.

"Let us talk about happy things," Lauren said. "I have had enough sadness to last me a lifetime. What good news have ye brought?"

"Aye, I would like to hear some good news as well." Iona carried a tray with tea and the bread cakes she had baked earlier in anticipation of their visit. She poured the first cup and handed it to Kathleen.

"That reminds me." Kathleen pulled open her reticule and dug into it. She pulled out a folded letter. "This came for ye, Iona. The postmaster asked if I would bring it since I planned to visit."

Iona accepted it but handed it right back. "No need in pretendin' I can read it." She tilted her head with discomfort in her eyes. "Would ye mind?"

"Of course not." Kathleen split the seal and unfolded the thick parchment. "Dear Mrs. MacGregor. I received your letter inquiring after your daughter, Carleen MacGregor. I did purchase her indenture to serve on my rice plantation for seven years. She is here and doing well. You should be proud. She is one of the hardest workers I have seen. I myself was an indentured servant when I came here fifteen years ago. If you would like to visit, my place is located in New Hanover County, North Carolina, about ten miles south of Wilmington, one of our port cities. Sincerely, Oliver Bates."

Silent tears crawled down Iona's cheeks. After a few moments, she smiled and gasped with relief. "Thank the good Lord, she is well." She wiped at her eyes. "We need to tell Malcolm."

"I shall do it." Deidra bounced to her feet and rushed out the chamber door, much like an excited child. "Malcolm, we have great news!"

Iona came and sat on the side of the bed and took Lauren's hand in hers. "As soon as ye're able to travel, we will go to North Carolina."

"But that may not be for another couple of weeks." Lauren sputtered, surprised by Iona's generosity to include her. "I would not dream of making ye wait on me. Ye should go as soon as possible. Mayhap, I could continue recovering at Deidra's house." Lauren glanced at her friend for confirmation as she returned to the chamber with Malcolm and Logan on her heels.

"I would consider it a blessin' if ye stay with us." Deidra sat down and folded her hands. "I am sure Logan would not mind."

"But I would." Malcolm braced an arm against the threshold. "I promised myself that I would not let Lauren out of my sight after what happened to her. She is part of the family now."

"I agree." Iona nodded.

"But, Malcolm, Rob posted a letter to my father before I was forced to leave Mallard Plantation," Lauren said. "He could arrive in Charles Towne anytime. I canna leave."

Malcolm guided their new wagon on Meeting Street toward home. Over the past week, he had taken another logger position. It didn't pay as much as his previous position, but he couldn't afford to refuse it.

"I wish Lauren had been well enough to attend church this morning," his mother said. "I think it might have done her some good. She has been too depressed lately."

"Aye," Malcolm nodded. "I do not know how to help her. At least her ribs hurt her less."

"Only the Lord can help her right now, but she seems determined to reject Him." His mother dropped her head in sad disappointment. "I tried to pray with her the other night, but she refused."

"When we were on *The Sea Lady*, she prayed often. She shared her faith in how she lived." Malcolm cleared his throat and swallowed his emotions. "I do not understand what happened. I thought her faith was stronger than what happened."

"Her faith alone may not be strong enough, and that is the problem," she said. "Lauren is angry at God, and so she is not leaning on Him for the strength she needs to get through this."

Malcolm listened as he pulled the reins to the right and guided the horse onto Society Street. The wheels jostled over the cobbled road as the sun brightened the day. They rode under the shade of a tree, giving Malcolm better vision from the rays. A slight movement caught his attention by the side of the house. A saddled horse stood tethered to a tree.

"Who would be calling on a Sunday morning without notice?" Malcolm asked.

"I do not know." His mother leaned forward, shielding her eyes from the sun. "I do not recognize the horse."

Malcolm slapped the reins and urged the horse to increase his speed. Something didn't feel right. His gut twisted in eerie warning. He raced the wagon up to the house and set the brake.

"Stay here and scream if you see anyone ye do not know." Malcolm jumped to the ground and crept to the house.

"Malcolm, ye're being a bit extreme," she said. "I am sure 'tis someone paying Lauren a wee visit."

"Everyone we know is at church somewhere or on their way home this morning." After a closer inspection of the horse, he still didn't know to whom it belonged. His heart thumped as he peered around the corner toward the back. One of the guards from the Pink House picked at the door lock.

Rage ripped through Malcolm. He ran toward the man with a raised fist, breathing hard. The intruder sensed his presence and turned in time to deflect his attack. Malcolm blocked the blade coming at him with his other hand. It went flying into the grass. He took that moment to shove a fist into the man's stomach and rammed his other fist into his jaw, knocking him off balance. Malcolm stepped forward, taking advantage of his momentum and grabbed the man's shirt, jerking him.

"Why are ye here?" Malcolm demanded. Thoughts of how this man beat his wee Lauren made him want to give him a good beating. Instead, Malcolm slammed him up against the back of the house. "Ye had better speak up. I am in no humor to be toyed with."

His evil grin revealed a missing top tooth. Malcolm's stomach revolted at the stench of his body odor. Why wasn't he the least bit worried about his situation? Did the man have a death wish?

Frustrated beyond words, Malcolm punched the man's nose. "I asked ye a question." Blood spattered, and his expression lost some of his pleasure.

"Madame wanted her girl back." He shrugged. " 'Tis as simple as that. She made an investment, an' now she wants to make her money back."

"Tell her she made a bad investment." Malcolm shoved the man away from him and kicked the discarded blade into the grass. "Walk back on foot."

"But my horse . . ." He pointed to the side of the house.

"Is now mine," Malcolm said. "Anything ye bring while trespassing on my property, ye might as well consider it confiscated." Malcolm lifted a finger. "In fact, consider it payment for all the wrong ye did to Lauren—not that a price could be set for the kind of harm an' torture ye inflicted."

"Ye cannot steal a man's horse."

"But ye can go around stealin' people?" Malcolm raised his voice and came at him. The man backed up, an expression of fear finally registering in his dark eyes and twisted mouth. "Get out of my sight before I am tempted to do more."

The man turned and ran. Malcolm hurried back to the wagon to make sure his mother was well. He helped her down. "Come on. I need to see Lauren."

"Who was that man an' why was he bleedin'?" she asked, trying to keep up with Malcolm's pace.

"He was from the bordello. An' I hit him. He is blessed I did not do more." Grateful he had placed new locks on the doors, Malcolm fumbled putting the key into the lock. It finally gave way. He shoved the door open.

"Lauren?" No answer. He hurried to the kitchen in the back where she crouched on the floor, clutching an iron scoop from the fireplace. No doubt, she intended to use it as a weapon. Silent tears streamed down her face as she hugged her knees, trembling. "Lauren, he is gone. No one will hurt ye." Malcolm dropped to his knees in front of her. He wanted to pull her into his arms and comfort her, but he sensed he should approach her with caution. Instead, he touched her hands. "I promise ye're safe now."

She met his gaze, her blue eyes engulfed in a sea of red. "I made up my mind. I would rather die than go back to that place. At least heaven would be safer."

"True, but I am a wee bit selfish." He offered her a grin and squeezed her hand for emphasis. "I would rather keep ye here with me a while longer."

"Why? Why would ye want a broken woman who needs to be coddled and pampered to get through each day?" Her eyes narrowed.

"Because ye are not broken, only wounded. And God heals an' binds our wounds." He stroked her hair. "An' because I love ye."

"I am afraid ye love the woman I was." Tears slid down her face. "I canna even find myself—seems as if I am floating through the days in some foggy haze."

"Lauren, this morning, the pastor read something that I want to share with ye. I memorized it. Now that God is helping me be a better man, I want to love ye with the passion born from the fruit of the Spirit. 'Tis the everlasting love of joy, peace, longsuffering, gentleness, goodness, faith, meekness, and temperance. I want to give ye more than a passionate love that fades with time, age, and hardship. Through Christ, we can have true love—the way it is meant to be between a man an' a woman. I never realized it could be this way, 'til ye came into my life, an' I began to see God through yer eyes."

15

Lauren was speechless after Malcolm's declaration. He was too good to be true. In Scotland, she had dreamed of such a man, but back then she wouldn't have imagined that Malcolm MacGregor could turn out to be so principled and God-fearing. She reached out to hug him and seek the comfort he offered, but he misinterpreted her actions and helped her rise from the floor.

"Thank ye . . . for everything." Inadequate words compared to all the things he had done for her. Would he still feel the same way about her if he knew other men had seen her body? Shame crawled into her cheeks at the memories. She could never consider marriage without being honest about her past.

" 'Twas naught. I wish I could have saved ye from . . ." His neck and face turned the color of his russet hair.

The urge to run her fingers through it compelled her. Lauren dug her nails into her palm. What was wrong with her? She had never experienced such feelings before. Mayhap, her time at the Pink House had turned her into a wanton woman.

"I shall take ye back to yer chamber." He took her elbow and helped her stand.

"Aye, an' I shall get us some food cookin'." Iona pulled off her bonnet and tied an apron around her dress.

"Actually, now that I am up, I would like to sit for a while in the parlor," Lauren said. "A change in scenery will do me good. I am tired of lying in that bed staring at the same four walls."

"I suppose it is rather dreary." Iona paused in thought. "It should have occurred to me to decorate the walls with somethin'."

"I did not mean to sound ungrateful." Lauren touched her fingers to her lips. The last thing she wanted was to offend them when they had opened their home to her, served her daily, and shared their food with her. "I only meant that 'twould be more cheerful to be allowed outside my chamber now that I can sit up and move without pain. I like yer company . . . both of ye." Her gaze traveled from Iona to Malcolm.

"No need to explain yerself, lass." Iona gave her a genuine smile. "We understand. Malcolm, take her into the parlor and keep her company while I cook us a decent meal."

"Aye, I could use some stimulating conversation." Malcolm took her elbow and led her from the kitchen, down the narrow hallway, past the bedchambers, and to the parlor at the front of the house. As soon as he had her seated in a wooden chair with a thick cushion, someone knocked on the door.

"I wonder who that could be?" he muttered as he went to answer it.

"Malcolm MacGregor. 'Tis good to see ye, my friend." Pastor Brad's voice carried inside. "I preached a short sermon this morn so I could pay ye a wee visit."

"We are glad to have ye." Malcolm swung the door wide and stepped aside. The elder man's eyes landed on Lauren, and his grin broadened.

"Lass, ye're a sight for sore eyes." He strode across the hardwood floor and bent to take Lauren's hands in his own. "I am so glad to see ye up an' well. I have been thinkin' 'bout ye."

"Thank ye. Glad to see ye're well." Lauren forced a smile and pulled her hands away from his. She gestured to a chair across from her as Malcolm closed the front door. "Please, have a seat."

"I shall let Mither know we have a visitor." Malcolm glanced over his shoulder. "Pastor, I hope ye'll stay an' eat with us. 'Tis the first day Lauren will be joining us at the table." Malcolm winked in her direction. "A cause for celebration."

" 'Twould be honored." Pastor Brad looked at Lauren. "I came by because I thought ye might like to know what happened to yer friends."

"Indeed, I would." Lauren scooted to the edge of her seat. Guilt sliced through her already frazzled brain at being so immersed in her own worries, she hadn't considered her friends. Worse, she hadn't even thanked God for freeing them.

"Violet was taken in by a young couple who have a new infant son. The new mither is not recovering as fast as hoped. Violet will help with the household chores and the new bairn."

"Do they know about her past?" Lauren asked.

"Aye, in fact, they have agreed to help Violet find her parents." He held up a finger. "After learning that she was stolen at the age of ten and two and held prisoner in such a place, the deacons and elders of our church plan to petition Charles Towne to end such practices."

"What about Violet? Is she embarrassed by this? Some may not be so understanding." Lauren thought back to all the women she had known in Scotland who talked about the poor and anyone who had questionable behavior. "Has she attended yer church?"

"Aye," he nodded, "an' she was accepted by all. I canna speak for other churches, but our congregation wants to do something about this atrocity." He scratched his temple and cleared his throat as Malcolm entered the room and sat by Lauren. "I know ye might be questioning why God allowed this to happen, but look at all the good coming from it. Two other lasses were set free. People are now aware of it and trying to stop it from happening to others."

Lauren glanced at her hands in her lap. Such positive results should have made her feel better, but for some reason it didn't. She felt used.

"Rose, your other friend, has been given a room at a boarding-house. Her rent is free for the first couple of months to give her time to find a respectable position."

"Pastor Brad, I am verra happy for them, but they must be careful," Lauren said. "One of the guards from the bordello tried to break into our house while Malcolm and Iona were at church this morning."

"Aye." Malcolm nodded, linking his fingers and setting his elbows on his knees as he leaned forward. "When I demanded to know what he wanted, he said to get Madame's investment back." He rubbed the back of his neck. "If warned, they can take precaution."

"What are ye going to do, Malcolm?" Pastor Brad asked, rubbing his chin in thought. "If he came once, what is to keep him from coming back while ye're at work?"

"I have not thought of that." Lauren gasped, hating the immediate fear rising inside. She shot a glance in Malcolm's direction. Would it be improper to beg him to never leave her side again?

Malcolm couldn't get Lauren's stricken look out of his mind. Her fear was real and warranted. Pastor Brad agreed to come back on Monday to stay with Lauren and his mother while he worked, but that was only a temporary solution.

Malcolm spent a long day bringing down trees. He was dirty and sweaty, but he couldn't let that deter him. By late afternoon, Malcolm rode by Dr. Drake's house to see if he could speak with him. To his relief a candle burned in the upper window since the sun had set on the other side of the house. Dr. Drake's office was on the first floor, but his living compartments were on the second.

Malcolm reined in his horse and dismounted. He tied the animal to a post Dr. Drake had installed in front of his office for patients. Malcolm walked to the thick brown door. A bell hung from the top of the threshold with a string hanging down. Malcolm tugged, and the loud clinking sound echoed through the house.

Footsteps clambered down the stairs toward the door. The lock clicked, and the bolt slid to the side. Dr. Drake greeted him with a pair of spectacles perched on his nose. His somber expression lifted in surprise.

"Malcolm, how is Lauren?" Dr. Drake asked, pushing his spectacles higher on his nose.

"Fine, but I do have some concerns. Could we talk?" Malcolm pulled his hat off.

"Come in." Dr. Drake opened the door wider. "Would you like something to drink?"

"I am too dirty to ruin yer good furniture." Malcolm gestured to his rumpled and soiled breeches and shirt.

"Nonsense." Dr. Drake waved him inside and left him standing at the door. Malcolm had no choice but to follow if he wanted to talk to him. A sliver of light shone from the window as the sun faded from the sky. Malcolm trailed Dr. Drake past cabinets full of medicine bottles and medical tools he didn't recognize.

Dr. Drake lit a lantern and sat in a wooden chair by the empty fireplace. Malcolm stood. Books lined several bookcase shelves on the other side. "Sit down, Malcolm. 'Tisn't likely you will hurt a wooden chair."

With a sigh, Malcolm sat in the chair he indicated and launched into the story of how Lauren was still in danger from the guards at the bordello and his need to search for his sister. "I would like to leave the area as soon as possible. I do not want people to know 'bout our departure or where we are goin'." Malcolm crossed his booted ankle over his knee. "But I need to know if Lauren is well enough to travel. I canna do anything to harm her further, nor can I continue to work and allow her an' my mither to be unprotected."

Dr. Drake pressed his lips into a frown. "Ye do have a dilemma, but I would say the worst damage would be for those people to get her again." He stroked his mustache. "I had hoped to give her more time to heal before undertaking such travel. Do ye know how far ye will be going? There is naught but miles of wilderness outside of Charles Towne. The roads are treacherous and overgrown in areas. Ye could encounter danger from wild beasts or even Indians."

"I know, but the alternative to staying is not much better. We shall be going to Wilmington, North Carolina. I am not sure how far it is." Malcolm pinched his eyebrows in concern. "If they do not leave her alone, I shall be forced to protect her. What good would it do me to end up in jail?"

"I think you would have plenty of people to testify on your behalf, and if they trespass, it could be considered self-defense." Dr. Drake rubbed his mouth in distress. "I shall come by and see her tomorrow. I will let you know what I think. The last time I saw her, she was healing well, better than I thought she might."

"Thank ye." Malcolm sighed with relief.

"Try to create a padded pallet that she can lie on in the wagon bed so the jarring over uneven ground will not hurt her as much. I still do not want her lifting anything. 'Tis a long way. There is more land here in the colonies than England and Scotland combined."

"So I have heard." Malcolm grinned. "Mayhap, 'tis time we get a look at some of it. I might want to purchase a few acres myself. I have never had the chance to own land afore."

"I would feel more comfortable if you had others traveling with ye," Dr. Drake said. "There might be a few waterways you will need to cross. I shall try to get my hands on a map of the Carolinas for ye."

"That is more than I could hope for." Malcolm thought about what Pastor Brad said about his church petitioning the town and what Dr. Drake said about testifying on his behalf. "I have one more favor to ask."

"Name it." Dr. Drake sat back and waited.

"Pastor Brad has a small church in north Charles Towne. They saved two other lasses from the same bordello where Lauren was an' plan to petition the town to stop the practice of takin' lasses against their will. Can they count on yer support when the time comes?"

"Of course." He nodded. "I am appalled by what I have witnessed. Most people do not know about it, but we can change that."

"Not even Logan knows of our sudden plans to leave, only Pastor Brad." Malcolm rose, and Dr. Drake followed, holding out his hand.

"I will keep your confidence on the matter." Dr. Drake shook his hand. "I shall be over first thing in the morning."

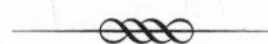

This time when Dr. Drake poked at Lauren and rolled her over, the experience wasn't as painful. He asked a few questions and nodded at her answers. Malcolm waited in the parlor, while Iona stayed in the chamber with her.

Afterward, Dr. Drake left her chamber and spoke to Malcolm outside her door. She could hear the rumble of their voices as Iona helped her rebutton her blouse.

"He seemed quite pleased with how well yer ribs are healin'," Iona said. She rubbed her hands in obvious excitement. "I have been prayin' for ye, lass. An' the good Lord has seen fit to answer my prayers."

"I appreciate all ye've done." Lauren touched her arm. "And for keeping my confidence. I am sure it is not easy, especially with a son like Malcolm asking so many questions."

" 'Tis the least I could do." Iona's smile faded, and she looked down at her feet. "We all know it would not have happened if I would have stayed at Mallard Plantation. No one in their right mind would have dragged an auld woman like me to a bordello."

"Iona, 'twas not yer fault." Lauren gripped her shoulders. "Please, do not think on it. The whole thing will make ye mad. Believe me, I know."

"I want ye to know Malcolm only asks about ye because he cares." Iona's brown eyes met hers, and Lauren sensed the concern of a mother's heart. "In fact, I have never known him to be so worried 'bout anyone afore."

"I know. Malcolm is a wonderful man." Lauren stepped back and glanced at the closed door. "I admit I did not realize it at first, but now I have no doubt."

A knock sounded at the door.

"Come in," Lauren called.

"Dr. Drake has left." Malcolm peered around the door. "He said ye're well enough to travel. The sooner we are out o' here, the better." He held up a rolled parchment tied with a black ribbon. "He also brought us a map. Would ye mind helping me read some of the markings?"

"Coming." Lauren gripped her skirt and joined Malcolm in the kitchen where he unrolled the map. He spread the ends out on the table and set small spice jars at the corners.

"I shall make us some tea." Iona sailed past them to the cooking pot and poured water from a pitcher.

"Here we are in Charles Towne." Malcolm pointed to an area of the map indicating a port city. "I have seen the name enough to recognize it."

"If ye would allow me, I could teach ye to read," Lauren offered, hoping he wouldn't be offended.

"There is naught I would love more." His grin widened as if he had been waiting for her to make the offer. No pride lurked in his expression. He leaned close and lowered his voice. "I look forward to the time it will bring us together."

"I shall be teaching ye with yer mither," Lauren whispered. "I plan to take up her lessons where we left off back in Scotland."

"Can I not have private lessons?" He raised an eyebrow.

"Nay," Lauren shook her head, smiling. "I must conserve my strength and teach ye both at once."

She knew her face flushed from Malcolm's flirtations, but she couldn't help it. The man affected her in ways no one else ever had. Now that he had made his peace with God, he fit all her dreams in a husband. His lack of fortune still wouldn't be good enough for her father, but that didn't matter here in the colonies. What if she never saw her father again? The thought didn't pain her as much as the fear of never seeing Malcolm again.

"Indeed, ye're right as usual." Malcolm twisted his lips and appeared to contemplate the matter.

"Malcolm, stop teasing the lass and let her take a look at that map." Iona winked at Lauren as she pulled down three mugs from a shelf.

"This is Wilmington—about one hundred eighty miles from here," Lauren said. "If we can travel twenty-five to thirty miles a day, we could make it in six or seven days."

"Looks like we will have to cross some waterways." Malcolm pointed at the water canals and rivers.

"We could try to purchase tickets to sail north. Would that be easier?" Lauren asked.

"Aye, it might be easier, but then we would have to wait for a ship goin' that way." Malcolm folded his arms. "We need money for the tickets, an' we might have to leave behind some of the things we have acquired an' start over again."

"But we would not have to worry about Indians, wild beasts, and criminals on the road." All of a sudden, the thought of traveling by land sounded daunting. Lauren wasn't sure she was up to it. "Will there even be roads in some places? Or will we be forced to traipse through the wilderness without any path?"

"According to Dr. Drake, the roads are more like pathways, but I am sure others have gone this route afore." Malcolm shrugged. " 'Tis too dangerous for ye to stay here, Lauren, an' I will not risk yer safety. We need to leave as soon as possible, an' I do not want anyone to know we are leavin'."

"Do not forget that Carleen already took this route." Iona poured tea in each cup. "We have multiple reasons for this trip. Mayhap we will meet up with people along the way who may have seen her."

Guilt tore at Lauren's conscience. How could she have forgotten about Carleen? Iona and Malcolm had put off this trip to rescue and take care of her, and here she complained about the discomfort of such a journey. She should be doing everything in her power to help them. What if Carleen had suffered a similar fate as hers or was beaten daily by a horrible overseer? What if her owner lied about her welfare in his letter?

"Ye're right." Lauren rubbed her lips together, determined to change her behavior.

"I plan to go out an' purchase a traveling trunk," Malcolm said. "Can ye both share it?"

"Of course." Iona nodded. "We do not have that much. Ye would not mind, would ye, lass?"

"Nay." Lauren shook her head, determined not to be more of a burden. Eventually she would have to find a way to support herself or return home to Scotland. The thought brought a twinge of pain to her chest, but what were her options? Malcolm said that he loved her but had not proposed.

"I would like to post a letter to my father before we leave," she said.

"Ye intend to return home?" Malcolm gave her a stricken look. Lauren wasn't sure if he was angry or disgusted that she still harbored sentiment for his great enemy—even if Duncan Campbell was her father. Malcolm straightened, staring at her. "The way ye've been talkin', I thought ye had set yer mind on stayin' here in the colonies."

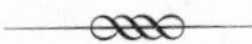

Lauren sat on the wagon seat next to Iona. After Malcolm returned home with their trunk, she and Iona packed their clothes and other possessions, but neither of them would allow Lauren to help with anything else.

Malcolm made a soft feather mattress and set it in the wagon bed for her. He wanted her to begin her journey lying on it, but she refused, saying she would lie down when she was tired or as the ground grew too bumpy and jarred her. Every few minutes he kept glancing in her direction. He wore a frown that made her uncomfortable. While his displeasure bothered her, she hated the thought of being in that covered wagon longer than necessary.

"Lad, stop glaring at the lass like that." Iona patted his arm. "I daresay, if Lauren begins to feel poorly, she will go inside an' lie down. Now let her enjoy the sunshine."

"Ye do not know her like I do." He shifted on his seat. "Back on the ship, she worked herself to the bone. She does not know when to take proper rest or nourishment."

"That is not so," Lauren said. "People were dying and depending on me. This is quite different."

She adjusted her bonnet to shield her eyes from the sun as they climbed a hill. They were three hours past Charles Towne, and Lauren estimated the time to be midmorning. Her stomach grumbled in spite of the porridge she consumed before they left. She figured it was a good sign that she was mending.

The sound of birds chirping in the trees, the clip-clop of the horse's hooves, and the rolling of the wagon wheels were enough to lull anyone to sleep. Lauren longed for conversation. She had spent too much time in her chamber alone, even though Iona and Malcolm often came to visit.

It felt wonderful to be outdoors again, breathing in the fresh air. The bordello had reeked of too many stenches she wished would leave her memory. She filled her lungs with the aroma of pine trees, grass, and earth. It was refreshing now that breathing no longer hurt.

"I believe the country suits me." She smiled, looking up at the blue sky, glad there wasn't a cloud around.

"This is beyond country," Iona said, her face taking on an unpleasant expression. " 'Tis pure wilderness. For myself, I would prefer a few neighbors, mind ye, nice neighbors."

"I would not." Malcolm shook his head. "Look at all this vast land. 'Tis waitin' to be explored." He gestured to the empty field around them. A mixture of wild daisies, dandelions, and small yellow flowers nestled among the tall grass. "I could see a beautiful farm with grazing animals. 'Twould be a pity for people to ruin it with houses so close together one could not fit a carriage between them or with roads going in all directions."

"Aye, I think ye're right, Malcolm." Lauren gripped the seat to steady her balance. "I would much rather have my home someplace out here." She wanted to add the words "with you" but dared not. Instead, her gaze rested on Malcolm's eyes, willing him to see the love she harbored for him. They stared at each other over his mother's gray head.

"Do ye really feel that way, lass?" He dipped his head toward her, his hat casting his hopeful expression in the shade. "I thought ladies loved being 'round society an' all the parties?"

"I thought ye knew me better than that by now." She couldn't hide the disappointment in her tone. After traveling halfway around the world and enduring so much together, did he not know that society could never dictate her actions or be her self-fulfillment? " 'Tis one of the things I always enjoyed about Kilchurn Manor. Our remote lands were well away from big cities like Edinburgh and Galloway."

At the mention of Kilchurn, his smile faded, and he turned to face the terrain in front of them. Lauren wondered if it was because it reminded him of her father or if he missed Scotland and his brothers. What was he thinking?

"Kilchurn always was such a lovely place," Iona said. "Too bad the castle is now crumbling."

"Aye, the place has so much history to it." Lauren nodded. "Do ye miss Scotland, Malcolm?"

"Do ye?"

His clipped words confused her, and she looked down, folding her hands on her lap. "Not as much as I thought I would. Other than my forced stay at the bordello, I like it here in the colonies. But I do miss my wee sister, Blair."

"What about yer da?" He gripped the reins, clutching his hands into fists. "Do ye plan to go back home to 'im?"

"I do not know. He has not come for me, and I wrote him again before we left." The reminder of her father's neglect stung her heart. "I am not sure why I would want to go home to a family that has not bothered to try and find me or at least return my letters."

"Och, lass!" Iona wrapped a thin arm around her shoulders. "Mayhap he has tried to write ye an' somethin' happened to it. Too many things can go wrong across that huge ocean." She squeezed Lauren in a hug. "He might have even come after ye, an' that is why ye have not received a letter. It took us a lot of lookin' to find ye in that terrible bordello ye was in."

"Mither is right, Lauren." Malcolm's voice softened. She wasn't sure what had caused the transformation in his tone, but she appreciated his compassion. "Duncan loves ye. I am sure of it."

"I know ye do not like him, Malcolm. And ye have every right to be cross with him, but please understand he is still my father." Lauren looked out at the woods and a shimmering lake in the distance. "I do not really know how to support myself here in the colonies. I may be forced to leave."

"Ye'll always have a place in our home. Right?" Iona elbowed him in the ribs. He didn't seem to mind as he nodded.

"Aye, so quit frettin' about goin' back." He adjusted his hat lower over his forehead. "Ye'll stay with us. Of course, 'twill not be as fancy as ye're used to, but I shall do my best by ye."

"Ye worry too much, lass." Iona covered Lauren's hands. "None o' us will see ye cast into the streets." She patted Lauren. "Let us think on something more pleasant. Would ye mind readin' the letters again?"

"Of course not." Lauren took the folded pieces of paper Iona handed her.

> Dear Sister,
>
> I cannot begin to explain the relief and joy we all felt at receiving your letter. We are pleased to know you are alive and well. None of us had any doubt that Malcolm would find you. We will continue to pray you both find Carleen. Be encouraged and do not give up hope.
>
> Both your sons made it here safe. I will be honest. The travel was tough on Graham in his condition. Thomas took excellent care of him, and our physician assures us he is healing well. I have arranged a tutor for both lads. Soon they will be able to write you by their own hands. I have enclosed a letter from Thomas.
>
> Please write soon and do not keep us in suspense of your success in finding Carleen.
>
> Your brother,
> Athol Ferguson

Lauren refolded the first letter and unfolded the second letter. She cleared her throat and began reading.

Dear Mother and Malcolm,

We are so grateful you are both well. We hope you will soon find Carleen. Graham is much better, but he no longer talks or jokes as he used to. I miss his energy and wit. He spends much of his time sitting on a boulder overlooking a nearby loch.

Mother, you will be pleased to know Graham started attending church again on the last Sabbath.

Once you find Carleen, let us know where you settle and we shall join you directly. I think a change of scenery and having our family reunited will cheer Graham. I think he blames himself for failing to protect Mither and Carleen, as well as for not preventing William's death. I have tried to tell him it is not his fault, but he is about as stubborn as Malcolm.

We are eager to receive your next letter.

With much love,
Thomas

16

By the third day, Malcolm was convinced most of the scenery looked all the same: thick woods, bushes, and fields of wild weeds and flowers. By midday they came upon several small huts that mirrored log cabins without windows. Small children with black hair and dark brown skin played nearby. Their clothes were tan leather and exposed more skin than they were used to seeing. They were about to meet Indians for the first time.

His mother grabbed his arm, her nails digging into his skin. At least, Lauren rested inside. He didn't think he could survive multiple nail attacks.

"What do ye suppose they want?" she whispered.

"Well, I imagine it might be the other way around. Since we are here on their land, they might be wondering what we want." Malcolm lowered his voice and kept a watchful eye on the people who stopped what they were doing to either watch them pass or point at them and talk in their language. He had no idea what they were saying, but he could imagine. "Let us hope they are friendly."

They followed the dirt road that led right into the center of the village. Indians gathered around them, making their progression difficult. Malcolm didn't want to hurt anyone so he slowed the horse until they came to a complete stop.

Bursts of conversations floated through the air. Malcolm smiled and nodded, hoping they interpreted his expression and behavior as friendly. More Indians crowded around their wagon. Malcolm exchanged a bewildered look with his mother. It was impossible to continue.

"Does anyone speak English?" Malcolm asked. No one responded. Disappointment stirred his gut with unease. How was he to communicate that they had to move on without offending them?

A group of six men came toward the wagon. They were different from the rest with more adornments around their necks and heads. Gray streaks blended in their black hair. They walked with an air of authority as the crowd parted for them. Malcolm tensed. What did this mean?

A piercing cry ripped through the air. It came from the back of the wagon, and the woman's voice was all too familiar. Fear ignited in Malcolm's gut.

"Lauren?"

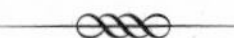

Lauren stared at the half-clad Indian peering in the back of the covered wagon. She pulled her blanket up to her chin in spite of the heat and scooted as far away as possible. What was he doing here and what did he want?

"Lauren, are ye all right?" Malcolm's voice carried through the front flap.

Just hearing him calmed her nerves. "There is an Indian watching me!"

"Aye, try not to panic, but they have surrounded us." This time she recognized the worry in Malcolm's tone. "Why do ye not come up here so I can see ye?"

A second dark head appeared, a wide grin upon his face. Lauren searched for a weapon, but everything was secured in the trunk.

They would be over the side and upon her before she could manage to get one of the lids open.

"Another one is here," she said, afraid to take her eyes off them long enough to crawl up front with Malcolm and Iona.

"Come on, Lauren." Malcolm reached a strong arm through the flap. Lauren clutched him, rose up on her knees, and tried to maneuver onto the bench without hurting her ribs. Once Lauren was settled beside Iona, her heart lurched, making it hard to breathe. An entire tribe surrounded them with six formidable men standing in front. Their arms were crossed over their chests, and they had somber expressions. If they intended no harm, would it hurt them to offer a smile?

"Lord, please have mercy on us," Lauren whispered.

"I see ye're on speaking terms with God again." Malcolm rubbed his chin as he continued to stare at their company.

How could he tease her at a moment like this? "I have always been on speaking terms with God, especially now." Lauren wrung her hands together and took a deep breath to ease her trembling. She feared her ribs would soon start aching again. "God and I just had a few weeks of silence. 'Tis now over."

"I am Speaking Arrow," one of the men in front said. "Have you come to see us, or are you passing through?"

"Ye speak English?" Malcolm wiped his brow, a sigh of relief escaping his lips.

"Some." The man nodded. "We are Cherokee."

"We are passing through to Wilmington, North Carolina. We are peaceful."

"We did not want to scare your woman." The man pointed at Lauren. "Look for armed men inside."

"Oh, he is not—"

Malcolm reached across his mother and clamped a hand on her arm in a firm grip to silence her. "I thank ye. Will we be allowed to pass through?"

"Yes, you eat with us. We make sorry to woman. We have deer meat." He pointed toward a circle of their log cabin homes where smoke drifted into the air. "Come, eat. We trade."

"All right." Malcolm shrugged and set the brake. He assisted his mother and Lauren down, keeping a firm grip on the hands of each woman as the crowd closed in on them.

"Move back!" Speaking Arrow commanded, and people dispersed, creating a wide circle of space. Malcolm couldn't remember meeting a man who commanded so much respect. Their obedience to him was instant. As he marveled, Speaking Arrow led him through their village to where the deer meat cooked over a fire. The animal's skin hung to dry, stretched and tied to two poles. He hoped they would be sitting in a location where the image would not be in view. Lauren and his mother needed nourishment, and such a display might make their stomachs queasy.

Speaking Arrow sat at an angle and crossed his legs, motioning for them to join him. Others sat nearby, and the smoke drifted up into the breeze in the other direction.

"A man came with black book and spoke from it. Good Book. You have black book?" Speaking Arrow lifted an eyebrow in Malcolm's direction.

"Do ye know the title? What did he call it?" Malcolm searched his mind for what he could mean. There were many black books in print. How could he possibly know which one? He searched his mind but came up blank. Since he couldn't read, Malcolm wasn't very familiar with book titles.

"He called it Good Book," Speaking Arrow said, blinking at him as if that explained it.

Malcolm glanced in Lauren's direction for help.

"I believe he is referring to the Bible. So many people call it the Good Book." Lauren met Speaking Arrow's gaze. "I have it in the wagon. Would ye like for me to read it?"

"Yes." He nodded, his somber expression breaking into a smile. Wrinkles framed his dark eyes as excitement lit them. This was most unexpected. She couldn't deny God's sense of humor. If the Lord wanted her to read the Bible again, this was one way to do it.

She started to rise, but Malcolm touched her shoulder. "I will get it."

Knowing he would find it in the trunk she shared with his mother, Lauren settled back down. She adjusted her skirts around her legs and stared at the grass.

Speaking Arrow spoke to the others in their native tongue. A few moments later, Malcolm returned with her Bible. The others stopped talking and gathered around as if waiting for a bedtime story.

Lauren flipped to the Book of Esther and began reading. They listened with more enthusiasm than she would have ever imagined. She wondered if they understood the story.

By the time she finished, a woman served them hot pieces of deer meat. Lauren didn't mind not having a plate. She bit into the meat and chewed, reveling at the grilled taste.

"I trade for Good Book," Speaking Arrow said.

Lauren coughed, nearly choking on her food. While she had been angry at God, she wasn't ready to give up her Bible, especially since it was a gift from Malcolm. "Can ye read it?"

"Read?" Speaking Arrow repeated with a blank look. "You teach me."

Lauren's mouth dropped open, but words evaded her. Would God be displeased with her if she refused to trade her only Bible? Was this a punishment for how she had behaved these past few weeks?

"We can trade the Bible, but we will not be able to teach ye to read it," Malcolm said. "We must leave on the morrow, an' it will take more time."

"The Great Spirit will bring someone to teach us."

His faith pierced her heart as she contemplated her own shallow thoughts. How could she deny this man God's written word? What kind of witness would she be?

The morning sun shone bright, promising another day of burning heat, the kind that suffocated the breath out of a man. Rob wiped his brow and paused as the birds tweeted and sang in the distant woods. Crates of ripe strawberries filled the wagon. They had a decent size crop, something to bring in a little cash while they waited on the big tobacco crop in the fall. Soon their peach trees would be ready.

He counted the rows and stacks and marked his log. If he counted and logged the numbers at the same time rather than relying on his memory the way Fairbanks did, their inventory was more accurate.

He had given a trusted slave Fairbanks's previous position. The man could count well and learned his sums and subtraction quicker than Rob anticipated. With a little instruction, Rob would soon have him reading and could turn over the books to him. In exchange for such loyalty and dependability, Rob gave him permission to move his family into Fairbanks's old house, and to fix it up as he liked.

At first, his father tried to fight him on all the improvements, but he realized that Rob refused to budge on his decisions. He had the choice of disinheriting Rob or waiting until his demise for Rob to implement the changes. In the end, his father decided to step out of the way and lead a life of leisure.

"Mastah Rob!" Henry ran toward him. "There is a group o' men comin' up the drive an' I's need help to see to all their horses."

"How many? Do they look familiar?" Rob wondered if a group of his father's political friends could be making an unannounced visit.

"Naw," Young Henry shook his head. "They's look different. Like that fella that came here with Miz Lauren awhile back. There is 'bout eight to ten o' them."

"Malcolm MacGregor?"

"Yes, sir. But it ain't 'im."

"Get a couple of men to help you from the strawberry field," Rob said, pointing to the right where others were still filling crates. "I will go to the main house to wash up and greet them."

"Yes, sir." Henry hurried away.

Rob closed the ink bottle and grabbed his quill. After a quick inspection, he ensured the tip was dry and so were the ledger pages before he closed them. He walked to the house. At least, he wasn't out in the far fields and could make it in decent time. They would only have to wait a short while in the parlor.

He entered the side door and took the stairs two at a time leading to the second-level chambers. By the time he washed and put on a fresh shirt, George knocked on his door.

"Come in," Rob called.

The doorknob twisted, and in walked George. "Sir, a Mr. Duncan Campbell of Argyll, Scotland, has arrived. He has seven other men with him. I put them in the parlor."

"Very good, George. I will be down directly." Alone again, Rob took a deep breath and stared into the looking glass. He appeared more confident than he felt. Lauren's father had finally arrived. How much should he tell the man? What if Lauren didn't want him to know everything? Could she have written and already told him what she wanted him to know? Time would tell.

"Thank ye for writing me, Mr. Robert Mallard." A man's deep voice carried out into the hallway before Rob's arrival.

"I did not write you," his father replied. Rob's stomach sank, knowing he would now have to deal with his father on top of everything else.

"I wrote to you, Mr. Campbell. I am the one who slipped your daughter's letter inside mine." Rob walked in with his hand held out. He forced an open smile as he kept his posture straight and his stride authoritative. Familiar blue eyes turned to gaze at him, much like Lauren's, but his were cold and calculating. Confusion and distrust lingered in his round face, behind a layered gray beard and mustache.

"Thank ye for the letter. I was disappointed to see that yers was more informative than Lauren's. I did not know what to make of it." he said. "As ye know, we have traveled a long way, an' I am eager to see my daughter."

"Have a seat and I shall tell you what I can." Rob gestured around the room to the couch by the window, the two chairs by the empty hearth, and two wooden chairs on the other side of the room under a framed landscape painting.

With obvious reluctance, Duncan sighed, clenching his jaw. "I am not interested in formalities. I want my daughter . . . and I want her now!" His voice rose to a new level as he paced back and forth in front of Rob like a caged lion.

"My word, what is the meaning of this?" Rob's father demanded.

One of Duncan's men grabbed him by the shirt and slammed him against the wall. Rob's father clutched his chest as his eyes widened. For a moment, Rob feared he might have a heart attack.

"Tell me what I want to know or he will pay the consequence." Duncan pointed at Rob's father.

"Lauren is not here." Now shaking inside, Rob scratched his neck.

"What do ye mean?" Duncan glared at him, a pulse beating through his temple. "Yer letter indicated she was here. What happened to her?"

"That is what I wanted to tell you." Rob launched into the story of how she was kidnapped from their plantation while the family was away. The only detail he omitted was his father's orders to Fairbanks to remove her from the property. He didn't reveal Fairbanks's identity, fearing the Scotsman would go after Fairbanks and a murder would be on his conscience. These men looked like fierce warriors, and he had no idea what they were capable of.

"Da, I told ye Malcolm MacGregor would be involved somehow." Scott Campbell leaned forward, rubbing a hand over the back of his head. "We canna allow him to get away with all he has done to Lauren. He had no right taking her aboard that ship."

"You might want to wait and hear the rest of the story before passing judgment on Malcolm," Rob said. "He helped us get Lauren out of that place. Not only that, but he and his mother nursed her back to health for weeks. He paid for her medical care and did everything possible to ensure her full recovery."

" 'Tis the least he could do after stealing her from home and sailing her halfway around the world." Duncan's temper rose as his face turned darker. "He risked her reputation, put her in harm's way, and caused her to suffer humiliation. God only knows what else she has been through. Malcolm knows I will come after him. He is no fool."

Rob thought back to the way Lauren had looked at Malcolm when they rescued her. He, Logan, and Pastor Brad had all been part of the plan, but Malcolm had been the hero in her eyes. "Certain things change people, especially the kind of things Lauren has been through. Have you considered what you will do if Lauren refuses to go back to Scotland?"

"She will return with us to Scotland!" Duncan roared, his voice echoing through the room. "Now where is she?"

"I do not know." Rob braced himself. "The MacGregors packed up and left town without telling anyone where they went. I suspect they might have gone looking for Carleen MacGregor. Malcolm and Iona were searching for her. Other than that, I have no information."

Malcolm drove the wagon into a budding community he could only assume was Wilmington. He followed the road up the Cape Fear River. Several brick buildings were of various sizes. Others were in the process of being built. Homes varied in shapes and sizes from painted wood structures to homes of wealth made of brick and layered up to three stories with balconies.

The town was nowhere near as large as Charles Towne, but it was a decent start in the middle of the wilderness. He could feel excitement building in his mother as they took in the sights of the new town. She craned her neck to view each sandy street, no doubt looking for a sign of Carleen.

He couldn't find an inn as he drove down Front Street, but when he turned down Dock Street, Lauren spotted a three-story brick house with a sign that said Boarders Welcome. The windows were draped in black shutters while the rest of the house was trimmed in white. Even the front door looked as if it had a fresh coat of white paint. Malcolm pulled behind a black carriage and set the brake.

"Wait here while I see if they have any vacant space." He jumped down. He landed in a layer of powdered sand, which covered his black boots. His quiet footsteps left the soft sand and crunched the pebbled walkway leading up to the shaded porch with three white pillars.

Malcolm used the brass knocker in the shape of a clamshell. It reverberated through the house as he waited for someone to answer. A middle-aged man opened the door. He was round with gray hair and a thick mustache. His lips turned into a friendly smile as his round cheeks widened and his blue eyes lit.

"Welcome," he said. "My name is Mr. Saunders. What can we do for you?"

"I would like to rent a couple of rooms if ye have any available. We just arrived from Charles Towne."

"How many do you have with ya?" Mr. Saunders leaned around to see past Malcolm since he was too short to view over his shoulder.

"Just my mither an' her companion," Malcolm said, stepping aside so the man could see out to the wagon.

"I see. So you shall be wantin' a room for them an' one for yourself?"

"Aye, if ye have it. Give them the best one." Malcolm gestured his thumb over his shoulder. "I can take whatever ye got."

"Well, I have a decent-size room on the second floor for the ladies." He scratched his wrinkled forehead. "But as for you, the best I can do is a small attic room on the third floor. The bed is narrow and the ceiling low for such a big man as yourself, but if you think you can handle the cramped quarters, the space is yours. Come on in an' we shall discuss the arrangements."

He swung the door wide and motioned for Malcolm to step into the parlor. They crossed from hardwood floors to a plush rug with an intricate design of dark red and black. They both sat in facing chairs while Mr. Saunders outlined the price of each room and the included meals. Once the details were agreed upon and Malcolm paid the first month's rent, they stood and shook hands.

"Do ye know a Mr. Oliver Bates?" Malcolm asked.

"Indeed." Mr. Saunders nodded. "He attends church when the weather is well. He lives out in the country where he runs a small rice plantation. How did you come to hear of him?"

Malcolm told him about Carleen and how they had come to Wilmington to find her.

"Such a sad story about her wrongful indenture, but I can assure ya, she is in good hands with Mr. Oliver Bates. He treats his servants well."

"That is good to know." Malcolm walked to the foyer, not wanting to take up too much time from Mr. Saunders. "One last question if ye do not mind." At his nod of agreement, Malcolm continued, "Where is his plantation located?"

"Half a day's drive up the inland river, but why not get settled in first? My wife will take care of the ladies." He gestured down the hall. Malcolm didn't see anyone, and he wondered if he and his wife ran this place by themselves without any servants. "There is a livery up the street where you will wanna park your wagon an' make arrangements for your horse."

"Thank ye." Malcolm bowed and stepped out onto the gray porch. Lauren and his mother wore eager, hopeful expressions as they watched him approach. At least he had good news to impart. They had a warm and comfortable place to stay for the next few weeks until he could figure out the rest of their plans.

While Mrs. Saunders took Lauren and his mother to their chamber, Malcolm carried in their trunk and his roll of personal belongings. Mr. and Mrs. Saunders prepared a nice warm bath for the women.

Once he secured the horse and wagon at the livery, Malcolm went for a walk to explore the town. He liked Wilmington. The place didn't have as many bordellos and questionable taverns like Charles Towne. While less formal, there was a small Presbyterian church, a tiny shop, and the *Cape Fear Mercury*, the local newspaper. He found a tavern on Front Street and went inside to see if he could discover some local news.

It looked like a decent place. Seven square wooden tables dotted the room. Malcolm slid into a seat next to a window. The location gave him the perfect opportunity to observe passersby and hear any local gossip in the small tavern. A woman wearing a simple blouse and skirt that covered her modestly came over to his table.

"Sir, what will you be havin'?" She placed her hands on her hips and tilted her head to the side. "My husband is the cook. I have never known a dish he could not prepare."

"I shall wait to eat with my mother and her companion this evening, but I would like a cup of water."

"Suit yourself. You might wanna bring them here for a good meal this evenin'." She sauntered off, leaving Malcolm to his thoughts.

Two men sat at a table behind him, deep in a discussion. "I have applied for a patent for a headright land grant. 'Tis fifty free acres. You will not find aught like it in jolly ole England," said one man.

"I have been wondering 'bout those grants. I heard 'bout them sailin' here, but I thought it was too good to be true," said the other.

"True enough. It may not be for indentured servants, but for those who pay their own way an' intend to settle the area an' pay annual taxes to the king's coffers."

"Here ya go." The woman returned with a cup of water.

"Thank ye," Malcolm said, picking up the wooden cup. He drained the contents like a man who had been laboring out in the hot sun. The news about the headright grant rolled around in his mind. He had purchased his own ticket here and still had the paperwork of the sale. Malcolm had no idea why he kept it, but now he was glad he did. If he chose to stay, he could apply for a patent of fifty acres as well.

"Pardon the interruption, but do either of ye know where I could find work?" Malcolm asked as the two men paused to consider his question.

The older one stroked his brown beard. "I heard the shipyard is needing men. They have an order for three new vessels."

"Where is it?" Malcolm lifted an eyebrow, intrigued by the idea of doing something different.

"Between Church and Castle Streets," the younger man answered. "You will want to speak to Mr. Pryer."

"Thank ye." Malcolm committed to memory what he had heard. Was it possible all he had heard about the colonies was true? A simple man like himself could be given free land without being born to it? And an opportunity to make his own way?

Thankful for a warm bath and her hair washed, Lauren felt as if she could purr like a contented cat. Now she and Iona were dressed in clean clothes and ready for dinner. She looked forward to seeing Malcolm again.

They arrived downstairs promptly at seven as told. The elegant dining room had dark paneled walls on the lower half and painted walls of solid maroon on the upper half. A brass chandelier hung over the oblong dining table made of cherry. Over the fireplace mantel hung a large painting of a basket of fruit encased in a golden frame. The image made Lauren's mouth water and her stomach growl in hunger.

Upon their entrance, Mr. Saunders and another man stood with a bow. Iona and Lauren curtsied and slid into their seats. Mrs. Saunders sat at the end of the table across from her husband.

Malcolm's seat remained empty across from Iona. Lauren thought she heard him return above their room, but now she wondered if she was mistaken.

Mrs. Saunders followed her gaze to the empty chair. "Mr. MacGregor will be with us shortly. He returned a little while ago and requested a bath," Mrs. Saunders said. "Please, let us pray."

With heads bowed, Mr. Saunders prayed, "Lord, we thank You for the new company and fellowship we have this night. Let each one find their way on Your path as they spend a portion of their time with us. We thank You for the food and for the nourishment it will provide. In Jesus' name, amen."

They passed around a plate of fried chicken, a bowl of mashed potatoes, and one with green beans. The bread basket passed around and Lauren picked out a warm, flaky biscuit. The food was delicious.

Malcolm finally arrived with a wet head neatly combed. He smelled like fresh soap as he sat next to her, across from his mother. "Sorry I am late." He bowed his head in a silent prayer.

"Did ya have any luck?" Mr. Saunders asked.

"Aye, I learned that the shipyard is hiring. I thought I would try to get on with them for a while." He bit into a chicken leg.

"What about Mr. Oliver Bates?" Iona asked, her brown eyes wide with hope.

"I thought we would go there on the morrow," Malcolm said.

Iona covered her mouth as tears sprang to her eyes. For a moment, she couldn't speak as tears spilled over, pooling in the wrinkled lines around her eyes. Her nose turned red as she dropped her gaze and covered her face with her palms. "I am so sorry." Her voice sounded strained. "Please forgive me."

"Mither, Carleen is fine." Malcolm said, reaching across the table and giving her his handkerchief. "Mr. Saunders says that Mr. Bates treats his servants well. Most likely, she has not endured any of the trials ye an' Lauren endured."

Iona cried even harder as she turned away from them in embarrassment and buried her face into the handkerchief. "I am so relieved 'tis nearly over. It almost killed me when they took her away, not knowing if we would ever see each other again."

"This should be a joyous occasion. You will be seeing her tomorrow," Mrs. Saunders said. "Poor thing." She glanced from Iona to Lauren.

"These are tears of joy an' relief, I assure ye," Iona said, wiping her eyes and sniffing.

"You know I have five grown children, three daughters an' two sons. I think I would feel much like you if they were taken from me. They have all married, except my youngest. He lives in Charles Towne."

"Our eldest lives nearby with his wife an' family," Mr. Saunders said. "The rest live on the New Brunswick side. We do feel empathy with you, Mrs. MacGregor."

Iona wiped her eyes and resumed eating as everyone lapsed into an awkward silence.

"Tell me about the headright land grants. I am interested in applying for a patent of fifty acres." Malcolm scooped up a forkful of mashed potatoes. "Is it really free?"

"It is. The Crown is desperate to colonize as much of the New World as possible. The more landowners there are, the more taxes can be collected for the Crown." Mr. Saunders chuckled. "The truth is, land here is unlimited."

"So it seems." Malcolm took another bite.

"Can anyone apply for a free land grant?" Lauren asked, now curious. She had never heard of such a thing. At home, only wealthy men were born into the privilege of being landowners. It was not something a person could aspire to, but the colonies changed things.

"No, indentured servants and slaves are not eligible. People have to come from abroad and pay their own passage." Mr. Saunders leaned back. "Do you fit the requirements?"

"I do." Malcolm nodded. "You know, when I first left Scotland, it was my full intention to return once I found Mither an' Carleen, but now I might stay here. I like the idea of receiving fifty free acres of land. 'Twould be a nice start for a new family. I could send for my brothers an' they could experience the same blessings."

"Aye, there is so much more for ye here than in Scotland." Lauren met his gaze. His hazel eyes softened her heart like no other. She couldn't imagine him going back to the same poverty and humiliation the Campbells put him through. She wanted more for him. Whether or not he realized it, God had brought him here for a reason—to make things better in the long term.

Had God not done the same thing for her?

17

They set out for the Bates plantation by early morning. Malcolm realized his mother was so excited she could hardly eat enough to break her fast. He was grateful Lauren managed to coax her until she ate a piece of toast and drank a half cup of coffee.

They traveled down the narrow dirt road by the Cape Fear River. The sun grew hot and bright fast. Crickets sang in the thicket while frogs called through the morning. Birds chirped and flew from tree to tree as if playing a game in flight. White seagulls squawked overhead and perched themselves on wooden docks.

They passed two farms, but neither of them had signs posted to identify their names. Mr. Saunders indicated the Baker place would be the third home, but there were plenty of acres between each. By the time they reached the Baker property, they were hot, sweating, and thirsty.

Malcolm guided the wagon up the sandy drive toward the two-story white house. His mother scooted to the edge of the wagon bench, and Lauren reached for her hand in support. Malcolm glanced at Lauren's profile, and sentiment overwhelmed him. She wore her blonde hair up under a white bonnet, and her blue gown complemented her azure blue eyes.

Malcolm rolled the wagon to a stop. Before he could set the brake, his mother crawled over Lauren and climbed down.

"Wait, Mither." Malcolm jumped down and hurried around to catch her. "I do not want ye to fall. If Carleen is here, she is not about to disappear before ye get to the front door."

"I have been patient long enough." She paid him no heed as she scrambled down to the ground and shook out her skirts. She set her determined jaw at an angle and gave him a glare that dared him to defy her.

Malcolm drew up short and melted before the tiny woman in front of him. With a sigh, he held out his elbow to escort her. "Let us at least appear to have some decorum."

"Verra well." She laid her hand on his arm, her nails digging into his skin. "How else is a mither to act in my position?"

Malcolm didn't answer. He used the knocker to announce their arrival. Feet shuffled on the other side. The bolt slid back and clicked. The door creaked open like a heavy vault. A Negro man stared at them. He had gray hair that encircled his round head and a full beard and mustache to match. His brown eyes peered at Malcolm.

"May I help yous?" He quirked a dark eyebrow in a serious expression.

"We came all the way from Scotland to see Miss Carleen MacGregor. I am Malcolm MacGregor, her brother." Malcolm inclined his head toward his mother. "This is Iona MacGregor, her mither." Glancing at Lauren, he said, "And Miss Lauren Campbell, a friend."

"I am sure Mistah an' Mrs. Bates will want to meet y'all. Pleaz, come in." Although his speech wasn't as refined as the Mallard Plantation butler, his manners were. He led them through the small foyer to the parlor.

The walls were a forest green with white trim. Portraits hung all about the room in thick gold frames. Bright brass candelabra were on the walls between the portraits. A fireplace with a white marble mantel was on one end of the room, and a pianoforte sat on the side between two oblong windows with white drapes pulled to the side by golden ties. The floor was dark wood, a shade Malcolm hadn't seen before.

"Yous may wait here while I inform the Mastah of your arrival," the butler said.

Lauren and his mother sank on the white couch while Malcolm paced in front of the windows, taking in the side view of the river from the southeast angle.

A door shut above them and footsteps walked across the room, then silence. Malcolm clenched his fists behind his back. "Lord, please make them let us see her." He whispered the prayer low enough to keep the women from hearing. It would do no good to upset his mother with his private concerns. She had enough anxiety. He glanced over at them, pleased that Lauren continued to give his mother the support she needed. Lauren understood his mother in ways he could not. Her attention to such details and her selfless devotion to his mother made him love her all the more.

If only he could erase all her memories of home and quash her desire to go back with her father, he would be a content man. He wanted nothing more than for her to stay here and marry him—to be Mrs. Malcolm MacGregor. The only thing holding him back was his uncertainty of how she felt about him. She had not returned the same sentiments when he had expressed his love to her. Soon her father would come for her, and he feared she would leave.

"Mither!" Footsteps hurried toward the parlor, and the door flung open. Carleen ran in with tears brimming from her long eyelashes. A broad smile glowed on her face, showing robust health. "Mither, it is ye?"

"Aye, lass, did ye not know I would find ye when I got free of that awful place?" Iona held out her arms. Carleen flew into them even though her height now towered over her mother. A flood of tears shook them both as they hung onto each other, reluctant to let go.

Malcolm hung back, allowing them this special moment as an older man entered, wearing a pensive expression. His brown-eyed gaze met Malcolm's, and the two of them exchanged a nod in acknowledgment. To Malcolm's relief, he didn't appear upset or disapproving of Carleen's behavior.

He walked over and reached out a hand. "My name is Mr. Oliver Bates. You must be the brother I heard about." He lifted an eyebrow in question. "Malcolm MacGregor?"

"Aye. Thank ye for allowing us to see her." Malcolm gripped his hand in a firm handshake. "She appears to be in excellent shape, an' I want to thank ye for that."

"Nonsense. We think the world of your sister. In fact, we believe she has been a gift to our family." Mr. Bates glanced up. "Carleen has been a tremendous comfort to my wife in her last days. The doctor says her heart is getting weak and may have only a month or two at the most."

"I am sorry." Malcolm hoped his expression appeared sincere as he wrestled with the surprising news. "I am glad Carleen has been a comfort to your family."

" 'Tis my prayer that you do not intend to take her away—at least not yet. I doubt my wife could take such a blow."

Malcolm's stomach plummeted to his feet as he witnessed his mother embrace Carleen. How would he break the news to his mother after all she had endured? Had she heard their discussion?

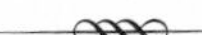

Lauren's heart constricted at the stricken look on Malcolm's face. His hope of rescuing his sister must have been dashed as obvious indecision wrestled across his face. Silence lengthened between the two men as Malcolm struggled to form an appropriate response to Mr. Bates.

Driven to save the situation, Lauren stepped forward and gripped Malcolm's arm in what she hoped would convey strength and comfort. She gave him a compassionate smile. "Mr. Bates, please accept our sincere condolences for yer wife. It sounds like yer family is experiencing a difficult time."

Carleen and Iona pulled apart, wiping at their tear-stained faces. Iona took a deep breath as she laid her hand across her heart and smiled up at them with blessed contentment.

"Malcolm! I am so glad to see ye." Carleen rushed over and threw her arms around him. Lauren let go so he could hug her. He swallowed with difficulty and squeezed his eyes closed as he fought the rising emotion. Malcolm's face turned a darker shade, and he shook like a man who had lost his voice and had so much to say.

"I am all right," Carleen whispered in his ear. "I have been blessed. God took care of me in yer place."

The dam of emotion exploded from Malcolm. He blinked several times, but the red in his eyes and the tension inside him rose until an agonizing groan escaped his throat with unbidden tears. His chest rose and fell as he tried to calm his erratic breathing. He swallowed. "Aye lass, He did at that. An' He did a much better job than I ever could."

"Malcolm?" Carleen leaned back in hesitation. She bit her bottom lip in confusion. "Ye mean ye're no longer mad at God, thinking our family is cursed?"

"Nay, how can I? He has turned what seemed like the most horrible thing into so many blessings." Malcolm reached for his mother and hugged them both. "I took Lauren, planning a forbidden conquest I knew was wrong and against God's will for the purpose of revenge against her father. But instead, God made a conquest of me, an' I have never been happier."

He smiled as he kissed both of them on top of the head. Lauren's heart lifted through her own tears, and a new peace settled over her. She realized he spoke the truth. Malcolm was happy, and that is why he planned to stay—for the opportunities here.

"The quest of the MacGregors has always been to gain freedom—freedom from tyranny and unjust persecution," Malcolm said. "In being forced to come here, we have all found a freedom that we could only dream of in Scotland. Here, the king does not forbid our name. We can freely be MacGregors an' serve God as He intended."

"Lauren, I canna fathom how ye came to be here, but 'tis good to see ye." Carleen reached out for her, and they embraced like old friends. Carleen studied her with a curious eye. "Ye look different somehow." She crossed her arms and touched a finger to her lips. "Ye've lost weight to be sure, but there is something else . . ."

"The story of how I came to be here is a long one." Lauren gripped her hands with a genuine smile. "Allow me to say how deeply sorry I am for what my father has done."

Nonsense, 'tis not your burden to bear. Mither an' I knew ye had naught to do with it." She took Lauren's hands in her own and met Lauren's gaze. "We are still friends as we have always been."

"I am so thankful." Lauren let go of Carleen's hand to wipe her eyes as relief poured through her. Her hand trembled. "Let us discuss ye and all that has happened since we last saw ye."

"I imagine you shall have much catching up to do," Mr. Bates said. "I do not wish to be insensitive to your reunion, so I shall take my leave." He folded his hands behind him. "My wife will be sorry to miss Carleen's family since she is lying down with the headache. My sons as well. They are out overseeing and working the affairs of the plantation." He lifted a thick gray eyebrow and looked at Malcolm. "Unless you stay and have supper with us?"

"We would not want to inconvenience ye," Iona said, but the hopeful look on her face gave away her true wishes. She wanted to stay.

"Not at all. 'Twill give the rest of the family a chance to meet you." He gestured around the parlor. "Make yourselves comfortable." Mr. Bates stepped out into the hall and called a servant to inform the cook their guests would be staying for supper.

Carleen spread her gray skirts and sat on a nearby chair. Each of them found a place to settle. Iona chose a chair next to Carleen. Lauren glanced at Malcolm, but he turned and paced toward the window. She sank onto a wooden chair with a tall back.

Mr. Bates returned and settled by the dark fireplace. He crossed a leg over his ankle and rubbed his hands together. "You may have noticed we treat our servants different here." Mr. Bates nodded in Carleen's direction. "That is because my wife and I arrived here in the colonies as indentured servants ourselves."

"An' ye have all this?" Malcolm turned around in a full circle with his hands out.

"Indeed, but I only started with a few acres. I worked hard and kept investing. This is the land where dreams come true for men like you and me." Mr. Bates grinned at Carleen. "Now, on with your story. Do not leave us in suspense a moment longer."

Malcolm listened as Carleen told funny tales about Mr. Benjamin Shore and her frightening experience in being at his mercy. He had purchased her and seven other indentures straight from the ship. His intention was to take them to North Carolina where laborers were scarce and in more demand. This way he could set a higher price and make more profit off his investment.

"For all his scruffy and unkempt appearance, he is quite smart." Carleen linked her hands in her lap, a pensive expression on her smooth face. Light freckles dotted the bridge of her nose. When she was a child, the slight imperfection made her adorable, but it gave her distinction as an adult. Watching her now, Malcolm missed her as a wee lass, but he was also proud of her.

"A true man of wit keeps himself bathed and clean, my dear." Mrs. Bates had joined them in the parlor, as had her three grown sons. Her skin looked pale and dark circles framed her brown eyes, but a spirit of light still shone through her.

"Aye, but his situation is so sad," Carleen said. "He is a lonely man who needs to feel loved by someone. I canna help thinking that if he had someone around to keep him accountable, he would take better care of himself."

"That has been my experience with people as well," Lauren said. "No one is a lost cause, even if it seems like it. God still provides miracles."

"I wish He would give us one for Mother," Randall Bates said. "I am not ready to say good-bye." An angry frown marred his young face as he turned and stared at the wall. Silence followed the awkward moment. The youngest Bates son stood and walked out.

The middle son rose to go after him.

"Nathan," his mother's voice halted him. "Let your brother go. He needs time alone. He will be all right, as you all will be."

Once settled again, Carleen glanced from Malcolm to Lauren. "Now that I have shared my wee boring story, tell us how Lauren came to be here with us."

They launched into the details of what Malcolm discovered when he returned to the village and discovered she and their mother had been taken by Duncan Campbell. Lauren interjected her reaction to the news, and together they told the story of their adventures on *The Sea Lady*, their arrival in Charles Towne, Lauren's decision to take Iona's place at Mallard Plantation, her abduction to the Pink House, and her rescue.

"How horrid!" Carleen covered her mouth, blinking back compassionate tears. "I am overwhelmed by it all, but now that it is all behind ye, can ye not see how God's hand was in the situation all along?"

"What do ye mean?" Lauren gave her a skeptical glance as she gripped her knees like she needed something to hold onto.

"Well . . . 'tis as Malcolm said, what looked like the worst situation has turned out to be an opportunity of a lifetime." Carleen gestured at Lauren. "An' ye've always wanted to serve those who are less fortunate. 'Tis yer callin' an' gift. That is why ye always came to the village to bring us food an' taught us things. Now, God has opened yer eyes to an even greater need, to save young lasses from being sold into prostitution against their will. It was not by accident that they were savin' ye for the auction. 'Twas a way of protectin' yer virtue while exposing ye to something He needs yer help to solve."

"I see what ye mean, Carleen." Iona reached over and covered Lauren's hand with her own. "When ye were rescued, two other lasses were saved as well. An' now that Pastor Brad is rallying the town with a petition, more lasses will be saved." Iona squeezed her hand. "My dear, yer experience was not in vain. Somethin' good came of it in spite of yer pain."

Lauren's blue eyes filled with a pool of tears. "I . . . I know . . . but it has been so hard to forgive Him." She covered her face and took a deep breath. "Please, excuse me." The rushed words were a whisper as she turned and fled the room.

Malcolm's heart raced, each pulse digging a deeper ache into his soul than the one before. He knew Lauren had struggled with her faith since her rescue, but he wasn't sure how rooted the problem had grown inside her. If she couldn't forgive God, what chance did he have? If he had not tried to use her as revenge against her father, she wouldn't have endured all the horrible things that had happened to her. Worse, how could he forgive himself?

It didn't matter. He wouldn't allow her to face this struggle alone. Malcolm pushed to his feet and went in pursuit of her, not caring what the others thought.

Lauren stepped out onto the front porch. She leaned against a white pillar and took a deep breath to steady her vibrating heart. Why had she been so stubborn? Deep down she knew God would never forsake her and her life was not her own. The moment she dedicated her life to the Lord, it was His to use as He pleased. He had broken no vow or promise, but He had saved lives, including hers.

The front door creaked open and out stepped Malcolm. Lauren pressed her back against the pillar, wishing she could disappear. She needed a few moments alone—to reconnect with God—to reconnect with herself.

To her relief, Malcolm remained silent. He moved to stand beside her, his arm brushing against hers. His warmth sent a trail of shivers that tingled up her spine to the base of her neck. She closed her eyes. "I am not good company right now."

"Good. I am not here to talk, only listen. Whatever is needed."

She tried to smile, but her guilty tears burst through her fragile façade. Her shoulders shook and trembled against the hard surface.

Malcolm turned toward Lauren without touching her. Lauren turned toward him and burst into tears. "I blamed God, but it is not His fault."

Malcolm closed the distance between them, holding out his arms. She stepped into his embrace and laid her cheek against his shoulder.

As the crickets sang around them, the evening sun lowered inch by inch while Lauren wept. Malcolm consoled her but not with false words of comfort. He said naught, and she preferred it that way.

After a while her tears subsided, and Lauren lifted her chin to seek Malcolm's expression. Did he think she had no backbone? Was he now sorry he brought her along?

The sun's orange rays slanted over the land, casting shadows in various places but managed to highlight Malcolm's hair like a golden halo. His hazel eyes roamed over her face until she felt as warm as a bright summer day. He lowered his head toward her. Lauren braced herself. Malcolm's mouth touched hers, his firm lips molding to become one with hers. She breathed in the fresh scent of earth and pine clinging to him. Lauren's hands inched up around his neck and encircled him. In return, Malcolm's hands gripped her around the waist.

Her head danced with a light-hearted sensation she didn't want to end. Malcolm leaned back, breaking his lips from hers. Indecision wrestled in his gaze, but his hands came to rest on each side of her face. "Lauren, ye make my heart beat as if I have run a race." He grinned, leaning his forehead against hers.

"Aye, I know the feeling well," she said.

"Good, then I am not alone." He gave her a grin that warmed her heart all way way down to her toes.

Once Lauren recovered, they returned to the others and departed a couple of hours later. Iona wept silent tears as they drove down the path back to Wilmington. No one spoke as each of them tumbled through private thoughts.

Over the next week, Malcolm took a job as a laborer at the shipyard. That Sunday they attended the local church. It was much smaller and less formal than they were used to, but being able to attend gave them a chance to meet more Wilmington residents.

One afternoon, Malcolm came home early, beaming with a broad smile. Lauren and Iona were sitting out on the front porch of the boardinghouse, rocking in the shade. Both of them were sewing.

"Get ready for a wee drive. I have somethin' I want to show ye." Malcolm rubbed his hands together. "I shall fetch the wagon from the livery, an' when I return, both of ye need to be ready."

"Malcolm, why are ye home so early?" Lauren asked. She stopped rocking and stood. "Have ye lost yer job?"

"Nay." He shook his head as he bounced down the porch steps. "They gave me the rest o' the day off. 'Tis a special day. Ye will see."

Lauren gasped as she stared at his retreating back and then turned to Iona. "Ye suppose there is some strange holiday the colonists celebrate?"

"I do not know, but the lad is actin' a wee bit mysterious." Iona gathered her sewing materials. "I suppose we should do as he asked an' get ready. I am quite curious to know what this is all 'bout."

"Aye." Lauren followed her inside.

By the time, they freshened up, donned their bonnets, and made it outside again, Malcolm pulled up alongside them. He set the brake and swung down to assist them. First, he helped his mother and then reached for Lauren's hand. He leaned forward, his breath tickling her ear. "This is for ye." The whispered words sank through to her heart, planting a seed of hope for their future—together.

Instead of heading north as she expected, Malcolm turned them south toward the sea. They passed Green's Sawmill and the swamp and came to a tract of land on Cape Fear River with tall grass. A large stake stood in the middle with a red ribbon tied to it.

Malcolm walked out to the stake, threw his arms wide, and turned in a circle. "This is ours. I signed the deed this morn . . . with my own signature, I might add." He pointed at Lauren. "Thanks to ye, I will never sign my name with an X again."

"Lad, ye mean ye bought this land?" Iona laid a hand on her chest as she looked around them, taking in the sight. "The view of the river will be splendid, to be sure."

"Aye." He nodded, walking toward the road where he parked the wagon. "Imagine a drive from the road, coming up to the house like this and going into a circle in front of the house." He swung his arm around. " 'Twill be a large two-story facing at an angle. That way, the front will have a slight view of both the road and the river."

" 'Tis magnificent," Lauren said. "Will ye need to worry about floods?"

"I suppose that could always be a concern, but I consulted Mr. Bates an' Mr. Saunders. They both said they have only witnessed minor flooding in the few years they have been here. Fire seems to be Wilmington's worst problem. They suffered a fire back in fifty-six that almost destroyed everything. That is why most of their new structures are being made of brick."

"The spot where ye plan to build the house is on a natural incline." Lauren gestured to the area.

"True." Malcolm rubbed the back of his neck as he walked toward them. "To answer yer other question, I did not buy this land. I petitioned for a free land grant from His Majesty's court. Since no one had snatched up this tract, an' I wanted us to be on the river near the sea, I requested this land."

"I can hardly believe this is all ours," Iona said. "How many acres?"

"Fifty. For all its advantages, it does have its disadvantages." He pointed north. "Few people want to be next to a swamp, but that means we will not have any close neighbors in that direction, only the family on the south side." He took a deep breath. "An' there is one other thing. No one wanted this area because they say it is a den of alligators."

"Alligators!" Lauren gasped. "Ye put us in the middle of a den of alligators? Are we safe as long as we stay away from the water?" Lauren scratched her arm in sudden discomfort.

"In truth, the whole area is full of alligators. I have already seen them hovering in the water in Wilmington and in the swamps on the way to the shipyard. Enjoy the water from a distance, an' we shall dig a well near the house."

"That sounds reasonable." Lauren nodded. "I am so happy for ye, Malcolm. I know this is something ye've always wanted."

He waved to her and held out his hands. In confusion, Lauren placed her hands in his. "Remember what I whispered in yer ear back at the boardinghouse?"

"Aye?" Excitement raced through her as she waited.

The sound of horses racing up the dirt road distracted them from the tender moment. "Malcolm MacGregor!" bellowed an angry but familiar voice. A mixture of dread and fear flooded Lauren as she turned and saw her father with a raised fist riding toward them. Seven other men kept pace with him. Shock reverberated through her veins, paralyzing her until Malcolm shoved her and Iona behind him. Several times, she had envisioned him coming for her but never like this, in a cloud of vengeance and hate. Somehow, she had been naïve in hoping time and distance would dissolve his cold heart and open his eyes to his own guilt. She was wrong.

"Get yerself an' Mither to a safe distance." Malcolm pushed her behind him. "Lauren, whatever happens, please know that I love ye, lass." He pushed her away. "Now go!"

Could he not have picked a better time to tell her? Torn between staying by his side and getting Iona to a safe place, Lauren grabbed the elder woman's arm. "Come, Iona. My father is in no mood to talk."

"Malcolm canna fight all those men by himself. 'Tis Inverawe all over again." She covered her mouth on a sob, hesitating to leave her eldest son.

"Go to the wagon!" Lauren nudged her. "I will stay to help Malcolm. My father might listen to me."

"Lads, Malcolm MacGregor is mine!" her father shouted above the others as they slowed their horses to a stop behind him.

Her father dismounted and strode toward Malcolm as he unsheathed his sword. Malcolm had no weapon to protect himself.

With her heart twisting in agony, Lauren ran toward them. "Nay!"

"Malcolm, this man says he is Lauren's father, but I did not expect him to come at you like this." Mr. Saunders struggled down the side of his horse, his black hat askew upon his head.

Her father reached Malcolm and swung his sword at him, but Malcolm ducked and moved to the side. "I am not fighting ye, Duncan."

"Aye, ye will." He took a deep breath and swung again. "Or ye'll die a coward's death."

Malcolm rolled away and kicked him from behind. Her father stumbled forward but soon regained his balance.

"Uncle, he is unarmed," Keith Campbell said, coming toward them.

"Ye stole my daughter an' for that ye'll pay." His forehead wrinkled in anger, her father glared at Malcolm. " 'Twas the one thing ye could do that would make me follow ye across the Atlantic."

"I told ye, Duncan. I will not fight ye." Malcolm stood tall and still. " 'Twould hurt Lauren, and I will not do it."

"Oh? Since when did Lauren start mattering to ye, MacGregor? What lies have ye promised my daughter?" He raised his broadsword high above his head. Malcolm stiffened, clenching his fists at his side, bracing himself. Would he simply stand there and allow her father to slice him to death?

"Nay!" Lauren screamed as she ran in front of Malcolm.

Duncan brought down his sword.

18

Malcolm's heartbeat thundered in his ears. He shot an arm around Lauren's waist and pulled her against him as he side-stepped and twisted, hoping to shield her with his body. Immense pain sliced through his shoulder. It was as if coals of fire pulsated through his head. Nausea rumbled through his stomach, and the rest of his body went numb. He couldn't feel his legs as they crumbled beneath him.

He tried to lean to the side to keep from crushing Lauren under him, but his sense of balance also left him, and he couldn't tell which way he fell. A pool of blood soaked his shirt. Had Duncan hit an artery? His vision blurred, but his hearing remained intact as Lauren screamed.

Had he hurt her when he fell? He couldn't tell. "I am . . ." Words failed him. He wanted to say he was sorry, but he needed air.

"Now look at what ye've done." Anger carried in Lauren's voice. "Malcolm, I am here. Can ye hear me? I will not leave ye."

Duncan stumbled backward. "Why are ye defendin' him?"

"Aye . . . keep . . . talkin', lass," Malcolm mumbled.

"Malcolm, my lad!" Tears carried in Iona's voice as she rushed toward them.

"I am pressing the wound with his plaid to stop some of the bleeding." Lauren leaned over him. "Mr. Saunders, fetch us a doctor. He will need stitches. Hurry!"

"Has he washed yer brain of all ye know 'bout the MacGregors?" Duncan demanded.

"Aye, Lauren, what are ye thinkin'?" Scott Campbell came up behind her father, confusion swirling in his blue-eyed expression. His blond hair was a shade darker than she remembered.

"If Da's blade had tipped forward an eighth of an inch more, he would have severed a main artery," Lauren said, ignoring her father and brother. "Still, I think he sliced through an important vein. Ye're losing a lot of blood. I am afraid to move ye." She closed her eyes. "Lord, please let Malcolm live. Help Mr. Saunders bring back the doctor in time."

"Ye're prayin' for him now? The verra mon who stole ye from yer family an' country? Who caused ye to be beaten in a bordello?" Duncan smacked his forehead in disbelief. His red face tightened in anger as his veins pulsated through his neck and temples. He grabbed Lauren's arm. "Come on. I came here to take ye home. Let us go."

"Nay!" Lauren jerked away and continued to press Malcolm's wound. "I will never go back home. I am staying here with Malcolm. If ye had not taken his family, he never would have been tempted to take me." Tears soaked Lauren's voice as she brushed his hair over his forehead. "Why did ye do it, Da? Iona and Carleen never did anything against ye."

"Yer mither died because of her." Duncan pointed at Iona. "An' ye were becoming just like her. Goin' over to Inverawe to take care of the poor an' catch their diseases. The more I forbade it, the more ye would sneak away an' do it. Ye thought I did not know. Well, I did, an' I saved yer life by sendin' them away."

"Mither died giving birth to Blair. 'Tis a lie. All ye ever do is lie." More tears streamed down Lauren's face as she watched Malcolm's life drain from him. His skin looked too pale.

"Da, what are ye sayin'?" Scott leaned forward, his eyes narrowing. "I remember her dyin' after Blair was born. 'Twas childbirth."

"He is talking 'bout the time I nearly died with a case of pneumonia," Iona said. "My husband had died in the Jacobite war, my children were young, an' most o' my family was in Glenstrae. Mrs. Campbell learned of my situation an' came to nurse me back to health. She even cared for my children."

"Aye, an' she had just given birth to our own bairn. She was too weak to be caring for all of ye." Duncan's harsh voice vibrated through them. "Ye lived while my children's mither perished."

"I am sorry." Iona rubbed her tired eyes, red with tears. "I heard she had died soon after, but I never knew 'tis from me."

"Aye, a combination from being weak with childbirth an' the pneumonia ye gave her." Duncan's voice hardened. "I was not 'bout to let the same thing happen to Lauren."

"Ye wasted yer time coming here. I will not go anywhere with ye." Bitterness brought a hard edge to Lauren's tone.

"Ye'll do as I say!" Duncan grabbed her arm and jerked her away from Malcolm as he tried to reach for her, but his reflexes were too slow. His head hit the sandy ground. Blood gushed from his wound, soaking his shirt with more warmth that quickly turned cold. Malcolm lay shivering in his own blood.

"Iona, press the wound hard to stop the bleeding," Lauren said over her shoulder. She kicked and clawed at her father. "Let go of me. I am grown and will choose my own fate."

Malcolm leaned up, but dizziness clouded his vision.

"Nay, lad." Gentle hands pushed him back. "This is a battle between Lauren an' her da."

"She does not wanna go with 'im." Malcolm groaned, blinking as if to clear his vision. Taking a deep breath, Malcolm struggled to his feet in spite of his mother's protests. "Duncan Campbell, are ye forgetting somethin'?"

Duncan turned and, with an evil grin, shoved his daughter from him. "I have never known a MacGregor to give up a fight. Glad to know ye will not be the first." He licked his bottom lip and spat on the ground. Taking a warrior's stance, he leaned forward, bracing his legs. "Glad to know ye will not be disappointing me."

"Nay, Da, he is wounded." Lauren grabbed his arm, but he shoved her back.

"Scott, get yer sister, an' keep her away." He stalked toward Malcolm, who struggled to his feet. "I told ye, did I not? That ye would fight me?"

"Aye, ye did." Malcolm nodded, motioning for Scott to move Lauren farther back and out of the way. Her brother held an arm around her waist and swung her up each time she kicked back at him. Malcolm turned his attention to Duncan. "At least I now know why ye have such a strong vendetta against our family."

Malcolm kept blinking, as if trying to focus. He staggered to the side.

Duncan charged, his sword at the ready. Malcolm groaned as more blood soaked his shirt. When he lunged toward the right, Malcolm tumbled to the ground, the side of his face plowed into the gritty sand. The air in his lungs crushed out of him. He waited for Duncan's sword to pierce his back. Instead, steel clashed against steel.

"Sorry, Uncle, but I canna stand by an' watch ye murder a mon in cold blood," Keith Campbell said. "I am no match against yer sword, but at least I can stand on my feet."

"Well, ye will not be standin' for long." Duncan lunged at him and their swords clashed again.

"Da, nay!" Scott let go of Lauren and pulled his own sword against his father. "Keith is not only our kinsman, but he is now a vicar. Are ye willin' to murder one o' the Lord's verra own?"

"I am willin' to take down anyone who gets in my way. Now move, son," he said, clenching his fists. His angry scowl resembled a bear more than a man.

"Malcolm is down. Ye have Lauren, an' she is why we came. Let us be gone from here afore that other mon returns."

"Move!" Duncan breathed heavy like an ox pulling a load up a mountain. He lifted his sword and swung it against his only son. "Get out o' my way, lad!" he growled through his teeth.

"Malcolm, you better not dare leave me." Lauren crawled to Malcolm and lifted his head onto her warm lap. "Stay with me."

"Uncle, stop afore ye hurt Scott." Keith charged at Duncan. The men charged each other, their swords clanging like short bells. Scott could not match his father's broad strength, but he made up for it in agility and speed. Keith stepped back but stayed nearby with his sword ready lest Scott needed his resistance.

"My own family has turned against me." Duncan paused. "I never thought I would see the day. Ye're all Campbells, or have ye forgotten?"

"Aye, an' none o' us is willin' to hurt a vicar," one of the other men said.

"I think my da has gone mad," Lauren said. She brushed some of the sand from Malcolm's face. "I love ye, Malcolm MacGregor, no matter what happens."

"Ye what?" Rage coursed through her father at her words. "I shall finish him, I will." He thrust his sword out and ran toward Malcolm. Lauren threw herself over Malcolm.

"Da, ye'll hurt Lauren!" Scott chased after him, moving with the speed of a cheetah.

Both Scott and Keith lunged at Dunccan from opposite directions, grunting in the effort. The three of them collided. Keith was able to deflect Duncan's sword, scraping against it, while Scott stumbled over Malcolm's feet. The sword went spiraling down as Scott fell into the blade's path. It sliced into Scott's chest. He moaned and landed with a thud on his back. A stunned expression painted his face as the glow of life paled to an ashen gray.

Duncan shuddered with horror as he realized what had just happened. He fumbled to his knees beside his son, blinking in disbelief. Unusual pain and remorse reflected in his eyes as the lines in his face deepened and his forehead wrinkled. Keith dropped to the ground on the other side of Scott.

"Son, I am sorry. 'Twas an accident," he said, touching his son's shoulder.

Keith scrambled to grab Scott's hand and leaned over him. "Scott, God saw what ye did in saving Malcolm an' myself, but now ye have to save yerself. Do ye believe an' accept Christ?"

Scott tried to speak, but all he could manage was a gurgling sound.

Lauren wept.

"If ye canna talk, blink." Scott blinked, his lips trembling and turning blue. He gasped for air, severe pain etched in his smooth face. "If ye believe an' accept Christ, blink again." Scott blinked. Blood dribbled out of his mouth and down his chin. A few moments later, his labored breath grew silent. His eyes stared. He was gone.

Lauren sobbed as she leaned over Malcolm, wetting him with her salty tears. Malcolm's grip on her hand went limp. "Malcolm?" He didn't respond. "Nay!"

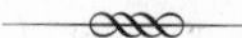

Lauren's eyelids felt heavy and swollen. Her tears had soaked her sleeves where she kept wiping her face. She continued to press against Malcolm's wound. It had been a while since he had moved or spoken. She tucked her finger under his chin and turned him to face her. His eyes were closed and his face deathly pale. Fear punctured her heart as she slid her fingers over the pulse at his neck. It beat slow and steady. He was alive.

Horses raced down the road toward them, and relief filled her. They could still save Malcolm. Remorse scratched at her grief-stricken heart as she glanced over at her brother. He was so young—too young to die.

Her father's men tried to convince him to leave and avoid being arrested. They tugged at his arms, but he jerked away. "I am not leavin' my son!"

"We canna stay," one man said as they mounted their horses and rode away. Only Keith and her father remained.

Lauren stroked Malcolm's hair as Iona sat beside her. Silent tears crawled down her weathered wrinkles, and her shoulders slumped.

Mr. Saunders arrived with the doctor and the magistrate and a few local men. Two of them set out after the other Campbells while the magistrate questioned Keith.

The doctor slid to his knees next to Malcolm. He ripped open Malcolm's shirt and assessed the wound. " 'Tis a good thing he is already unconscious. He has lost a lot of blood." The doctor sighed as he looked from Iona to Lauren. "I need to sew him up right away before we move him."

He pulled out a flask of water and cleaned the wound. The bleeding had finally slowed enough for him to pull a needle and thread through. Lauren closed her eyes and looked away.

"If he gets proper rest and nourishment over the next few days, he will make it. The main thing we need to watch for is infection. I shall leave a bottle of laudanum for the pain."

"Thank ye, Doctor," Iona said, brushing her gray hair from her forehead. A layer of perspiration broke out on her forehead.

"Where will you be taking him?" the doctor asked. "I would like to stop by and check on him sometime tomorrow."

"We will be going back to Mr. Saunders's boardinghouse," Lauren said.

The doctor looked at the magistrate. "We need to get Malcolm MacGregor back to the boardinghouse as soon as possible. Can you finish questioning the women from there?"

"Indeed, but I am taking these two in first." The magistrate pointed a thumb at Keith and Duncan. "Sounds like this one accidentally killed his son while trying to murder Malcolm. His son tried to stop him and got in the way." He turned to his men. "Tie them up."

"I must see to my son's burial." The moment they touched Duncan, he punched one man and jerked away from another. He elbowed another man and kicked at one behind him.

Lauren closed her eyes and looked away. She couldn't bear to see anymore. She listened to the grunts and blows they delivered as tears slid down her face and blinded her. Why couldn't he go in peacefully? Why did violence always have to be his way?

"Da, stop!" Her scream ripped through the air. She wiped the tears from her face as she marched over to where a man held him by each arm. A third punched the resistance out of him. The blows stopped. Blood gushed from his nose and the side of his cut and swollen lip. The skin around his eye began to swell. "Why are ye doing this to yerself? Why can ye not go peacefully like Keith? Do ye want them to beat ye to death?"

"I killed my only son, Lauren." His chin trembled. "I do not deserve to live."

"What 'bout Blair? Do ye think 'tis fair for her to lose all of us? Mither and Scott are gone. I am not going back . . . ever. Who will finish raising Blair if ye're in prison here in the colonies?"

"Too late." Blood sputtered from his mouth as he shook his head.

"Mayhap, this time it is." Lauren swallowed. "Look where yer vengeance and hate have taken us. I will make my statement to the magistrate, and believe me, he will hear the complete truth."

"What 'bout yer loyalty to yer father?"

"It no longer matters." She shook her head. "When I look at ye, I feel naught. No love, no pain, not even hate. Pure numbness. Right now, I do not know what that means, but I hope it means the beginning of my healing."

She moved past her father and climbed into the wagon bed where they had laid Malcolm and where Iona sat beside him. She had already started a new life with Malcolm's family. As soon as she could, she would send for Blair.

Malcolm woke lying on his stomach in a bedchamber. Searing pain shot through his shoulder. It felt tight and heavy. As awareness grew, the ache in his shoulder increased. He reached up and felt the bandages.

"Nay." Lauren stilled his hand. "Do not scratch at it."

"Lauren?" He tried to lean back so he could see her, but all he saw were moving shadows.

"Aye, I am here. Yer mither as well." Her smooth voice coated him with warmth, especially since he didn't recognize this room and a searing pain kept shooting his shoulder and into his head.

"We will not leave ye, lad." His mother's voice poured over him like sweet honey.

Malcolm blinked as his blurry vision came back into focus. He mustered some strength and rolled over on his good side. With a determined will, he wiggled to a sitting position. Iona repositioned his covers while Lauren set his pillows behind him.

"Ye've got several stitches in that shoulder, so ye must be careful," Lauren said, gripping his chin and staring him in the eyes. Her gaze narrowed in the midst of her inspection.

"I am thirsty," he said, smacking his lips and disliking the dryness in his mouth.

"I shall get ye some water." Iona stood to leave the chamber. "An' I will let the others know ye're awake. The magistrate wants to talk to ye."

The memory of Duncan Campbell swinging a sword at him came to mind. His addled brain struggled to conjure up the images of what had happened. The pressure was so intense, it felt like someone had squeezed his head in a large nutcracker. Scott Campbell had fallen under Duncan's sword. Malcolm turned to Lauren and winced from the sudden movement. "Lauren, are ye all right? What 'bout yer brother an' da?"

"Aye, my father has been arrested, and I am in the process of planning my brother's funeral." She gulped as her chin trembled, and she wrung her hands in her lap. "I have been sitting here trying to figure out how life can take such a dramatic turn. I am confused, heartbroken, and relieved all at once."

"Relieved? Why?" Malcolm lifted an eyebrow, thankful that his mind had begun to work again—at least enough to carry on a conversation.

"Revenge is more important to him than his daughter. I knew he would eventually come for ye, Malcolm, even if not for me." Lauren rubbed the back of her neck and took a deep breath. "Now we no longer have to wait and worry. 'Tis done."

"Lauren, please forgive me. I never meant to hurt ye." He closed his eyes, willing the right words to come. "Before I left Scotland, the desire for revenge burned in my heart almost as deep as yer father's. I am grateful that God used ye to change me."

"Malcolm, I have already told ye, I forgave ye a long time ago." She brought his hand up and kissed his knuckles. "I refuse to hold grudges. I do not wish to be a product of my father's hate, but of Christ's love."

"All this time ye talked 'bout yer da comin' for ye an' I feared ye might intend to go back to Scotland." He cupped her cheek and offered her a weak smile.

"An' now, Da will not be going back anytime soon either." She shook her head in disbelief. "After questioning Keith, they let him go. I am hoping he will be willing to go back to Scotland and bring Blair to me."

"If not, I could always write Thomas an' Graham. They could bring her with them when they come." He would do whatever it took to reunite Lauren with her sister.

"Here is yer water." His mother returned, handing him a cup.

"Thank ye." Malcolm accepted it and gulped the water. He handed her the empty cup. "Mither, will ye give us a few minutes?"

"Of course." She nodded and left the room.

Malcolm looked at Lauren. "When I signed for that piece of property by the river, it was ye I imagined spendin' the rest o' my life with. 'Tis ye I want to be the mither of my children. I know I canna give ye the kind of life ye had in Scotland, but I shall give ye all my love an' will do my best by ye. I will work hard an' provide what I can." He traced his knuckles over her cheek. "Mayhap, in time, ye'll come to love me as well."

"Malcolm MacGregor, I already love ye. Why do ye think I jumped in front of ye when I thought my da would stab ye?" Glassy tears magnified her eyes before spilling onto her cheeks. "I thought he might stop for me, but I was wrong. Scott made the same mistake, and it cost him his life."

"I think he would have stopped for both of ye, but he had too much momentum going to pull back in time." Malcolm moved his hand to the back of her neck and pulled her close. "Marry me, lass. Please? Let us end the MacGregor and Campbell feud right here in the colonies." Their lips touched, sealing their fate and future together. The warm feel of her eased the tension in his head as a light-headed surge raced up his spine.

"I have been wondering how long it would take ye to ask me." She leaned back, searching his face. "I will marry ye, Malcolm MacGregor, on one condition."

"Which is?" He lifted an eyebrow, waiting to hear what this one obstacle would be.

"Ye name our land the MacGregor Quest as a reminder of what ye came here to achieve, but as the gift ye received from the Lord instead." She bit her bottom lip in a mischievous grin.

"Done." He pointed to his lips. "An' might we seal that agreement with another kiss as well?"

"Absolutely." Lauren burst into laughter as she leaned toward him.

Aye, the Lord had made him a contented man, indeed.

Epilogue

Lauren stood on the shore between Malcolm and Iona, waiting for the ship that had anchored to bring in a small boat full of passengers. There were no loading docks or wharfs like in Charles Towne. Lauren squeezed Malcolm's hand. They had waited to marry so the rest of their family could be with them during the celebration. This time next month in October, she and Malcolm would be speaking their vows before God and making a lifelong commitment to each other.

As the boat came closer, Lauren grew more excited. She couldn't wait to see Blair. Her sister would now be ten and three. Lauren walked to the water's edge. Her bare feet sank into the warm sand. She could make out her sister's long sandy brown hair flapping in the breeze. Beside her sat Keith and on the other side were Malcolm's brothers, Thomas and Graham.

Keith picked up Blair and carried her through the water to the shore. Once he set her down, she broke into a run. Lauren let go of Malcolm and rushed to her. She was taller than Lauren remembered with the top of her head reaching Lauren's nose instead of her chin. They embraced with tears of joy.

"I feared I would never see ye again." Blair's thin arms squeezed Lauren so tight that she almost cut off Lauren's breath. "I read yer letter again and again. I could hardly believe that ye planned to marry the verra mon who took ye from us."

"We have so much to talk about," Lauren said. "I am not sure how much Keith told ye."

"I know about Scott's death, an' how da was involved." Blair pulled back, her watery eyes meeting Lauren's. "I am so glad Keith was there to tell me, and I did not have to learn about it from a letter. Malcolm's brothers have been nice but at times distant. 'Twould have been verra awkward if Keith had not been traveling with us. His presence made me feel much better."

"Aye, I would imagine our wedding is hard for them to take as well, especially for Graham." Lauren lowered her voice as she glanced at Malcolm greeting his brothers in a hug. "Were they civil?"

"Indeed, they were quite protective on the ship. Looked after me, as well as Keith. If any lads showed me too much attention, their scowls scared them away."

"So they are already acting like the good brothers-in-law they should be?"

"I suppose so." Blair giggled. "They seem to be under the impression that Malcolm would beat them if something happened to me." She wrinkled her brow. "I wonder what he wrote in the last letter they received from him?"

"I am sure we will soon find out." Lauren wrapped her arm around her sister's shoulders and led her over to the men. "I think 'tis time ye meet my soon-to-be husband and his mither."

Lauren introduced her to Malcolm. He bowed. Blair stared up at him in awe. She seemed to remember her manners and dipped into a curtsey. Her gaze slid over to Graham. "I did not think anyone could be as tall as ye, but now I realize I was indeed wrong."

"Aye, but he lacks wit." Graham grinned, pointing at his head and slapping Malcolm on the shoulder.

Lauren exchanged a look with Malcolm and Thomas, knowing how relieved they were to hear their younger brother joking again. Graham had healed well. He didn't have any scars that she noticed, but he now possessed a careful wariness he didn't have before.

Once they loaded the trunks onto the wagon, Malcolm turned and held his hands up. "Shall we show ye the MacGregor Quest? 'Tis on the way to the inn."

"MacGregor what?" Thomas asked as he assisted his mother to the wagon and up on the front bench.

" 'Twas Lauren's idea," Malcolm said as he assisted Lauren up beside his mother.

Graham swung Blair into the back. He jumped up and settled beside her. Thomas joined them a moment later. Malcolm clicked his tongue and tapped the reins, and the horses lunged forward. They followed the dirt road until they came to a two-story white house up on a hill with a circular drive. "Welcome to the MacGregor Quest."

"Is this yer house?" Graham asked, sitting up on his knees and leaning over the side. His eyes were wide and his jaw slack. No doubt, this house looked like a mansion compared to the rock hut and dirt floor they had back in Scotland. "I never dreamed one of us MacGregors could own somethin' so grand."

"Aye, 'tis ours. We will be moving in after our wedding next month," Malcolm said. "Lads, ye can apply for a land grant just like I did. Here, we are not the poor, but free men with opportunity—the way God created us to be."

Discussion Questions

1. Lauren did an honorable thing in trading her life for Malcolm's mom's, yet she had to endure mistreatment, beatings, and slavery afterward. How do you learn to lean on God when doing good for others brings you nothing but pain and sorrow?

2. God's plan for Malcolm and Lauren was to leave Scotland to come to America so they could have a better life. Would you be willing to allow God to move you from your current home for a better life?

3. Malcolm was able to subdue Lauren with chamomile tea to make her sleep. What other herbs and home remedies could have been used during this time period?

4. Indentured servitude was the only way many could come to America. Can you trace your ancestry back to anyone who was an indentured servant?

5. Lauren and Malcolm were at odds because they saw each other only on the surface before fate got them to see the people they truly were on the inside. Is there anyone in your life who you

have judged on the surface without taking n the time to get to truly get to know them?

6. With all that Lauren endured, how do you think God will use this trial in her life to strengthen her as a person?

7. Malcolm started out on his journey to find Duncan Campbell on a mission of revenge. How did God use time to change Malcolm's heart?

8. In this story we see life in Scotland, life on the ship, and life on the plantation. Put yourself in the shoes of a wealthy person in charge as well as a poor person, and discuss the differences in the realities of their lives.

We hope you enjoyed Jennifer Hudson Taylor's *For Love or Loyalty*, the first book in the MacGregor Legacy series. Here's an excerpt from the next book in the series, *For Love or Country*.

1

Christmas 1780

Tyra MacGregor did not want the Christmas feast to end. She leaned back in her wooden chair and peered at her family gathered around the long dining table, laughing and talking in jovial spirits. That her father, Lieutenant Malcolm MacGregor, and her elder brothers, Callum and Scott, had been allowed a few days off from the Continental Army to spend Christmas with them felt like a miracle. But this time when they left, they would be taking another brother, Alec, now that he had turned ten and five. Tyra blinked back sudden tears as a searing ache twisted her insides.

"Lauren, that was a delicious meal." Da leaned over and gave their mother a kiss on her rosy cheek. They shared an intimate glance of love and devotion. Tears sprang to her mother's blue eyes. Tyra looked away, unable to witness the emotional exchange as the back of her own throat constricted.

"I did not prepare it alone, Malcolm." Mama's voice carried down the long table. "Tyra's cooking skills have greatly improved since you've been away at war."

"Indeed?" Her father lifted a russet eyebrow, as the corners of his mouth curled in an approving grin. A full reddish-golden beard and thick mustache layered with gray specks branded its mark into her memory. "Then I daresay, well done, lass."

"Thank you, Da." Tyra forced a tender smile to hide her fearful worry. Thinking of her gift to them, genuine joy crept into the muscles of her tense face. "And now I have a surprise for you all."

"Dessert?" Kirk's voice cracked as he shoved his empty plate aside. At ten and three, her youngest brother often suffered the embarrassment of the tones vibrating from his throat. He rubbed his hands. "I thought I smelled a sweet treat earlier."

Tyra took his empty plate and placed it on top of hers, biting her bottom lip to keep from blurting out the answer. She whirled and stepped toward Alec.

"No, leave mine." Alec threw a hand out to protect his unfinished plate. "I intend to eat every bite." He glanced at their father and older brother, Scott. "I do not know when I might have the blessing of another home-cooked meal after this day."

Tyra paused, her gaze meeting Alec's brown eyes. Her heart thumped against her ribs in an attempt to stomp down the rising grief welling inside her. Even though she was only ten and seven, she believed Alec was too young for war. She didn't care that other lads his age had already signed up these past five years. Many of them were gone from this world. That knowledge alone made her want to drop the plates, wrap her arms around Alec, and beg him to stay. Others who had enlisted at his age continued to survive, like her eldest brother, Scott. They had grown into fine young men, accustomed to the ways of war, always fighting for their freedom.

"I wanna go!" Kirk plopped his elbow on the table and set his chin on his palm. A disgruntled expression marred his forehead. "I'm not that much younger than Alec."

"Hold your tongue." Mama's blue eyes were like the crystal frost outside as late evening approached. She toyed with the wrist of her cream-colored blouse, her dark blond hair coiled into a French bun. " 'Tis bad enough I must part with three sons and a husband. They can at least leave me one son."

Tyra gulped, hating the tide of emotion that kept threatening their last moments together. She carried the plates from the dining room to the kitchen where she placed them on the table. As she pulled out the dessert plates, her mother entered. She wiped at her eyes and took a deep breath. At five feet and eleven inches, Tyra towered over her mother by at least five inches, but she didn't let that stop her as she threw a comforting arm around her mother's shoulders.

"Mama, don't worry. God will keep them safe." Tyra hoped her voice sounded more certain than she felt. "Da, Callum, and Scott have been safe these past few years. We must have faith for Alec as well."

"Of course, you're quite right." Mama grabbed the extra plates and gave her a grateful smile as she reached up and cupped Tyra's cheek. Thin lines framed the corner of her mother's eyes, but she still looked young at two scores and one. "I am thankful I have you here to remind me, lass." She motioned to the dessert tray and waved Tyra forward. "Now on with you, they are waiting."

Tyra hurried to the dining room and set the tray before her father. "I hope you all saved room for my cinnamon gingerbread cake. 'Tis a small Christmas gift I want to give each of you."

"Then we shall cherish it." Her father rewarded her with a wide grin, reaching for the small plate with eager anticipation. He grabbed a fork and carved out a bite. With slow precision, he slid it into his mouth as he watched Tyra and chewed. He nodded in appreciation. "Mmm, quite good."

"Thank you, Da." Tyra said, pleased her father liked it. "Now, the rest of you must try it."

"I am ready." Kirk leaned up on his elbows against the dining table and drummed his hands on the surface. He beat out a ditty of

"Free America." "See? I could be a drummer. Plenty of boys my age have enlisted."

"Well, you shall not be one of them," Mama said, as she set a plate by Alec and Scott. "Mind your manners, lad."

Tyra cut slices for each of them before carving a slice for herself. She enjoyed the sweet taste of the moist cake on her tongue. With the British blockade along the coast, they had learned to do without certain supplies and cooking ingredients. Sugar was rare, but Tyra was blessed to have as friends the Tuscarora Indians who lived in the nearby swamp. She had been able to barter for some honey to save what little sugar they had left over the past couple of months in anticipation of their upcoming Christmas feast.

"Someone has been making you into a fine cook while we have been gone." Callum sat back with a satisfied grin and pushed his empty plate aside. " 'Tis good to be home again, all of us together one more time. I will cherish this fond memory in the months to come." His brown eyes glistened in the candlelight as he blinked back moisture and looked away. When he had first arrived yesterday, she had hardly recognized him with a full beard and mustache. She was glad he had shaved it off. He now looked more like the brother she remembered, although he'd come home with a much more somber mood than he'd left with. Tyra could only imagine what horrible images lurked in his mind from the war. He no longer acted like a young, vibrant man of only a score of years to his credit, but a seasoned man who had seen too much of life.

Tyra glanced at Scott to see if he shared the same sentiment as Callum. Scott cleared his throat and looked down, hiding his blue-eyed gaze. His blond hair looked darker than she remembered, most definitely longer, tied back in a ribbon at his neck like her father wore his hair.

Always the charmer in their family, Scott had changed as well. He was more pensive and quiet than she had ever known him to be.

At ten and eight, he had only been serving for three years, unlike her father and Callum.

"Mama is a very patient teacher," Tyra said, breaking the silence. She glanced at her mother, knowing herself to be a difficult pupil with her unladylike qualities and lack of interest in domestic skills. She and her mother had been forced to set aside their differences and work together while the men were away from their rice plantation. Tyra had taught her mother to shoot a rifle and a pistol, while she made more of an effort to wear constricting gowns and assisted with more household chores—like cooking.

"Tyra has turned out to be quite a teacher herself." Mama winked at her as she took a bite of her cake. "There has been too much strife in Wilmington of late between the Whigs and the Tories, so I decided the boys should receive their education here under Tyra's guidance."

"Aye, she is more like a growling bear," Kirk grumbled, reaching for another slice of cake.

"No!" Tyra snatched the plate from his grasp, covering its contents with a protective hand. "The rest are for Da and our brothers. I wanted them to have at least one more slice to remind them of home whence they leave on the morrow."

Kirk gave her a scowl but sat back without another protest. He glanced at his father and brothers, his green eyes wide with concern. Tyra knew he felt the same fear as she—that it might be the last time they were all together. Most of his childhood had been stolen by the War of Independence.

"Let us retire to the parlor." Mama stood. Her smile brightened the candle-lit room as shadows danced upon the paneled walls. Even the fruit painting by a local artist seemed ominous in the dim, flickering light. A slight chill hovered at the glass windows of the dining room with no fire to warm them. "Kirk, go build us a warm fire in the parlor." Her brother hurried to carry out their father's bidding.

Frantic beating on the front door sent alarm through Tyra as she exchanged worried glances with the rest of the family. Who would dare interrupt their Christmas? Most of their neighbors would be at home celebrating with their own families. "Lieutenant MacGregor! I have new orders for you." A man's voice called through the door. More knocking followed.

"Wait here. I shall only be a moment." Da's boots clicked across the wooden floor as he left the dining room and entered the foyer. The sound of him unlocking the latch and sliding it back grated on Tyra's nerves. The hinges creaked, and low voices conversed. A few moments later, he closed the door and walked back into the dining room. Tyra held her breath.

"I am sorry," Da said, standing at the threshold. "General Greene has gained new information and is calling all the troops back to service. We must leave now."

"Can it not wait till the morn?" Disappointment carried in Mama's tone. Her chin trembled as she lifted fingers to her lips as if to still the motion. Her gaze slid to each son and lingered on the three eldest. "I had hoped to have a wee bit more time."

"Me too, my love, but 'tis not to be." Da took a deep breath of regret. "Leaving now will make the difference of eight hours of travel."

"When will ye sleep?" Mama asked.

"War does not always give us time to sleep." Callum stood to his feet. Scott and Alec followed his example. "Da, I shall prepare the horses."

"Excellent." He motioned to Scott. "Pack us some food."

"I'll help." Tyra launched into action, standing to her feet. Her head swirled in denial as her legs moved on their own accord. The back of her throat went dry, and it seemed as if stones churned in her stomach. The moment she had dreaded was now upon them.

Captain Donahue Morgan bristled as the hairs upon his neck and arms rose and goose pimples crawled over his flesh. They were being watched, and their red uniforms were like a bull's target. He held up his hand to signal the four soldiers following his lead. Their mounts slowed to a stop. Hugh listened as he gazed into the layered forest of green pine needles and bare branches of oak and poplar trees. The earthy scent of fresh pine and melted snow drifted through the air. No sound of human life caught his notice, but winter birds sang and flew above them. Wiry bushes dotted the thick woods full of dark shadows where anyone could be crouched in hiding, waiting to ambush them.

The only map in his possession wasn't drawn to scale, so he feared they might have wandered off the path to Wilmington. The drawing lacked significant landmarks that could have been more insightful. His superior officer had given it to him when he commissioned Hugh to find two of their ranking officers and negotiate their freedom from the rebel Continentals. Hugh could not fail. One of them was Colonel Neil Morgan, his elder brother.

A shiver of foreboding slithered up his spine and branched over his neck and shoulders. If Hugh had learned anything during his time in the colonies, it was the fact that these rebels did not fight fair like an upstanding British soldier, full of honor and courage. Instead, they would take cover behind rocks and trees, picking off His Majesty's Royal Army one by one like the red-skinned savages he had heard about.

"Get ready." Hugh unsheathed his sword from his side. "We are not alone." He kept his voice low as he continued to watch the woods around them. Hugh saw and heard nothing that would alert him to danger, but surviving the last three ambushes in South Carolina with his full regiment had given him enough experience to trust his instincts.

The birds above flew away. Eerie silence followed. Hugh tensed. The sound of a rushing wind sailed by him. A low thud hit the man behind him and a gut wrenching moan wrestled from him. Hugh twisted to see his comrade clutch the arrow in his chest, a look of shock and pain carving his expression into a memory of guilt that would not soon leave Hugh. His friend paled and fell from his horse.

"Go!" Hugh urged his mount forward. Arrows whistled past them from every direction. They were surrounded and outnumbered. Strangely dressed men left the cover of the trees with loud shrilling sounds that vibrated through Hugh's head. He maneuvered his horse around one dark-skinned man who met his gaze, lifted his bow and arrow, and took aim. On instinct, Hugh dropped his head and tried to crouch his large frame behind his horse's mighty neck. As Hugh raced by the man, pain sliced into his left side, like someone had branded him with the end of a red-hot iron poker, fresh from a burning fire.

Air gushed from Hugh's lungs as another fallen comrade landed in the dirt behind him. The man's horse neighed and reared up on its hind legs, its hooves pounding thin air. Hugh raced on, eager to escape the same fate. He could not fail in this mission. Who else would rescue his brother? Clenching his teeth against the increasing pain in his side, Hugh blinked to clear his vision and leaned forward with determination.

More shrieks and warrior cries bounced through the forest, and they followed him. As near as he could tell, most of the Indians were on foot. Two of them climbed up on the horses of his two fallen comrades and chased after Hugh and his last remaining companion. They knew the layout of the land better than Hugh, and it showed as they caught up with them. Hugh ducked and leaned to the left and right to avoid the large tree branches, but he couldn't avoid the sting of some of the smaller ones as they slashed across his face and neck. A cut above his eyes poured blood into his blurry vision. With each breath, his heart continued striking against the inside of his chest like a fist that wouldn't stop.

"Argh! They got me, Hugh!" Miles called to him.

"Just hang on and keep going." Hugh glanced over his shoulder. The movement twisted the arrow still lanced into his side and caused a wave of dizziness to wash over him.

Something pierced his left thigh, stinging his flesh. Shock reverberated through his system as he glanced down to see another arrow had hit his leg. Warm blood oozed over his breeches, soaking and discoloring the white material. Hugh struggled to stay seated as his energy evaporated, and his remaining strength drained with his life's blood. The jarring of his winded horse pushed both arrows deeper. Hugh groaned from the pain and almost lost consciousness.

The two Indians closed in on him from the front, and Hugh couldn't find the strength to guide his horse in another direction. Instead, the animal slowed to a trot, then walked, until he stopped altogether. The Indians grabbed the reins and pulled Hugh down. Hugh grabbed his side as he landed on his right hip and gritted his teeth in agony.

A moment later, Miles landed beside him. Blood now soaked his shirt beneath the opening of his red coat. His pale face was testament to how much blood he had already lost. Hugh hoped their end would be swift and merciful. The thought of more torture was enough to make him pray for death. Instead, he sat still and held his head up when he could find the strength. He would not be a coward. If he had to die, he wanted it to be with honor.

"I am Red Fox," said the man who had stared at Hugh and shot him in the side. "You are on MacGregor land. They fight redcoats." He pointed at them. "You are the enemy. We take you to War Woman." He bent and broke the long stems of the arrows sticking out of Hugh's thigh and side. Red Fox moved over and did the same for Miles.

"A woman?" Hugh blinked with a weary sigh. His body swayed one way and then the other, his head numb from a loss of blood. "Dying . . . by the hand . . . of a woman . . ." Hugh took a deep breath to gather what little strength he had left, " . . . has no honor."

His head rolled back on his shoulders and his blurry vision saw a mixture of colors and light. "Kill us now."

The next morning Tyra slid the latch back and swung open the side kitchen door. The rising sun cast an orange-pink glow across the slanted gray clouds. The frigid air promised another cold day, but it didn't look like more snow would fall. As much as she enjoyed the rare snow, she rubbed her hands in a silent thank you to the Almighty. Harsh weather would make things harder on her father and brothers.

Since the MacGregor Quest plantation was located southeast of Wilmington, their homestead overlooked the road and a semi-circle dirt drive. On the other side lay the Cape Fear River, shimmering like diamonds when the sun's rays angled upon the surface of the water. The swampy woods served as their only neighbors on the right, and on the left their rice fields extended for several acres beyond the stables. Tyra followed the familiar path to the well on the swampy side. Patches of snow still lingered where their house shaded the ground. A thick white frost covered the rest.

As she walked toward the well, her black boots crunched against the stiff white frost layering the grass like thick pie crust. She breathed in the crisp air, allowing it to cleanse her lungs. Now that winter was here, they kept the doors and windows closed and the hearths burning; at times it almost stifled her.

The sound of men's voices carried in the breeze. Tyra paused and tilted her head to hear better. A horse snorted. It sounded like they were on the other side of the house by the swamp. She rushed back to the house and entered through the front door to keep from alarming her mother who was no doubt still in the kitchen.

Hurrying down the hall, Tyra tried to keep her footsteps light. She opened her father's study and reached above the hearth to lift the rifle from where it hung on the wall. A quick search in the desk drawer revealed a pouch containing a round bullet and gun powder. Tyra loaded the rifle as her father had shown her and slipped out of the study. She rushed down the hall and out the front door, determined to meet the men before they reached the house. Lifting the hem of her brown skirt, Tyra ran down the porch steps, hoping she wouldn't trip. She rounded the corner and lifted the rifle, taking aim.

"War Woman, we bring you redcoats!" Red Fox called out. He led two horses carrying wounded British soldiers. Both men looked unconscious as they lay over the back of each horse with broken arrows sticking out of them. Tyra's gaze scanned the somber expression of the other ten Tuscarora Indians surrounding them. She lowered her rifle in stark confusion.

"They were on MacGregor Land. Redcoats are enemy to MacGregor."

"What happened?" The words slipped from Tyra's mouth before she could halt them. She hoped her tone did not sound like an accusation. Would this deed now bring British wrath down upon their heads? They had heard rumors that the British were heading toward Wilmington. She had to find a way to protect her mother and Kirk. How could she make this right?

"We bring them for justice." Red Fox continued walking toward her. Tyra knew him to be a fair man, but he did not always understand the white man's ways. She wished her father was here to speak for her.

"You found them on MacGregor land?" Fear iced up Tyra's spine, but she stiffened to keep from shivering. Fear would not aid her now. Instead, she hoped to draw strength from the Lord and the wits He gave her just as her mother had always done. She lifted her chin and met his gaze. "Were there more of them?"

"We killed two others." Red Fox turned to glance back at the wounded men and nodded his dark head toward them. "These two live. We bring them to War Woman. You decide fate."

"What were they doing?" she asked.

"Riding to your house. We stop them." He pointed to one of the men with an arrow in his side and thigh. "This one must be the leader."

"What did you do with the others?" Tyra accepted the reins of the two horses he handed over to her. "I have heard that more redcoats are coming. I do not want your tribe to be in danger." Tyra thought of his wife and daughter, a close friend from childhood. "Their army has far more soldiers than the small tribe you have left in the swamps."

"We bury them as your people do." He nodded his head to the two wounded men. "How will you judge them?"

"I shall try and get them to talk. I cannot fight hundreds of soldiers when they come, but if I save their lives, the new soldiers may give my family mercy."

Red Fox laughed and exchanged doubtful glances with his friends. "Few white men understand mercy. Your father and brothers are rare."

Tyra swallowed at the memory of her family's smiling faces at the Christmas feast. A hollow spot formed in her throat. She gripped the reins tight in her hand. "You speak the truth, but I must try. I am only one woman. I cannot fight hundreds of soldiers."

"War Woman fight with wisdom." Red Fox pointed to his own head. "If you need us, you find us in swamp."

"Indeed, I will." Tyra nodded.

Red Fox motioned to his men, and they followed him back to the woods.

A groan caught Tyra's attention. She looked over to see the one with two arrows grimacing in his semi-conscious state. If she didn't hurry, he would soon awaken, and the pain would be unbearable.

Tyra led the horses to the front of the house where it would be easier to carry them inside. Indecision wrestled in her heart. How would she get them down and drag them inside without causing them further damage and pain? She couldn't leave them like this to die.

Want to learn more about author
Jennifer Hudson Taylor and check out other great
fiction from Abingdon Press?

Sign up for our fiction newsletter at
www.AbingdonPress.com
to read interviews with your favorite authors, find tips
for starting a reading group, and stay posted on what
new titles are on the horizon. It's a place to connect
with other fiction readers or post a comment about this book.

Be sure to visit Jennifer online!

www.jenniferhudsontaylor.com
http://jenniferswriting.blogspot.com
http://carolinascots-irish.blogspot.com